CLOSING BOOKS

Trisha Grace

To Jesus, the one who made it all possible.
To my dear fiancé, who is always so supportive of me.
To my mom, who is always encouraging of whatever choice I make.

Prologue

Evelyn and Dan strolled through the park. The light pink cherry blossoms hanging low above them. She took off her coat, folding it over her arm.

Spring was warmer than usual this year.

Children were already out in full force, running around in T-shirts and jeans.

She glanced toward the playground and smiled ruefully as she saw the huge grins plastered on the children's faces.

She loved watching children at playgrounds. She loved listening to the high-pitch, carefree laughter and shrieks of joy as they ran spiritedly, flailing their hands about.

"I used to love playing at the playground until my parents forced me to take my sister along," Dan suddenly said.

She shook her head with a grin, but didn't say anything. She felt Dan's eyes on her, waiting, she supposed, for her to share an anecdote of her own.

But she didn't like to think about the past—no, she didn't *allow* herself to think of the past.

"Do you want to head over to the mansion for dinner tonight? Or would you rather we go somewhere else?" Dan asked after a moment.

She turned her head back to him and pursed her lips. It felt weird going over to Kate's house when she wasn't around. "Somewhere else."

"Are you going to stay away from the mansion until they come back from their honeymoon?"

One of her shoulders inched up as she gave him a nonchalant shrug.

"You can still head over even though she isn't around, you know?"

"I know." She smiled, then continued. "Where do you want to go for dinner?"

She was glad that Kate's wedding had resulted in the need for her and Dan to work together. She was reluctant at first, thinking it was better that she stayed away from him.

Things between them were complicated.

They were good together, but they weren't meant to be.

She wasn't meant to be someone's girlfriend; she wasn't meant to be in a relationship.

She wished things between them could remain like this forever —simple, just two friends hanging out together.

"How about—" Dan looked down toward the floor.

A young girl wearing a bright-pink dress printed with large blue flowers ran right into Dan's legs, fell back, and landed heavily on her bum.

Dan immediately knelt down and lifted the young girl to her feet.

The young girl stared at him with wide, frightened eyes, seemingly ready to burst into tears.

Even being down on one knee, Dan towered over the girl. And his broad shoulders must have made him seem like a giant to her.

"Are you all right?" Dan asked with a small smile and a light pat on her head.

The girl nodded slowly, her lips curling to reflect Dan's.

"Are you hurt?"

"No," the young girl replied.

"Abi!" A woman wearing a light purple top came running over. "I'm so sorry; she never looks where she's going," the woman said as she scooped the young girl into her arms.

"It's okay," Dan said, grinning at the girl. "Don't worry about it."

"Bye." The young girl grinned and waved as her mother carried her back toward the playground.

Evelyn watched Dan return the girl's wave.

Dan would make a great father. The kind of father who would be there for their children; the kind of father a kid would be proud to have.

He was responsible and extremely patient.

She'd worked with him and seen how he was with his staff. When things went wrong, he never lost his temper. Instead, he always focused on solving the problem. Then he would give a stern warning that such mistakes should be avoided.

What she admired most was how he would never bring up the subject again.

Even with her, even after all that she'd put him through, he would always turn up whenever she needed him.

"Cute girl," Dan commented.

"You think every child is cute."

He grinned and shrugged.

"You'll be a great father."

"I sure hope so. I've been babysitting Joanne forever," he said. "And I'm sure you would be a great mother."

She hitched her handbag higher up against her shoulder.

"Don't you want to have a family?"

Her fingers tightened around the strap of her handbag.

This was why they weren't meant to be; they were so different. "I know you do."

"Yeah, and you don't?"

Again, she adjusted the strap on her shoulder. "I already have a family. I have Kate."

Though Kate wasn't related to her, they were closer than most sisters were. Kate would probably be the only family that Evelyn would ever have.

His head bobbed up and down as he stared ahead.

They continued strolling through the park, walking side by side, neither saying anything.

Evelyn gazed at a mother walking past them. The young mother held a baby in her arms, rocking gently as she cooed the baby back to sleep.

She turned her head from the mother and child.

She wouldn't know how to be a mother anyway. She didn't know a single lullaby. She didn't know how to bake cookies. She didn't even know what a normal childhood was.

It was better that someone like her didn't have children.

"So what do you want to have for dinner?" Dan asked.

Dan deserved better. He shouldn't be wasting time on someone who could never give him what he wanted.

Pressing her lips into a thin line, she turned to him. "Actually …" She paused as she felt the vibrations in her bag. "One minute."

She pulled out her phone and frowned at the unfamiliar number. "Hello?"

"Hi, Mandy."

Evelyn's face blanked. "Wrong number," she said and ended the call.

"Is everything all right?"

She forced a smile as she looked up at Dan. "Yeah, but I have to go."

"Now?"

"Yeah." She turned and walked away from Dan without another word.

"And dinner?"

She drew a deep breath and turned back to him. "I don't think that's a good idea."

"Eve—"

"I really have to go."

She spun around and strode toward the parking lot, still clenching the phone in her hand.

Chapter One

Evelyn stared at the phone number displayed on the screen of her vibrating cell phone. The originally unfamiliar number had become a source of fear and was probably the cause of the migraine she'd been suffering from.

She buried her face in her hands and let the phone vibrate a few more times before sighing and picking it up.

"I thought you were going to ignore my call," the monotonous voice said.

Tightening her grip on the phone, Evelyn clenched her jaws. She took a deep breath and quietly cleared her throat of the frustration that had lodged itself there before replying. "What do you want?"

"Money, of course. I've run out."

"I'm not your bank."

"You can always say no. But I can't say you'll like what follows."

Evelyn shut her eyes and reminded herself to take slow, deep breaths. All she wanted to do was to smash her phone into the wall and leave, to disappear to a place where no one knew her.

If only life was that easy.

"How much do you want?"

"Three thousand. Six o'clock, same place."

Evelyn ended the call without another word. Leaning back against the chair, she shut her eyes and swallowed hard. Crying wouldn't solve the problem. She needed a solution; she needed to think.

She had contemplated on making a police report, but that meant revealing the secret she'd so adamantly refused to speak of. She had thought of changing her phone number so she could live in denial. Perhaps things would simply return to normal as long as she could no longer be reached.

But as much as she tried to convince herself, she knew things wouldn't just vanish by feigning ignorance.

Since receiving the first call less than a month ago, Evelyn's bank account had been set back by over six thousand dollars, and there didn't seem to be an end to it.

Straightening herself, she stared at the photos playing as the default screensaver on her laptop, photos taken on her best friend's wedding. She stared blankly at the pictures from Kate's wedding, seeing smile after smile until a photo of her and Dan appeared.

Evelyn tilted her head back and took a deep breath, but tears still went tumbling down her cheeks. Tears stemmed from the nostalgia of joy she'd felt in the picture; a joy that seemed so far away and unattainable at the moment.

Life had been good since she got out of the foster system. She had worked hard, and now she had a successful career and a great life.

She had thought that if she were to keep her past a secret, she could bury it deep enough that someday she'd completely forget about it.

Thus far, time had proven her theory to be entirely wrong. Ghosts of the past had a way of haunting one no matter how much one had changed.

After so many years, Evelyn thought her past was so far behind that the only remnant of it was in her mind.

Again, she was wrong.

She was beginning to doubt if she would ever be free from the past she couldn't shake.

There was a simple solution, and she knew it.

All she had to do was to spill the beans. If everyone knew what had happened, the blackmailer wouldn't have anything to threaten her with.

It should have been an easy thing to do.

All those things happened so many years ago. But even after a decade, it was difficult for her to open up and talk about what had happened to her or what she had done.

Kate was the only one who knew her secret, and Evelyn was sure that Kate would never reveal it to anyone unless she allowed it.

Before, she had kept it a secret because she didn't want to talk about it. She didn't want to discuss it with anyone and relive her nightmare.

Now, even though she didn't want to admit it, the truth behind her silence was her hope to keep Dan from ever finding out what she'd done.

She'd battled with the decision of telling Dan in order to end everything once and for all, but the resolve to do so always disappeared before it ever took root in her heart.

Each time she made up her mind to tell Dan, fear would creep in.

Fear, with its sneaky little voice, would tell her that Dan would never accept her after what she'd done and that he would be disgusted with her.

The little voice, which seemed ridiculous in the beginning, began to grow louder until she could no longer ignore it.

Soon, the voice in her mind dropped into her heart, and she was convinced that Dan would scorn her when he found out what had happened.

Though she was no longer seeing Dan, though they were never officially dating, she couldn't bear the thought of Dan finding out her past. She couldn't bear to see his reaction.

It didn't take much for the fear to convince her that she was alone in this matter. No one, not Dan, not Kate, would want to be involved with her shady past.

Brusquely, she wiped the tears on the back of her hand and picked up her bag by the side of the table. Another trip to the bank was necessary.

Evelyn drove up the lone, single driveway that led to the

mansion. Green towering trees that stood throughout all seasons flanked both sides of the road. For a moment, her eyes flickered onto the trees. She forced herself to focus on the road and kept her eyes away from the never-ending woods.

Even after a year, Evelyn couldn't get over how creepy and isolated the mansion was.

Whenever her eyes wandered to the trees, thoughts of someone or something suddenly appearing out of the forest to attack her would surface.

Even with her wild imagination aside, she hated the drive up to the mansion.

She wasn't sure if it was the scenery of the impenetrable forest or the solitary drive, but a sense of melancholy always accompanied her on the drive.

If only Kate had chosen to live somewhere else, then she wouldn't have to make this drive up every other day.

She tightened the grip on her steering wheel as she turned into the mansion and saw Dan's car.

She hadn't seen him for weeks, not since Kate went on her honeymoon, not since that day at the park. But that hadn't stopped her from thinking about him.

She sighed, pushing the thoughts from her head.

They were no longer together, and for good reason.

Stepping out of the car, she strode up to the door and turned the knob. As expected, it wasn't locked.

With so many people going in and out of the house, Marianne had made it a policy to leave the door unlocked during meal times.

Evelyn stepped through the doorway, and her entrance was immediately announced by the motion sensor alarm.

She didn't understand why Tyler had bothered with that thing. The kitchen didn't offer a direct view of the main door, so the alarm did nothing to indicate who was coming in. For all they knew, she could have been a burglar.

Strolling past the luggage in the living room, she headed straight into the kitchen.

She forced her lips into a wide grin. "Hey!"

Kate turned around with a blissful smile and gave her a hug. "Sit! I'm giving out presents. These are yours," Kate said, giving the two large paper bags on the oval dining table a slight nudge.

Without even looking, Evelyn knew it was probably two new branded bags.

Bags were her sole indulgence.

Having grown up with barely anything instilled some habits in her.

She always made sure she set aside more than half of her income in the bank. She didn't go for expensive food and had been driving the same secondhand car for years.

But bags, she was always willing to cut back on other expenses for her bags.

She sat beside Kate and watched her dole out presents to Dan and Marianne. It was strange to see so few people in the usually crowded kitchen.

Kate's husband, Tyler, sat back against his chair with his arm draped lazily across Kate's chair.

The past year had brought about many changes to all their lives.

A year ago, a will left behind by Tyler's grandfather ended up bringing Kate and Tyler together. Along with Tyler, Dan, Ryan, and Joseph all tagged along. They had all become part of the regular people in her life now.

Besides Dan, she wasn't close with any of the guys.

She wasn't a sociable person in the first place. She was the sort who fared better at being alone than having to mingle with people. Having one friend was more than enough for her.

Her on-and-off relationship with Dan didn't help her score any points with the other guys as well.

Joseph, in particular, was exceptionally cold toward her. He never spoke to her directly unless necessary.

Even Ryan, the friendliest in the group, hadn't warmed up to her.

But she did have to admit that everyone had been cordial with her for Kate's sake. Even Marianne, Tyler's housekeeper, who loved all the boys like her own children, never showed any disapproval of her despite the things she had going on with Dan.

Evelyn hadn't meant to keep Dan in her craziness. Each time she had walked away from him, she'd promised herself that it was the last time and that she wouldn't get involved with him again.

Logic and rationale told her that they weren't meant to be. But each time she needed someone, she couldn't stop herself from reaching for her phone and calling Dan.

"How was the honeymoon?" Marianne asked.

As Kate launched into a speech about how perfect everything was, Evelyn took the chance to steal a glimpse of Dan.

She hadn't spoken to him since the whole blackmail began.

It was her decision, her own doing, but that didn't stop her from missing him.

She smiled ruefully as Dan ran his hand through his blond hair, causing the sleeve of his shirt to inch up, revealing the muscles under it.

Though he wasn't the largest guy in the group, his tendency to work alongside his men in his construction firm had built quite a few sturdy muscles.

Dan hated folding up the long sleeves of his shirt. He hated having to pull the edge back down his elbow whenever he lifted his arms.

Her smile faded as the dull ache in her heart worsened.

All the details she remembered about him only reminded her of how happy she was whenever they were together.

But people like her didn't get happily-ever-afters.

The blackmail she had been receiving was a reinforcement of the different world they belonged in.

Dan grew up in a complete family. It wasn't perfect, but at least he grew up safe.

The horrors she'd gone through and the things she'd done were beyond the worst nightmares that someone like Dan could ever imagine.

Pushing the thoughts from her mind, she reached into one of the paper bags on the table and took out the leather bag within. She twirled the new handbag, pretending to examine it while her thoughts were consumed by the payment due later that night.

Money was draining out of her bank account faster than before. Just two days ago, she had paid off her blackmailer. Now, she was to prepare another three thousand dollars.

It had started out with a few hundred dollars. Within two weeks, her blackmailer had quickly upgraded the demands. Besides demanding more money, her blackmailer was increasing the frequency of the demands as well.

"You don't like them?"

Kate's voice broke her thoughts. Evelyn looked up and quickly gave her a small, pleasant smile. "You know I love them. I was just thinking about some stuff at work. Speaking of which, I brought some new projects that you might be interested in. They're in my car, I'll get them."

Before anyone else could say another word, she was up from her chair and out of the kitchen, heading toward the main door.

Evelyn knew she wasn't acting like her usual self very well. Before driving up to the mansion, she'd reminded herself to behave as normally as she could. Kate was particularly astute at picking up emotional disturbances in people, and Evelyn knew she had to be careful or Kate would be all over her.

She tried; she genuinely did. But it was difficult to keep up her smile with the apprehension of meeting a ghost that had latched onto her.

Halfway through the living room, she heard the familiar ringtone she'd grown to dread.

Crap. She spun around and sprinted back toward the kitchen.

Why did she put down her phone to play with her new bag?

The moment she got back to the kitchen, she saw her phone in Kate's hand.

Without thinking, Kate tapped on the screen and answered the call. "Hello?"

Evelyn's eyes widened, and she snatched the phone from Kate's hand. "Don't pick up my calls."

She could see the confusion on Kate's face and felt the stares directed at her. She knew her strong reaction would appear to border along temporary insanity, especially when they all knew how close she was to Kate.

"I always answer your phone when you're not around," Kate stated hesitantly while Evelyn checked who the caller was.

"Stop doing that," she hissed and headed out of the kitchen with the phone in her hand.

Hastening her steps, she exited the mansion. Once the door was closed behind her, she lifted the phone to her ear. "What do you want? I know I'm supposed to hand you three thousand dollars tonight."

"Is that your friend?"

"What do you want?" Evelyn repeated, irate at the situation she was in and at how senseless she was behaving toward the only person who actually cared about her.

"I changed my mind. I need five."

"Don't push it," she said through clenched jaws.

"No, Evelyn, don't push me. I'm sure you don't want the-one-who-always-answers-your-phone-when-you-are-not-around to know what's going on, right?"

Evelyn ended the call and clenched her phone. Boiling, but with nowhere to vent, she got into her car and began to beat up her steering wheel.

She slammed her arms against the steering wheel, sending jolts of pain through them. Though her hands became the eventual victims, her anger was slightly appeased.

Pinching the bridge of her nose, she forced herself to take a few deep breaths while her arms burnt with a dull pain.

After a minute, she rearranged her features into a carefully placed smile and got out of the car.

As she entered the kitchen, everyone kept their eyes on the food that was on the table, and no one said a word to her. Although they had all been polite to her, they had never been overly concerned about her.

Evelyn didn't blame them. She was the one who kept everything to herself, and that had the tendency to keep everyone out.

In fact, she rather enjoyed people staying out of her business. It saved a lot of time and effort from having to explain things she'd rather not talk about.

Kate looked up from the table and smiled at her; a smile that didn't reach her eyes.

Behave normally. Evelyn sat and slotted her phone into her back pocket.

From the corner of her eye, she noticed Kate staring at her arms, which were red and slightly purple at certain areas where bruises were beginning to form. She quickly pulled her hands back and placed them on her legs. She was certain that if she refused to speak about it, Kate wouldn't pry it out of her, not right now anyway.

And she was right.

After a moment, Kate turned away from her and casually asked, "Where's the work you mentioned?"

"Oh, right." She got up, shaking her head at her absentmindedness. "I'll get it."

She turned and left the kitchen again. This time, she cast a brief glance over her shoulder; a glance long enough to see Dan staring at her. Their gaze held for a moment before she tore her eyes from him.

It pained her to see the questions, or maybe accusations, in his eyes.

She had only turned from Dan when he tried pushing her into a serious, committed relationship.

This time, she had simply shut him out of her life for what would appear to him as no apparent reason.

It was difficult to be so near to him and yet be so clearly separated that they might as well be a thousand miles apart. She wanted so badly to let him understand why she pulled away from him, but she could never find the words and didn't know where to begin.

Taking the files from her car, she ran her finger down one side of the files while she kicked the door close.

This was exactly what she needed—work.

With Kate being on honeymoon for the past few weeks, as her business partner, Evelyn should have been free as a bird. Instead, she scoured through the projects handled by the different teams they had and insisted on custom making pieces of furniture that were readily available in stores.

She had even begun trying her hands at keeping a good set of accounts, something she'd always avoided at all cost.

Her work was the one escape that kept her from thinking how screwed up the other aspects of her life were.

"Here are the few projects I thought you might be interested in. If you don't want them, we can assign them to the teams. Let me know," she said the moment she got back to the kitchen. "I have to go."

"Where are you going?" Kate asked as she took the files, staring intently at Evelyn.

Pausing by the chair, Evelyn hesitated a moment. A moment that turned the curiosity on Kate's face into suspicion.

"Nowhere," Evelyn quickly said. "I just need to run some errands."

Be casual, Evelyn reminded herself. She smiled and gave Kate a pat on her shoulder. "See you tomorrow."

Not giving Kate a chance to ask another question, Evelyn grabbed her bag and presents, made sure she kept a smile on her face, then left without saying goodbye.

Chapter Two

Dan forced himself to keep his eyes on his plate instead of looking up at Evelyn's disappearing figure.

"What's wrong with her?" Kate asked. "You haven't gone out with her since we went on our honeymoon?"

He pushed the food around on his plate as he looked up at Kate. "Something like that." He tried to speak as nonchalantly as possible, but when he saw Kate's lips thinning, he realized he wasn't doing a terrific job of concealing his feelings.

Months before the wedding, someone had set fire to Kate's house; a fire that almost killed both Kate and Evelyn. Immediately after, Evelyn retreated into her shell, barely speaking to him.

He'd thought that experiencing a life and death situation would bring about the epiphany of living life to the fullest and treasuring people she loved. Either that was a whole load of nonsense or Evelyn just wasn't like normal people.

Evelyn's cold-shoulder treatment toward him continued until the preparations for Kate and Tyler's wedding kicked into high gear. The planning for the wedding and the renovation of the mansion forced them to work together.

And it was clear that whenever they were together, they couldn't get enough of each other.

It was undeniable that they had terrific chemistry.

Whenever they were working together or going out on a date, they would spend half the night laughing away, and time always flew by way too quickly.

But despite all the laughter they shared, there was always an invisible barrier between them—the past she refused to speak of.

He didn't mind. He believed that with time she would trust him enough to tell him what had happened, and he was willing to wait.

When Evelyn wasn't busy pulling away from him or being all mysterious, she had a genuinely open and candid personality. He had never met anyone like her before.

He hadn't been with many women in his life. The two most prominent ones were already too much for him to handle. Throughout his life, his dramatic mother never spoke her mind and loved resorting to theatrics to instill guilt in him. Guilt was his mother's sole weapon of manipulating him into doing things her way.

Unfortunately, that unbearable characteristic had passed down to his sister as well.

Evelyn's frankness was a refreshing change. She had no problem telling the truth about anything, and they could chat about everything under the sun; everything except relationships and her past.

Each time he spoke of something that had happened when he was young, she'd laugh at his anecdote but never reveal any of hers. On occasions when Dan asked about her childhood, she would clam up and simply state that there wasn't much to talk about.

Though they weren't officially in a relationship, they spent all their time together and didn't date anyone else.

But Dan wasn't satisfied with their ambiguous status.

He knew what he wanted in life. He wasn't one of those who had flings and left a trail of broken hearts behind. He took each relationship he had seriously.

With Evelyn, he didn't even know if what they had qualified to be considered a relationship.

They always had a great time, and he couldn't think of any reason why they shouldn't be together.

But whenever he tried to push Evelyn into a relationship, she'd push as well; she would push him away. All communications would cease to exist between them, and she would treat him as if he never existed.

Initially, everyone assumed they had a fight and were in a cold war. Dan never explained to them either. How was he supposed to explain when he had no idea what was going on?

A week later, sometimes longer, sometimes shorter, she would call in the middle of the night and ask to meet up for supper. They would then begin to talk and go out again until Dan took another shot at pushing her into a relationship.

After so many cycles of this ridiculous routine, he thought he would have gotten used to it.

He tapped his fork against the plate, then pushed it away.

Everyone, especially Marianne, had been asking him about the situation between Evelyn and him. To get himself out of the need to answer the questions, he had adopted Tyler's classic style of shrugging then keeping his lips locked.

Eventually, the guys learned to stop asking questions. Marianne, on the other hand, wouldn't stop bugging him about it.

Perhaps that was how real mothers behaved. He couldn't be sure. His own mother was always more concerned about herself and his younger sister. To him, Marianne was more of a mother than his parents ever were. Despite that, it didn't change the fact that her questions were getting on his nerves.

Sometimes, he wished he had an answer for Marianne.

Despite Evelyn's straightforward personality, there was plenty that he didn't understand about her.

For one, he didn't understand why Evelyn always isolated herself and pretended she didn't care about anyone else. He was sure Evelyn wasn't such a person, and the kitchen he was sitting in proved it.

He looked up from his food and turned to the newly renovated kitchen.

The cherry wood cabinets that had been in the house for nearly three decades had been removed and was now furnished with dark brown cabinets. The wooden countertop had also been replaced with a light gray slab of granite. Those were the basic designs that Kate had chosen, but the degree that Evelyn went to customize it for Marianne showed how much she cared.

Every cabinet was designed specifically to suit Marianne's needs.

Instead of the standard shelf height, Evelyn had noted down all the things that Marianne had placed in the different cabinets and adjusted the height of the new shelves to fit those needs. She even solved Marianne's problem of having too many spices and not enough places to store them by completely revamping one of the cabinets into a multi-layered turning tray that allowed Marianne to store and reach her spices easily.

Evelyn had noted every complaint that Marianne ever had about the kitchen and designed the new cabinets to suit her needs. And she did all of that without even having to ask Marianne or Kate.

"Ryan and Joseph working?" Kate asked, bringing his thoughts back to reality.

Though Dan was glad that Kate wasn't harping on the problem between him and Evelyn, he was hoping that he didn't have to be the one to break the bad news.

He looked over at Marianne, then back to Kate. "Joseph's working while Ryan's in the hospital."

Kate's eyes widened, and Tyler's gaze finally shifted from his beloved wife.

"He got injured at work; part of a wall fell on him," Marianne clarified. "He's recovering now, so there's nothing to worry about."

"How is he? When did that happen? Why didn't you guys tell us earlier?"

"He's fine, around a week ago, and we didn't want to disturb your honeymoon. We knew you'd want to return immediately if we had told you," Dan answered and flashed a bright smile at Kate.

Kate narrowed her eyes at his condescending answer. "I called Eve so many times, and not once did she think to tell me what happened."

"She didn't know."

"Huh," Kate said, studying his expression before she continued. "We should visit him, *now*."

Tyler hesitated. "Are you sure? I thought you were tired?"

"I'm fine. We should go see him. How bad is it?" She turned back to Dan and glared at him, warning him from lying to her.

"Got some slight burns, dislocated his right arm from his shoulder, and tore a ligament in his leg."

Kate cringed.

"There's good news, though; for him at least," Dan said and continued when he saw Kate frowning. "He gets to stay home for three whole months. And since Marianne didn't want him staying in his apartment alone, he'd accepted the invitation to crash here until he recovers." As Dan finished his sentence, he turned to look at Tyler, grinning when he saw Tyler shaking his head.

Before Kate came into his life, the guys always made sure they gave Tyler his space. They only appeared to devour Marianne's cooking before disappearing. Now, all of them had become semi-permanent residents of the mansion.

Before, Tyler had no qualms about chasing them out of his house, but Kate loved their presence in the mansion and he loved seeing her smile.

"I can't believe you're joking about his injuries. It sounds serious; we should visit him right away."

Tyler smiled and stood, stretching out his hand for Kate.

"I'll drive," Dan volunteered. He didn't want to be left behind in the house, where he was certain Marianne would ask him over and over again if he was serious about Evelyn and why hadn't he taken a stand on the relationship he wanted them to have.

He trailed out of the mansion along with Kate and Tyler, watching Tyler run his fingers down Kate's hair.

When Tyler met Kate, his personality changed so drastically that it made Dan believed it was possible for things to turn around with Evelyn, too.

Kate had once told him that Evelyn treated him differently, and it was something she hadn't seen before, just like how Tyler treated Kate completely different from everyone else. Dan had come to believe that he would be different enough for Evelyn to break free from the mysterious shadow of her past.

The secretive past that Kate refused to talk about, even to her dear husband.

The two women were like sisters, and Kate guarded Evelyn's secret fiercely.

Dan understood Kate's reason; it wasn't her story to tell. Still, it didn't change the fact that the whole secrecy around it was frustrating.

Tempted as he was to ask Evelyn, Dan hadn't dared to step over that particular boundary. Each time he'd pushed Evelyn into taking a step closer, he'd only succeeded in pushing her further away. He had an inkling that if he did push Evelyn on this particular subject, she would close her door to him completely.

Looking up at the genuine smile on Tyler's face, a smile that was non-existent until Kate appeared in his life, Dan felt a sense of jealousy surging through him. In spite of the many things Tyler had, Dan never coveted any of them except for what he now had. Someone whom he could love; someone who would reflect the joy that he had; someone who only had eyes for him.

"Are you all right?" Kate asked when they got into his car.

Dan's face blanked, and he stared back at her. He had missed her question.

"What happened this time?"

She didn't have to elaborate; Dan knew exactly what she meant. Though she was the newest member of his group of friends, Kate was the only one Dan had spoken to about Evelyn. Perhaps he was hoping that Kate's understanding of Evelyn would help shed some light on what he was doing wrong.

"I don't know. I swear I didn't push her this time." He thought back on the last time they met. "She had this strange look after picking up a call, then she hurried away. After that, she just cut me off," he said. "Maybe she's seeing someone else."

Kate nodded. "She's acting weird over the phone, but I'm sure she isn't dating someone. She would've told me."

He didn't make any comment. He didn't believe Evelyn would hide such information from Kate, but based on her behavior, he couldn't help thinking otherwise.

Evelyn was clearly secretive when it came to those calls, even Kate wasn't allowed to answer her phone.

"I'm sorry. I wish I could help. It's just that she's *really* touchy when it comes to relationships. I love her, but I hate to see you like this. Maybe you should stop running around in circles with her."

Dan sighed heavily. Of course he'd thought about that. Basic logic told him that they weren't going anywhere and that he should put a stop to the crazy cycles. Yet whenever she called, his logic and reasoning would leave him.

Whenever they were in the cold stages, he couldn't stop checking his phone to make sure that he hadn't missed her call. And when she did call, he couldn't help but feel relieved. "I tried." *I really did.*

He heard Kate sighing softly before she changed the subject. "When is Ryan getting discharged from the hospital? He'll need someone to help him up and down the stairs. And his clothes? Anyone helping him to bring them over?"

He grinned and looked at Kate through the rear-view mirror.

Since Kate entered their lives, she had become the linchpin that held all of them closely together. With Kate, they'd all become a family, all except Evelyn.

He wasn't sure if it was the way she refused to reveal information about herself or the formality with which she treated everyone, but there always seemed to be a wall between her and everyone else.

Refusing to dwell on thoughts of Evelyn, Dan shook his head and returned his focus to the conversation. "Marianne has already brought his stuff over. He'll be staying with her in the other wing."

"Why? That's quite a long walk from the kitchen, and we all know how much he loves the kitchen." Kate looked up and grinned at Tyler.

Tyler beamed back in return and said, "There are three guest rooms near our room. He can stay there."

"Marianne says it's easier for her to take care of him. Plus, there's a room right on the first floor, so he won't have to climb the stairs." He kept his eyes on the road and smiled to himself. That was the exact reason Marianne had told them though they all knew Marianne just didn't want anyone disturbing the newlyweds.

When they got to the hospital, Dan and Tyler gave a nonchalant "hi" to Ryan before settling on the couch while Kate went to fuss over him.

Among all the guys, Ryan was the muscular one. His shirts always fitted him so snugly that the contours of the muscles were easily seen through the stretched T-shirts.

Dan knew Kate would be shocked to see their own giant lying in bed with a heavy cast on his arm and a huge brace on his leg.

"Gosh, I'm so sorry we didn't visit you earlier," she said, sitting on the edge of the bed.

"Don't be. I was in on the decision of not telling you guys. Where's my present?" Ryan asked with his boyish grin and usual upbeat tone.

"Back at the mansion. Don't worry, she knows you love her. She won't forget your present," Tyler answered from the couch.

Dan laughed when he heard how disgruntled Tyler was.

Besides being the strongest among all of them, Ryan was also the friendliest. His initial friendliness toward Kate had bothered Tyler, especially when Ryan openly professed how he loved her. Tyler knew Ryan had spoken jokingly, but he simply refused to let it go.

"How are you doing?" Kate asked after shaking her head at Tyler's childish behavior.

"Great, especially since I get to stay at the mansion for three whole months. I'll get to eat Marianne's food for three whole months!"

Kate laughed softly at Ryan's equally childish answer. "You guys deserve each other."

Dan joined in the laughter. "I think he won't mind being paralyzed if you tell him that he'll get to enjoy Marianne's food for the rest of his life."

Tyler grinned at Dan's words.

"When will you be discharged? We'll come and get you," Tyler said.

"You can take him back now if you want."

Everyone turned toward the door as Joseph entered. Kate got up from Ryan's bed and gave him a hug. "Are you coming with us? We can wait for your shift to end."

"That's still hours away. You guys must be tired from your flight. Go back and rest. How are your eyes?"

After much pushing, Kate finally found time to get her Lasik surgery done before the wedding. In the beginning, she had complained that her eyes felt dry rather easily, so Tyler had bugged Joseph on checking her eyes whenever he was at the mansion.

"Fine. I still can't believe I have perfect eyesight. Sometimes I go to bed thinking I should remove my contacts."

Tyler walked up to his wife and ran his fingers through her hair. In reaction, Kate gazed up at him and leaned against the length of his arm.

Again, the simple intimacy they displayed reminded Dan of the ache in his heart. "I'll get the papers settled while Kate fills him in on Marianne's menu for the night." He stood and walked out without a second look at the rest of them.

"Hey," Joseph said as he followed him. "Evelyn again?"

"I'm fine." There wasn't much he could say. How was he supposed to explain to his friends that Kate's best friend was driving him crazy, but he couldn't get himself to stay away from her?

"Ryan may be quitting his job," Joseph said after a moment of silence.

"Really? I thought he loved being a firefighter."

"Actually, after the fire at Kate's house, he started having second thoughts. Then this accident."

"So what is he going to do?"

Joseph shrugged. "I don't think he's put much thought into it."

Chapter Three

"Good morning," Evelyn said as she entered the kitchen. The kitchen was crowded with the entire gang, all of them sitting in their respective seats around the dining table. Only plates and utensils were on the table, but the aroma from the food was already making her stomach growl.

Evelyn's brows flitted up when she saw Joanne sitting next to Dan.

Since the fire, Evelyn had been working with Joanne on her application for an interior design course. They had looked at dozens of schools, narrowed them, prepared her portfolio, and submitted applications.

Helping Joanne was another secret that Evelyn had been keeping from Dan.

Initially, she was surprised that Joanne came to her for advice. She wasn't the kind of person whom people looked to for help, but she couldn't turn Joanne down. She knew Dan had hoped that Joanne would grow up and stop behaving like his mother. He wanted Joanne to have a life of her own, to have her own ambitions and desires beyond having Tyler as her boyfriend.

Evelyn smiled as she thought about the series of debacles that Joanne had resorted to when Kate first moved in.

Things were different now. Joanne was no longer creating problems for Kate and was serious about finding a future for herself.

Evelyn was glad to help. She was certain Dan would be elated to know that his sister was finally ready to start living her own life.

She pulled out the chair between Kate and Dan, joining the rest of the group around the crowded table.

The mansion was now the focal point of their lives. Even with the crazy work schedules that Ryan and Joseph had, they always came over whenever they had the time. If they couldn't make it for dinner, they'd turn up for breakfast or lunch or to chat with Kate and Marianne for a while before heading to crash in the guest rooms.

Evelyn didn't stay over as the guys did, except during the brief period of time when Kate had received threatening notes.

She didn't like staying anywhere except her own apartment. Her apartment was a place where she was used to, a place where the noises at night wouldn't startle her, and a place where she could lock her bedroom door without having to explain why.

"Hey! The food will be ready soon," Ryan said.

"How are you feeling? Kate told me what happened."

"Good. Still in one piece."

Evelyn smiled and stole a glimpse of Dan as she pulled her chair closer to the table, slightly disappointed that he wasn't looking at her.

She had no right to be, but she was.

She knew what Dan wanted: relationship, marriage, family. Everything that she couldn't give him. Everything that he wouldn't want from her if he found out about her past.

But when she wasn't with him, all she could think about was him. When she tried seeing other guys, all she could see was how they failed to compare to him. When she told herself that she wasn't going to keep Dan in her craziness and that it was time to bring things to a complete end, she'd have an overwhelming urge to see him.

Her hands would then betray her, picking up the phone and calling Dan before she could stop herself.

Dan would turn up; he always did. And they would have as much fun as they always had. They'd laugh and flirt. Dan would lean in close, push her hair back, then skim his finger down her cheek.

His soft touch, along with his warm and clear emerald eyes gazing into hers, never failed to capture her heart. His gentleness with her spoke of more affection than any words ever did. Selfishly, she didn't want to let that feeling go, so she persuaded herself into believing that they could always remain the way they were.

But what she wanted wasn't good enough for Dan. He'd always push her into formalizing their relationship, and she would take a thousand steps back away from him.

She didn't do that to punish him or to prove her point. She needed to stay away from him to remind herself that she wasn't girlfriend or wife material. She was damaged beyond repair; it was impossible to fix her.

Things that are impossible to men are possible with God.

Evelyn shook Kate's voice out of her head.

She had to remind herself that she and Dan were only meant to be friends, and she had to stay away to make sure she got her perspective right.

When she was with him, she sometimes fell into the daydream on the possibility of a future together with Dan. She'd allow herself to play with the thought for a few minutes, just a few minutes.

She wasn't the naive sort of person.

No one would ever want someone like her as his girlfriend or wife.

As if the universe were reminding her of why she could never be in a relationship, her phone buzzed, and she jumped from the shock of the vibration. She checked her phone, then dropped it back onto the table when she saw that it was just an advertisement.

The reminder of the blackmail took her mind into a dark turn.

What had she done to God to make Him abandon her and be so cruel to her?

She didn't doubt that a God existed.

He existed for Kate. He protected Kate when she was in trouble, but He had never bothered with her. If He did, He shouldn't have allowed her to go through what she did.

Unconsciously, her hand moved toward her left shoulder and her fingers grazed across her shirt, over where the scar was located.

Who would be interested in a woman with such a dark history?

"Ryan, Joe said you're thinking of quitting your job," Dan said.

Dan's voice easily cut through her thoughts, capturing her attention. Realizing where her hand was, she immediately dropped her arm back onto her legs.

Ryan nodded. "Maybe, but I don't know what else I can do."

"Open your own gym and produce more incredible hulks," Joanne teased.

"That's actually a brilliant idea," Kate said. "That way, you don't have to work those horrible shifts, and it's much, much, *much* safer than being a firefighter."

All of them echoed their support of the idea.

"Are you guys serious?" Ryan asked, half laughing.

"Why not?" Kate said. "You can get Joseph to come up with healthy meals that would help in weight loss or muscle gain. He can even give check-ups to track their progress."

Ryan turned to Joseph with a raised brow.

Joseph brows drew closer together, seemingly considering the possibility of doing so.

While Marianne began placing food on the table, more ideas were thrown around.

Evelyn tuned out the conversation and turned to Dan again.

She was tempted to talk to him, to ask him about his day. She missed hearing his voice, seeing the smile he always had for her, and feeling the warmth of his finger skimming down her cheek.

She closed her eyes, hoping that removing him from her sight would get rid of the thoughts in her mind.

This is better for everyone, she reminded herself.

Just then, her phone vibrated again, and another jolt of shock reverberated down her spine. Hastily, she grabbed the phone from the table. Relieved that it was just about work, she sighed softly and returned the phone to its position on the table. When she glanced up from her phone, she found Kate staring at her, probably waiting for an explanation on her neurotic behavior over her phone.

"Lack of sleep." A pang of guilt besieged her as she looked away from Kate. Though it was true that she wasn't sleeping well and her nightmares were back, compared to the other problem she was facing, the nightmares were insignificant.

She hated having to lie to Kate, and Kate's response only doubled her guilt.

"Do you want me to stay over at your house tonight? If you want, I can accompany you. Maybe tomorrow we can buy some chamomile tea and essential oils. I heard they work miracles for some who can't sleep."

"Don't worry, I'm fine." Evelyn kept her eyes from Kate, letting her know she had no intention of continuing that particular line of conversation.

It was better for Kate to know nothing about what was going on. There wasn't any need to pull another person into her mess.

The next morning, Evelyn pulled up in front of the mansion, surprised to see Lydia's car parked by Joanne's pink mini.

Everyone, including herself, had treated Kate's sister like an outcast since the fire. Though only her and Kate confronted Lydia, everyone else blamed Lydia for what happened as well.

Since finding out that their parents didn't die from an accident like their grandparents had told them, Lydia had been obsessed with finding out what caused their brutal murder.

Even though Lydia wasn't the one who set the fire, she was undeniably the cause of it.

To Evelyn, the actual fire didn't scare her; it was the events leading right up to it that did. The whole incident brought back the unwanted memories that she'd been trying to bury.

Even seeing Lydia's car brought back those memories.

She remembered how her heart pounded while she hid in the bathroom with Kate. She remembered how she kept her gun aimed at the door while fear ran rampant in her mind.

The suspense of knowing someone was heading for them

reminded her of how she had felt while hiding in the bathroom as a child, of the futile prayers she had made, and of the eventual punishment she had to endure.

She was no longer a child, and she had practiced hard at using her gun. Still, no amount of logic helped as the same fear that used to surge through her veins every night raked her once again.

Evelyn rubbed her palms against her arms, getting some warmth back to her suddenly cold hands.

"Hey, you're late," Ryan said as she entered the kitchen.

Everyone else echoed some form of greeting and went back to the food on the table.

Without command, her eyes moved in search of Dan's, then immediately darted away the moment they met his.

She took her usual spot, sitting between Kate and Dan. Since his eyes were obviously avoiding her, Evelyn took the chance to observe him.

He kept his eyes on his plate, taking a bite of food then looking up at the selection on the table. He looked well to her. The brilliant smile he used to wear was missing. But besides that, he appeared to be doing fine without her.

She couldn't help wondering if he was already seeing someone new and if she could handle sitting at the same table with whoever it was.

"Now that you're here, we're ready to make the major announcement," Ryan said, swallowing a mouthful of food. He nudged Joseph and gestured for him to continue.

Seeing Ryan's excitement made her smile.

She wished she had his personality; he was always smiling and chirpy. She wondered how he did that. The things he must have seen in his line of work: the carnage, the deaths … Yet he seemed untouched by them.

"We've decided to leave our jobs and start a gym like you guys suggested."

Joanne laughed. "Are you guys serious? I was only joking."

"We are. The only gym in this area isn't very good. Many of Ryan's fellow firefighters and friends he worked out with had complained about it. It's definitely viable," Joseph answered.

"That will be great," Kate said, her eyes bright. "That way, you guys won't have to deal with all the shifts anymore."

Dan nodded. "That's true. I can help with the finding of a location; I have contacts."

"And of course, Evelyn and I will design the place for you guys," Kate added.

"Before any of that, we'll have to come up with an actual proposal and get a bank loan," Joseph interjected before anyone else could continue.

Dan's brows drew closer in confusion. "You do know there are a few multi-millionaires sitting around this particular table, right? If the richest guy …" He cocked his head in Tyler's direction and continued. "Isn't willing, his wife definitely is."

Kate's smile widened. "Of course I'd support you guys. I've lots of money, and I can't find anywhere to use it."

Evelyn cleared her throat to conceal her laugh and hid her smile behind her hand.

Kate had inherited a sizable amount of money from Tyler's grandfather; money that was doing nothing but lying around in the bank. Since they got married, Tyler had refused to let her pay for anything.

"I have money," Tyler stated. "You guys get it from me."

Kate rolled her eyes. "Seriously? I can't even support them? What's the point of having all that money in the bank if I can't spend it?"

"You bought Evelyn's handbags with your money."

That began a banter that lasted for a few minutes, ending with Tyler hooking his arm over Kate and holding her against his chest.

Dan shook his head as Tyler grinned despite Kate's struggle to get out of his arms. "I don't think there ever was any couple who vies for the chance to pay for stuff."

Ryan nudged Joseph in his elbow. "Told you they'd help." Then he turned back to Tyler. "But no charity, we'll repay it. I'm sure Mr. Sawyer can draw something up for us."

"Of course," Mr. Sawyer said.

Evelyn looked at the now-retired lawyer sitting next to

Marianne, another addition to the group due to the will left behind by Tyler's grandfather. Mr. Sawyer had moved in last year to ensure that every condition of the late Mr. Hayes's will was met.

Now that Kate and Tyler were married, Mr. Sawyer had moved back into his own house, but that hadn't stopped him from dropping by during meal times.

The difference between him and everyone else who was there to sponge off Marianne was that he wasn't there for the food.

"So, what are you guys intending to do?" Tyler asked.

Kate elbowed Tyler softly in his ribs and finally managed to break free from his arms. "Yeah, what's the plan?"

Evelyn leaned on her arm and looked at the blissful couple beside her.

A corner of her lips curled as she thought about the shopping trip she had with Kate. They were at the counter, getting ready to pay for their stuff, when Kate took out her wallet and noticed the cards. Kate pulled out all the credit cards in her wallet with a gaping mouth, surprised that Tyler had substituted all her cards without telling her about it.

The bewilderment caused by the sight of the new cards was quick to pass while annoyance took over.

Once they were out of the shop, Kate called Tyler and gave him an earful. Despite her rant, Evelyn knew Kate hadn't been happier.

Whenever Evelyn looked at how Tyler and Kate interacted, a part of her longed for a relationship like theirs; a relationship where she would be loved and accepted despite all she'd done and all she might do.

She blinked, feeling a hint of moisture at the corner of her eyes, and turned away from the blissful couple.

Such fairytale love was for people like Kate, the kind of woman everyone loved. She was always sweet and amiable, and she never turned anyone down whenever they needed help. In less than a year, Kate was able to turn the aloof Tyler into someone who could never stop smiling whenever she was around. In less than a year, everyone in the room loved her like a princess.

Evelyn, on the other hand, wasn't that kind of lady.

She was one who could never trust enough to be nice to everyone.

While Ryan and Joseph rattled off their plans for the place, Evelyn suddenly felt a gentle squeeze of her hand.

She looked down at Dan's hand, and her head snapped over to him.

She pulled her hand back as she looked away. She couldn't allow herself to become needy now. Now, more than ever, she had to be strong. She promised herself that she wouldn't let a demon from her past destroy what she'd built for herself, and she couldn't be the tough Evelyn when she had Dan to rely on.

She had grown so used to Dan being her comfort that each time she woke from her nightmare, her thumb would hover over the phone while her heart and mind went into battle; a battle between satisfying what her heart wanted and complying with what her mind knew was right.

She wanted to kick herself when Dan withdrew his hand and pretended as though nothing happened.

She shouldn't have pulled her hand back that way. He was merely concerned about her, and all she did was hurt him in return.

Dan could see that Evelyn was already deep in her own thoughts, dismissing him from whatever or whoever was occupying her thoughts.

He looked away and caught Marianne staring at him.

Throughout the whole hot and cold cycle that Evelyn and Dan were going through, Marianne had been nagging him to step up and show Evelyn that he was serious about being together.

Each time, he had trusted Marianne and did what she said.

Each time, the result that followed was a period when he became the invisible man to Evelyn.

When that happened, Marianne would tell him that he wasn't serious enough, and he didn't show her that he'd meant what he said.

Sometimes, he was tempted to snap back at Marianne and tell

her to stop meddling in his business. It was easy to blame Marianne for things going downhill, but he had to admit that she was only giving him the push he needed.

He did know what he wanted, and he wanted everything with her.

He'd heard people talk about how they knew the person they were with was *the one*, and he knew.

It didn't matter that they were running in a circle. It didn't matter that they might be with someone else in between. There was a knowing in his heart that they would end up together.

She would be the one he would grow old with; the one he would create great memories with; the one he would have a family with.

Dan had lost count of the number of times he'd looked at Evelyn and heard the small voice in his heart telling him that they belonged together.

But Evelyn didn't seem to agree. She knew what she wanted as well.

She had told him right from the start that she wasn't interested in relationships, never had and never will. Still, he dove in head first, thinking things would change.

There was nothing for him to complain about. Evelyn did tell him straight to his face; it was purely his stupidity in thinking that he could change things.

Maybe he was wrong. Maybe it was just the spillover effect of Tyler finding love that made him think otherwise. Maybe this time, things were really through between them.

Pushing the food away from him, he tuned in to the conversation around the table.

"Eve always said she wanted to learn self-defense. We just never got to it. If you start one, I bet she'll be your first customer," Kate said.

He had tuned in just in time to disapprove of Kate's idea.

"Yeah, of course," Evelyn replied after a moment's lapse as if she, too, was daydreaming. "It shouldn't be too difficult for you guys to come up with the lessons. You guys learned judo, right?"

Ryan raised his brows. "True."

"Will you ladies be our guinea pigs?" Joseph asked Kate.

"Why not?" "No."

Two people spoke at the same time, but all heads turned toward Tyler. Even if they hadn't recognized his voice, it was obvious he was the one rejecting the idea.

"They're clumsy; you might get hurt," Tyler said to Kate.

"Thanks for thinking about me, too," Evelyn stated sarcastically.

"*Both* of you may get hurt," Tyler corrected.

For once, Dan was grateful for Tyler's protective nature.

Dan grew up with the guys and had lost count of the injuries he'd sustained while playing basketball with them. He didn't think it would be dangerous; he knew it would be. But unlike Tyler, he'd no right to speak up about it.

A silent frustration over the ambiguity of their relationship bubbled within him; a frustration over his lack of rights to be frustrated.

Though he never fooled around in relationships, he'd never felt so possessive over someone, especially someone whom he wasn't even officially dating.

The worst of it was knowing how ridiculous it all seemed. He wasn't in high school anymore; such trivial and petty relationship problems should no longer be an issue. Why couldn't he just close the chapter he had with Evelyn and move on?

"I don't think Ryan's in a position to hurt anyone," Kate said, pointing to the cast on his hand. "And Joseph is a doctor, I'm sure he'll be careful. *And* I'm going to ignore you now."

"Don't worry, Ty. We won't risk your *precious* in any way. I promise," Joseph assured.

There wasn't any point in trying to fight it, Tyler seemed to know it was a lost cause. He shrugged and smiled at Kate. "You do know they'll be dead if you end up getting hurt."

"Ignore him," Kate said.

Dan turned to Evelyn and saw, for just a moment, the hint of sadness in her eyes.

Perhaps her words meant more than she let on.

His fingers twitched as he fought to keep his behavior in check.

She didn't want him touching her, not even to comfort her, so he pulled his hand back a few inches and tightened his grip on his fork.

A moment of silence took over as everyone continued to devour the food Marianne had prepared. There was nothing more to discuss until Ryan and Joseph put more work into the gym.

"Are you interested in being part of the self-defense guinea pigs?" Mr. Sawyer said to Lydia. "After all, lawyers work horrible hours. It's good to learn something to keep yourself safe."

Lydia's head shot up. She blinked and looked around the table, clearly surprised that a question was directed at her.

Although Dan wasn't magnanimous enough to forgive Lydia, he did admire her courage to show up each time Kate invited her over. Everyone was angry with Lydia for various reasons. For Dan, it was because Evelyn could have died in the fire.

The thought of losing Evelyn in the fire was too much to think about, and each time he saw Lydia, he was reminded of the fact that the arsonist was still at large and Evelyn's life might still be in danger.

"Sorry, maybe another time," Lydia finally said.

Without much subtlety, Ryan rolled his eyes.

Lydia didn't have to explain her lack of time. Everyone knew she was still obsessed with the cold case.

Then, Ryan suddenly asked, "What about you, Joanne? Everyone's offering some form of help. What are *you* going to do?"

"Marianne and Mr. Sawyer didn't offer their help," Joanne retorted.

Laughing, Marianne said, "If Joe is planning healthy meals, who do you think will make it edible? And of course, Mr. Sawyer will be taking care of all the legal matters."

Having no other defense, Joanne turned and shared a look with Evelyn.

"Stop disturbing her," Evelyn interjected.

Dan narrowed his eyes at Joanne. He saw the look between Joanne and Evelyn; something was wrong.

Joanne had been disappearing a lot lately, and she would get all flustered each time he asked her what she was up to. Now, there seemed to be some shared camaraderie between Evelyn and Joanne.

"Yeah. What are you so busy with that you can't help? You've been rather secretive lately, Anne." Dan stared at his sister, worried that she was getting into some sort of trouble.

"Everyone has secrets. Let her be," Evelyn stated.

You definitely have yours. He pried his eyes from Evelyn and turned back to Joanne, waiting for her explanation.

Dan saw Joanne swallowing hard and ducking her head as her eyes moved to her plate.

He held his stare; he wasn't going to back down. If Joanne was up to something, he was going to find out right now.

"I'm leaving for Paris next week, and I won't be back for at least a year," Joanne rushed through her words while her eyes remained fixated on the plate.

"What?" Dan exclaimed. "Why?"

"To study. I'm going to study interior design. Everything is settled. Evelyn found an apartment for me and went shopping with me for all the necessities I need."

Evelyn knew all along? "And how long ago was this decision made? Do Mom and Dad know about this? You've never been away on your own for so long. How are you going to survive?"

"Oh, Dan, you should be glad. It's a fantastic opportunity; it'll be good for her," Marianne said. "Good luck with your studies, Joanne."

"Glad? She's never done her own laundry. She doesn't know how to cook—"

"This is why I didn't want to tell you. I'm always just your baby sister. I don't want to be just your sister anymore."

Clueless about what Joanne was talking about, Dan turned to Evelyn with a slight frown.

"Let her go. She'll be fine," Evelyn stated simply.

Dan sighed softly.

"Look, Evelyn taught me how to do my laundry, how to cook can food and ramen noodles," Joanne said.

Evelyn taught her?

Joanne continued to rattle on, "Always lock my doors and windows when leaving the house and when going to bed. Do not walk in dark alleys. Always be aware of my surroundings, and a whole load of other stuff that Evelyn has already been nagging me about."

"Nagging?" Evelyn arched a brow.

"Kidding … kidding." Joanne gave Evelyn a nervous smile.

"How long have you been preparing for this?" he asked.

"A while."

And Evelyn had been helping her.

Evelyn wasn't fond of Joanne at all, not after all that Joanne had done to Kate. So why was she doing this?

His gaze fell on Evelyn. If only he could read minds.

"I'll be fine," Joanne continued when he said nothing.

Evelyn had been living on her own since she was sixteen. There couldn't be a better person helping Joanne. And for the first time since the conversation took a turn, he finally breathed easier.

He leaned back and nodded. "When were you intending to tell me?"

"Soon, in a less public scene."

His head bobbed up and down as he thought things through. "Everything is settled? School admissions … money?"

"Yes, and probably yes. Evelyn settled all the admission stuff for me. I *think* Mom and Dad will help me with the money. Otherwise, Kate has agreed to help me with whatever I need while I find a part-time job."

He turned to Kate and smiled gratefully. Though he was somewhat offended that Joanne hadn't come to him for help, he was glad that she'd chosen the next best alternative.

"I'm sorry. She made me promise not to tell," Kate said with a wry smile.

He already knew how good Kate was at keeping secrets, but he couldn't believe that Evelyn hadn't told him anything when they were going out. Then, a sudden realization hit him. "Kate knew, so that means you knew," he said while glaring at Tyler.

Applying his signature style to avoid talking, Tyler merely shrugged.

"I made him promise not to tell," Kate interjected. "Joanne wanted to make sure that everything was settled before announcing it."

There was no way he was going to win the war. Putting aside his bruised ego for being blindsided, he had to admit that it was a positive step forward for Joanne. "Looks like you've got everything covered. If you need anything else, I hope you'll remember that you have a brother."

Joanne laughed. "I will. Now that I know you're not going to stop me, I will."

With that, all the guys wished her well while Dan dove into his own interrogation, prying all the details from Joanne.

When everyone was done with breakfast, Joseph helped Ryan back to his room, and Lydia left for her own house. Dan lingered in the kitchen; he wasn't through with Joanne.

"Going to the office today?" Evelyn asked Kate.

"Yup."

"All right. Tyler can drop you off, right? I'm going to head off first," Evelyn said and strode out of the kitchen.

Kate made no objection, but Dan saw how her eyes bore into Evelyn's back. Kate wasn't the sort who'd pry information out of people, but she'd definitely be keeping a closer watch on Evelyn.

Since he wasn't able to do so, he was glad someone would be watching Evelyn's back.

Chapter Four

Lydia stood outside a small diner and squinted as she took a look inside. She hitched her handbag onto her shoulder and checked her watch for the fifth time. She knew she was early, but her nerves were escalating her impatience.

Again, she peered into the diner to make sure that Suzanne Harrison hadn't slipped by her or entered through other entrances. Tapping her feet against the concrete floor, she looked away from the diner and scanned her surroundings.

Since the last dinner that Lydia had at the mansion, she'd been propelled into a new aspect of her investigation. Mr. Sawyer had noticed that no one was speaking to her and tried to engage her in a conversation.

The short conversation between them caused light bulbs to go off in her head.

She'd been looking at her parents' case through the lens of it being a simple, straightforward murder and had focused her investigation on Detective Cooper, the detective in charge of her parents' case. After going through it for months, there weren't any new leads for her to follow.

Then, Mr. Sawyer's words gave her a new perspective.

When Lydia told him that she intended to pursue a career as a public prosecutor, Mr. Sawyer mentioned the hazards that many public prosecutors faced; the possibility of threats brought about from the job.

It was certainly reasonable, and she couldn't believe she hadn't thought about that. Her father was a public prosecutor. Perhaps the murder of her parents wasn't a random homicide. It could have been an attempt to stop her father from prosecuting the case he was on.

The moment she got home that night, Lydia switched on her computer and combed through the Internet, searching for information. Then she hit the library archives, gathering as many newspaper clippings as she could. Years of studying law had honed her research skills. Within weeks, she was able to sift out the possible suspects. After some cross-referencing, the main suspects quickly became clear.

The information she found wasn't good enough. She wanted to make sure of things herself. Since the fire incident, she'd learned it was better to stay away from the main suspects until she had something concrete. This time, she was taking the roundabout route.

Lydia didn't know why Detective Allen was helping Tyler, but she'd managed to pester him into helping her find some of the people involved in the case her father was working on before his death.

Peering into the diner again, Lydia sighed and wondered if Suzanne Harrison was ever going to show up. Just as she was about to begin pacing, she noticed the petite middle-aged lady who was hastening toward the diner. She was clad in the same cyan uniform that the other waitresses in the diner were wearing.

Slipping her hand into her bag, Lydia took out her phone and opened the PDF file she had stored in it. She broke into a smile as a younger version of Suzanne's face popped into her cell phone's screen. "Suzanne Harrison?" She stepped in front of her, stretching her hand toward the woman. "I'm Lydia Mitchell."

"Mitchell?" Suzanne mumbled and hesitantly took her hand as she gave her a look over.

She could see the blend of confusion and suspicion on Suzanne's face. "I'm a law student. I'm working on a report for a cold case, and I'd like to interview you to find out more about it."

Lydia didn't have to elaborate or point out the particular cold case she was working on.

Once the words 'cold case' left her lips, Suzanne blanched and took a small step away from her.

"Please, I just have a few simple questions."

"It happened a long time ago. I don't remember anything. I don't know anything." Suzanne's words came out in a rush as she took a side step, trying to move away from her.

"You can just tell me what you remember." Lydia moved and walked by Suzanne's side.

"I've got to work."

"I understand. I can come back later after your shift."

Suzanne stopped and stared straight into Lydia's eyes while her fingers reached out and formed a vice-like grip on her arm. "Please, I don't want to get involved in anything about the case," Suzanne said in a harsh whisper.

The fear in Suzanne's eyes revealed so much more than Lydia had anticipated and indirectly answered the questions she had in mind.

"I understand. I'm sorry to disturb you."

Evelyn and Kate trotted along the corridor, heading toward Lydia's apartment.

"Are you all right?" Kate asked, her eyes looking ahead.

Evelyn continued walking, twirling her cell phone in her hand. "Yeah, why?"

"I don't know. You've been rather weird lately."

"Weird?"

"You've been disappearing a lot."

"No, I haven't."

Kate rolled her eyes and stared at Evelyn. "Seriously, what have you been up to? Are you seeing someone?"

"I've been up to nothing, and I'm not seeing anyone," she answered as she stole a peek at her phone's screen.

They stopped in front of the door, and Kate rang the bell. "If there's anything, you'll tell me, right?"

"Of course." Evelyn turned away from Kate, looking at her phone again. "You told Dan to pick you up later, right? I haven't been feeling too well, think I'll get some gastric pills then head home after this."

She could feel Kate scrutinizing her face.

After a long pause, Kate finally said, "Yeah, I did."

Evelyn tapped her feet against the floor and stared at the door. *Come on, Lydia. Open the door.*

When no one came to the door, Kate pulled out her cell phone from the bag and called Lydia. From outside the door, they could hear the phone ringing. Since they were already standing outside, Kate opened the door using the spare key that Lydia had given her and stepped in gingerly.

Evelyn entered after Kate and immediately heard the water running. "Showering," she said and followed Kate into the living room.

Kate shook her head as she took in the sight of the incredibly messy room. "Look at this place."

Though they were sisters, Kate and Lydia couldn't be more different. Kate was an excellent housekeeper. She kept her house spick and span, never having to worry if anyone dropped by her house unannounced.

Lydia was the complete opposite; Lydia was like her.

Clothes and shoes were strewn all over the place, half-eaten food was on the table, and a pile of unfolded clothes sat on the couch, taking up two seats on the three-seater.

Lydia would make the perfect roommate for her, and together, they would be the ultimate nightmare for the landlord.

She grinned as she glanced around at the reflection of her own house, her eyes stopping on the gigantic whiteboard standing in the middle of the room. Even with all the clutter in the living room, it was way too prominent to miss.

With a frown, she approached the unusual piece of furniture. At first glance, the whiteboard was another mess that matched the state of Lydia's living room. Thick nylon strings were sprawled across the board, leading to different pictures and Post-it notes.

Right in the middle of the whiteboard, the origin of where all the nylon strings branched out from, was a photograph that Evelyn had seen before. The photograph that was inside the locket that Kate used to wear.

The locket had belonged to Kate's mother, and Kate had treasured it. But after the fire, Kate was done with Lydia's obsession, so she handed the locket over to Lydia and washed her hands off the investigation.

Kate's finger skimmed down the side of her mother's smiling face.

Evelyn looked over at her. "Are you all right?".

"Yeah." Kate nodded and moved on to study the rest of the board. Her finger followed a thick nylon string linking the complex web of information on the board. On one side of the board were pictures of the threats that Kate had received not too long ago.

Kate's finger trembled slightly when she saw the picture on the aftermath of the fire, of the charred remains they almost became part of. Kate forced her eyes shut, and her fingers moved to fiddle with the angel pendant on her neck.

Evelyn gave Kate a gentle squeeze on her arm before she took over and traced another thick nylon string, leading to the name David Morgan. From his name, several branches shot out, stating several different years along with various sexual crimes. One particular year was circled with a red marker. *1997*. Beside the year stood the words, *Rape & Murder. 6.*

1997, the year Lydia and Kate's parents were murdered.

Evelyn continued down the links to another Morgan, Richard Morgan.

"Richard Morgan," Kate said, her brows furrowing. "The name sounds familiar."

A sudden gasp sent both their heads turning.

Lydia stood, wide-eyed, looking at them. "What … Why …" she fumbled for words.

"You promised to keep me updated on whatever you were doing on this case." Kate stood with her arms akimbo.

"Yes, I know that," Lydia said, finally regaining her ability to form a sentence, albeit a short one.

"Then what's this?" Kate asked, tapping on the board, pointing to the name *David Morgan*.

Evelyn rolled her eyes. She couldn't help feeling annoyed at Lydia. Even after the fire, Lydia was still adamant about solving their parents' murder. She had apologized, but apparently their almost-death wasn't good enough reason for her to stop the investigation.

Raising her palms, Lydia took a step back. "I only found out about this when you left for your honeymoon. I was waiting for you to come home and settle down before I dump this on you."

"Who is this David Morgan?"

"Rich young heir. Son of Richard Morgan." Lydia moved over to the coffee table and opened her laptop.

From where she was standing, Evelyn could see the laptop loading immediately.

Lydia clearly hadn't bothered to shut down her laptop, and that made Evelyn wonder how much time Lydia was spending on the case.

"David Morgan had been accused of several different sexual crimes: sexual harassment, attempted rape, rape, and aggravated sexual assaults. In 1997, he was formally charged with six cases of rape and murder." She paused, looking over at Evelyn then back at Kate. "Dad was the prosecutor in charge of the case."

"That doesn't mean he has anything to do with their deaths."

"Yes, but listen. Out of the string of cases that involved David Morgan, only two made it to court. For the rest of the cases, the witnesses, and sometimes the victims, backed out or disappeared before the trial began. Of the two that made it to court, the witnesses recanted their statements, claiming that the police forced them to appear on the stand and threatened them to feed a story to the court or they'd be arrested."

"If they could make witnesses disappear or change their words, I suppose they are rich or have some serious connections," Evelyn said.

"Rich, very rich." Lydia turned her laptop over to face them.

"My point is." Evelyn turned the laptop back toward Lydia. "Please don't do anything stupid."

"Your present." Kate shook the paper bag that was hooked to her index finger and placed it down by the table. "And please, be careful."

"That's a polite rendition of what I just said, but your sister meant the same thing." Evelyn turned toward the door. "Are you waiting here?"

Kate checked her phone. "Dan's already here," she said and turned to her sister. "Make sure you tell me everything that's going on. No more secrets or lies."

Evelyn opened the door and stepped out, waiting for Kate.

"Yes, ma'am," Lydia said.

"Are you sure you can't join us?" Kate asked Evelyn when Lydia closed the door.

"Yeah, I want to get some rest."

"Eve—"

"Don't start with me," Evelyn snapped before Kate could continue. Evelyn knew Kate had been dancing around the subject since she'd been back. "Nothing is wrong with me. Nothing is wrong with Dan and me. We were friends, and we are still friends."

She saw Kate reaching for her necklace and sighed softly. "I'm sorry. I'm just … Nothing is wrong, all right?"

Kate nodded then turned toward Dan's car.

"See you tomorrow." Evelyn turned from Kate and walked toward her own car while Kate got into Dan's black Dodge Dakota truck.

Dan watched Evelyn hurry away as Kate entered the car. Not once did she turn to look at him.

He took his focus off Evelyn's disappearing figure and looked at the line etched between Kate's brows. "Are you okay?"

"She never walks away from me to answer a call, not until now. Something is up with those calls," she said, her eyes staring out the windshield.

He pulled out of the lot and drove toward the mansion. "Did you ask?"

"Not specifically about the phone calls. I only asked what she'd been up to."

"And?"

"She said she was up to nothing." Kate sighed softly. "If she doesn't want to discuss something, she won't."

He knew that well from personal experience.

"Maybe it's nothing. Maybe it's like what she said; she just hasn't been feeling well," Kate continued.

"Gastric?"

"Yeah."

"She's been looking tired; maybe it's the nightmares."

Kate took her eyes off the road and looked at him with raised brows.

"She never told me anything. She just used to call me at night when she couldn't sleep. I surmised as much."

She didn't say anything for the next minute, but he could feel her eyes studying him.

"How are you?"

"Good."

She grunted and looked away.

"That's very unladylike of you."

She kept quiet again; this time, looking out of the window. "I'm sorry I can't be of more help."

"If it's something serious, she'll tell you, right?"

"I'd like to say yes."

"But?"

"But she went through so many things on her own. I think her first instinct is to solve her own problems. I think deep down she still has the concept that no one would be there to help her."

"But you've always been there for her."

"Not always, not before." She drew a deep breath. "I guess some memories can cripple you."

Though he was frustrated with whatever secret Kate was referring to, he had to ask, "Will she be all right?"

"She will; she's survived everything this far. And like I said, it's probably nothing."

He couldn't help thinking that her last sentence seemed directed at comforting him rather than being the truth.

Chapter Five

Evelyn jolted upright on the couch and shook her head, trying to get rid of the drowsiness that was making her head swirl. Squinting at the clock mounted on the wall, she realized she'd dozed off on her couch. She reached over to the phone lying next to her, pressed the home button, and cringed as the bright light from the cell phone came on.

Forcing her eyes open, she sighed when the screen showed no new notifications.

Groggily, Evelyn pushed herself off the couch and plodded over to the door, almost tripping over a lone black heel lying in the middle of her living room. She shouldn't be stumbling around in her living room while her mind was still fogged with sleepiness.

Though she didn't mind stepping on her clothes, entrapment might be lying beneath the deceptive jackets, and she could easily hurt herself.

Annoyed, she kicked the black heel aside to join the rest of the shoes and went over to look at the electronic security display that Tyler had installed for her.

Dan? He never turned up unannounced whenever they were in one of their cold stages.

She was instantly worried that something was wrong. Why else would he be here?

Her hand moved toward the knob just as she caught sight of herself in the mirror hung on the adjacent wall.

Using her fingers as a comb, she brushed through her

wayward auburn hair. She always tossed around when sleeping, so whenever she woke, her hair always looked as if it had survived a hurricane.

Once she was presentable, she opened the door.

Dan leaned casually by the door, wearing a clean white shirt with jeans. He flashed a brilliant smile and waved the can of chicken soup in his hand. "Hungry?"

Unconsciously, her lips curled to reflect his. Her hands moved to her stomach. "Yeah, I think so," she answered and stepped aside for Dan to enter.

"Feeling better?"

"Huh?" Evelyn closed the door and turned back to him.

"Kate said your gastric was acting up."

"Oh, right. I'm fine. Drank some milk."

Dan easily crossed over the clutter without stepping or tripping over anything.

She crossed over the messy living room, picking up some of her clothes. She had three tops draped over her arm when she gave up. There wasn't much she could do to rectify her messy habits at that moment. Besides, Dan had been at her house before, and he had never complained.

She transferred the clothes onto the nearest dining chair and joined Dan on the couch.

Placing the can down on one of the few spots available on her coffee table, Dan tilted his head and watched her. "Have you eaten anything? If you have the appetite, we can order take out."

"Hmm …" Evelyn considered Dan's question for a moment as she swept all the magazines on the coffee table into her hands and stacked them up.

She hadn't had anything to eat since the few bites of sandwich from lunch; she hadn't had much appetite lately. Though she was feeling kind of hungry now, she wasn't sure if she could stomach heavy food. "I think soup is enough."

"Okay." His finger traced her fringe, sliding across her forehead and down her temple.

"I missed you." The words escaped her lips before she could stop them.

"What should I do with you?"

She chewed on a corner of her lower lip and looked away from him. As she turned, she felt his finger on her chin.

Gently, he turned her face back toward him. "Don't turn away. I like it when your eyes are on me." His eyes bore into hers, holding her captive.

The sincerity in his eyes always caught her off guard. No matter how many times he looked at her that way, she never knew how to react. All she could do was to gaze right back at him.

At times like this, she wanted so much to lean in and kiss him.

She wanted to believe she could be one of those lucky enough to live happily ever after, to believe someone would still love her after knowing everything about her.

But even in times like this, the nagging voice of fear and accusation never left.

She sighed softly.

"I'll do anything to have you look at me like this for the rest of my life," he whispered. Then, without waiting for a response from her, Dan took the can from the table and stood. "It should be ready in fifteen minutes."

Dan went into the kitchen while she remained seated on the couch.

She wanted so much to go after him and tell him what he wanted to hear, but she couldn't get herself off the couch.

He won't want that from you, not after he knows what you've done, the voice of fear, loud and clear, reminded her.

She buried her face in her hands and swallowed hard.

And you know you can never give him what he wants.

Her eyes burnt behind her lids.

How could all her resolution to stay away from him disappear the moment she saw his face on the security screen?

She had thought about the situation between them over and over again, and each time the conclusion was always the same— he was better off without her.

She should have told him to leave when she opened the door. No, she shouldn't even have opened it in the first place.

Taking a deep breath, she pinched the bridge of her nose and forced all emotions from her face. Then she got to her feet and trotted over to the kitchen.

"You should go." Evelyn folded her arms, her fingers digging into them.

"What's wrong?" Dan asked, moving over to her, and ran his hand down her arm.

As though his mere touch burnt her, she yanked her arm from him and retreated a few steps back.

His eyes widened, and he stood where he was with his arms raised by his chest.

"You should go," she repeated.

Dan crooked his lower jaw and drew a deep breath through his nose.

Without another word, he made his way out of the kitchen and stalked toward the door. Pausing right in front of it, he hesitated for a moment.

She closed her eyes and turned away from him. She couldn't stand watching him leave; she was afraid her will to send him away would dissipate.

"I can't do this anymore," Dan said, almost in a whisper.

She didn't allow herself to turn around, not even as she felt his eyes on her back. *This is better for everyone,* she reminded herself.

"Goodnight." He opened the door and stepped out.

That one word, coupled with the click of the door, sounded so final.

She took a ragged breath and staggered to the wall just as her legs lost all their strength.

With her back against the wall, she crumpled onto the floor. Tears streamed down her face while her hands cupped tightly over her mouth. She forced herself to breathe through her nose and soften her cries.

No one else was in the house. No one would hear her cry. It was simply a habit ingrained in her.

She didn't grow up with the notion that wailing would bring about help and kind attention from adults. Since she could remember, being seen crying was a sign of weakness, and any sign of weakness would make her a target.

She gasped and drew small, rapid breaths as she wiped her tears away. *This is better for everyone,* she repeated that thought over and over again. She wasn't suitable for a relationship, and it was never going to work anyway.

Even if she did tell him everything about her past, she couldn't expect him to accept her when she couldn't give him the future he so desired.

Her hands dropped from her mouth, and she wrapped them across her abdomen.

She shut her eyes and drew a shaky breath.

Stop crying. Crying doesn't solve anything. She tried shoving all her feelings into a box and throwing it away, just as she had done so many times when she was in the foster system.

There was no point crying; no one would help her.

There was no point feeling sad; nothing would change.

But she couldn't.

She pulled her legs against her chest and hid her face between her knees as a new wave of hopelessness crashed against her.

A whimper escaped her throat, and she immediately silenced herself.

Slowly, the palpitations faded. She picked herself off the floor and staggered back onto her couch. Picking up her cell phone, she called the only comfort she had left.

"Hey, Eve, feeling better?"

She didn't answer Kate. She took a moment and cleared her throat softly, making sure her voice wouldn't break before she asked, "Will you come over and stay tonight?"

"I'll be there in half an hour."

She hung up the phone without saying goodbye and pulled her fleece throw over her shoulders.

It wasn't a cold night. In fact, it was a warm, stuffy summer night; a night where even the occasional breeze brought nothing to relieve the heat within the house. Still, she couldn't help shivering.

As she lay on the couch, she stared at the cell phone in front of her. Frustrated, she picked it up and sent the phone flying across the room. The phone smashed against the wall and fell heavily onto the floor. Turning her head away, she tossed onto her side and squeezed her eyes shut.

Though the phone wasn't the cause of her problem, lately, it had become a reminder of how she'd never have a happily-ever-after, something she was beginning to yearn.

She never imagined herself needing such a frivolous thing. To her, survival was the only thing she needed. She'd always worked to make sure she earned enough so she would never require any help. Everything she'd done in life was to make sure she could survive on her own.

But nowadays, with each call came the reminder of what she could never have with Dan, and with each call came a new injection of despair.

When Evelyn heard the keys, she rubbed the throw brusquely over her face before pushing it aside and sitting up just as Kate entered.

She forced a smile when she saw Kate closing the door behind her. The last thing she needed was Tyler seeing her in such a state. "You're alone."

"He walked me to the door and left after I came in. What's wrong?"

She looked away from Kate, staring at the lone black heel she'd kicked aside while scooting over on the couch to make room for Kate.

"I don't know," she said with a sigh and shook her head. "I don't know."

This was what she wanted right from the start; she wanted Dan to know they would never be more than just friends.

Now that she had gotten what she wanted, she couldn't ignore the ache in her heart. "It's over. It's really over."

Then she felt the heavy droplets of tears on her legs as Kate moved closer to her, gently rubbing her back.

"I'm so sorry."

Dan took a swig of his beer and scanned through the channels, trying to find something to occupy his mind. He wasn't paying attention to anything on the screen. He simply wanted to vent on something, and the incessant pressing of his remote control was rather therapeutic.

The ache in his heart had faded and was replaced with frustration.

He should've headed to the gym to vent it off instead of sulking at home. But he didn't feel like going anywhere, so the buttons on the remote control would have to bear his vexation.

He couldn't get over what a complete idiot he was.

Why did he even bother to turn up at her apartment? Why couldn't he stop worrying about her when he heard about her gastric?

He should've known it was going to end this way; it always did.

How could he still be deceived into thinking that her smile was evidence of her missing him? Her sweet smile, revealing a hint of nervousness, was nothing but a fragment of his imagination.

Sighing, he took another gulp of beer before tossing the empty bottle into the nearby trash can.

Until an hour ago, he would still swear that he could see the feelings Evelyn had for him. He was sure of the yearning he saw in her eyes, and he was certain she felt the same way about him.

Now, he realized he merely saw what he wanted to see. He was merely pulling things out of nowhere to convince himself of what he wanted so much to be true.

The more he thought about what happened, the more idiotic he felt.

When she had told him to leave, all he wanted was to talk to her, to ask her what was wrong, and to make her feel better. But he knew Evelyn wouldn't entertain him. If he hadn't left, she would start screaming at him to do so in the next second.

Even when he was standing at the door, he had paused and hoped that Evelyn would change her mind and ask him to stay. But his heart was crushed by her silence.

On his drive back, a new sense of determination rose.

Evelyn wasn't ready, and he was beginning to doubt if she ever would be.

His thoughts were interrupted by the doorbell. He groaned,

then chose to ignore it.

But whoever was outside wasn't cooperating. Whoever it was, he or she wasn't giving up.

With an annoyed sigh, he got off the couch and opened the door, ready to unleash some of his peevishness.

"Hey!"

"What are you doing here?" Dan asked as he peered over Ryan's shoulder. "You came here alone? How did you get up the steps?"

Looping his hand over Dan's shoulder and using him as a crutch, Ryan leaned onto Dan and half hopped his way in.

"Tyler dropped me off, then I got up the steps on my own. He thinks I'm Superman. That guy didn't even bother to help me get out of the car. The whole 'new Tyler' thing only exists when Kate is around."

Dan laughed at Ryan's ramble. "Did he kick you out? You should've asked Marianne or Mr. Sawyer to drive you over," he said while helping Ryan to the couch.

"Kate went over to Evelyn's house. Though Ty was too idiotic to bother with helping me up the stairs, he's smart enough to know that he isn't the perfect candidate to come and talk to you. So, here I am."

"Don't be so proud of yourself. I'm sure you got assigned the task due to the lack of other available candidates."

Ryan gave him a mock punch, picked up the remote, and proceeded to change the channel. He sighed as he lazed against the couch. Lifting one of his legs onto the coffee table, he asked, "Beer?"

"You treat every one of our house as your own, don't you?"

Ryan gave him a quick brow raise and went back to scanning the channels.

Dan went into the kitchen and came back with two beers in his hands, handing one to Ryan.

They sat and watched the television quietly until Ryan said, "So what happened with Evelyn?"

"It's over."

"When did it start?" Ryan asked with a smirk.

Dan made a sound between a grunt and a laugh.

"Look, I never understood what's with you and Evelyn. Why are you playing this merry-go-round with her?"

Dan sighed and took a mouthful of beer. Ryan was the last person he wanted to discuss the topic of love with. Relationship wise, Ryan was a complete opposite of him.

"I know she's hot and all."

Dan rolled his eyes and continued before he had to punch Ryan. "She's different from everyone I know."

"If you're talking about Joanne and your parents, then yeah, of course she's different."

"It isn't just that. I want her to get over whatever happened in the past; I want to make things better for her. She's more than the person she lets the world see."

"So it's a damsel in distress situation?"

"No. She doesn't need me to take care of her, but I *want* to. I don't know, we're … we're good together. When she lets her guard down, we have so much fun," Dan said, thinking back to the times they'd spent together.

He remembered the silly jokes they made, how she'd laugh at everything he talked about; a genuine laughter, unlike the polite smile she always had. Sometimes when they were together, he'd look into her eyes, and he could see beyond the dark brown eyes and feel the pain she had buried within.

Though he didn't know the details of what had happened in her past, all he could think about was to protect her and tell her that he would never leave her alone to deal with anything.

"If it helps, I think she feels the same. Her eyes always light up when she's talking to you. With Kate, she seems comfortable. With you, she seems happy."

"So it's not just me who thinks that."

"What is she afraid of?"

"The damn secret that Evelyn refuses to tell. The same damn secret that Kate is guarding for her."

"Huh. Maybe I can help you charm it out of Kate."

Dan had to laugh. "I'm pretty sure that unless Evelyn allows it, Kate is going to carry the secret to her grave."

"But she loves me."

Dan continued laughing, and after struggling for a while, he finally managed to reply. "Someday, Ty will kill you over this Kate-loves-me thing."

"Is it really over?" Ryan asked.

"Yes." The same determination he had felt when walking out of Evelyn's house rose again. "Yes," Dan repeated, though this time, even as the word left his lips, he wondered how Evelyn was doing. "Kate is over at Evelyn's?"

"Tell you what," Ryan said with a pat on Dan's back. "As your friend, I'm going to pretend that you never asked that question. It's my way of helping you get over her."

Ryan was right. Kate would be with her anyway. It was high time he stopped worrying about her. She was the one who wanted nothing to do with him.

Chapter Six

The next morning, the atmosphere at breakfast was awkward. Besides Marianne, all the ladies were missing that morning.

Dan could sense Marianne's eyes flickering toward him every couple of minutes. She was clearly waiting for him to say something.

It wasn't possible to keep anything a secret from the group. Everyone knew what had happened, but no one knew what to say about it.

Even Marianne was being more subdued than usual, giving him a break and not bugging him about what was going on.

Maybe this time, everyone could sense that things between him and Evelyn were truly over.

"Kate! Good morning!" Ryan exclaimed.

Tyler swiveled around. "I thought you said you'd call me to pick you up?"

"She finally fell asleep, and I was tired. So I just called a cab." She pulled out the chair next to Tyler's and sat.

Dan hadn't realized he was staring at Kate until her eyes met his.

"You came from Evelyn's?" he asked before remembering he wasn't supposed to care.

Kate pursed her lips into a thin line and twirled the pendant around her fingers. "I can't. I can't be on both your sides at the same time. I'm all she has."

Trying to be understanding of Evelyn's closely guarded secret was vexing enough, but not being able to get an answer to his simple question compounded his frustrations further. "I just wanted to make sure she was okay. Do you have to be so difficult about it?"

The uncomfortable silence that was lingering got heavier, and everyone had a sudden newfound interest in the food on their plates.

"Remember whose house you're in," Tyler stated with as much annoyance as Dan had expressed with his question. "Vent your frustrations on someone else."

"I tried to be patient; I tried to be understanding. But seriously, does everything about her have to be a secret? What the hell is so scary that she can't get over after so many years?" Dan said, louder than necessary.

Kate got to her feet and turned away from them, moving to leave the kitchen.

Immediately, Tyler got up alongside her. He reached over and grabbed her arm, his head shaking slightly. "This is your house; you don't have to leave."

"I don't want this to erupt into a fight."

"Have you lost your ability to speak your mind, too?" Dan uttered under his breath and jabbed his fork into a piece of scrambled egg.

Tyler turned his head toward him and said, "Dan, get out."

Though the words were spoken in an even tone, Dan knew it was a command. He placed his utensils down and was ready to leave when Kate turned back to face him.

"No, it's fine. You want me to speak my mind? You judge her based on *your* experience. All you had to deal with in life was your manipulative mom. Eve would've given her soul to the devil to exchange her childhood with yours. You can make the decision to end things with her, but you have no right to judge her."

Dan stared blankly at Kate. The usually sweet and amiable Kate morphed into a mother hen in an instant.

Though Kate's words were harsh, it was nothing compared to the seriousness he saw in her eyes.

He'd never seen her fly into such rage, not even when Lydia almost killed her.

He had been frustrated with Evelyn for keeping her secret, for behaving the way she did. But seeing how worked up Kate was at the mention of what had happened to Evelyn was making him wonder if he'd taken for granted his childhood and expected too much of Evelyn.

This wasn't how he'd intended to start his day. He couldn't believe he lost control like this.

He got up and stepped away from the table. "I should go, or Ty will throw me out anyway." The last thing Dan had wanted was to upset Kate. He should've kept his mouth shut. *So much for being done with Evelyn.*

Over the next few days, Dan found himself having too much free time on his hand. Without the long dinners at the mansion, he found himself thinking too much about everything.

Initially, he distracted himself by fussing over Joanne, checking and double-checking that she had everything needed for her studies in Paris. Then, he had to deal with his over-dramatic mother when she found out about the news.

After sending Joanne to the airport, he turned his attention to work, working harder than ever, both at work and at his current gym.

He'd thought he was succeeding in putting Evelyn out of his mind until he found himself rushing to pick up every call, hoping it was Evelyn. He was, of course, sorely disappointed.

The only redeeming factor of the calls was a call from Ryan, asking him out for lunch.

As he made his way into the restaurant for lunch with Ryan and Joseph, Dan could see the apprehension on their faces. "I'm fine. Is Kate still angry?"

"She regretted it almost as soon as you left, but we all backed her up. You shouldn't have vented your anger on her," Joseph stated matter-of-factly.

"But we get it, this thing with you and Evelyn is eating at you," Ryan added. "At least, it's over."

Yes, at least it is over.

The past week had been quiet. He didn't offer any news of himself, and neither did he receive any news of Evelyn. It was a good thing that the chapter with her had finally ended.

"So you guys are really over?" Joseph asked.

"Yeah," Dan answered.

"So anyway, we've signed the lease for the gym. Thanks again for helping us find the place," Joseph said.

"And, I've got a friend joining us for lunch. I'm thinking of getting her to teach some yoga classes at the gym," Ryan said.

Dan shrugged. "Sure."

Just as they were about to order, a long-legged, tanned, and extremely well-toned brunette walked toward their table.

Ryan waved his hand to get her attention. "Hey, Chris! I want to get up to give you a hug, but it would be a long and difficult affair."

She waved him off, then took a quick glance at Joseph and Dan. With a broad smile, she took the guys' hands as Ryan introduced her.

Dan then pulled out the chair for her, bringing about a look of surprise from Christine.

"Thanks," she said and sat. "Not many guys pull out chairs for women anymore."

"That's because I don't want to insult you. I'm sure you're more than capable of pulling out your own chair," Ryan said.

"Right."

After ordering their food, Ryan immediately dove into the discussion of the plan for the new gym.

While Ryan, Joseph, and Christine discussed work, Dan immediately saw the similarity between Christine and Evelyn. She was candid and frank, speaking things as they were. This, in turn, allowed Ryan to get straight to the point, settling their cooperation before lunch was over.

"So, Dan, will you be there at the gym as well?" Christine asked when her discussion with Ryan and Joseph ended.

"Yeah, I think I'm in line to be the first customer."

"Good, so I'll see you around."

He smiled politely, not saying anything else.

For the rest of lunch, Christine continued flirting with him. Though she would serve as a good distraction, the last thing Dan needed right now was another woman. So, he continued behaving like a courteous gentleman.

When they were leaving the restaurant, Christine suddenly asked, "So, Dan, are you doing anything tonight?"

"I think I'll be having dinner with them," Dan said, tilting his head toward Ryan and Joseph.

"If you're tired of seeing them all the time, I don't mind accompanying you for dinner."

He blinked and found himself at a loss for words. "Are you asking me out?"

Christine laughed. "You mean I wasn't obvious enough?"

"No, I'm just not used to …"

"Being asked out? You don't expect me to believe that." She smiled, then continued. "So, dinner?"

He tried to come up with an excuse to let her down gently.

"Yes, he's sick of seeing us, and he'll pick you up at seven tonight," Ryan interjected. "Dan, open the door for her before she changes her mind."

He smiled awkwardly at Christine and opened the door. While Christine strode through the door, he turned around and glared at Ryan.

"It's all right, you don't have to—"

"No, he's right. I'm sick of seeing them. I'll pick you up at seven?"

Christine's smile grew wider. "Great. Give me your phone." She gave Dan her number and address, then returned the phone to him. "See you tonight."

Dan shifted the flowers to his left hand and knocked on Christine's door.

"Right on time," Christine said as she opened the door.

He nodded and couldn't help but take another look at the bright red strapless dress that fitted her toned body so snugly.

"Like what you see?" Christine asked while she put on her earrings.

He smiled sheepishly, feeling silly that he was caught staring. "You look great."

She grinned and took the flowers from Dan's outstretched hand. "Aw … you shouldn't have. Come in, take a seat. I'll be ready in five minutes." Christine smiled, then disappeared into her room.

Dan moved toward the couch, stepping over the yoga mat that lay opened right beside it. The house was clean, and though it wasn't large, the minimal furniture she had created a sense of spaciousness.

Across from the couch was a plasma TV that was hung on the wall and a plain, uncluttered TV console holding a photo frame and a remote. Instead of a coffee table, a white furry rug took up the space between the couch and TV, opening up more space in the living room.

Even the dining table was small. It was a table meant for four, tucked away in the corner of the room.

He leaned back and took in the view of the living room, grinning as he thought about the huge difference between Christine's and Evelyn's apartments. Catching himself in his thoughts, he turned as Christine strutted out of her room.

"Do you want something to drink? Otherwise, I'm ready to go."

"I'm good. Let's go, then."

By the time they got out from his car, Dan realized that being with Christine was like being with a female version of Ryan. They laughed and chatted with each other as if they were long-time friends.

He opened the door for her and took a quick scan of the restaurant as they entered. He was glad it wasn't the romantic kind of restaurant where tables were placed wide apart, giving couples their space.

Smiling politely to the couple next to them, Dan and Christine took their seats. Immediately, Dan noticed the slight color difference in the wooden beams of the table. The dark chocolate-brown paint on the beam wasn't even, revealing a lighter shade of brown in the deeper grains of the wood.

Shoddy workmanship. His lips curled as he heard Evelyn's voice in his head.

It took certain skills and lots of practice to get such details right, details that Evelyn always paid attention to.

"What's good here?"

He looked up from the table leg and noticed the menu on the table. He didn't even realize that a waiter had come by. "I believe steak is their specialty," he quickly answered.

Christine nodded just as the waiter returned and took their orders. Once the waiter left, she turned to Dan and started asking him about work.

Five minutes into the conversation, Christine suddenly narrowed her eyes and leaned forward. Resting her chin on her hand, she asked, "Am I boring you? Or is there someplace else you have to be?"

"What? No, you're not boring me, and I have nowhere else to go."

"Who is she?"

He choked on the wine he was drinking. "What?" he said after coughing into his fist to clear his throat.

"Who is she?" Christine repeated.

"No one, no one important."

"I can see how upset you are just to say she's no one important."

"Do you always talk about other women when you're on a date?"

"Is this a date?" Taking a sip of wine, she smiled coyly at him. "I have no problem with holding a guy's interest when I want to, but I also know when things aren't mine to take."

Dan smiled wryly as he shook his head.

"Oh, come on. Sometimes it's easier to talk to people you don't really know than friends you've known for years." She paused, continuing only when Dan grinned at her words. "So, who is she? And why are you here with me instead of her?"

"She's made it clear that she isn't interested."

"But you were and still are."

"No." He shook his head again. "It's over between us."

"Then you're lying to yourself."

"I'm trying," he said after a moment. "I don't know what's

wrong with me. She keeps slamming the door in my face, and I still keep going back."

"True love."

Dan laughed and leaned forward on his arms. "True love?"

"Yeah. I believe everyone has their one true love; someone they're meant to be with."

"Then why are you here with me?"

"Because I haven't found mine. But you." She pointed her finger at him as she leaned forward. "You seem to have found yours."

"Isn't true love supposed to conquer all? And I'm sure it's supposed to have a better ending than mine."

"Even fairy tales have their evil witches and stepmothers, you just need to conquer them."

"It's not easy when the princess involved doesn't want to be rescued."

"I've never seen the prince ask for permission."

"I don't even know what's the monster haunting her."

She took another sip of her wine and leaned back against the chair. "What do you love about fairy tales?"

His brows drew closer. "The happily-ever-after?"

"I love that in every story, the prince doesn't give up no matter what." She paused, giving him an encouraging smile. "In reality, we never know what's going to happen. The only way you can get your happily-ever-after is the commitment to never give up no matter what; that's all the magic and love potion you need."

He grinned, observing her for a moment.

"What?"

"You don't look like the sort who believe so wholeheartedly in true love."

"Why? Because I'm toned and sporty, so unlike the princesses in Disney?"

He laughed. "Maybe."

"I think every girl, despite what she says or how she looks, yearns for a prince and a happily-ever-after."

"Well, at the risk of sounding like a brat, true love sucks."

Christine laughed and raised her glass. "To friendship, then."

"To friendship."

The rest of the night, after much persuasion, Dan told Christine everything that had happened with Evelyn. It was much easier to talk to her about Evelyn than it was to the guys or even Kate. Since Christine didn't know Evelyn, he didn't have to consider his words before speaking. He didn't have to worry if he sounded judgmental or if Christine would judge him.

When he was done with his story, he listened to Christine list all the possibilities of what could have happened to Evelyn. After running out of ideas, Christine asked for his thoughts.

For once, Dan speculated aloud.

Everyone in their group knew Evelyn held a secret about her past. But the secret was a taboo topic. There was somehow an unspoken rule on keeping mum about it.

He hated the secret. He hated pretending that it didn't exist when it had built such a massive wall between them, and keeping mum about it only seemed to magnify the situation and distance between him and Evelyn.

Simply chatting about it with Christine seemed to remove the stress behind it. Being able to speak freely, without worrying that someone might get angry or hurt was exactly what he needed.

At the end of the night, after dropping Christine off, Dan drove back with a genuine smile. He wouldn't call that a successful date, but he definitely had more fun than sulking at the gym or trying to bury himself with work.

Chapter Seven

Evelyn threw her keys and bag onto the dining table and dragged her feet across the living room. She dropped onto the couch and kicked off her shoes, not giving a hoot about where they landed.

After checking her phone again, she tossed it onto the coffee table and lay down on her couch.

Since paying the five thousand dollars to her blackmailer, everything had been quiet.

It had been a week, and she wanted to believe that the worst was over, that the blackmailer had gotten the money and she would be left alone.

But she was certain that once the money was gone, the calls would return.

She closed her eyes, draping her arm over them while her head throbbed. She should've just stayed home instead of going to the mansion for dinner.

When Dan didn't turn up for dinner that night, she thought he was still avoiding her. It didn't take long for her to realize that she wasn't the one keeping him from the mansion or his friends.

Ryan had enthusiastically volunteered the information that Dan was out on a date with his friend, and new yoga instructor for the gym, Christine Skyler.

Evelyn kept her face straight.

Ryan had obviously dropped that piece of information for her ears, probably trying to goad her into some form of reaction.

But she'd grown up in an environment where the ability to keep a straight face was a vital survival tool. Such a minor event was nothing compared to the things she'd trained herself to endure.

Since Ryan couldn't get her to react, the topic was dropped when Kate distracted them with the design she'd drawn up for the gym.

A drop of tear rolled down her eye, and she brushed it away angrily. There was no reason for her to feel this way. When she made the choice to shut Dan out, she knew this would happen; she knew he would move on and find someone who deserved him.

She forced her eyes to remain shut even as another tear escaped.

Slowly, she drifted off to sleep.

When her eyes opened, she found herself lying on a pillow.

She frowned, her head swirling, and pushed herself off the couch.

But she wasn't on her couch.

She was sitting on a small single-size bed with plain off-white sheets. She looked around and saw two other girls sleeping on the double-decker bed next to her.

No. She squeezed her eyes shut. *Wake up,* she told herself.

When she opened her eyes, she was still trapped in the last foster home she was in.

Then, she heard the footsteps coming up the wooden stairs. With each step, the floor creaked and her fear doubled. Her chest heaved up and down rapidly as the creak grew more prominent.

The monster was getting closer.

She knew what was coming, and she didn't have much time.

She had to run.

The door was always locked from the outside, and the window grill was nailed down to keep them from opening it.

Still, she had to try.

She tried to push herself off the bed, to get to her feet and search for an escape, but she couldn't move.

She lay frozen on the bed, her heart pounding so hard that the rapid thumps rang in her ears.

As the creaks got louder, her fingers dug into the sheets.

She turned toward the other two girls. The older girl, Leah, was sitting up on the lower deck. Her tangled chestnut hair and wide eyes could almost be mistaken for hysteria. Though fear was apparent in her eyes, Leah didn't make a single sound. She only stared at the door while her hands clenched onto the blanket as if her life depended on it.

On the upper deck, the youngest girl among them hid under her blanket. Evelyn could hear the soft sobs coming from Amy even as she fought against her own tears.

Evelyn refused to cry. She dearly wanted to, but she gulped down her tears. Showing any sign of weakness now would only make the she-devil happier, and she wasn't going to let the monster get any satisfaction out of her.

She shot up straight and turned to face the door just as the she-devil burst through it.

She was always the first to go.

The she-devil pointed the gun at her and pressed her back against the bed. The monster hovered over her and tried to stuff a piece of rag into her mouth. Evelyn immediately tightened her jaws, flinging her head from side to side, trying to avoid getting gagged.

"You always have to fight me, don't you?" The she-devil jammed the gun into Evelyn's stomach.

The sudden pain caused Evelyn to release the tension she held on her jaws.

One blow was enough, but the she-devil relished such display of pain.

Again, the monster slammed the back of the gun against her stomach while Evelyn's hands tried to ward off its attack.

Evelyn's efforts were pointless; she was too slow, she often was.

The pain drew her hands to her abdomen, and she curled into a ball while the she-devil laughed at her pathetic position.

Then, the she-devil forced Evelyn's mouth open with sharpened fingernails and stuffed the rag deep into her mouth, making her gagged.

She coughed and choked.

With another blow to her stomach, the she-devil dragged

Evelyn out of bed by her legs, pulling her down the stairs.

Evelyn's hands flew up, forming a cage over her head. She ducked her head and clenched her jaws as she felt the edge of the steps knocking and scraping across the vertebrates of her spine.

At the end of the steps, the she-devil let go of Evelyn's legs and stormed on her stomach before dragging her down into the basement.

Though she was drained, the moment Evelyn was done with the stairs, she would pull the gag out of her mouth and try to twist her legs from the she-devil's arms.

But it was useless.

She was too young and too small in stature for her struggles to cause any impact.

The she-devil was accustomed to the fight she put up every night and would only release her legs after shutting the basement door. Once the door shut, the she-devil would point the gun at Evelyn and force her toward the metal cage before kicking her into it.

While she went sprawling into the cage, the she-devil locked up her cage and return to the bedroom to retrieve the other two girls.

The metal cage, like that for dogs, encased her. The cage was large enough for her to sit up straight, but she would have to bend over if she stood.

She got on her knees, crawled toward the lock, and pushed at the cage. When the lock refused to budge, she leaned back and used her legs to kick against the edge of the cage.

The whole cage shook, but the lock stubbornly remained in place.

Soon, the other two girls staggered into the basement at gunpoint. Unlike Evelyn, they weren't gagged or shoved into the cage. They went in on their own, huddling into the far end of the cage while the she-devil took her time to lock them up.

Tears poured down Leah's cheeks, but she was old enough to understand that the she-devil didn't appreciate any noise, so she bit down on her lips to keep as quiet as possible.

Amy, on the other hand, cried as any young six-year-old would. She wailed and begged, repeating between each sob, "Mrs. Moore, please …"

It was too late to scream or wail. They were in a basement that was built as a bomb shelter; no amount of yelling would help them now.

They should have done so when they were being dragged down from their room, but they never did.

"Quiet!" Mrs. Moore shouted.

"Mrs. Moore, please …"

Begging never helped. The she-devil didn't have any ounce of conscience or sympathy, and begging only irritated her.

The she-devil retrieved her box of torture tools from a concealed compartment in the floor and opened it. Picking up the elongated Taser, a corner her lips morphed sinisterly into a sneer as she moved toward Amy's cage.

Amy's wails instantly ceased.

Amy scampered to the other end of the cage, hugging her legs against herself. She was trapped and surrounded by metal. There was no place for her to hide.

The she-devil circled Amy's cage, humming the same tune she always did whenever she was enjoying herself, while Amy frantically huddled into the opposite corner of wherever the she-devil was.

Without warning, the she-devil jammed the Taser into Amy's cage, aiming straight for Amy and laughing as Amy's ear-piercing scream got cut off.

Amy fell on her back, unable to move.

Evelyn knew from experience that nothing she did would help Amy. It would only direct attention to herself—something she should avoid at all cost. She stared, watching as the she-devil once again stepped toward Amy's cage.

"Stop it!" Evelyn screamed as her fingers slipped through the small rectangular grids, clinging to a side of the cage. "Stop it!"

Amy was too young, too young to be going through any of this.

"Always trying to be the hero. You never learn." Mrs. Moore

said, moving toward her.

Wake up now! Wake up now!

As Mrs. Moore neared her, instinct made Evelyn want to huddle against the opposite side of the cage. But she wasn't going to give that sick woman the satisfaction of seeing her cower.

Her fingers tightened their grip on the cage, and she held her position.

She stared up defiantly at the she-devil, at the woman who was supposed to take care of her, and clenched her jaws when she saw the tip of the Taser being jabbed in her direction.

In an instant, she felt all the muscles in her body tense and she couldn't move. She fell back against the cage like a block of wood as the sting of electricity ran through her body. Soon, the sting subsided and a burning sensation pulsated through her.

The pain gradually eased, and she could once again hear the she-devil humming. Even as the pain slowly subsided, Evelyn was already bracing for the next zap. After another few zaps and some cursing, Mrs. Moore moved to her box and pulled out a small knife. The monster was much more cautious with the knife, careful to make cuts in places that were easily covered by their clothes.

Twirling the knife in her hands, the she-devil circled their cages and stopped by hers. Evelyn clenched her jaws and tensed her arms and back, bracing for the pain as her skin got sliced open.

Suddenly, she felt herself falling.

She screamed and flailed her arms as her eyes flew opened. She stared up at the ceiling while her senses slowly registered where she was.

She'd fallen onto the floor from her couch.

Using her elbow, she pushed her back off the floor and sat up. Her hair clung around her neck and hot, angry tears gushed from her eyes.

She closed her eyes and let the tears fall. She was too tired to do anything about them.

The trip down memory lane had left her more exhausted than before, but she didn't dare to go back to sleep.

Pushing herself off the floor, she tottered to her bathroom. She stepped into the shower with her clothes on and let the water cascade down her already wet face and shivering body.

Dan checked the time again before getting out of his car. He had waited outside the mansion for over fifteen minutes, hoping that Kate was up and in the kitchen before he headed in. Otherwise, Tyler might throw him out before he could apologize to Kate.

"Good morning," Dan announced as he stepped into the kitchen, immediately noticing that Evelyn wasn't around.

"Look who's back," Ryan said. "I told you he won't be able to stay away from your food for long."

Marianne shook her head indulgently. "Sit. Eat," she instructed, placing a plate in front of him.

No one spoke of the spat Dan and Kate had. Everyone chatted, catching up with one another. When all the food on the table was gone, Dan suddenly turned to Kate and said, "I'll drive you to work."

Tyler looked at Kate and waited for her reaction.

"You know, guys, I do have a car. A car that's just sitting and rotting away in the garage."

Tyler's lips turned up and he shrugged. "I'm helping to save the earth. We shouldn't be wasting precious resources."

Kate rolled her eyes, turned to Dan, and said, "Can you believe him? He'll say *anything* to get his way." Standing, she grabbed her bag and turned to Dan. "I guess you're my ride to the office."

Tyler kissed her goodbye, and she strolled out with Dan.

"I must say, I'm surprised that he didn't flat out reject my offer to drive you," Dan admitted when they got into the car.

"He trusts you. He's protective of me, but he trusts you."

"I'm sorry about the other day. I shouldn't have vented my frustrations on you."

"I'm sorry I overreacted."

"So we're good?" Dan asked, looking over at her.

She chuckled softly. "Yeah, of course. I can't believe you'd think I'm so petty."

A few moments of silence lingered as Dan tried to find something to talk about. They never lacked in topics, especially when they both worked in the same line. He loved joking about the stupidity of some interior designers while she complained about the brainlessness of certain contractors.

They could go on quipping for hours, each trying to prove their profession being the better half of the construction line.

Turning the key in the ignition, he struggled to come up with some line of conversation while a battle went on in his mind. He fought to stop himself from asking about Evelyn; his logic reminding him of all the reasons why he should forget about her.

"How's things going with Christine?"

His head snapped toward her. His brows furrowed and he stared at her, wondering how she found out. Then, almost immediately, realization hit him. "Ryan can never keep his mouth shut."

Kate laughed. "He was trying to rattle some nerves. Since Joanne is gone, he had to find someone else to tease. Christine was just good material."

To tease? "Someone else as in Evelyn?"

"It was bound to come out sooner or later anyway."

He would choose 'later' or 'never.'

Unable to contain his question any further, he finally asked, "How's she doing?"

"She's fine," Kate said after a moment's hesitation. "She's fine."

He noticed how Kate's eyes lost their focus and drifted into thoughts. He was about to ask her what was wrong when he forced his mouth close. If she'd kept it from him, it was probably something she believed Evelyn wouldn't want her to share.

"You haven't answered my question. How are things going with Christine?"

"Nothing much. We've been out a few times. That's it."

"You must kind of like her to go out with her a few times, right?" Kate turned to him with her brows raised, then suddenly raised her arms and looked away. "You know what? Don't tell me."

Laughing at her reaction, he answered her anyway, "She's nice."

From their first date, it was clear that there would be nothing more than friendship between them. But Christine didn't mind hanging out with him, until she met her true love, of course. Then she'd kick him to the curb.

He loved chatting with Christine. With her, he didn't have to worry about their conversations leaking to the rest of the group.

A sudden loud alert on his phone caused Kate to jump in her seat.

"I'm sorry," he said.

"Why do you have to set it so loud?"

Dan didn't offer any explanation. He merely gave her a sheepish smile and apologized again.

Before he formally ended things with Evelyn, she would, at times, call him up in the middle of the night, asking if he was interested in some late-night supper.

She always sounded depressed, but whenever he asked, she'd simply shrugged it off and said she just couldn't sleep.

He didn't mind not knowing the reason. He always met her whenever she wanted and accompanied her for as long as she liked. He knew there were more to those late-night suppers than her insomnia, but he never forced an answer out of her.

When Evelyn refused to talk about something, nothing could change her mind.

Since there was nothing he could do to change Evelyn, he did what he could on his part.

Each night, before heading to bed, he'd set his phone to the maximum volume, just so he wouldn't miss any of Evelyn's calls. Though she probably would never call him again, the ritual had already become a habit.

Lowering the volume on his phone, he asked, "Any news on the arson case?"

Kate turned and looked out the window. "Nope, Detective Allen hadn't found anything new. I guess you can call it a cold case."

"But Ty's better now. He lets you meet your clients on your

own and all."

"Yeah." Her hand reached over to her necklace. "Thanks to this." Her fingers tugged on the necklace that Tyler found around her neck after the fire. The same necklace that Tyler had given to his mother when he was young, and the same necklace that his mom never took off.

No one said much about it, but no rational reason could explain how Kate got the necklace that was lost for twenty years.

"I still think you should join the self-defense class that Joe is organizing."

"Really? You *really* think I can do damage just by attending self-defense classes? If Eve hadn't been with me that day, I probably would've fainted from a panic attack."

He gave her a dry laugh.

A few moments of silence followed, and he noticed Kate playing with the pendant around her neck.

"What is it?" he asked.

"I know what Eve has been doing to you is horrible, but she isn't doing it on purpose. She's stuck in her thinking that no one would want her or love her if he knew what happened. She's never really gotten over her past."

He didn't know how to react.

Neither Kate nor Evelyn was willing to divulge the truth of the horrible past they kept talking about. He couldn't help getting annoyed at being asked to be understanding while being kept in the dark. "Look, I know she's been through something horrible, and I want to understand and help. But I can't do anything when you ladies aren't willing to talk, so let's just put all this behind us."

Kate nodded, then bit down on her lips and turned to Dan. "She wouldn't let me tell you, but you can guess. Yes and no questions."

"Whatever for?"

"Because I want you to understand. I know a lot of them in the house think she's aloof, and they aren't happy about what she's doing to you. The thing is, she isn't like that. She's more than her craziness. I just wish all of you could understand, especially you. I know she doesn't show it, but you're important to her. I'm not trying to change your mind about ending things with her; I just don't want you to hate her."

"I don't hate her."

"But you're pissed with all these secrets, so guess."

Oh, what the hell. "Abused?"

"Yes."

"Abused by her foster parents?"

"Yes."

He hesitated at his next question. "Rape?"

"No."

Abuse. He'd guessed as much. Still, her absolute distrust seemed too extreme. He didn't dare to say that out loud. He didn't want Kate to think he couldn't sympathize with the things Evelyn had gone through.

But even without him saying a word, Kate picked it up.

"It wasn't just abuse. It was much worse. It was torture, it was evil." Her voice softened, and he turned, seeing tears in her eyes.

He was stumped for a moment. Whenever his mom or Joanne started the waterworks, it was a signal for him to clear out of their zone. He knew Kate wasn't trying to manipulate him with her tears, but after years of walking away from crying women, he didn't know what to do.

"Okay …" he said, searching for a tissue. He should have a box somewhere.

Kate dabbed at her tears and gave a strangled laugh. "I'm sorry, I just … No one should've been made to go through what she did."

He took his eyes off Kate and stared at the road ahead. He understood what she was trying to get through to him.

Evelyn wasn't using the past as an excuse to hide behind her walls. Something so terrible happened that she hadn't dared to step out from behind it.

The only way you can get your happily-ever-after is the commitment to never give up no matter what; that's all the magic and love potion you need. He ran his hand through his hair as he heard Christine's words in his head.

He sighed softly. He should've stayed angry instead of asking his questions.

Chapter Eight

Evelyn flipped onto her back. Her room illuminated in a warm, yellow glow from the small night lamp plugged into the electricity outlet on the table across her bed.

She stared up at the sky blue ceiling above her. She had painted it herself on the first day she moved in. She hated white ceilings. It reminded her too much of all the sleepless nights she'd spent staring at the lines in the cotton-white ceiling while she waited for the creaks creeping up the stairs.

She looked at the clock on the wall and groaned. It was already four in the morning.

Despite having been in bed since nine, she hadn't slept a wink.

She pushed her blanket aside and reached across to pick up the bottle of sleeping pills on the nightstand. She sat up straight, twirling the bottle in her hand.

With a frustrated sigh, she twisted the cap off the bottle and shook out one of the pills. She was tempted to pop it into her mouth and continue to lie in bed until she could fall asleep.

At the last moment, she changed her mind and dumped the pill back into the bottle. If she were to take the pill now, she wouldn't be able to wake up in the morning.

Besides, an unwelcome side effect from the sleeping pills was negating her initial reason for taking them.

Puffing her cheeks, she blew out a breath and threw the bottle into a nearby trash can.

She got off her bed, trudged over to the window, and glanced out of her apartment.

The silence outside was accompanied by a stillness. Even the leaves appeared to have frozen in place, making it look as if time had slowed down.

Staring at the empty streets only reminded her of how alone she was. Even now, as she stood in front of her window, she was awake while the rest of the world slept.

The universe seemed to be showing her how out of place she was, how she would never belong.

Once again, tears slipped down her eyes.

This routine wasn't new to her.

Initially, when she was on her sleeping pills, she would be able to enjoy a good night's rest for most of the night. Sleep that was free from all nightmares. But soon, one pill was no longer sufficient. She began taking two, then three, and still she'd find herself waking in the middle of the night.

She had enough common sense to know she was popping way too many pills just to get some rest, but common sense wasn't good enough an incentive for her to stop. Each nightmare-free sleep was a slice of paradise for her, and she wasn't willing to give that up.

The newly-acquired motivation to stop taking the pills stemmed mainly from the fear of the scarier side effects.

Instead of nightmare-free sleep, her nightmares returned in full force, and it became more difficult to wake up from them.

The start of the nightmare varied. Sometimes, she would be immobilized on the bed. Sometimes, she would be hiding in the bathroom, her arms pulling against the doorknob as she tried her best to keep the door shut.

No matter how it began, the next stage of her nightmare always remained the same.

She would have to endure the sharp jolt of electricity from the Taser surging through her body, the tension of clenching her jaws so tightly that she was sure her teeth would shatter, the sting of sharp blades skimming across her skin, and the distinct feeling of warmth as blood oozed out of her.

Usually, she would wake up by then. She would be drenched in cold sweat and be shivering as she wrapped her arms around herself. But she would be awake and could remind herself that she was no longer in that hell hole.

The pills, however, were trapping her inside for a longer time.

She could bear the tortures in the nightmare. After all, she'd lived through it once. The true pain, the pain she couldn't bear, wasn't from the wounds inflicted by the torture. It was the feeling of abandonment and betrayal.

The abandonment of the people who were supposed to protect her.

The betrayal of the one person she had tried, in spite of her own position, to help and protect.

So instead of heaven, the sleeping pills were keeping her longer in hell.

Evelyn shook her head and brushed her tears on her shoulders.

Since going cold turkey, her sleep dropped into two main categories.

On the 'good' nights, she would toss for two to three hours before finally falling asleep, then waking up from her nightmare in the early hours of the morning.

On the 'bad' nights, such as the one she was having, she would try, but no matter how she forced her eyes shut and made herself relax, her mind simply refused to shut off.

She'd tried imagining herself drifting on a smooth, serene lake. She'd tried counting sheep. She'd tried using all those essential oils that Kate had bought for her, but none worked.

Regardless if it was a 'good' or 'bad' night, not taking her sleeping pills summed up to only one fact; she would end up crying away whatever was left of the night.

During the day, she could be the strong Evelyn. The Evelyn who told herself that what didn't kill her only made her stronger. The Evelyn who had turned out to be a better person despite the things she had experienced and done, and the Evelyn whom no one would dare mess around with.

The nights were another matter.

Each night, her insecurities and nightmares took turns to taunt and remind her of how unworthy she was.

Nightmares, insecurities, loneliness, and fear; her old companions of the night had all returned together.

Her hands moved toward her phone, and she dialed Dan's number. Her thumb hovered over the call button while her sleep-deprived, slow-witted brain informed her that she no longer had the right to call him.

Things were no longer the same.

This time around, Dan was the one who told her that he was done, and he was already seeing someone else.

He deserved to be free from someone as damaged as she was.

She let her new phone slip from her hand and allowed it to drop onto the floor.

Giving one last look at the pill bottle in the trash can, she crawled back into bed and opened her nightstand's drawer.

She took out the leather pouch and ran her index finger along the edges.

Kate had given this to her years ago, but Evelyn had never opened it.

She knew what was inside and never saw the need for it.

But she figured nothing was better at boring her to sleep than a thick Bible.

Sighing softly, she unzipped the pouch and pulled out an almost new leather-bound Bible. Her brows drew closer as she saw the various Post-it tags throughout the pages of the Bible.

Thumbing through it, there were highlighted phrases and handwritten notes throughout. She flipped to the front page and smiled wryly as she saw Kate's note.

Evelyn,

I don't know when you will, or if you will ever, open up the Bible to see this. But I pray that on the day when you do reach for this, you will finally see how much God loves you. What men cannot do, what men cannot solve, Jesus can.

I know and can even understand your resentment of God. I can't explain why you went through what you did, but I know God didn't cause it, and He never abandoned you. Sometimes, life isn't what we expect it to be.

When Lazarus was ill, Jesus delayed going to him. Jesus waited until Lazarus was dead before showing up. For without Lazarus's death, Jesus couldn't show the world His power of resurrection.

I know you have been through a lot, but I know for everything you have been through, God will give you double the reward. All you have to do is ask Him for help, and He will help you.

Kate.

Evelyn looked through the Bible again, and another tear slipped from her eye.

Kate must have spent hours highlighting, tagging, and copying in the notes. And Kate did all that without knowing if Evelyn would ever see what she had done.

Placing her thumb on one of the translucent blue tags with the word 'Sleep' written on it, Evelyn flipped it open to see a verse highlighted in blue.

In peace I will lie down and sleep, for you alone, O Lord, will keep me safe.

It wasn't easy for her to accept God's words. The first thought that entered her mind when reading the verse was how God had failed her in that as well.

She was tempted to close the Bible and put it back into the drawer, but she wasn't going to get any sleep, and she didn't have anything else to do.

So she continued reading through all the verses that Kate had highlighted and tagged in blue. If she couldn't find comfort from the words she was reading, she could at least find comfort in the effort her best friend had put in for her.

The summer heat outside wasn't helping the temperature within the gym. With dust swarming the place, they couldn't switch on the air conditioners or fans, and the heat was getting on everyone's nerves.

Though Dan hadn't done much heavy-duty work, his T-shirt was getting wet from the heat trapped in the gym.

"What the hell are you doing? Move over!" one of his men

shouted from across the gym.

For a moment, he thought he was the intended recipient of the message. He took a step aside and knocked into another of his men. "Sorry."

"Are you okay?" his staff asked.

"Why?"

"I don't know. You're just moving around, doing nothing."

Dan frowned, then turned and walked away.

His staff was right.

Confusion was clouding his mind, making it impossible for him to concentrate on anything. Instead of being any real help, he'd basically been floating around the gym, checking everything but registering nothing.

The determination he'd felt last week was fading.

Instead of taking his mind off Evelyn, he had started to hope, hope planted by Christine's continual speech on true love.

There was also the little Q&A session that he had with Kate. That short chat was making him question the frustrations he thought was justified.

Even with his cluttered mind, he instantly noticed Evelyn as she strolled through the gym's doors. He watched as she yawned and stretched her back, her hand holding a rolled-up piece of paper.

She waved the paper before her nose, trying to push the dust from her face.

He couldn't help but grin as he thought about the irony of Evelyn hating dust. Putting aside her house that was a permanent setting of the aftermath of a hurricane sweeping through the ladies departmental store, there was no way she could avoid dust whenever she had to work on a piece of custom-made furniture.

She was so particular with details and quality that she tended to build them from scratch instead of finding parts and piecing them together, then passing it off as her own.

When Evelyn's eyes began scanning the gym, Dan was tempted to hold his gaze to see if she was searching for him. But he decided that he wasn't up for another round of disappointment so early in the morning.

He dropped his gaze and searched for something he could busy his hand with.

Carefully, he maneuvered through the main area of the gym that was acting as a storage and work area. Wood paneling for the floors, sound-proof doors, and several large mirrors leaned against one of the walls while another was lined with a few pieces of equipment.

He went over to a group of his men who were throwing around suggestions on how best to move the huge mirror without causing any damage. Everyone looked up at him, seemingly expecting him to put in some suggestions or give some commands. Instead, he simply looked away from them and back to Evelyn.

The instant their eyes met, his legs twitched as they instinctively wanted to move toward her. But he forced his heels back down and glued his legs to the floor. He turned his attention to his men who were beginning to yell at each other.

"Watch your hands!"

"You're not holding it properly. Look at how I'm doing it," another man shouted.

He had no idea what they were trying to do, but his hand gripped the edge, and he moved along with the rest of the guys.

The shouting continued while they tried to get the right angle to maneuver the piece of mirror around the cluttered place. His focus was required for the task, but he couldn't help feeling the strong sensation that someone was staring at him.

He looked up from the mirror and saw Evelyn's gaze on him.

This time, Evelyn tore her eyes away and turned her back to him.

He sighed softly, but his disappointment quickly became irritation when he found himself wishing she hadn't done so. He should know how good Evelyn was at pretending that he didn't exist; he'd already experienced it uncountable times.

He took a deep breath and adjusted his grip, fixing the piece of mirror for the studio.

"Hi, handsome!"

Dan looked over his shoulder, his hands still supporting the mirror against the wall, waiting for the industrial superglue to dry. "Chris, what are you doing here?"

"I was in the neighborhood. I thought I'd drop by and see if you're free to go out for coffee or something."

He hesitated for a moment. Without control, his eyes darted toward Evelyn.

Christine noticed and followed his gaze. She looked over just in time to see Evelyn hastily moving away in the opposite direction. "So she's Evelyn? That explains the look she gave me when she saw me walking in."

"The look?"

Christine nodded while Dan's eyes flickered over to Evelyn again. She was no longer looking at them and was busy texting on her phone. Just then, Evelyn turned and moved toward the door. Her eyes were fixated on her phone, completely unaware that she was heading right into a few men whose eyes were glued to the large piece of mirror they were gingerly handling.

"Eve!" Dan shouted and sprinted toward her.

His shout effectively stopped Evelyn in her tracks, and her head snapped right up.

Evelyn saw the mirror, saw her eyes widened in the reflection. Her knees locked and she froze in place. But it wasn't enough. The men carrying the mirrors heard Dan's shout as well, and in a panic, the mirror slipped from one of their hands.

She saw the corner of the mirror making its descent toward the floor. She should get out of the way before the mirror shattered right before her face, but there was only enough time for her to shut her eyes and brace for the pain.

Instead, she felt a strong tug followed by warmth, security, and the thumps of heartbeats.

Then, she heard the mirror smashing, heard the men's shouts, but that was it.

She didn't feel any sting from the pieces of mirror that should have rained down on her.

Slowly, she raised her head and saw that her hands were fisted up in a black T-shirt; the same black T-shirt that Dan was wearing.

She looked up as Dan's hands moved from the back of her head and cupped against her neck, one of his thumbs gently rubbing against her cheek.

"Are you all right? Did you get hurt?" His eyes searched her face, then moved onto her neck.

When she continued to stare blankly at him, Dan took her hands and stepped back, giving her a look over. "Eve," he said softly as he squeezed her hand. "Eve, talk to me."

"She's fine! You're not!" "Dan, I'm so sorry." His men spoke at the same time, but his eyes didn't shift an inch from hers.

Evelyn blinked when she heard the statements, and she finally snapped out of her trance. "You're hurt?" She pulled her hands from Dan's and ran her hands down his arm. "Where are you hurt?"

"I'm fine," Dan said softly, taking her hands back into his.

"Dan, you're bleeding," Christine stated, getting both Dan's and Evelyn's attention.

"Where are you hurt?" Evelyn asked again, peeling her eyes from Christine.

Dan's hand reached up to the back of his neck and pulled out a piece of mirror. He winced slightly as he casually cast it onto the floor. "Nothing serious."

Evelyn moved around him and brushed her hand against his hair, checking if he suffered any cuts on his head. She sighed, relieved that there didn't appear to be any serious injuries. His neck had a few cuts, with one that appeared deep. "We should call Joseph and ask him to take a look."

"I'm fine." Dan shifted and pulled Evelyn back in front of him. He pushed her hair behind her ears and asked again, "Are you all right?"

Nodding, her eyes searched the mess on the floor and found her phone. "I'm fine. I'm calling Joseph."

"I should go," Christine said with a smile. Then she turned to Evelyn, and with a wider grin, she continued. "He got injured because of you. You should stay with him and make sure he's fine."

Before Evelyn could say anything, Christine was out the door.

Evelyn frowned and watched Christine leave as she unlocked her phone. "You should go after her."

"I'm fine where I am. Besides, I'm hurt. I shouldn't be running around."

She would have felt guilty if she thought he meant what he said, but his goofy grin told her otherwise. She returned his smile, then turned away to speak to Joseph on the phone.

A few of the men continued staring at them until Dan shot them a glare.

Everyone around them got back to work, leaving the two of them alone. Dan placed his hand on Evelyn's back and led her out of the gym. Sitting on the curb, he waited for her to finish up the call and join him.

Instead of sitting beside Dan, she went over to her car and opened the trunk. She opened a bottle of water and poured some of the water onto a clean face towel. When she got back to Dan, she gently dabbed on the wounds to wipe away the blood, then handed the towel to him. "Apply some pressure to it."

Dan did as he was told. With a wry smile, he said, "I didn't think you were someone who would keep a water bottle and a towel in the trunk."

Sniggering with absolute understanding, she answered, "Not only do I have that, but I also I have a fresh set of clothes in a Ziploc bag and a first aid kit." Smiling at him, she continued. "Kate packed them for me."

"I knew it."

She chuckled softly. It was always easy to laugh around him. "I'm sorry for getting you hurt."

"I'm fine, really," Dan assured, flashing a wide grin.

She grinned and nodded, but her smile instantly evolved into a frown when her phone buzzed. She looked at the unsaved number and sighed.

"What's wrong?"

"Nothing; it's …" She wanted to come up with an excuse, but she was so tired of lying. "Nothing."

"Who's calling?"

Dan's voice had turned serious and stern. She stared at him, clutching the phone.

"Let me help."

She wanted so much to tell him everything. Everything that had happened during the last few years of her foster nightmare. Everything she'd been going through, but she couldn't bring herself to speak. Her voice disappeared, and she couldn't get it to work.

"Eve, you can trust me."

Again, she opened her mouth to speak. She wanted to tell him that she already did.

Since her foster days, she had found it difficult to ask for help.

She had asked for help once. She'd told her teacher what was happening in her foster home. Instead of the help she'd prayed for and expected, her teacher scorned her.

In hindsight, she could understand why her teacher didn't believe her. She wasn't the best student. She talked back to the teacher, never handed in her work, and was barely passing her tests.

She could understand, but she couldn't forgive.

Though she wasn't a perfect student, she didn't deserve to be scorned and told off.

Then, she had asked for help from her school nurse. Instead of telling her what happened, Evelyn had taken off her shirt and showed the nurse her wounds. Her school nurse immediately called in Evelyn's caseworker. But after an interview with the she-devil, her caseworker chose to believe that Evelyn got her wounds due to a fight she had gotten into.

A look at her wounds would have been clear that it was impossible for the she-devil's story to be true. All her wounds were carefully made such that they would be hidden by her clothes, but her caseworker never bothered. The result of her cry for help was another scathing remark from her caseworker, the cruel realization that she was indeed all alone, and the increased disproportionate torture toward her.

But even with all that, she trusted Dan.

Each time she picked up her phone to call him, no matter where they stood in their strange relationship, no matter how late it was, he'd always picked up her calls and showed up without demanding any explanation.

She trusted him with all her heart, but she didn't trust herself.

How could someone like her ever make Dan happy? How could she expect anything of Dan when she couldn't give him what he wanted?

In the end, she could only shake her head.

"Eve …"

"I'm sorry, I should go." If Dan hadn't been thoroughly disappointed by her, she was positive this would do so.

"Eve, wait."

She ran across the road, not caring about the cars rushing by and the angry honks she incurred. Without looking back, she slid into her car and drove off.

This is better for everyone, she reminded herself and peeled her eyes off the reflection of Dan's disappointed face in her rear-view mirror.

Chapter Nine

After a whole day of working at her workshop, carving intricate flowers into the chest she had made, Evelyn was just stepping into the office when her phone vibrated. She threw her head back, giving a loud, annoyed sigh before reaching into her bag to dig for her phone.

Her morning with Dan already had her mood rocking between throwing herself off the building and having a volcano eruption. After an unsuccessful day of trying to drown herself in work, her mood was definitely tilting toward a major volcano eruption.

As she took out her phone, she caught a glimpse of Kate walking out of the pantry. Without thinking, she turned around, hurried away from the office and down the corridor she'd just come from. "Again? I just gave you a thousand this morning. Do you know how much you've taken from me already? Do you really think I'm a bank? I don't have any more money."

"Well, you'd better find some in the next hour. I want two thousand. You know where to find me." The line went dead, leaving behind the monotonous beep to mock her.

The elevator's door flew open, and she jabbed impatiently at the button, even as it was already descending.

She kept her feet moving and managed to keep her tears at bay until she got into her car. Her tears fell in unison with the groaning of her car's engine. Tears slid down her cheeks and landed on her ebony skirt, seeping into it and disappearing within moments of their landing.

Again, she flung her arms against the steering wheel, fighting a losing battle against it.

She wasn't sure how long it was, but eventually, her arms lost their strength and she dropped them onto her legs.

Between sobs, she reached for a piece of tissue and dabbed at the tears on her face.

Leaning back against the leather-cushioned seat, Evelyn closed her eyes and focused her attention on the radiating pain in her arms. The pain, in an uncanny way, was a reminder of what she'd overcome. And that gave her hope; something that had been missing in the recent weeks.

Tucking her hair behind her ear, she took a slow, deep breath, easing away all emotions from her face. She locked all her fear, shame, and pain away into a small box and shoved it into a deep corner of her heart.

She took her bag from the passenger seat and pulled out her pocket mirror and makeup to touch up the washed-off concealer around her eyes. *Thank God for waterproof mascara.*

When she decided she looked decent enough, she pulled the car out of the building and made a quick stop to withdraw the two thousand dollars she needed before driving toward the meeting point.

The towering trees and well-mowed grass faded as she drove toward an area where decent people avoided. Soon, the suit-wearing crowd was replaced by sparse, loitering crowds wearing hooded sweatshirts and jeans that were hanging low on their hips.

Bored faces gathered along fences, some in groups while others idled alone. Most had their hoods over their heads while their watchful, skeptical eyes darted around.

The solitary colored, high-rise buildings disappeared as well. In place of it were low-rise buildings that lined both sides of the roads. A layer of grayish dust had settled over the neglected walls. The only hint of fresh colors was the vibrant red, yellow, and blue graffiti that overlaid the dullish walls.

Words and random symbols were drawn over one another, making the task of deciphering them near impossible.

The whole neighborhood brought up one word in her mind. Despair.

She could see herself in the jaded looks of the teens; teens who shouldn't be out on a street like that.

Months ago, she would have driven through a neighborhood like this and thought she was done with that life; life with a sense of hopelessness, with nothing to look forward to.

Evelyn sighed and crooked her lower jaw as she stopped on the same street that she had become a frequent visitor to.

The street was still relatively deserted. But in a few hours, it would be teeming with women standing on the sidewalk, and there would be plenty of cars driving by.

While sitting in her car, Evelyn stared down everyone who walked by. Looking away from the stares would only make her look weak, and being weak in such an area equated to becoming a victim.

She knew most of the stares she was receiving were out of pure curiosity. Her car, though old, was polished, cleaned, and without any signs of bullet holes; an unusual sight in this neighborhood.

As another curious teen went by, her mind wandered off to the younger version of her blackmailer.

Amy was only six when Evelyn met her.

No, Evelyn hadn't met Amy, Mandy did.

Mandy Shannon; the young girl who was thrown from foster home to foster home, carrying all her possessions in a black plastic bag.

Plastic bag was a nice term; it was really just a trash bag.

A black trash bag they gave to foster children to keep their belongings. It was as if all of her things were garbage, just as she was.

She was thrown from homes with parents who promised to care for her to another when she was no longer wanted.

They always had a reason.

The foster parents finally conceived and needed to spend more time with their own flesh and blood. The foster parents couldn't afford to keep her; the checks received from the government weren't enough. The foster parents' children didn't like her, so she had to go.

With each home, the young, naive Mandy Shannon quickly died, and an older, colder, and angrier Mandy Shannon appeared.

She learned never to trust the words of adults. No one truly cared for her, not her caseworker and definitely not her foster parents. She was only at a house until she was no longer needed or wanted.

Like her stuff, she was disposable garbage to them.

By the time she had gotten to Mrs. Moore, Mandy was by all means a problematic child. She stood and gave no reaction when the seemingly cordial Mrs. Moore introduced Amy and Leah to her.

Her caseworker had smiled politely to Mrs. Moore before whispering harshly into her ear, warning her to behave. Then the adults led all of them to a dull, yellowish couch where they had their own conversation. While the adults chatted, Mandy took the chance to steal glimpses of the living room and the other two girls who were already under Mrs. Moore's care.

Under her feet, the floor was covered with an old, algae green carpet, its fiber completely flat. Though the walls were white, there seemed to be a gloom in the house.

There wasn't much decoration in the house either. Besides the couch they were sitting on, there was a set of ugly olive curtains with hideous red flowers printed all over it and a small television in front of them.

She wasn't expecting a grand house with antiques displayed all over, but there wasn't a single picture or book. It felt like an empty shell; it felt as if the house was merely for show.

Mandy had shrugged off those thoughts and turned to the girls.

The girls' hair hung neatly around their shoulders, covering the nape of their necks, and their clothes appeared fresh and clean. They seemed to have just taken a bath, but instead of the freshness she'd expected, they appeared weary and somewhat demoralized.

Leah sat like a statue, blending in so well with the furniture in the background that she was almost invisible. Amy, on the other hand, sat quietly, but her hands were clasped so tightly that her knuckles were turning whiter than her already pale skin.

But what truly struck her as odd was how subdued the girls were. They kept their eyes on the floor, occasionally gazing outside as though they were daydreaming, but never directly at anyone—not even at each other.

Despite having acted out in the last foster home, she kept her behavior in check. Something about the house was weird.

She toed the line and did whatever Mrs. Moore told her in the first few days.

Things were normal then, and Mandy never suspected anything was wrong. She merely thought Mrs. Moore ran her house with an iron fist, which was why the other two girls were always so quiet.

No matter where she'd gone, foster kids always stuck together. They would talk or warn each other about the parents and watch each other's back. But Leah and Amy kept to themselves. They didn't speak to her or each other. The only time she heard them speak was when they answered Mrs. Moore's questions.

Mandy didn't care how they behaved. She kept to herself as much as they did.

There wasn't any point in making friends when she could be thrown out anytime.

What she didn't know then was that she wouldn't be discarded this time. Mrs. Moore was determined to keep her in the hell hole for as long as she could.

It didn't take long for Mrs. Moore to peel off her mask. Just four days into her stay, the torture began.

Mandy fought hard. She screamed, yelled, and thrashed her hands about, but she was always overpowered in the end.

After a year, the torture became routine. And though it was weird, Mandy got used to it.

She feared it tremendously; she couldn't sleep and found herself listening out for the dreaded footsteps that would come up the stairs each night.

Even on the rare occasions when the she-devil decided to take a break, Mandy still couldn't sleep. Her ears would be on alert for the slightest movement on the wooden stairs that creaked with each step. Still, despite it all, she grew to accept it as a situation she couldn't get out of.

Her defiance, her stubbornness, her fights; none of it helped her.

In desperation, she turned to the people she'd grown to distrust—adults. She tried to ask for help, only to be turned down and scorned.

To top it off, her cry for help only made Mrs. Moore transfer more of the torture toward her.

To a fourteen-year-old, there was nothing else she could do.

She was certain that the rest of her life would be subjected to the sadistic tortures of Mrs. Moore. She was sure she would die in the she-devil's hands.

The only way she could make herself get out of bed each morning was to be angry.

Anger that gave rise to stubbornness and determination.

Her stubbornness kept her alive. Her determination to make it difficult for Mrs. Moore in whatever small, tiny ways gave her satisfaction whenever she succeeded.

She didn't care if she died in the she-devil's hands, at least she was going down defiant.

Mrs. Moore continued in her attempt to break Mandy with all sorts of torture, but that only aggravated Mandy's rage.

When checks from the government and torture were no longer enough to keep Mrs. Moore happy, the she-devil decided to pimp them out.

The same rage that had given her the will to live supplied her with a resolution to fight to her death before she became anyone's sex slave.

She scratched and bit Mrs. Moore, swearing she would hurt the men so badly that they would come after her. The she-devil didn't care much for her threats, but Mandy wasn't going to give up. She fought so hard that Mrs. Moore got frustrated and eventually gave up, turning her attention to Amy.

Self-preservation should have been all she cared about. She was safe and should be celebrating.

Amy and Leah never lifted a finger to help her whenever she was being tortured. In fact, they seemed relieved that the torture was geared toward her instead of them.

Still, she couldn't let Mrs. Moore take Amy.

Amy had just turned seven. She couldn't allow Mrs. Moore to do that to Amy. So, she fought and held on to Amy as if she were her lifeline.

In the end, both of them were given a good beating while Leah quietly obeyed her orders.

She had never expected gratitude from Amy, but she never expected Amy to take Mrs. Moore's side and turn on her.

She knew Mrs. Moore was simply trying to prove a point, to show her that being a hero didn't bring any rewards.

Mrs. Moore made Amy hurt her on purpose. The she-devil wanted her to know that no matter what she did, she was always the odd-one-out, the one nobody would give a second thought about when discarding.

Amy, of course, did as she was told. She tortured her just as the she-devil did. Amy was clearly relieved that she was no longer the victim, and she couldn't care less that she was hurting someone else.

Evelyn clamped her jaws down and swallowed her tears as her hand moved over to her left shoulder, feeling the bump of the scar that Amy had given her.

She was no longer the silly Mandy Shannon.

Each time she stepped into the shower, each time she looked in the mirror, she would be reminded that she should never expect anyone to help her.

Evelyn continued to sit in the car, waiting for another fifteen minutes before she saw the reason behind her current situation.

Clenching her jaws, she grabbed her bag and got out of her car. She kept her chin up as she strode forward, her eyes focused on the pasty woman whose dark, haunting eyes stared right back at her.

Clad in a midriff, low-cut halter top and a miniskirt that barely covered her bottom, the slim, petite woman leaned lazily against a lamppost. Besides the thick eyeliner and mascara she had on, Amy wore a sneer on her face as she watched Evelyn stalk toward her. "Hi, Mandy."

That name irked her.

It made her feel small and weak. It reminded her of the helplessness she felt each night at the foster home and the hopelessness of her situation. But Amy brought up that name for the sole purpose of taunting her, and the same anger Evelyn once held on to survive gave her the ability to conjure up a smile.

As she drew nearer to Amy, Evelyn scanned the area around her, making sure there weren't any threats nearby. "This is the last time I'm giving you money." Taking out the wad of notes, she thrust it forward.

Evelyn already knew Amy wasn't going to let her cash cow off, but with the memories of Amy's betrayal fresh on her mind, Evelyn was itching for a fight.

"That was what you said the last time." Taking the money from Evelyn's hand, Amy licked her finger before counting the notes, her sneer growing more prominent with each passing second. "Oh, come on. You have a good life now. I'm sure you don't want to ruin everything because of the past you had."

"Amy, call me again and I'll kill you. You, of all people, should know I'm capable of that."

She could see Amy's jaws tightening, but it was only for a split second. Almost immediately, the fear vanished and the smirk returned. "Then you should do it now. Because, Mandy, I'll be calling again," she said as she waved the thick stack of cash in Evelyn's face.

Irate, Evelyn slapped Amy's hands away, spilling the money onto the floor.

The forced cordiality between the two came to an instant halt.

Amy scowled at her, and Evelyn knew she would be getting the fight she wanted.

Soon, each had their fingers digging deeply into the other's arm.

Being taller, Evelyn was able to keep Amy at arm's length,

preventing Amy's sharpened nails from clawing across her face.

Living life on the street had clearly toughened Amy. She was no longer the young, helpless girl who would cave to anyone's commands.

Since Amy couldn't get to Evelyn's face, her nails went for another target, scraping lines and drawing blood from Evelyn's arms.

With the adrenaline pumping through her body, Evelyn barely felt the pain. She pried Amy's fingers from her arm and struggled to keep Amy's hands from grabbing her hair.

Out of nowhere, a large brown handbag came between Amy and Evelyn.

As the handbag assaulted Amy's face, Evelyn stumbled back, bringing the owner of the bag into her sight. "Kate!"

Kate continued swinging her bag at Amy, pushing her away from Evelyn, ceasing only when Amy fell onto the floor. Taking a step back from Amy, Kate turned back to check on Evelyn.

Evelyn's focus immediately shifted to Amy; an experienced fighter would never take her eyes away from the danger.

While on the floor, Amy pulled out a pocketknife and flipped it open in an instant. Without much effort, she pushed herself off the ground, drew her arm back, and was ready to take a swing at Kate.

Kate must've seen the horror on Evelyn's face because she turned around, instinctively raising her arms up before her face.

Still, flesh was by no means a good shield.

Evelyn lunged forward and collapsed onto Amy, sending both of them crashing back onto the floor. The impact on Amy's head knocked her out cold. Evelyn pushed herself up and hurried back to Kate.

Kate was still standing with her arms in front of her face. A deep, slanted slash lay across both her arms while crimson blood streamed down from it.

"Damn it! Kate, are you all right?"

Hearing Evelyn's voice, Kate lowered her arms and stared at Evelyn for a couple of dazed seconds before turning to her arms and wincing. The pain must have finally gotten to her.

Evelyn couldn't control the guilt ballooning in her, but that had to wait. She had to get them out first.

"Listen, we need to go." She looked over her shoulder at Amy again, making sure she was still unconscious. Then glancing around anxiously, Evelyn repeated, "We need to go. We need to take you to the hospital."

She didn't know if Kate's silence was stemmed from anger or the remnants of shock.

Regardless, their commotion had attracted the attention of quite a few people. Though Evelyn was sure that minding-your-own-business was a norm in this neighborhood, and the money on the floor provided a good enough distraction, she didn't want to risk it.

She cupped her hand under Kate's arm and led her away from the unconscious Amy.

Kate allowed Evelyn to drag her along. But when Evelyn opened her car door, Kate suddenly turned away and got into a nearby taxi instead.

When the fog of confusion lifted, Evelyn turned and went after Kate, but the cab sped away before her hand could touch the handle.

"Kate!"

Not knowing what else to do, Evelyn got behind her wheel and followed the speeding cab. She sped and ran the red light, determined to keep the cab within her sight.

She heaved a sigh of relief when the familiar sight of the woods appeared. She had never been this happy to see the creepy woods.

For the first time since Kate got hurt, Evelyn could finally process what had happened. All the way here, she had been concerned with only one thing—not losing sight of the cab.

Now that her mind was off the chase, all sorts of emotions assaulted her.

And the vanguard for the besiege—frustration. Evelyn was frustrated with herself for being so consumed by thoughts of Amy and herself that she hadn't realized Kate had tailed her.

Anxiety came crashing right after. She'd been so concerned

with getting them out of the neighborhood that she didn't get a good look at Kate's wounds.

She never wanted things to end like this.

Evelyn had kept the blackmail from Kate so she didn't have to get dragged into this dark world of hers.

Her decision had completely backfired.

Before today, she was certain her reasons for keeping the blackmail a secret were justified. Right now, she couldn't even remember what her reasons were.

She should've just asked for help.

After so many years, she should've moved on from her past. Why was she still so afraid to ask or even hope that someone would help her out?

Kate wasn't like any of those who had scorned her. She had always been there for her.

And Dan. Dan had given her so many chances to ask for his help.

Still, she'd chosen to keep her lips sealed.

Because of her choice to keep her mouth shut and close the rest of the world out, she was going to lose her only friend.

Kate would never speak to her again.

Kate had told Evelyn how betrayed she felt when Lydia chose to lie and keep her in the dark about the investigation that eventually led to the fire.

Evelyn had been irate at Lydia, too. Yet, when she was subjected to the same dilemma, she chose to do exactly what Lydia did.

She kept Kate in the dark and lied whenever necessary to keep the blackmail a secret from everyone.

Kate always gave her the space she needed, trusting that she would go to her when she was ready. This time, she chose to betray Kate's trust.

As the mansion came into view, Evelyn could see Tyler pacing, then rushing up to the cab even before it came to a stop. She pulled up right behind the cab and stepped out just as Tyler shouted for Joseph.

"Joe!" Tyler yelled again while helping Kate out from the cab.

Evelyn took a step closer to Kate, but Tyler immediately moved between her and Kate. His back was facing her, and he didn't take his eyes off Kate. But Evelyn got his message.

Nodding, she took a step back. She couldn't blame Tyler. Like Lydia, she wasn't the direct cause of Kate's injuries, but none of it would have happened if it wasn't for her.

With his arm tight around Kate's waist, Tyler pressed Kate against him and led her into the mansion, nearly knocking into Joseph.

Joseph stepped aside for them to enter. "What happened?" he asked when he saw the blood on Kate's arm.

"It was me," Evelyn said softly. "It was me."

No one made any comments about Evelyn's statement. Tyler's attention was solely on Kate while Joseph ran back to get a first aid kit.

By then, Marianne and Mr. Sawyer had joined them in the living room. Marianne gasped and hurried over to sit by Kate. "Oh, Lord. What happened?"

Kate turned to Evelyn and said, "I don't know."

Evelyn could see the anger burning in Kate's eyes before Kate returned her gaze to Marianne, then turned to rest her forehead on Tyler's shoulder.

Evelyn watched as all of them took their places.

Tyler and Marianne were right beside Kate. Mr. Sawyer went out of the house and spoke with the cab driver while Joseph knelt in front of Kate and checked her wounds.

She was the only one standing around doing nothing.

She stood and watched for a moment, realizing how out of place she was. Kate had a new family now, and there wasn't any place for a person like her.

"You're lucky you didn't get slashed on the ventral side of your arms. You could lose the ability to move your fingers," Joseph said as he turned Kate's arms to examine the wounds. "This is going to sting."

Kate winced as Joseph sprayed a generous amount of antiseptic over her wounds.

"What were you cut with?" Joseph asked.

"Pocket knife," Evelyn answered, turning all eyes to her.

"Was it rusty?"

Evelyn blinked and stammered, "I … I don't know. Maybe. Is she going to be all right?"

Again, no one replied.

She pursed her lips and turned away from the group. She didn't know what to do with herself. She couldn't leave or walk away from them right now; she had to make sure Kate would be fine.

"We need to take her to the hospital. The wound on her left hand is too deep. She needs stitches, and she should get a tetanus shot, just in case." As he spoke, Joseph bandaged the wounds. "This should slow the bleeding."

Tyler's brows were etched in a permanent frown. He nodded and was about to scoop Kate up into his arms when she stopped him.

"I'm fine. I can walk."

"Ty, drive ahead. I'll call the hospital and let them know to expect you." Then, turning to Evelyn, Joseph said, "You're with me."

While Joseph called the hospital, Evelyn walked out to pay the cab driver, but he wasn't there anymore.

"I've settled the bill. Don't worry about it," Mr. Sawyer said and gave her a pat on her back. "Are *you* all right?"

Evelyn blinked as her eyes burned. "I'm fine." She swallowed her tears and forced herself to smile.

"If there's one thing I learned in life, it is that everything will work out fine in the end."

"Thank you."

Mr. Sawyer gave her an encouraging smile and went back into the house when Joseph came trotting out.

"Your arms have some scratches, too. Do you want me to—"

"It's nothing. We should go."

Joseph signaled for her to throw the car key over. She threw it over without an argument and got into the car.

"What happened?" Joseph asked, his tone even, but Evelyn knew his dislike of her was probably doubling with each passing second.

She turned her head away, quietly trying to stop herself from crying. She took a moment to clear her throat before asking, "Will she be all right?"

"The knife didn't slash any major arteries. Some stitches and a tetanus shot should fix her right up." Joseph peered over at Evelyn, but she kept her back to him and didn't give any reaction.

After a few minutes, Evelyn said softly, "Is Dan home? Will you drop me off at his house instead?"

"You don't want to—"

"Just drop me off at Dan's place."

Joseph sighed and shrugged.

Chapter Ten

"Are you sure you don't want to head down to the hospital?" Joseph asked again when Evelyn was about to open the car door.

"Text me. Let me know how she's doing." Then she got out and closed the door behind her.

Evelyn waited until her car was out of sight before heading up the steps toward Dan's house. She rang the bell and waited.

The whole situation had spun out of control, and there was no way things would go back to the way they were.

The efforts she'd spent on guarding her past and new secret that ended up hurting her best friend were just too much. She couldn't endure all these secrets anymore. It was time to cut away every possible aspect that she was afraid would be affected by the blackmail.

Dan opened the door in sweats and T-shirt, his towel still hanging over his shoulders. "Eve? What happened?"

She looked up at him, confused by what he was asking.

"You're a mess. How did you get hurt?"

Following his stare, Evelyn turned to her arms and saw the bright red scratches across them. She waved it off just as Dan reached out to soothe her hair. She closed her eyes and smiled at his gentleness with her.

"What happened?" Dan asked again, leading her into his house. "Does Kate know? Do you want me to call her?"

She shook her head and turned away as tears fell.

"Eve …" Dan blinked. He took a step forward and pulled her into his arms. "It's all right. No matter what it is, it'll be all right."

Again, she shook her head and continued weeping. "No, it won't. It won't be all right." She pushed her arms against his chest and took a step back. Turning away from him, she brushed the tears from her eyes.

"We should take care of your wounds first."

"No, don't bother."

Dan sighed softly. "I'll call Kate."

"No, she's at the hospital. She's hurt; she got hurt because of me." She paused and sniffed. "She'll never forgive me."

Right from the start, she should never have chosen this path. She should've just told Kate the truth. "I need to tell you something."

"Okay …"

"You should sit."

Dan moved to sit on the couch and patted the seat next to his. But instead of joining him, Evelyn moved to an adjacent couch, leaving some space between them.

He reached toward her, but stopped midway when he saw her drawing her hands back.

"What is it?"

"The secret that Kate has been keeping for me. I want to tell you about it myself. You shouldn't have to hear it from someone else."

She was done with hiding. She was done with Amy. This time, she was going to get rid of Amy once and for all.

After what had happened, Amy was either going to demand more money or go all out to destroy her reputation. Either way, Evelyn was going to make sure that no one she cared about would get hurt because of her.

She considered for a moment on how to begin her torrid story.

Drawing in a deep breath, she decided it was best to start from the beginning. "My name wasn't Evelyn Jordan. It was Mandy Shannon.

"You already know my mom abandoned me at the hospital, so I was put into the foster system. I was moved from home to home for various reasons, but my nightmare began in my sixth foster home." She stopped then, taking another deep breath. She tilted her chin up to stop the tears from brimming over.

Dan leaned forward, his hand once again reaching over for hers.

But she pulled her hand up by her chest. "Don't, I need to finish this. If you hold me now, I'll start crying and I won't be able to continue."

He hesitated for a moment, then pulled his hands back and clenched them together, placing them on his legs.

She told him everything about the torture Mrs. Moore inflicted on her for almost every night during the three years she was there. She told him how she had asked for help only to be labeled as a lying, ungrateful child. She told him how she almost became a sex slave and how Amy turned on her.

Surprisingly, she managed to keep herself from breaking down and told him everything as calmly as she could.

She paused a few times when Dan turned away from her, his finger rubbing his chin as if he'd just been punched.

She knew her story wasn't one that was music to the ears. It was uncomfortable and perfect for one of those horror stories people would tell around campfires, but she needed to finish it. So, she continued even as Dan kept his face from her.

"The whole thing lasted three years before it was finally over."

Dan finally returned his gaze to her. "What happened?"

"It was like every night. Amy was listening to the she-devil's instruction, doing everything she said. Then suddenly, the she-devil started waving her gun about, saying we were all doomed to be her slaves forever. Amy got distracted, and the she-devil wasn't paying attention.

"That was the chance I was conserving my energy for. I jumped up, and we struggled for the gun until it went off …" Evelyn cleared her throat as the memories came flooding back. "At first, I thought I was the one who got shot. But suddenly, the she-devil collapsed onto the ground, her hand pressed against her dress. Then I saw the blood spreading out from where her hands were and realized I shot her. I killed her." Her voice trembled as she said those words.

It wasn't until Dan took her hand that Evelyn realized she had it pressed to her abdomen, the same location where she'd shot Mrs. Moore. She swallowed and continued. "I can't remember much after that. I remember being in the hospital. I remember the police questioning me. I remember seeing my story all over the news. Then some hotshot lawyer helped me sue the state, got some money for me, and got me emancipated from the system."

"You're sure she's dead?" Dan asked through clenched teeth.

"Absolutely." She had stood over the she-devil and watched the life fade from her eyes.

Dan nodded. "What's that got to do with what happened to Kate today?"

"The she-devil is dead, but Amy isn't. Somehow, she managed to track me down and has been blackmailing me."

"The calls you've been getting."

She nodded slowly.

"Why didn't you tell me? Why didn't you tell Kate?"

"Because I didn't want to drag anyone into my past. I thought … I thought I could do this on my own. I didn't think anyone would get hurt. I was a complete idiot."

"I wasn't trying to—"

"I was afraid it'd be too much for anyone to accept. I thought I could solve this on my own." She stopped and shook her head at her idiotic decision. "I think Kate followed me today. When Amy and I started fighting, she jumped in and ended up getting hurt. Amy slashed her across her arms. Joseph said her left hand needs stitches, and she'd need a tetanus shot. Will you check on her and make sure she's fine?"

"She has Tyler; he'll make sure she's fine. We should do something about your wounds. I'm not taking no for an answer." He stood and headed upstairs to retrieve the first aid kit.

Evelyn waited until she heard the bathroom door close before she headed out of his house.

She had to close this chapter.

Enough damage had been done. She hastened down the stairs and waved for a cab, heading home to pack.

If she left, Kate and Dan wouldn't have to get involved in

anything. No one else would get hurt because of her.

If she left right now, she wouldn't have to face the pity or disdain on their faces.

She closed her eyes as the taxi pulled away from Dan's house.

If You can hear me, if all I really have to do is ask, then I ask that You make sure Kate is fine and make sure Amy doesn't bother any of them anymore.

Dan closed the bathroom door behind him, stepped forward, and pressed his palms against the edge of the sink. Lifting one of his hands, he turned on the tap and splashed some water onto his face.

He'd suspected that Evelyn's childhood was bad, and Kate had hinted that there was more, but what he'd just heard was sadistic. He never would have guessed the extent of horror she went through each night in those three years.

The story explained a lot.

Who could blame her for her lack of trust?

Her mother abandoned her. The adults who were supposed to protect her only turned their backs to her. The girl she'd risked her own safety to protect not only betrayed her once, but turned up after so many years to remind her of the horrifying memories.

His fingers clenched the surface of the glass sink, turning his knuckles white.

This Amy person was despicable. After all that Evelyn had done, this was how she was repaying her.

Sighing, he ran his hand through his hair and grabbed the first aid kit from the top shelf. There would be time for him to deal with the Amy situation later.

He wanted to do something about her wounds before helping Evelyn patch things up with Kate.

He half ran down the stairs and skidded to a halt as he stepped off it. Staring at the empty living room, he frowned and peered toward the kitchen, wondering if she'd gone to get a glass of water.

"Evelyn?" He went into the kitchen and realized he was alone. "Ugh!"

Flinging the first aid kit onto the dining table, he grabbed his car key and drove over to her house. On the way, he tried calling Evelyn several times, but it kept going straight to her voicemail.

Exasperated, he called Joseph and asked if they were still at the hospital. Perhaps Evelyn had headed over on her own.

"Yeah, but we're leaving now."

He hung up without saying goodbye. *She won't get to the hospital in time.*

If she got to the hospital and found out that Kate had already left, she'd probably head to the mansion.

Since he'd be stuck outside the mansion while waiting for the rest to arrive, he thought he'd swing by Evelyn's house to make sure she hadn't gone home.

He drove around her block twice and searched for her car. When he was positive that it wasn't there, he headed toward the mansion.

Coincidentally, he arrived at the mansion just as Tyler and Evelyn's car came to a stop.

When they stepped out of the cars, Dan was surprised to see Marianne, Mr. Sawyer, and Joseph streaming out of Evelyn's car, with Joseph stepping out from the driver seat.

He turned to Tyler's car, but only Tyler and Kate were standing beside the silver beamer. "Where's Eve?"

Joseph looked over at him, his brows raised and eyes widened. "I dropped her off at *your* house. I saw the lights in your house and assumed you were home."

"I saw her, but she left while I went to get the first aid kit. Why are you driving her car?"

"She appeared to be in a state of shock, so I thought it was better for me to drive. I didn't expect her to change her mind at the last minute, insisting on going to your house instead of the hospital."

"What did she say?" Kate asked.

"Everything."

He saw Kate's astonishment, but he wasn't interested in explaining what had happened. Turning back to Joseph, he asked, "Why didn't you do something about her wounds?"

"I wanted to, but she brushed me off. Kate's wounds were deeper, so I attended to her first. Whoever wielded the knife at her didn't hesitate."

Dan glanced toward the house.

"She's not inside. No one's home; there isn't anyone to open the door for her," Kate answered the question in his head.

"I'm going to look for her."

"Where?" Kate shouted as he ran back to his car.

"Her house."

Again, he drove toward Evelyn's apartment, redialing her number over and over. His concern was quickly morphing into annoyance. He didn't understand why she'd leave the house without telling him or why she'd go off on her own, especially after what happened that day.

What if that Amy woman went after her again?

Once he got out of his car, he buzzed her apartment, but there was no answer. He continued pressing the button, pausing for a few seconds in between each buzz.

Nothing.

Either she wasn't in her apartment or she was simply ignoring him.

He sighed, then grinned when he saw an elderly man pulling out a security card from the pocket. Stepping away from the door, he pretended to sift through his pockets. With a look of utter frustration, he took out his wallet and checked each compartment.

"Need help?"

Dan looked up and gave the white-haired man a sheepish smile. "I can't find my card, and my girlfriend isn't home."

"Here." The man scanned his card and the door popped opened. "Problem solved."

He held the door open while the old man strode in. "Thank you so much."

Instead of waiting for the lift, he walked up the first flight of stairs. Once he was out of the old man's sight, he sprinted all the way up to Evelyn's apartment.

There, he kept knocking on Evelyn's door until the door next to Evelyn's opened.

He turned, seeing a disgruntled neighbor.

"What are you doing?"

Dan stopped his knocking and smiled politely. "Hi, I'm looking for Evelyn Jordan. Is she inside?"

"I don't think so. I saw her heading out with two suitcases when I got home. Looks like she'll be gone for a while."

"When was that?"

"Less than an hour ago."

Resisting the urge to groan aloud, he ran his hand through his hair. "Thanks. I need to make a call."

"All right. And stop knocking on the door, it's annoying."

Dan nodded as he pulled his phone from the pocket and called Kate. "Kate, can you—"

"She's bathing."

"Ty? I know Kate has Evelyn's spare key. Can you ask Joe to bring it over?"

"I'll ask her when she's out."

"No, ask her now." Dan rolled his eyes at the signature silence from Tyler. "Look, I know you're pissed about what happened. But something's wrong, and Kate will be furious if she finds out that you did nothing to help her best friend."

Tyler sighed audibly, and Dan knew he'd won.

"Hang on."

Dan heard the water running on the other end, the muffled voice of Tyler, then Kate finally picked up the phone. "Why do you need her key?"

Another of Evelyn's neighbor opened the door, and Dan realized he'd been pacing up and down the corridor. He smiled and waved, then moved to sit on the stairs. "Her neighbor said she left the house with two suitcases a while ago."

"Suitcases?"

"Quote, looks like she'll be gone for a while."

"Ugh! She's exceptionally good at making destructive choices. I'll head over now."

Dan sat and twirled the phone in his hand, wishing there were something he could do instead of sitting there while Evelyn slipped further away from him.

Chapter Eleven

Dan stared at his phone, willing it to ring with a text reply or call from Evelyn. He'd already left a voicemail and sent her a text. He was tempted to spam her phone with text messages, but he didn't think that would help in bringing Evelyn back to him.

Eve, I'm really worried about you. Please call me when you see my text.

He stared at the blue bubble containing his message and continued to wait for a reply.

It was tough to remain seated. He was getting antsier by the minute.

He pressed the home button on his phone and checked the time again. He jumped to his feet when he thought he heard footsteps coming up the stairs.

False alarm.

The young teenager clipped his skateboard tighter under his arm and stared suspiciously at Dan while walking by. He returned to his position on the step, hoping no one would call the cops on him before Kate got here.

"Dan?"

Dan got up and looked down the stairwell.

Tyler must have seen how anxious he was. Taking the key from Kate, Tyler jogged up the steps and threw it to Dan when he neared.

Once Dan had the key in his hand, he headed back to Evelyn's apartment.

The moment he opened the door, he was sure Evelyn's neighbor was right. There were still clutters of shoes and clothes on the floor, but it was significantly neater. He stepped into the house and crossed the living room without bothering to avoid what was scattered around.

Once he was in Evelyn's room, he opened her wardrobe. The only things Evelyn always took great care of were her handbags.

If she were intending to leave for good, she would take her bags.

"Her bags are missing."

"That's not good." Kate ended her words with a sigh.

That wasn't the reaction he was hoping for, but the exact one he'd expected.

He turned as Kate got onto Evelyn's bed. She lifted the pillows and tossed them over her shoulders, then stuffed her hand into the edge of the bed that was against the wall.

"Kate, your hand," Tyler reminded.

"She took her gun, too."

Dan stared at Kate while she reached into the rest of the edges around the bed.

"She always sleeps with a gun near her," Kate explained.

Dan didn't blame her; he would, too.

In fact, if he had been through what she did, he would probably install bolts on his bedroom door.

Standing in her bedroom, Dan suddenly saw the prison that Evelyn had kept herself in and realized she was still a captive to the horrors she had been through.

On those nights that he had come by to accompany her, he noticed how she would jump at the slightest sound in the corridor; sounds that he might not even have noticed.

She might think that keeping herself in a locked bedroom with her gun under the pillow was dealing with her fears, but she was only suppressing them.

Everything was still trapped within her, fresh in her mind, which was probably why she couldn't bring herself to speak about it, which was why she didn't want anyone else to find out.

Though the physical torture had ended years ago, its clutches were still on her, and she was as trapped as the young Mandy Shannon was.

His heart was getting heavier with each moment spent in her room. He sighed, wishing he was with her.

He needed to make her understand that she wasn't Mandy Shannon anymore. She no longer had to deal with monsters on her own.

"She'll be fine," Tyler said.

Dan managed a half smile. "She's all alone."

"She'll be fine," Kate repeated softly.

"And how would you know that?" Dan said, taking a step forward toward Kate. "Because she'd survived it before?"

"Dan," Tyler warned, but Dan had turned away and continued his rant.

"You shouldn't have gotten angry with her. I know you got injured, but she's been suffering through this whole thing alone. She was so upset that she caused you to get hurt—"

"Really? You're going to blame Kate for what happened? She should've just told us the truth. We would've helped her. Then Kate wouldn't have been hurt, and she wouldn't have to do this."

"She couldn't ask for help! She may think she has a legitimate reason. But the truth is, she just didn't think anyone would help her."

"Then she was being stupid, wasn't she?"

"You have no idea what she went through."

"Again, because *she* didn't want it told."

For a moment, Dan was at a loss for words.

Another epiphany.

He had been whining about Evelyn keeping the secret and how frustrating it was for him. He had been vexed at Evelyn for choosing to run each time he wanted more.

He had thought that whatever he was doing was enough. But as it turned out, Marianne was right. He hadn't stepped up.

Each time she had run behind the gates of her prison, he had stood and watched her lock herself up. Then he would complain about it like a spoiled brat thinking she was being unfair to him.

"You have no idea what she went through," he repeated, softer this time.

He ran his hand through his hair and sighed heavily while

Kate began digging into Tyler's pocket. "What the hell are you doing?"

"When are you going to learn that Kate isn't here for you to vent your anger?" Tyler said, pulling Kate behind him.

Kate shook her head as she got her phone out of Tyler's pocket and staggered a few steps back from Tyler's manhandling.

He ignored Tyler; he wasn't interested in getting into a fight with him. He continued staring at Kate, waiting for an answer.

"What? I thought you guys were having so much fun yelling at each other. Go ahead, be idiotic. Don't worry, I'll find her," she said sarcastically and moved to sit on the couch.

"I thought you didn't know where she was," Dan said and sat beside her.

Kate rolled her eyes but didn't bother answering him.

He turned to Tyler, wondering what was going on.

"Don't look at me. I don't know what she's doing."

"I know her iTunes account. I can track her phone's GPS through the *Find my iPhone* app. That was how I found her earlier." She glanced up at Tyler and gave him a small, embarrassed smile.

"So can you tell me the full story now?"

"She hadn't told you? By the way, her phone is switched off. You won't be able to locate the phone."

"You mean you didn't know Kate always kept Evelyn's secret for her?"

Immediately, he was remorseful of his words. Even after all this, Kate was still guarding Evelyn's secret. "I'm pretty sure she wouldn't care if you told them now."

Her head bobbed up and down while her thumbs continued working on the phone. "Sorry, honey. I'll tell you everything I know on the way home, but I don't have the full story. Like I said, I saw her fighting with that woman and I helped."

"You do know that the email notification will be sent to *her* email when she turns on the phone," he said as he looked at what Kate was doing.

"Dan, if you continue to treat me like some bimbo …" She paused, taking the time to glare at Dan before returning to the phone. "I know her email password, too. I just need to add her email account to my phone and set it to check every fifteen minutes. This way, there's a higher chance of us seeing the notification before she does. Then she won't know we're trying to track her through the phone."

"So what do we do now?" he asked while Kate continued with the configuration.

"Think of the possible places she'd go," Tyler said.

Dan turned to look at Kate, expecting her to start churning out a list of all the possible places.

"She would stay home and call me over, or she would come over to my house; that was how things were."

Since Kate was of no help, he decided to come up with a list of his own. "She needs a place to stay, so nearby hotels?"

"I hope you're not suggesting that we call each and every hotel," Kate said, handing her phone over to Tyler. "Even if we do, I doubt the receptionists at the hotels will just tell us if she's staying there."

"You can call Detective Allen and ask him to send patrol cars to search for her."

"Have you gone out of your mind?" Tyler asked.

He glowered, irritated at the hypocrisy of Tyler's statement. If Kate were the one missing, he would call Detective Allen without a second thought.

"Guys."

Both Tyler and Dan turned their attention to Kate. She had successfully prevented another shouting match that Dan was ready to enter.

"Everyone has a place they'll go when they want to think, right? Where's that place for her?" Tyler smiled at Kate and continued softly. "Take your time. I'm sure you know it."

"Playgrounds." Dan suddenly interjected. "Whenever we walked by one, she loved to sit on one of the benches and watch the children."

"Which playground?" Tyler asked.

"Every playground. Was there one she loved in particular?" Dan stood as he asked, confident that Kate would have the answer. His initial confidence disappeared when he saw Kate playing with the angel pendant on her necklace. "You have no idea."

Kate sighed. "I'm sorry, Dan. I know she does that. But like you said, it's every playground."

"It's all right. I'll just drive around and look for her."

"We'll go with you," Kate said.

Dan shook his head. "She's already upset that she got you hurt. If she finds out that you're going around looking for her, she'll never forgive herself." That was when Dan saw Kate's eyes lighting up.

"Does she know where the woman stays?" Kate asked.

"Amy?"

"Amy—I figured it was one of them. Does she know where Amy stays?"

Running through Evelyn's account, he couldn't recall her saying anything about that. "I don't think so."

"Then she should be waiting at one of the places they met. I don't know if they have a usual meeting place, but we can try the street where I saw them."

"And where's that?" he asked.

Kate threw her head back and groaned. "I don't know. I gave the driver my phone and told him to follow the GPS."

"Mr. Sawyer took down the cab driver's details while we were checking your wounds, just in case we needed a witness to prosecute the woman," Tyler said as he pulled out his phone, calling Mr. Sawyer.

The moment Mr. Sawyer answered the phone, Tyler stood and signaled for them to get moving while he got the information they needed from Mr. Sawyer. Tyler repeated the address aloud for Dan and hung up after thanking Mr. Sawyer.

Without waiting for the couple, Dan sprinted down the steps. "We'll take separate cars in case we need to split and search for her later."

Not having been in the neighborhood before, Dan had to rely on the GPS in his car. Slowly, he cruised around the neighborhood, keeping his eyes out for Evelyn or anyone who resembled her. It wasn't a difficult task; she'd stick out like a sore thumb in this neighborhood.

The women, either standing on or trotting down the sidewalk, were clad in provocatively scanty clothing. In comparison, the dress that Evelyn was wearing, despite barely touching her knees, would be considered highly conservative.

His speed, which would usually elicit immediate honks from impatient drivers, wasn't giving him any problem. All the drivers were taking their own sweet time driving along as they looked out at the women on display.

Dan gave a frustrated sigh as he cleared another block with no sign of Evelyn.

He was certain that Kate was right. After what Amy had done to Kate, there was no way Evelyn would let her off. With the growing conviction of that reasoning, Dan's grip tightened on the steering wheel as his concern and fear escalated.

This wasn't a neighborhood where a woman should be walking alone, not even if she had a gun with her.

He slowed his car further and pulled to a stop at the end of the street. Parking his car, Dan watched as car after car drove past him.

Running his hand through his hair, Dan closed his eyes and forced his over-anxious mind to calm down. He didn't know what else to do. If Evelyn wasn't here, he had no idea where she'd be.

He took his phone and sent another text.

Eve, I don't know when you'll see this, but I need you to know that you don't have to do this alone. I'm really worried. Please call me. Please let me help.

The ringing of his phone broke the silence in his car. He picked it up immediately when he saw that it was Kate calling. "Tell me you found her."

The awkward silence and the same tension resonated on the other end of the phone. "She isn't here. Maybe we should move on and drive by some playgrounds nearby instead of circling around here. Maybe that Amy woman lives around here."

He sighed. That was the only solution left. He nodded,

completely forgetting that Kate wouldn't be able to see him.

"Dan, she's extremely streetwise and …"

He was glad that Kate let her words trail off. He knew she wanted to tell him that Evelyn had a gun, that she could protect herself, and that she'd be safe. But with how things had unfolded, Amy didn't seem like someone who would back off without a fight. "Go ahead. I'll drive another round, just to make sure."

After another fruitless round, he decided that if she weren't already there, she probably wouldn't turn up regardless of the number of rounds he made.

When he was turning out of the neighborhood, he got a call from Tyler. The moment he picked up the call, Kate said, "The GPS notification came back. I'm texting you the address now. I'll log into the app and let you know if she moves. We're already on the way; look for our car."

Thank God for best friends. He knew they were invading Evelyn's privacy, but right now he couldn't love Kate more.

As he drove into the familiar neighborhood, he was slightly relieved that Evelyn had the sense to choose a safer neighborhood than the one they had been at.

It was the park they were at when she first picked up the call and walked away from him.

He parked his car right beside Tyler's silver beamer and checked his phone again. If Evelyn had switched on her phone, she should have seen his messages.

Then why hasn't she replied?

Pushing the door open, Dan stepped out and immediately noticed Joseph's car parked behind Tyler's. He twirled the phone in his hand, refusing to put it back into his pocket; he didn't want to miss her call or text.

"What are you guys doing here?" he asked, getting into the back seat.

"We were heading out to help search for your sort-of-girlfriend when Kate called us to meet them here," Ryan said. Then he jerked his chin forward and continued. "She's right there, at least Kate insists it's her."

"I'm sure. I have better than perfect eyesight, remember?" she said without taking her eyes off the target.

Dan looked ahead and narrowed his eyes, squinting at the silhouette standing by the playground that wasn't far from them. Kate seemed to be right. The way the woman paced, the way she hitched her bag up on her shoulder, and above all else, the way she kept glancing over her shoulders.

Whenever they were out in the open, Evelyn would often turn her head periodically and systematically in all directions as though she was scanning the area for potential danger. She never did that when they were in a place or room filled with people. It didn't matter if she knew the people or if they were strangers she'd never met; crowds just seemed to ease her nerves.

Still, he had to ask, "How can you be sure? She isn't *that* near to us."

"It's her; I can tell. Plus, I'll recognize that bag anywhere."

"Kate, I don't mean to question you, but it's just a bag," Joseph said when he noticed Dan hesitating. "You didn't piss her off again, did you?" Joseph shook his head when he saw Dan giving him a quick brow raise.

"I'm going to make him pay for whatever he said later. As for the bag, it's *not* just a bag. I remember it because it's a limited edition bag, and I searched all over the place for it."

"Then why are we still sitting here?" Dan asked, his hand already reaching for the door.

Taking a quick glance over at him, Kate answered, "Ty says she looks like she's waiting for someone."

"Probably crazy Amy," Ryan added.

Dan pulled his hand back. "So all of you know what's going on?"

"Kate filled us in."

"I still think it's better for us to wait with her rather than stalk her like this," Joseph said, turning to Dan for his opinion.

He sighed and nodded. "I know that's the right thing to do, but if we all storm the playground, she's going to freak and it won't be a nice scene. We should just wait it out."

"We don't have to storm in. We can wait for her while you and Kate go ahead. And probably Ty, since he's never going to let

Kate out of his sight ever again," Ryan said, giving Kate his teasing smile.

Everyone laughed while Kate grinned and ran her hand down Tyler's arm.

"Maybe, but I'd rather not risk it. If we screw up, she's really going to disappear. I mean, right now, she probably doesn't know that her best friend has hacked her account and tracked her phone. If she sees us, I'm pretty sure she'll suspect something."

He continued staring at the figure walking up and down the edge of the playground, constantly glancing over her shoulders and fiddling her bag.

"It'll be all right. We're all here; no one can hurt her," Joseph said with a pat on his back.

He smiled and nodded. "Thanks for helping."

"I was wrong to judge."

He nodded again and looked out at the pacing figure. "We all were."

Chapter Twelve

Evelyn twirled the phone in her hand and hitched the bag higher on her shoulder as she continued pacing up and down along the edge of the playground. Pausing for a moment, she forced herself to take a deep breath.

There was no need to be nervous. This would be the last time she'd ever see Amy. It was exactly what she wanted right from the start, closing the books on her past once and for all.

She was done getting hauled back into her past, living in fear of her ugly secret being exposed and having to hide and lie to people who cared about her.

Checking the time on her phone, she glanced around at the empty park and sat on the bench that had been waiting, for the past forty-five minutes, to serve its purpose. It wasn't a sensible idea to be alone in the park at such late hours, but she didn't know where else to go. She wasn't sure how things would go down, and she didn't want to be in public scrutiny when that happened.

With her back against the bench, she looked over her shoulders again, making sure no one else was in the vicinity. She pulled the bag higher up on her shoulder, slightly comforted by the gun in her bag.

After another scan of the surroundings, she slipped the bag off her shoulder and placed it on her lap. She looped the handle of her bag over one of her wrists and watched idly as the breeze rocked the swing back and forth.

Her mind wandered to how a childhood involving swings,

picnics, and amusement parks would be like.

How would it feel to be a child, playing, laughing, and running wild across the park? How would it feel to look over at a bench and see an encouraging smile from someone who loved her more than anything in the world? How would it feel to walk over and have someone's hand held out, ready to take her home?

Unconsciously, a teardrop slipped down the corner of her eye. She quickly brushed the tear away and tipped her head back.

She closed her eyes and exhaled slowly, regaining her composure.

Trying to distract herself, she rummaged through her bag and took out her cell phone. Again, she read the texts that Dan had sent. She had already read them several times and had been meaning to reply; she just didn't know what to say.

Looking into the distance, her mind spaced out for a moment before she returned to her phone, her fingers skimming across the screen of the phone as if she could touch Dan through the messages.

She'd thought Dan wouldn't want to be associated with her once he'd heard her story. And now, his text messages were giving her second thoughts about leaving.

But even if he didn't mind her past, he wouldn't be able to accept the future she couldn't give him.

Her hand wrapped over her abdomen, and she clutched onto her dress.

"I was expecting you to bring reinforcements."

She dropped her phone into her bag and wiped all expressions from her face before standing to her feet. "You shouldn't have done that today. You just solved my problem. The cat's out of the bag, so this is over."

"This is over for Evelyn. As for you, Amy, it depends."

Though Evelyn recognized that voice anywhere, her hand instinctively reached for her gun. "What are you doing here?" she asked, releasing the grip on the gun and casting a quick glance over her shoulder to keep an eye on Amy.

"To help you put a stop to her nonsense and bring you home," Dan answered, stepping closer.

"I—"

"You don't need to do everything by yourself," Kate interrupted, stepping out from behind Dan.

Evelyn took her eyes off Dan and peered behind him to see the rest of the guys.

Before she could get her throat working again, Dan stepped forward and pulled her to his side in time for her to see the smirk on Amy's face.

"If you think that the few of you will scare me, you think wrong. You," Amy said, pointing her index finger at Evelyn. "You're going to keep paying me as long as I want, or I'll haunt you; I'll tell all your colleagues and clients about your past."

"Tell them what? That she's a survivor? A successful business owner? Her only colleague is standing right here with her infuriated husband."

"Oh, the prince is upset that the princess got hurt? That's what happens to people who get in *my* way. That slash is my warning. The next time, it'll be on your pretty little face."

Evelyn couldn't stop the corners of her lips from turning up. She shook her head as Amy took an audacious step forward, clearly intending to continue her threats in Kate's face.

Tyler stepped forward calmly—way too calmly.

She watched Tyler reach into his pocket and pull out his cell phone. She frowned, and the etch between her brows deepened as Tyler tapped something on his phone before looking up at Amy.

"I highly suggest that you watch your tone." Then with another tap on his phone, Tyler turned the phone toward Amy.

Though soft, Evelyn could hear the conversation they had with Amy over the past few minutes.

Amy stepped forward and tried to grab the phone from Tyler. But compared to him, Amy was a dwarf.

Tyler merely raised his arm above him while the other hand pushed into Amy's face, forcing her to stagger back.

"That's my first warning to you. I don't want you anywhere near my wife. If you step forward again, I'll break you."

When Evelyn saw the disorientation in Amy's eyes, she gave up trying to conceal her smile and broke into a wide grin.

"On top of this recording, a veteran lawyer is now getting an official statement from the cab driver who saw everything you did, and he's more than willing to appear as a witness," Dan added.

Scoffing at Dan's words, the smirk returned to Amy's face. "I've been to jail before. It's nothing."

Evelyn shifted uncomfortably. The problem with dealing with people like Amy was that they had nothing to lose. Dan must have felt her anxiety; he took her hand and gave it a gentle squeeze.

"You stay in a neighborhood with quite a lot of gang influence, and Tyler won't have a problem getting detectives to arrest certain gang leaders and give them the impression that you're the cause of the harassment. I wonder what trouble that would bring you." Dan paused for a moment before continuing. "We can start with your drug supplier," Dan said, staring at the bruises right below Amy's elbow.

Amy's face blanched, but she quickly composed herself. "All your reputations will be ruined when people find out you associate with a woman like her." Amy's index finger jabbed forward again as she took a step nearer.

Evelyn wanted to reach out and snap Amy's finger, but Dan tightened his grip and pulled Evelyn a step back before grabbing Amy's finger and twisting her arm backward in an awkward position. "Don't struggle. Your arm will pop out of your socket."

"I think we forgot to mention that we're all judo black belt. You should stop stepping within our reach," Ryan said while Joseph pulled Evelyn back farther from Amy.

Before she knew it, she was half a step behind the group while the guys stood protectively in front of her.

She stared blankly, looking at the backs of the guys. For the first time in her life, she didn't have to fight her own battle. Ironically, it was also when she had the epiphany on why Kate got irritated whenever the guys jumped in front of her for every problem she had.

It was slightly demeaning. It was as if they all thought she wasn't capable of solving her problems, and the feminist in her was tempted to shove her way back to the frontline and take Amy on herself.

Then again, she'd never felt so protected in her life.

Evelyn glanced to her side and saw the small smile Kate was displaying.

"I'm so sorry for getting you hurt," she said, forgetting about Amy.

Kate's smile was immediately replaced by the rolling of her eyes, followed by an unforgiving glare. "I'm not angry with you for this," Kate said, raising her arms with the bandages. "I'm disappointed that you chose to keep this to yourself instead of telling me. I already knew what happened before. Why didn't you just tell me about this? I would've helped."

Evelyn nodded.

"Then to top it all off, you ran off after talking to Dan. What were you thinking? Do you know how worried we were? Did you think we'd just let you walk out of our lives?" Kate continued her tirade, her volume increasing with each question.

When Kate stopped speaking, Evelyn suddenly realized how quiet it was. She turned and noticed all eyes on them. With a quick glance over at Kate, the two of them burst out laughing.

"I see what you mean about her monstrous side," Ryan joked.

"I'll see how long your friendship lasts when everyone knows about her past."

Evelyn's laughter got choked in her throat, and she clenched her jaws as she took a deep breath through her nose.

"You think I'll be embarrassed?" Kate asked, looking right at her.

Softly, she finally admitted, "Everyone will know I'm a murderer. None of you should be linked to a murderer."

Kate's head swayed side to side. "Really, Eve, sometimes you can be rather thick-headed." Looking at Ryan, Kate gave him a mischievous smile. "I'll show you *my* monstrous side."

Striding forward, Kate moved to stand right in front of Amy. "Amy, you're a prostitute and you've been to jail, right?" She smiled and fluttered her eyelids innocently. "Besides you, none of us here has a record. In our group, we have successful business owners, a firefighter, and a doctor. Even if you speak to everyone we've ever met, how many of them will choose to believe you instead of me?" Softening her voice further, Kate continued. "If we were to both cry wolf, who will the people run to protect?" Again, she paused, allowing Amy to take in her words. "So, Amy, unless Evelyn allows it, I *will* keep her secret and defend her to the end. You, on the other hand, are on your own. She has all of us."

With her polite smile, her fluttering eyelids, and her soft, sweetened voice, Kate was able to do what the threats hadn't; she removed the carefully placed facade on Amy's face.

"All yours," Kate said as she gave Dan a pat on his arm, returning to Evelyn's side.

"Wow," Evelyn uttered under her lips.

Leaning closer to her, Kate whispered, "I think I did pretty well."

She shook her head and whispered back, "You did much better than *pretty well*."

"Here's how it'll go," Dan said. "You keep your mouth shut and disappear from all of our lives. That way, we all get our peace."

Amy tried wrenching her hand from Dan's grip, but immediately winced and stopped. "Bullies. You're all behaving like Mrs. Moore."

Evelyn stared at Amy, dumbfounded.

Kate stepped forward. "Maybe, but who are you to complain? You should be glad we're standing here, speaking to you as if you're a sensible human being instead of the animal you truly are."

Amy scowled and struggled against Dan's grip, trying to pounce on Kate. It was ludicrous for Amy to think she could ever hurt Kate with all the guys around, but she tried anyway.

Dan deepened the angle of her already awkward arm position, causing her to scream from the sudden pain. "Disappear from our lives, do you understand?"

"Let me go!"

"Do you understand?" Dan asked again.

Curtly, Amy nodded and stepped away when Dan released her arm.

Amy glared at Evelyn while her fingers kneaded the strain on her arm.

Evelyn supposed Amy was considering her next move. The odds weren't in her favor, and she appeared to have finally understood that.

With her fingers still on her arm, Amy turned and was about to walk away when Evelyn stopped her.

"How did you know where to find me?"

That question had puzzled her from day one. Since they were minors when the investigation on Mrs. Moore began, the records would have been sealed. There was no way Amy could find out her new identity.

With a smugness fused with contempt, Amy replied, "You'll find out soon enough."

It was nowhere near a satisfying answer. She was tempted to ask more questions, but she didn't want to waste her breath on Amy.

Quietly, they all watched as the figure of Amy's back got smaller before disappearing into the darkness of the park.

"What does that even mean?" Evelyn asked, her eyes still staring in the direction where Amy had disappeared to.

Kate shrugged nonchalantly. "I'm sure it's nothing. She's probably trying to scare you or something." Turning toward Evelyn, she continued. "You need to get your stuff from wherever you've taken them and go home." She returned to Tyler's side, taking his hand as they headed back toward their car.

"Kate, I really am sorry."

Kate stopped and turned back to her. "I just hope that next time, if ever such things happen again, you'll choose to trust us instead of trying to handle things on your own. I know what you've gone through, but I hope this proves that we're not like those people you met in the past."

Evelyn nodded and turned to the rest of the guys. "Sorry for the trouble."

"You're sounding a lot like Kate now. You should stop apologizing," Joseph said. "You're our friend, too. We'll help as long as you allow us to."

"Actually, we'll help even if you don't allow us to." Ryan gave Evelyn a soft nudge on her arm before leading the group back toward the cars.

"See you for breakfast in the morning?" Kate asked.

Evelyn smiled and gave Kate a tight hug. "Thanks."

Kate returned her hug and whispered into her ear, "If you ever do such a thing again, I'll kill you."

They laughed, breaking off the hug and getting stares from the rest of the guys.

"Goodnight," Kate said and got into Tyler's car.

Dan leaned against the passenger side of his car and waited for Evelyn to walk over.

"I'm not going to eat you," he said when he saw Evelyn dragging her feet.

"I'm sorry."

He ran his hand through his hair and sighed. "You can't dump your life story on me then disappear while I'm getting the first aid kit."

"I didn't think you'd want to be associated with me, not after what I told you."

Dan moved and closed the distance between them, speaking in a low, soft tone, "Tell me, what did I do to make you think so low of me?"

"I just …"

Clipping his finger under her chin, he tilted her face up to him. "I never know what to do with you." Then he wrapped his arms around her waist and pulled her closer, holding her tightly in his arms. "Don't ever do this to me again."

Evelyn tensed up in his arms.

She stood, not moving, not saying anything.

"What's wrong?" He released his arms around her. "I don't care what happened in the past. I don't care what people say. I want you; that's all I care about."

Evelyn sighed and looked down.

The light from the lamppost glistened off the drops of tears that fell heavily onto the ground.

She stepped back from him and turned away. "I can't give you what you want."

"You don't want to be with me?"

She spun around. "No, not that."

"Then?"

She swallowed hard and tipped her head back with a heavy sigh. "Remember the last time we were here? Remember what you told me?"

"That I want a family?"

"I can't give you that."

"I'm lost. Are you saying that you don't want a family? I—"

"I'm saying that I can't." She looked up at him and waited for the information to sink in. "I can't get pregnant."

His eyes widened. "Was it because of …"

"No, I don't think so. I'm not sure. I didn't really hear what the doctor said; it wasn't as if I understood the medical terms. And I never thought I'd want children anyway." Her tongue pushed against the inner side of her cheek. "So you see, it isn't just my past. I can't give you the future you want."

He drew in a slow, deep breath and nodded. "Is that all?"

Evelyn blinked. "So this is it, I guess."

"No, it isn't." He took a step toward her. "Marianne kept saying that I wasn't stepping up and going after what I really wanted. I thought I'd done what I could, but I always gave in to your decisions because I thought you knew what *you* wanted—and it wasn't me."

"That's not—"

"Hear me out. I want you; I've told you that more than once, and each time you've turned me down. And when that happened, I moved back and gave you space. This time, we're doing it my way. You try me out. We go out as a couple, for say … three months. If at the end of it, you decide that I'm not what you want, then fine. But until the end of the third month, no matter what happens, you'll try to work it out with me instead of running away."

"Dan, did you hear what I say? I can't—"

"We'll adopt, or if you'd rather just have me to yourself."

"You're going to regret this."

"You don't understand," he said, tucking her hair behind her ear. "Everything I want, I want it with you. It doesn't matter to me if we can't have our own children. We can always adopt. We can take in foster kids and give them a home; a safe home that you didn't have."

Tears brimmed over her eyes. "You'll do that?"

He smiled, his thumb wiping her tears away. "If that's what you want."

She gave a strangled laugh and brushed her tears away on the back of her hand. "Are you sure?"

"Yes."

"And my past … I killed someone."

"In self-defense. She would've killed you."

"I still get nightmares; sometimes I wake up screaming."

He could see they weren't going to get anywhere until he could convince Evelyn that nothing was going to change his mind.

He had already waited this long; he didn't mind thrashing everything out now. "I've accompanied you when you couldn't sleep. If you wake me up, I'll accompany you as I always did."

"I don't know how families work. I didn't grow up playing with dolls; in fact, I didn't even own any toys. I didn't get to go to amusement parks or have family picnics."

"You said Kate was your family. You and Kate worked out just fine."

"I've never been in a serious relationship before; I don't know how to be a girlfriend."

"Then you ask. No drama, no secrets. You once told me that, remember?"

That drew a smile from her. "No drama, no secrets," she muttered under her breath. "I've been keeping such a huge secret from everyone, and even I would have to say that today has been a drama-filled day."

"Then starting tomorrow, promise me that."

She stared back at him, her face straight and without expression.

He narrowed his eyes, scrutinizing her face for any hint of what she was thinking. "This is the time when you should say something."

She chewed on her lips, and he saw the hesitation in her eyes.

"Give *us* a chance. Three months, that's all I'm asking."

"Three months?"

"Yes," he said, gazing into her eyes.

The corners of her lips curled. "I can do that."

"Finally." He closed the distance between them and pulled her into his arms.

Chapter Thirteen

Evelyn woke up the next day in Dan's arms. He'd sent her home and stayed to help her unpack. She fussed over returning her bags to their proper place while he helped with the folding and hanging of the clothes.

All he really had to do was to stuff it into her already messy wardrobe, but he insisted on packing everything.

After that, they had supper and chatted until she fell asleep.

She didn't know how she ended up snuggling on top of Dan while he took up whole of the couch underneath them, but she'd fallen asleep without any pills. And for the first time in a while, she didn't have a nightmare.

She tried to slide off Dan without waking him, but when she began moving, his arm tightened around her waist and he held her in place.

"Where are you going?"

"To wash up, then we're going to your house so you can change. Otherwise, we're not going to Kate's for breakfast."

Dan laughed and shifted his arm from under his head, wrapping it around her. "Five more minutes."

She smiled and leaned her head against his chest. "Five more minutes."

When they finally got to the mansion, all eyes turned toward them as they strode in.

"Good morning," she said.

Settling onto the chair that Dan had pulled out for her, she glanced around, glad that everyone was behaving as though nothing had changed.

On the drive over, she was worried about the looks of sympathy that they might start giving her. She smiled to herself, relieved that her needless worry was simply her over-active brain screwing around with her.

"Are you heading to the office?" Evelyn asked Kate.

Kate looked up at her, turned to her bandages, then cocked her head toward Tyler. "What do you think?"

Evelyn had to laugh. "I'll call or email if there's anything important. And Tyler, I'm sorry about getting Kate hurt."

Taking Kate's hand, he smiled and said, "I've been warned about giving you any trouble."

Evelyn smiled at Kate, mouthing a 'thank you' to her.

"Now that Dan will be busy going out with you—officially—will the progress at the gym be delayed?" Ryan asked with his goofy smile.

Rolling her eyes, Evelyn said, "Yes, we're *officially* going out. That's the real question, isn't it?"

"You're not much fun."

"It's going fine," Dan said. "We're ahead of time. If you can get yourself down there, you can see it for yourself. The studios should be ready by the end of this week."

"That's fast. Can we start using it for the practice lessons?" Joseph asked.

Dan's brows furrowed. "We'll need to put in the mats, but with the rest of the renovations, it's going to be a mess. Unless you're fine with cleaning it up yourself, I suggest you find another place for that."

The guys continued their conversation about the gym while she looked at the table of food. She hadn't felt this hungry in a while.

Feeling that someone was staring at her, Evelyn looked up and saw Marianne's eyes on her. "Is there something you want to ask?"

Marianne's gaze flickered onto Dan before returning to her.

"I don't mind you asking."

"Mrs. Moore is dead. You saw Amy last night … What about

Leah?"

Dan reached out and took her hand, watching her for a moment.

She pinched her lips together. "I don't know." Besides the nightmare, she hadn't thought much about Leah. Even back then, Leah seemed to have lost all determination to fight. "Once the police stepped in, they separated us and I haven't seen her since."

"Why are you so ashamed of it? You went through hell, but you're still here, successful and alive. You have nothing to be ashamed of," Joseph said.

A corner of her lips turned up.

She didn't have an answer for his question. She'd heard Kate say that so many times, and she'd repeated it to herself over and over, but she supposed she never believed it.

Part of her even thought she was somehow to blame for the situation.

"I, I didn't mean … don't …" Joseph said with his palms up, glancing over at Marianne and Kate for help.

Only when Dan pulled her into his arms did she realize she was crying. She hid her face in Dan's chest. "I'm fine, I'm fine. Really." She straightened herself, but Dan kept his arm around her.

"Because she's messed up, just like her house," Kate said and grinned at her.

"My house is perfectly fine." She turned to Dan. "Right?"

Dan hesitated for a moment, but he eventually figured out the right reaction. "Right, of course."

Everyone laughed while Evelyn narrowed her eyes and stared at Dan. "You know, from what I understand, you're supposed to stand by your girlfriend."

"I did." Dan glanced around the table and repeated, "I did!"

Tyler grinned and shook his head. "Keywords—I'm sorry."

"Wow, I never thought there'd be a day when I'd be taking relationship advice from Ty."

"Oh! That reminds me. Eve," Kate said, fluttering her eyelids at her. "Dan was *really* mean to me yesterday. He *shouted* at me."

With a small pout, she continued. "He says it was my fault that you went missing."

Dan raised his hands. "Wait, I didn't shout *at* you. My back was facing you, so that makes it impossible for me to yell *at* you. I was merely stating my opinion at a louder decibel."

Evelyn rolled her eyes at Dan. "Really? That's your excuse?"

"What happened to standing by your boyfriend?"

"There are exceptions."

"You're pure evil," Dan said as he looked over Evelyn's shoulder.

"That's my wife you're speaking to."

"That's how you should've reacted when I asked you about my house," Evelyn said.

Dan opened his mouth to speak but changed his mind at the last minute. He shook his head, and after a moment, he said, "I'm sorry."

Ryan leaned back and laughed at them. "I'm *never* going to end up like this." Pushing himself off the chair, he popped the last piece of hash brown into his mouth and hobbled out of the kitchen with Marianne's help.

Everyone finished up their food and headed to work after Kate shooed them off.

Just as Dan and Evelyn were getting into his car, Evelyn's phone rang. She took a quick look at the display and dropped her phone back into her bag before slipping into the car.

"Is that Amy?"

"No," she said, pulling the seat belt over herself. She turned to him when she noticed his awkward silence. "You know the bad-in-relationships thing that Kate said about me? That includes relationship with clients. It's better that Kate handles them."

Dan grinned and shook his head.

"And Dan, whatever happens between us, whatever stupid thing I do, please don't take it out on Kate."

"Eve, I wasn't—"

"I know, I know you didn't mean it. And trust me, she isn't angry. It's just … I *am* a ridiculous mess. The way I do things, the way I behave. I know she ends up being the one who cleans up my mess, but she never complains—except about the cleanliness of my house."

"And she keeps Ty in check. Even when he could've, and probably would've, been all crazy about Kate getting hurt."

Evelyn nodded. "Exactly. Remember what happened with Joanne?"

Dan laughed as he thought about his sister's crazy behavior. "So, if I ever get into a fight with Kate, it's safe to assume you'll *always* take her side?"

"Oh, come on, that isn't a fair question."

"Why not? I'll pick you over the guys anytime."

"Kate will never pick a fight with you for nothing; she isn't unreasonable."

"I'm saying what if. If she's being unreasonable, you'll be on my side?"

"No, but I'll probably tell her to be kind to you for my sake, and she will."

"Is that the best answer you can give?"

"Do you want me to lie? I can do that if you want," she said with a mischievous grin.

He laughed and shook his head. "And Eve, I've completely forgotten about Anne, but thanks for helping with her school admissions and all."

"I knew you'd want that for her."

"Thanks," he said, then continued. "My mom flew into a rage when she realized Anne was going to Paris."

"At Joanne? I didn't think that was possible."

"At me, of course. But it was the first time that Joanne actually looked apologetic about it."

"She emailed me; sent me quite a few photos and said she was having a lot of fun. She promised she was studying hard, too."

"That's good. I'll see you tonight?" Dan asked as he stopped his car right in front of the elevator of her office building.

She nodded and was about to get out when Dan stopped her, turning her head back toward him.

Leaning in close, Dan brushed her hair back and said, "Have a good day." Then, he closed in and kissed her.

* * *

Evelyn hung up the phone and checked the order list on her laptop, making sure she'd ordered everything she needed for the new project.

"Ready to go?"

She looked up from her laptop and smiled as she saw Dan leaning by the door. Then she noticed what he was wearing.

"I know I look good, but you don't have to ogle at me like that."

Of course he looked good. He wore a black suit with a midnight-blue shirt. He'd buttoned up the suit, showing off his sculpted body.

She glanced at her own attire; a black, three-quarter sleeve cotton shirt tugged into her faded jeans. "Where are we going? I think I'm underdressed."

Dan lifted the black paper bag he was holding and handed it over to her. "I asked Kate for the size, so if it's wrong …"

Laughing, she took the bag from him. "Give me a minute."

She changed into the simple, sleeveless black dress that ended slightly above her knees, all the while wondering where they were going.

She returned to her office and grinned at Dan. "Fits perfectly," she said. "So, are you going to tell me where are we heading?"

Dan shrugged. "You'll see."

He waited by the door while she grabbed her bag and followed him out.

She kept pestering him about the plans for the night, but Dan either shrugged or told her that she would find out soon enough. Eventually, she gave up. He was obviously determined to keep his mouth shut.

She looked out of the window and tried guessing where they were going, realizing she'd taken the same route so many times. "We're all dressed up to have dinner at the mansion?"

Again, Dan merely smiled, drawing another frustrated sigh from her.

Instead of driving all the way up to the mansion, Dan kept looking into the woods and parked his car by the start of a line of candles leading into it.

Her brows drew closer, and she turned to Dan. "All right, I know it's supposed to be some sort of surprise. But I've got to say, this is scaring me a bit."

Dan laughed as he got out of the car and jogged over to open the door for her. "Trust me," he said, stretching his hand out for her.

She sighed again, but took his hand anyway. As she stood by the car, she squinted, looking into the woods. "I hate the woods. I can't believe Kate chose to stay here."

Wrapping his arm across her waist, Dan pulled her closer toward him. "Don't worry, no serial killer is going to get you; not while I'm with you anyway."

Her brows rose and he noticed her astonishment.

"I called Kate to ask for help in preparing this. She told me about the *When a Stranger Calls* movie you girls watched."

She laughed and nodded. "Yeah, that's one reason. I just don't like quiet places; it feels as though someone can jump out at you anytime."

"Well, it's quiet now." Pointing toward the rest of the group, he continued. "But whenever Ryan is around …"

She laughed again, leaning closer to Dan.

Dan smiled and kissed her hair, tightening the grip around her waist.

"Is this supposed to be romantic? Because it feels kind of cultic with all the candles and all of us in black."

"You should stop watching horror movies."

"I don't believe in ghosts. It's psychos I'm afraid of." She smiled wryly, then shook her head and continued. "Are you going to tell me what are we doing here?"

"Soon," Dan answered.

"Why aren't you all dressed up like the rest of us?" Evelyn asked Ryan as they neared. Everyone else was dressed in their black, formal attire; only Ryan wore a T-shirt.

Raising his arm with the cast, Ryan said, "I know it's a thinner cast than before, but I still can't fit my arm through the sleeve. And do you know how much effort it takes for me to hop here?

Especially when Ty only has eyes for Kate, leaving me to Joe. Don't complain."

"What's wrong with me? At least I bothered to help," Joseph said.

Dan gave Ryan a mock punch on his arm, but it was enough to send him wobbling and everyone else laughing.

"Yeah, yeah. Get your cheap thrill, laugh at the cripple."

"All right, can someone tell me what are we doing here?"

"You haven't told her?" Kate asked, her eyes wide.

"We're here for a funeral," Dan said.

Evelyn leaned back, taking a better look at Dan. "Whose?"

"Mandy Shannon."

She took a step away from Dan, moving out from his arm. "What are you talking about?"

"You've changed your name and your life, but you haven't left your past behind. I think it's time to close the books and move on."

She continued staring at him, her face blank.

Dan took a step toward her and draped his arm over her shoulders. Nodding at Mr. Sawyer, Dan signaled for them to begin.

Clearing his throat before speaking, Mr. Sawyer said, "Dearly beloved, we're gathered here today in memory of Mandy Shannon."

Evelyn looked up and watched as Tyler reached into his pocket, taking out a piece of folded paper and handing it to her. She opened the paper, and immediately her hands began trembling.

Dan pulled her closer, running his palm up and down her arm.

Even with the friction, her skin couldn't seem to warm up.

She continued to stare at the picture of the house she was trapped in for over three years. Her tears formed blobs of circles on the picture, smudging some of the ink. She turned into Dan's chest, forcing herself to take a deep breath.

And as she did, an uncontrollable shiver reverberated down her back and arms.

Dan brushed down the length of her hair, his arm holding her tight against him. "It's all right. It's over."

Around them, all eyes teared. Marianne dabbed at her eyes with her handkerchief while Kate hid her face in Tyler's chest.

Ryan hobbled forward, nearly collapsing onto them. "I know she's yours, but I need to give her a hug." He hopped forward and wrapped his arms around Evelyn from behind.

Everyone, even Evelyn, laughed.

"Thank you," Evelyn said, sniffling.

Ryan hopped away, giving Evelyn some space. "When you're ready, you can put the picture in there," Ryan said, pointing to the small ditch that Joseph had dug.

Taking another glimpse at the house, she took a deep breath and bent down to place the picture into the ditch.

Mr. Sawyer then continued. "A girl who was made to go through what no one should ever have but survived it all." When he finished his sentence, he dropped a slip of paper, on which was written what he'd just said, into the same ditch.

"A girl who, somehow, throughout all the insanity, managed to stay honorable," Marianne added, bending down to place her slip of paper.

"A girl whose courage exceeds many men," Ryan said with a grin, then folded the paper and flung it in.

Joseph looked Evelyn right in her eyes and dropped his paper into the ditch as he said, "A girl who was completely misunderstood and neglected, but still managed to find her voice."

"A girl who never gave up in spite of the horrors she faced, who even after being abandoned and betrayed, never lost her spirit." Kate stepped toward Evelyn and gave her a hug before turning to place her paper on top of the stack.

"A living testimony that the past doesn't have to shape your future."

Evelyn nodded as Tyler placed his slip over Kate's.

"A girl who stared fear and demons in the eye and emerged triumphant." Giving her a peck on her forehead, Dan bent forward and dropped the paper in.

Tyler reached into his pocket and took out a pen and a blank slip of paper for Evelyn.

She looked down at the items then back at him, confused about what she was supposed to do.

"Everyone has to say something," Tyler explained.

As she took the pen and paper, she thought about what to write. She knew everyone had spoken of how Mandy had survived, but that wasn't all Mandy Shannon was. Since the purpose was to let go of Mandy, she decided to be the one to let go of what wasn't good about her.

She scribbled onto the paper before saying, "In memory of the girl who forgot how to trust."

While she placed her piece of paper on the top of the pile, Dan picked up a twig, and Marianne handed him a kitchen lighter. Dan paused and blinked.

"No one smokes," Marianne explained.

Dan took the lighter with a wry smile. He placed the fire right at the tip of the twig. Once it caught fire, Dan shifted his grip to the middle of the twig and handed the other end to Evelyn while cocking his head toward the pile of paper.

Evelyn took it and lit the slips of paper, watching them turn into ashes.

When the paper was completely gone, Dan kicked some soil over it to fill up the ditch. Joseph then went behind one of the trees and handed everyone a white rose. One by one, they stacked the roses above the newly covered ditch and headed back to the mansion, leaving Dan and Evelyn behind.

Evelyn stared at the white roses for another minute before closing her eyes. *Goodbye, Mandy,* she told herself.

She opened her eyes when she felt Dan running his hand down her back. "Are you all right?"

"Thanks for doing this." Evelyn tiptoed and gave Dan a peck on his lips.

After placing down her own rose, she strolled back to the car with Dan. They drove up to the mansion where, as usual, Marianne had prepared a sumptuous meal for everyone.

Chapter Fourteen

Evelyn opened her eyes and glanced over at the clock next to her bed.

"Ugh!" She jumped up and ran her hand through her hair. She couldn't believe she'd overslept, especially since she'd gone to bed earlier last night.

She smiled as she picked up her phone and saw Dan's text.

Will be there in fifteen minutes.

Tossing the phone back onto her bed, she tried to hurry, but when the doorbell rang, she had just stepped out of her bath in her bathrobe. She strode out and opened the door after checking the security screen. "You're early. Give me a few more minutes."

She turned to go back to her room, but Dan grabbed her arm and stopped her. "Take your time; we're not going to the mansion for breakfast."

She turned back to him and asked, "Why?"

"We're going out."

"Where? I need to work."

"No, you don't. Kate says it's fine if you disappear for a few days, as long as I get you back in one piece. So …" He reached to the side and pulled out an enormous pink Care Bear. "Happy birthday!"

Lifting the bear, he handed it over to an extremely confused Evelyn while he stepped in.

"It isn't my birthday." She struggled to carry the gigantic Care Bear. Even using both her arms, she couldn't get a firm grip on it. Using her leg, she hitched the bear up before grabbing it around the neck.

Dan had gone on into the living room, picking up magazines and pieces of clothing off the table. He held them in his hand, looked around for a moment, and eventually chucked them onto a corner of the couch. "I know. We had a funeral for Mandy Shannon; I thought Evelyn Jordan deserves a birthday."

Evelyn took a few steps and dropped the bear. She stood and considered the possibility of hauling it all the way into her room without dragging along the other stuff that was scattered around. "And why is there a need for such a huge toy?"

He looked around the house and grinned. "I was afraid you might lose it if it wasn't large enough to be covered by ..." He scanned the living room and said, "Stuff."

She narrowed her eyes at him, and he laughed.

"I'm kidding, I don't mind the mess—not that it's messy at all." Stepping forward, he pushed her damp hair behind her ear and took her hand. "You said you didn't own any toys, so I wanted to get you one that's ... special." He lifted her chin and kissed her softly on the lips. "Do you hate it?"

She smiled and returned his kiss. "No, I love it. I just need to find a way to get it into my room."

"You can always ask me to help."

"Why can't you just carry it in for me?"

"Because I think it's good practice for you to ask for help."

She wanted to retort. But after the stunt she'd pulled, she deserved it. Nodding, she cleared her throat dramatically and asked in the sweetest voice she could conjure, "Dan, would you *please* help me put this lovely present into my room?"

"Anything for you." He winked and easily picked the bear up.

While Evelyn got ready, Dan moved around the house, picking up pieces of clothing flung all over the floor and dining chair. Then he arranged her magazines, placing them neatly on a corner of the table.

"So, you haven't told me where we're going."

Though she only left him alone for less than fifteen minutes, her living room looked drastically cleaner than it was before, almost like how it looked after Kate had been over. She stood, distracted by the lack of clutter on her floor.

"Just thought I'd help you pack things up a little. I had nothing to do," Dan said.

Evelyn was used to Kate cleaning up her stuff. It didn't matter much to her. She knew many people who live messily always claimed to know exactly where their things were. Evelyn never bothered to lie about that; she never knew where her things were.

She knew, roughly, that she'd probably thrown something into a particular corner. But other than that, she was usually clueless. Whenever she was desperate to find something, she would simply call Kate and hope Kate had packed it away neatly.

"I didn't do much. Just picked up your clothes and gathered your magazines."

Evelyn smiled and shrugged. "I don't mind. I guess it's easier to find my clothes when they're in a heap as compared to all over my house. So, where are we going?"

"You'll see." A corner of Dan's lips turned up, almost into a smirk.

"You know, this whole secrecy thing let me learn something about myself—I. Do. Not. Like. Surprises."

"You'll love this."

She shook her head. His arrogance was annoying her, but she couldn't help thinking it was somewhat alluring.

Taking his arrogance as a challenge, she started her quest of prying information out of him. Throughout the whole drive, she tried asking him different questions in various ways. She tried goading, coaxing, and pleading with him, but none of it worked.

Having run out of creative ways to question Dan, she gave up and watched the passing scenery while her mind continued to muse over the possibilities of where they were heading.

When Dan finally pulled the car to a stop, she looked out at the park and wondered what they were doing there. She turned to ask him, but he'd already closed the door behind him and was moving over to her.

Once she stepped out, she glanced around and spotted Marianne waving at them.

Sitting in the shade of a tree, everyone except Joseph was

there. A large mat was spread out with all sorts of food that must have been prepared by Marianne. "A picnic?"

Dan grinned and, with his arm on her back, led her toward the group.

"Happy birthday!" Marianne smiled, pulling out a small cake from a chilled lunch bag. "I'm sorry, I didn't have much time to make it look better. Your boy there didn't bother telling me until after he sent you home last night."

"I didn't ask you to bake one. I asked you and Kate to *pick* one." Turning to look at Evelyn, Dan said, "I had to buy your present."

"Why would I *pick* one, when I can make one?"

Evelyn looked down at the cake. It already looked like a store-bought cake. "I'm not trying to be polite, but it looks beautiful as it is. Thank you."

"Oh, come. Sit. Kate said these are your favorite dishes. Try them!"

"Thanks, Marianne, for preparing all of these."

"Oh, Dan planned it. I just did what I do every day—cook! And you should know I love cooking."

She had just settled on the mat when Ryan suggested, "Try the cake first."

"Because Marianne says he can't have any until you take the first bite," Kate added.

Evelyn laughed softly. "Aren't you afraid you'll get fat from all the eating? You can't work out in your condition, and you're opening a gym."

"This boy still has his dumbbells in his room. And don't listen to him complain about having difficulties moving around; he's always moving around on his own. Can't sit still," Marianne complained, her head consistently swaying left and right throughout the whole time she was speaking.

Evelyn couldn't help smiling at Marianne's reaction.

She didn't have many memories of her mom. But when she was young, when things got tough, she would sometimes imagine having conversations with her mother.

Her imaginary mother would always be wearing an apron and

baking cookies for her. At times, when Evelyn knew she was doing something wrong, her imaginary mother would nag at her just as how Marianne often did with the guys.

"Joe's working?" Dan asked, breaking her thoughts.

Tyler nodded as he ran his fingers down Kate's hair.

For everything that you've been through, God will give you double the reward. Evelyn looked around as she thought about what Kate had written in the Bible.

She'd never thought she would one day belong in such a scene. She'd never imagined herself sitting idly under the clear blue sky and being among the smiling faces and laughter that filled the atmosphere.

She leaned onto Dan and whispered, "Thank you."

Pushing her hair behind her ear, Dan hooked his arm around Evelyn's shoulders and pulled her closer. "You're welcome."

They sat around eating and chatting the whole morning until Kate had to go meet a client. Tyler then drove Kate to work while Mr. Sawyer sent Marianne and Ryan home.

Evelyn and Dan lazed around in the park, chatting about nothing in particular. She laid her head on Dan's lap, watching the clouds drift along with the warm summer breeze. She listened to the children's laughter and mothers' chatters. Even though it wasn't really her birthday, so far, it was the best she ever had.

Kate always bought her something nice, but Evelyn was adamant that there be no celebrations.

She hated her birthdays; they reminded her of a time when she was naive enough to believe in birthday wishes, only to be disappointed.

Now, it didn't seem to matter what she'd believed.

It didn't matter that her birthday wishes never came true; it didn't matter that the only birthday cakes she'd ever seen were through the windows of a bakery.

All those memories hurt. And though she could still remember them, it didn't seem that important anymore.

They stayed until they were hungry before heading for lunch, which was another affair that lasted hours. By the time they stepped out of the restaurant, Evelyn thought they'd be heading back to the mansion to wait for the others to return for dinner.

"Tired?" Dan asked.

Evelyn shook her head; she hadn't done anything except eat and chat. There certainly wasn't any reason for her to be tired, but she was feeling rather lazy. The slow-paced day made her want to laze the rest of the day away.

"Good. I've got something else planned."

"And what's that?" She should have guessed that he wouldn't tell her anything.

As expected, he shrugged and grinned. "You'll love it."

With last night's and that morning's experience, she knew nothing would get him to tell her what he was up to. Dutifully, she strolled alongside Dan toward his car.

Periodically, as they chatted in the car, she would glance out at the scenery and try guessing where they were heading. Soon, they were out of the city area, and she didn't recognize the streets they were on. If Dan weren't the one driving, she'd probably be freaking out right now.

Instead, she turned to him and continued to list all sorts of ridiculous ideas. At first, she was simply trying to goad Dan into telling her what he was up to. But after a while, they were having so much fun with it that she just continued.

Not long after, she noticed the tiny glow of lights in the middle of the horizon. She leaned forward and squinted, wondering what it was. She could feel Dan's eyes on her, so she was certain that whatever she was looking at was their destination.

She continued staring at the lights, and as they got nearer, she could see the tip of a Ferris wheel. The round metal structure emerged further and more lights lit up at its base.

"Carnival! You're taking me to a carnival!" She turned to look at Dan for confirmation, but she immediately cleared her throat and forced her wide grin into a small smile when she saw the indulgent grin on Dan's face.

She hadn't meant to get all excited, but she couldn't help it; she'd never been to a carnival before.

She used to watch on television how kids played at amusement parks and fairs, but she never had the chance to do so herself. She never even allowed herself to dream of going to a carnival. Surviving the day itself was tough enough.

When she grew older, carnivals and amusement parks became reminders of a childhood she never had and the nightmares she wished to forget.

Getting out of the car, she leaned against the door and stared at the myriad of lights and blue-and-white awnings that stretched across the different stores. Loud music blared from the speakers placed randomly across the fair. And like the park, it was teeming with children, parents, and couples.

"Ready?" Dan asked, turning her attention back to him.

"Definitely."

Dan took her hand and led her into the crowd. Pulling her toward a store, he asked, "Anything you like?" His chin gesturing at the soft toys hung up against the wall.

Evelyn shook her head. "One huge bear is enough."

"Then there isn't any fun. Pick something."

She bit down on her lips and stared at the toys on the wall, hesitating.

"Humor me."

Sighing softly, she pointed to the purple Care Bear, a much smaller version of what he had bought.

"All right, our aim is to earn seventy-five tickets today."

"Is that difficult?"

"That depends."

"On?"

Dan pulled her close. "I'm pretty good at everything here, so …"

"I learn fast."

"Okay, then let's do it this way. Seventy-five is the number we need. Let's see who can get more tickets. Loser has to prepare dinner for the other."

"I like pizzas. Are you sure you know how to make them?"

"I like your confidence. Make sure you don't turn nasty when you lose."

They kicked off their competition with each having three

chances to bring down the tower of cans. Evelyn managed to hit two off while Dan got all three in one strike. They continued going from store to store, playing every game, then stuffing whatever tickets they received into their back pockets.

After the first few rounds, Evelyn was losing terribly. So whenever it was Dan's turn, she'd try her best to distract him.

At first, she was simply talking nonsense next to his ears, hoping it would make him laugh and lose his focus. When that didn't work, she resorted to pushing his hand away from whatever they were aiming at.

Dan laughed at her antics. Instead of keeping her at arm's length so that she couldn't disturb him, he wrapped his arm around her and pulled her in front of him. Most of the time, Evelyn would stop her antics and watch him play while she leaned against his chest. But whenever he was doing too well, Evelyn would start her distractions again.

Her strategy worked, and Dan was beginning to lose.

Taking a break from the games, Dan bought some popcorn and cotton candy, and they strolled around the fair. When they neared the merry-go-round, Dan pulled her toward it.

Once Evelyn noticed where they were heading, she started pulling back, refusing to move any further. "That's too childish for us. It's embarrassing."

"I'll be with you."

"That doesn't make a difference."

Her refusal didn't have much effect on Dan's decision. His hand tightened around hers, and he continued striding toward the horses dancing in circles.

The only other adults on the rides were parents accompanying their children. They got quite a few stares as they stepped up among the horses and children.

"Dan, seriously."

"Humor me," Dan said and pulled out his phone. He stood next to her and leaned in. "Smile!"

She did as she was told. A blinding flash went off, and she had to close her eyes for a few moments to get her vision back. She glanced around and turned back to Dan with a small frown.

"Everyone's staring."

"They're just checking out what a great couple we make." He grinned and, without any warning, grabbed Evelyn around her waist, lifting her up onto one of the horses.

Evelyn gasped and grabbed Dan's hand, worried she'd fall. "What do you think you're doing?"

"We've been walking. Rest for a while."

She turned to look around, but Dan gently held her chin and turned her face back toward him.

"Don't worry about everyone else. No one knows who you are. Just have fun, all right?"

She pursed her lips and cast another glance around, but she eventually nodded. Dan did bring her here to have fun.

She stretched her hand out, palm up, and gestured for Dan's phone. She took plenty of pictures, and when the ride finally ended, they got off the ride while scanning through the photographs on the phone.

"Rested?"

"How many more tickets do we need?"

They made a quick count of the tickets they had. They needed another twenty, with Evelyn losing to Dan by three tickets.

"Let's go, and stop cheating," he said.

She laughed and hooked her arm around Dan's, leaning against it. "The point is to have fun, right? I have fun when I do that."

For the rest of the games, instead of competing with each other, Dan always kept Evelyn close to him, helping or watching her play the games. Eventually, they got the tickets they wanted and headed to redeem the soft toy.

By the time Dan and Evelyn headed over to the Ferris wheel, the main crowd of families had dwindled down as the younger ones were sent home to bed.

Dan held Evelyn's hand and smiled at her.

Throughout the day, he had to fight the temptation to lean in and kiss her. Whenever she was close, he could smell the sweet and refreshing scent of green apple from her hair. It took all of his discipline to stop himself from turning her around and kissing her.

He was so distracted that he had completely forgotten about the competition they were having. But he wasn't too concerned with that. He was more upset when each game ended; because that meant he had to let go of her, and he didn't want to.

Now that he finally had her in his arms, he found it difficult to let go.

Stepping by one of the carriages, he helped her up before getting into it. "Ever been on one of these?"

Evelyn shook her head while her eyes scanned the surroundings. She watched every movement of the Ferris wheel, looking around as it slowly inched up. "You? How many women have you brought up here?"

Dan grinned at her question. "Two. Plenty of times with the first. First time with the second," he said, gazing right at Evelyn.

He waited for Evelyn to turn toward him, but she didn't, probably thinking of a reaction.

"Joanne was a sucker for these things. Usually my parents would accompany her, but those times when I had to take her, I'd be forced to take this stupid ride with her." His grin broadened as he saw the corners of her lips turning up.

"Why? You could've said no; you're the older brother."

"She knew my parents would kill me if she went home being anything less than completely entertained."

"If it's so boring for you, then why did you bring me to this now?"

"It isn't boring now. I've been waiting all day for this," he said as the Ferris wheel came to a halt while they were right at the top.

He placed his arm around her shoulders and pulled her closer as he leaned in, whispering, "I've been waiting all day to kiss you." Then he closed the distance and kissed her gently. Slipping his fingers into her hair, he moved her closer against his chest and deepened his kiss.

Her hands grazed across his chest, moving toward his neck. She looped her arms over his neck, keeping him in place.

"Mmm …" she moaned as he broke the kiss.

"Did you have fun today?" he asked, his nose still touching hers. He wanted to let her enjoy the lights from above, but it was difficult to pry himself away from her.

"Yeah," she answered, her voice as deep as his.

He sighed softly. "The view is extremely beautiful up here. You can see the city lights and—"

"One more minute," she said, her hands tugging at his neck.

Dan couldn't say no to that. He grinned and found her lips, returning to their kiss.

Chapter Fifteen

Evelyn grinned as she looked at the text on her phone. She leaned back with the phone in her hand, wishing last night could go on forever, wishing she could freeze the moment on the Ferris wheel.

"You look happy," Kate said as she entered her office.

"I am."

"So? Tell me."

Evelyn laughed and told Kate everything she and Dan did, pointing to the soft toy sitting on the edge of her table. "No one has ever done anything like that for me. Just because of what I said … he …"

What Dan did for her wasn't just sweet. He went over and beyond to help her close the ugly chapter behind her.

After all the insanity she'd put him through, after all that he'd learned about her, he was still around and still doing so much for her.

"I know," Kate said.

Evelyn smiled. Just as she finished her story, the new administrative temp walked into Evelyn's office with a bouquet of pink roses. "Miss Jordan, this just came for you."

Evelyn took the flowers from her with a grin.

Taking a deep breath, she breathed in the roses. Then she pushed the piles of files aside and placed the bouquet on the newly cleared space.

"If you clean up your office a little, there'll be plenty of room for Dan's flowers and presents."

"Actually, I wanted to ask you to help clean things up a little. Not today, though, I got some work to do. I'm a little behind time; I haven't found some of the furniture you wanted."

Kate blinked, her brows drawing closer. "Did I hear you correctly?"

Evelyn rolled her eyes and turned to her laptop.

"I never thought there will come a day when you'll admit that you're messy."

"I didn't say—"

"Yeah, yeah. I'm going down to the gym to check on things, and I'll help you sound out what Dan says."

Evelyn laughed at the notion of having to sound out what some guy thought of her. She never cared much about her dates. After all, she never went out with them more than once. "Kate, please don't do anything to embarrass me."

"I'm happy for you, I really am. And when have I ever embarrassed you?"

"Who's taking you there?"

Kate rolled her eyes and Evelyn chuckled at her frustrations.

Sighing out loud, she cocked her head toward the new temp staff. "Tiffany's dropping me off."

Evelyn nodded as Kate closed the door behind her.

She propped her elbows on the desk and scanned through the photos that Dan had sent her through an email. Picking a few, she sent them to Kate and asked her to print the photos.

Tyler knew Kate loved taking photos, and he had gotten her a photo printer so she didn't have to travel to get her photos printed.

And as her best friend, Evelyn was entitled to make use of her friend and photo printer.

Logging out of her email, she switched off the laptop and picked up her bag.

Though she was tempted to spend the rest of the day reminiscing, there was work to be done.

Dan stood behind his truck, his laptop opened, checking his email to make sure that the rest of his projects were on schedule.

He skimmed through his e-mail, smiling the moment he saw one from Evelyn.

He clicked on it and laughed when he saw a list of dishes she liked. Below the list was a short message telling him to pick from the list for the dinner he was to prepare.

"You look happy, too."

Dan turned around, surprised to see Kate. "Kate, I didn't know you were coming down."

"Hoping it'd be Evelyn?"

He smiled sheepishly. "No, I was surprised. That's all. She looks happy?"

"I'll tell you more if you take me out for lunch."

"Deal. Let me know when you're done."

Kate nodded and strode into the gym while Dan remained behind his truck and perused through the emails.

Less than fifteen minutes later, Kate was out. "You're the only contractor who hasn't given me any problem."

Dan laughed, understanding what Kate was referring to.

Though he tried as much as possible to follow the drawings provided by interior designers, often, some things that were feasible on paper just weren't possible in reality. Since he already knew Kate, he'd gone through the drawings and discussed with her some areas that had to be changed.

Once Dan had given her the explanation, she and Evelyn made the corrections and gave him the new drawings. That way, there wouldn't be a need to halt work while the contractors and designers thrashed things out.

"Ready? Give me five minutes."

Kate nodded, getting into Dan's car while he changed out of his dust-coated T-shirt.

When Dan got back into the car, he wasn't surprised to hear her talking to Tyler. The moment she hung up, she turned to him and asked how things went.

"I thought you were supposed to tell me what *she* thought?"

"I will. I'm just being your concerned friend."

"You mean nosy friend."

"You know, I heard you're supposed to cook for her, and I'm

betting that you're going to ask Marianne for help." Her lips curled and she continued. "And I can make it extremely difficult for you to do so."

"Sometimes, Kate, you're scary."

They laughed it off. Dan told her what happened in less than five sentences. His mind was too busy thinking about the kiss he had with Evelyn to provide any further details.

He sighed, missing her warmth within his arms.

"You skipped lots of details, but you obviously enjoyed yourself."

"So she shared the details with you?"

Kate gave him a what-do-you-think stare.

"All right, now can you tell me what she said?" He knew they had fun, but he had to hear it from someone close to Evelyn. He wanted to be more than sure.

"She had a great time, and she couldn't stop smiling at whatever you texted this morning. Oh, and she made space for the flowers you sent and the soft toy you guys won. The most significant thing she mentioned wasn't about your date, but definitely about you."

Dan cast a glance over at her, waiting for her to continue.

"She wants to clean up her house and her office. She asked me to help, so I suppose she expects you to be around quite a lot."

Dan grinned, relieved that Evelyn hadn't freaked out or began pulling herself away from him. "Her house *is* sort of messy." He laughed, remembering the conversation they had at the mansion.

"Sort of? Please," she said. "Afraid that I'll tell on you?"

"I'm just the polite sort of guy."

"That you are. And it's nice that you planned all this."

"I should've done so earlier. Marianne was right all along, but don't bother telling her; I'll never admit it in front of her."

At lunch, Kate told Dan in detail what Evelyn had said to her; details that didn't seem of much importance to Dan, but appeared severely important to Evelyn and Kate.

He wasn't entirely interested in the details. He was just glad it was a good report.

Since hearing what had happened to Evelyn, he wanted to

make things better for her. He wanted her to have everything she didn't have and everything she didn't experience. Above all else, he wanted to protect her from everything before and everything to come.

He knew Evelyn didn't want sympathy, but his heart ached each time he thought about what happened to her.

"May I ask why?"

Dan looked at Kate, uncertain of what she was referring to.

"Why are you still doing this after all that she'd put you through?"

His gaze shifted from Kate. He looked out of the glass panels in the restaurants and onto the streets. "You know how you see old couples on the streets, holding hands and smiling at each other? I can see us doing that. Not exactly see, but there's this knowing; gut feeling maybe."

"Aww …"

He didn't know if he should roll his eyes or smile.

"And if she starts freaking out and running away tomorrow?"

"We have a deal."

"I heard. But … just but."

"I'm not giving up no matter what happens. I'm not going to allow it," he said. After last night, after having her in his arms, after the kiss they shared, there was no way he was going to let her go.

He couldn't change her past, but from now on, he'd be there for her.

Since Dan was sending Kate back to work, he reasoned it was a good enough excuse to drop by the office and see Evelyn.

He couldn't stop thinking about her since he sent her home last night. They were both too tired to make it for breakfast at Tyler's house, and since Evelyn said she needed the car, Dan didn't send her to work.

They'd been texting each other all morning, but he wanted so badly to see her.

Stepping into the office with Kate, everyone looked up at him before returning to their work.

"Coffee?" Kate asked.

"No, thanks."

Dan strode over and peered through the glass into Evelyn's office, making sure he wasn't interrupting anything. Even through the glass, he could see stacks of magazines, files, and paper all over her desk.

A large cabinet stood by the wall, and Dan had to bite down on his lips to stop himself from smiling when he thought about the mess within the cabinet's doors.

The last time he was in her office, he was tempted to open a few of those cabinets and have a look inside, but he'd managed to suppress his curiosity.

Dan knocked softly and inched the door open. Sticking his head in, he winked as Evelyn looked away from her laptop.

Evelyn sat at her desk with the phone pressed against her ear.

Instantly, the frown she was wearing faded. "Dan," Evelyn said, putting down the phone without saying goodbye.

"You're done with your call?"

She glanced at her phone, and her face blanked for a moment. "Just an irritating supplier," she said, shrugging it off. "I'll call him back later. What are you doing here?"

Dan laughed and waved the brown bag he was holding. "Kate said you had some work to catch up on, and I was afraid you'd forget to eat."

"I'm always happy to take a break."

"Good." Dan took a glimpse at her table then around the room. "Is there a pantry?"

Evelyn lightly elbowed Dan in his chest before leading the way to their pantry. "How was lunch?"

"Good," Dan answered as they stepped into the pantry. There wasn't anyone around, and since it was all walled up, he closed the door behind him and pulled Evelyn into his arms. "I missed you so much."

She giggled as she wrapped her arms around his waist. "I missed you, too."

Dan loved her giggles. He loved being the source of her bubbly laughter, light-hearted and untroubled, the way he wanted her to be.

Shifting her weight onto the balls of her feet, she met Dan halfway as he bent down and kissed her.

They shouldn't be doing this in the office. It wouldn't be appropriate if someone came in and saw them kissing, but he couldn't help himself.

"You know, the glass walls of my office can be frosted. You don't have to pull me in here to kiss me," Evelyn said as she broke from the kiss and strode toward the table.

"I'll remember that."

He unpacked the food and placed it on the table for her while she made coffee.

"What are you busy with?" Dan asked as she returned to sit beside him.

"I'm looking for a lounge chair, but so far, none of the shops has one with the size I want. They're either too small or too large."

"I thought you always make it if you can't find what you want."

"Only as the last resort, or if the clients specifically want me to do something special for them."

"I can ask around and see if anyone has what you want."

Evelyn took a sip of her coffee then looked up at him. "I haven't asked for help. I thought you wanted me to learn to ask for help."

"I'm helping myself. By helping you, I'll get to spend more time with you."

"Great answer."

They continued to chat even after they'd finished up the food and coffee and would have continued if reality hadn't intercepted. Dan's phone began ringing non-stop, an indication that someone screwed something up at one of the work sites. So he helped clear up the pantry and left after telling Evelyn that he'd see her at the mansion for dinner.

Time couldn't go fast enough for Dan. Even after solving his problem at work and almost killing one of his men, there were still hours until dinner.

There wasn't a point in remaining at work. He was so distracted and would probably end up causing more problems. Since he needed to get the recipes from Marianne anyway, he decided to head over to the mansion.

When he got to the mansion, it was empty. So he sat outside for a while, wondering where Marianne and Ryan had gone. Thirty minutes into his wait, he saw Marianne and Mr. Sawyer strolling back hand-in-hand. They were so engrossed in their own world that they hadn't noticed Dan or his car.

He wanted to make himself scarce, but there wasn't anywhere he could hide. Even if he could, his car wasn't going anywhere.

While he was still wondering if he should pretend to do something on his phone, Marianne saw him staring and immediately let go of Mr. Sawyer's hand.

"Dan? What are you doing here so early? I haven't started cooking yet," Marianne said as she came hurrying back toward the house. "How long have you been sitting outside?"

"How long have you been out?"

Marianne turned and glared at him, so he bit down on his lips to remove the smile from his face.

He shouldn't tease her when he still needed her help. But after all this time of Marianne nagging him about Evelyn, he couldn't help himself. "I wanted to get some recipes from you. I lost a bet to Evelyn. Why isn't there anyone in the house?"

She opened the door and stepped in. "You can't even fry an egg, and you think somehow the recipes will help you cook?" She stepped aside for Mr. Sawyer to enter. "Joe drove Ryan to the hospital for his checkup."

"It's just following instructions; how difficult can that be?"

Smirking, Marianne nodded. "All right, what recipes do you need?"

Dan handed her the email he'd printed out. "Pick three of the easiest."

Marianne took the paper from him and strolled into the house. "Oh, what I'd give to watch you try cooking any of this."

Chapter Sixteen

Evelyn stepped out of the car and headed into the grocery store with Dan. He grabbed one of the grocery carts and pulled out the list of ingredients that Marianne had written for him.

"Shouldn't you have done this *before* picking me up?" Evelyn asked.

Dan looked over at her. "All my meals are settled outside; I thought it's better to come with someone who has more experience in cooking."

Chuckling, Evelyn shook her head as she wondered how the day would turn out. "Before Marianne, I had Kate. Haven't you noticed that my kitchen is the cleanest part of my house?"

"I'm sure we can figure it out. Let's start with the vegetables." The vegetables weren't difficult to find, but once they hit the mushroom section, they were stumped. "What's the difference between white button mushrooms and this mushroom?"

"What mushroom did Marianne say to get?"

"Mushrooms."

She shook her head again. The dinner would be disastrous.

Dan stood and examined the mushrooms in detail while she went to check out the various types of mushrooms on display. "This looks like the one Kate used to buy," Evelyn said, picking up one of the packets. "Let's just take this."

"Will they taste different?"

She stared at Dan. How was she supposed to know? "Maybe we should just order takeout. I don't mind. Or we can go out for dinner."

"I promised I'd cook."

"If it turns out horribly, can I order takeout then?"

"Come on, show some faith."

"I heard you can't even fry an egg."

"Marianne told you that?"

Her lips disappeared into a thin line. "Not exactly."

"*Kate* told you?"

She grinned and said, "Oh well, I appreciate that you're trying."

When Kate told her about Dan's cooking skills, she was sure he would come up with an excuse to get out of cooking. Then, when Dan told her that they were going to get groceries, she'd thought that maybe Marianne was comparing Dan's skills to hers, which of course would be horrible.

Now, Evelyn was certain the dinner was doomed.

Still, despite thinking that nothing good could result from a dinner prepared by someone who only entered the kitchen to eat, it was sweet of Dan to try.

"No. I'm going to get it right, you'll see." Picking up his phone, he called Marianne and asked about the mushrooms. "Yes, yes, but you didn't state the exact type of mushrooms. Do you know how many types of mushrooms there are?" He stepped away from her, seemingly getting a lecture from Marianne.

"Everything all right?" she asked when he returned.

"Yes. But I think from now on, I should just call Kate."

She laughed, hooking her arm around his. "Next on the list?"

They shopped around for nearly an hour, looking at everything and joking about all the stuff they'd never seen before. Their laughter attracted several unkind glares, but they couldn't care less. They were having fun, and that was enough for them.

Having enjoyed herself so much from the grocery shopping, she didn't care if the dinner turned out horrible.

Dan, on the other hand, seemed terribly excited about the cooking. Perhaps he was just determined to prove everyone wrong. When they got to his house, he didn't allow her to help. So she sat in his living room, scanning through the channels on the television until she got bored and turned to online shopping.

In the middle of deciding between two pairs of boots, she heard several loud clangs and curses.

She rushed toward the kitchen and saw Dan on all fours, wiping up what seemed to be linguine on the floor. She knelt across from him, intending to help in the clean up, when she noticed some sauce smeared on the bottom half of his shirt. "Did you spill it on yourself?"

His hand grabbed the edge of the shirt, and he flicked it a few times, allowing some air to go in. "It's nothing. Leave this to me," Dan said, reaching over to stop Evelyn's hand.

But she wasn't moving to clean up the mess on the floor. She pulled her hand from his and reached over to his shirt, lifting it to see if he'd scalded himself. Though there weren't any serious blisters, his skin was bright red. "Dan, forget about the mess; put some cream on that."

"It'll be fine after a while."

"Either you let me put some cream on you—now—or I'm leaving."

He stared at her for a moment, seemingly trying to gauge how serious she was.

"Now, Dan."

Dan stood, pulling her up along with him. "All right." He looked at the mess again, then turned back to her. "I'm sorry. There was so much multitasking to do that I couldn't focus on anything."

"Then you should've asked me to help. I can't do much, but we can always mess it up together," she said, dragging Dan out to the living room.

"I'm fine. I'll just splash some water on it."

Evelyn wasn't interested in standing around and debating with him on the right course of action to get rid of the redness. "Sit, and no cooking until I'm done with you. Where is the first aid kit?"

His thumb jerked upwards. "Bathroom."

Dan was scanning through the sports channel when Evelyn returned with the first aid box. She frowned when she saw the scalded area, and her brows drew closer as she applied the cream.

He laughed when he saw her expression.

"What's so funny about getting scalded?"

"Nothing," he quickly answered. "I never thought I'd see you so worried about me. I kind of like it."

Immediately, her gaze fell to the ground.

He cringed. "That came out wrong. I just meant that it's nice to see your concern for me."

"I've always been concerned about you."

He grinned. "I'm glad it's not just me," he said, taking the cream away from her and tossing it back into the first aid kit. Gently, he ran his finger down the side of her face.

Suddenly, Evelyn's head swiveled to the side, and she sniffed at the air.

He frowned and was about to ask her what was wrong when the smell hit him. "The food!"

He got up, sprinted toward the kitchen, and switched off the fire at the stove. "I think ordering takeout sounds like a fantastic idea," Dan said, looking at the charred salmon on the pan.

"And I think you'll need to throw that pan away." Evelyn wrapped her arm around his waist, careful to avoid the scalded area. "I'm sorry it didn't turn out well, but I can still tell Marianne that it did."

"She'll never believe it," he said and laughed. "You should've seen her face when I told her that it was just following instructions." Pulling open the top drawer, he took out a few menus and handed it to Evelyn.

"Oh well, we can just have our meals at Kate's place for the rest of our lives."

He turned away to hide his smile from her. In the past, she was always so careful with the words she used. She never spoke of anything that happened in the past and never mentioned any future, not even for herself.

"What?" Evelyn said, staring at him.

"Nothing."

"What's so funny?"

He placed the dishes into the sink and doused them with detergent, hoping it would somehow help to remove the dried sauce and burnt remains from the different pots.

"I'm still waiting for your answer."

He turned to Evelyn and pulled her close, looping his arms around her. "This is the first time you made a reference to our future."

Evelyn immediately looked away from him. But with his arms around her, she couldn't move away and pretend to be busy around the kitchen. "I was simply saying that we could."

"So you see us having dinner—together—for the rest of our lives?" Dan narrowed his eyes and waited for her reaction. He knew how she tended to find a way out of answering such questions.

As expected, she squirmed and tried stepping out of his arms.

But he wasn't going to let her go. His arms held their place, and he pulled her closer toward him. "I'm still waiting for your answer," he said.

Evelyn swallowed hard. Besides that, her face gave nothing away. The seconds ticked by, and she finally answered him. "Anything is possible, right?"

It wasn't exactly what he wanted to hear, but with Evelyn, this was good enough.

"Right," he said and released her from his arms. "Why don't you pick something for us to eat? I'll clean up." He bent down and gave her a peck on her lips before turning back to tackle the destroyed pans.

When Evelyn revealed her secret to Dan, she was prepared to be shunned by everyone. She'd thought she would need to move in order to save everyone from the awkward meetings.

Instead, she found herself suddenly having a family.

Joseph began to include her in the conversations around the table and, along with Ryan, was constantly checking up on her to make sure that Amy was no longer harassing her. Marianne was calling her at work to ask her preference of dishes and to check if she was coming over with Dan.

All this new attention was strange for her. She even felt guilty for being annoyed by Ryan and Joseph's over-concern of her. And she was mortified when she let slip and complained to Kate about it over lunch.

Kate had laughed, saying that if she had to feel guilty each time she was exasperated with their concern, then she would probably have to see a therapist.

So Evelyn learned.

She learned that it was all right to be vexed. It was all right for her to tell them to stop and let them know they were annoying her. It wouldn't stop them, but it was all right for her to say it. She wasn't going to lose their friendship for speaking her thoughts or feelings.

They accepted her for who she was; likewise, they expected her to accept the protective nature that she'd only recently found out was a group issue rather than just Tyler's.

The only one who hadn't been bugging her over the Amy problem was Tyler. Instead, he'd started giving her lessons on self-defense.

She had tried out some of the stuff that Joseph and Ryan came up with for their self-defense class, but the things they taught weren't self-defense. They were martial art skills; they were skills and techniques that required years of training before she could actually hurt someone.

Evelyn spoke honestly. She told Joseph and Ryan that if she were a student in their class, she wouldn't return after the first lesson.

She'd tried to be as honest as she could without hurting their feelings. It wasn't easy.

Kate's appreciation of her candidness, along with Evelyn's indifference to people's opinion of her, had allowed her to express her thoughts without much concern for whoever was listening.

Thankfully, honesty was what Joseph and Ryan were looking for.

They were disappointed that their lesson plans had failed, but were glad it happened in the trial class instead of the actual class for the gym. That was when Kate innocently commented that Tyler could help, that he had been teaching Kate self-defense on his own.

Apparently, Tyler didn't just dabble in Judo, he had gone on to learn Krav Manga and Kapap. And according to Kate, they were much more practical for normal people like herself.

No one asked if he would help. They simply assumed he would; that was how the group worked. Joseph told Tyler to hang on while he went to grab the video camera. And when Tyler began teaching, Evelyn had to admit that Kate wasn't bias toward her husband.

Since that day, Tyler had made it a point to teach Evelyn self-defense. Sometimes, when she stayed late after dinner, Tyler would ask if she wanted to practice, and he didn't mind teaching only her if Kate was busy.

Picking up the face towel that Marianne had prepared for her, Evelyn wiped the perspiration off her face. "Did Kate ask you to do this?" she asked Tyler as she sat with her back against the wall.

"Why? Because my humanity is only brought out by Kate?"

"I didn't say that." Evelyn tried not to laugh but failed. "But I can guess who did."

Tyler grinned. "No, Kate didn't ask me to do this."

"Then why?"

"That night at the park; you kept looking around even though there wasn't anyone there. Why?"

"I don't know. It always feels as though someone would spring out of nowhere and hurt me."

"So you learn; you learn how to protect yourself, then you won't have to be so afraid."

Evelyn studied him for a moment and smiled. This was his way of including her in his life. She supposed it was sort of like his gift for her. "Thanks."

He shrugged it off. "Dan is good for you. He's loyal, like Kate. You can trust him as much as you trust her."

"Now I'm feeling guilty."

"Why? Because you went on and on about what a bad

decision it was for her to move in here with me?"

"She told you that?" Evelyn quickly got rid of her disgruntled look and flashed a wide, toothy grin. "For what it's worth, I was wrong."

He shrugged again and stood. "Practice this with Joe."

"Done with my girlfriend?" Dan asked as he came out from the kitchen.

"Done with my wife?"

Evelyn laughed at how irritated Tyler sounded. Since coming back from their honeymoon, Kate had taken up several projects and was working with Dan on two of them.

"All done. Once the client approves it, and I'm sure he will, Kate's part will be done. Then, I can start working with you," Dan said, turning to Evelyn and tuning Tyler out.

He pulled her into his arms and leaned in to kiss her. Evelyn kissed him back, just a peck on his lips, and took a step back. By then, Tyler had made himself scarce and they were the only ones in the living room.

"So, how's this month coming along?" Dan asked after casting a glance over his shoulder.

"Good, very good. Everyone's been great."

"You know I'm not talking about that."

Evelyn blinked, wide-eyed, and gave him a sweet smile. "What are *you* talking about?"

"What happened to your straightforwardness?"

"I would be if I knew what you were talking about," Evelyn said and looped her arms over his neck.

"You've tried us out for a month. What do you think?"

"Oh, *that*. I can't say I have any complaints. I think I want to keep trying *us*."

"Good. Very good."

Chapter Seventeen

Lydia dug into her bag, searching for her keys. She frowned as her fingers felt around the base of her bag while she shook it, listening for the jingling of keys.

"Finally," she said, pulling them out from her bag. She opened the door as she swung her bag over her shoulder.

Behind! She paused for a moment as she heard the voice so clearly in her head. Before she could register what was going on, she heard the voice again. *Behind you!*

An uncontrolled shiver snaked down her spine, but she shook it off.

The moment she pushed her door open, a massive impact rammed into her back, shoving her into the house.

The shock stunned her, and she couldn't react.

She tried to scream, but her voice was abruptly cut off as her head got jerked back. She gasped as her hair was yanked further back while the door slammed closed.

Once the door clicked shut, her head was thrust toward the wall.

Everything happened so quickly that she didn't have time to react; she could only squeeze her eyes shut and try to turn her head away. But the grip on her hair was taut, and she couldn't move.

She heard the sickening crack of her nose and felt the shot of pain that went right to the back of her head before it got replaced by a dull burning sensation that slowly spread across her face.

"Stop," she pleaded.

While her head was still swirling, she was thrown back and felt the friction of the floor against her face. The corners of her vision blurred, and she struggled to keep her eyes open.

Stay awake, Lydia. Get up, you need to escape, the same voice she heard moments before coaxed.

Taking a deep breath, she tried getting her brain to work. She had to do something.

Using all her strength, she raised her head and searched for her bag. She had a Taser gun inside; she just needed to reach it.

She was certain her bag was nearby. She blinked as a stream of blood trickled down her forehead and tainted her eyes. Stretching out her hand, she reached for the bag that was mere inches from her. But once again, her hair was jerked back.

Instinctively, her hand reached behind her, and she tried to pry the hand from her hair. Before she could even reach the assailant's hand, her head was smashed against the floor.

Her hands fell limp beside her as pain radiated across her face.

Fight, Lydia, don't give up.

She felt herself being flipped over. She struggled to open her eyes, but she couldn't. Without any chance of reprieve, she felt a fist across her face.

A moment of numbness took over, but it didn't last. The numbness faded quickly, and a searing pain took over. She couldn't determine which part of her face was hit; the pain burned across half of it.

A weak sigh escaped her lips, and her head dropped to the side. She rested on a side of her face as a warm stream of blood flowed down her forehead. Her field of vision narrowed, and a darkness threatened to take over.

Fight, Lydia! Open your eyes! You need to fight back now!

The voice screaming in her head jolted her back to reality.

All of her things had spilled across the floor, but she couldn't see the Taser. Her hand reached out, and she felt the strap of her bag. Her fingers clutched over the strap, and she flung her bag at the person sitting on top of her.

Her attempt was futile.

Her bag was ripped from her hand. She screamed and flailed her arms wildly. Her fingernails scratched the face of her attacker. But instead of skin, she felt a rough, uneven surface, like that of a sock.

As her hands got pinned by her head, she opened her eyes as much as she could and squinted through the blood in her eyes. She saw nothing but a pair of dark brown eyes staring back at her.

He was wearing a mask.

"Back off or pay." The low voice was muffled through the mask.

She said nothing. She couldn't think; the pain was clouding her mind.

Taking a deep breath and gathering all the strength she had left, she let out a shrilling scream.

The attacker released her arms and cupped his hands over her mouth and throat. Her scream got choked off in her throat as she felt her windpipe constricting. She grabbed his hand and tried to release the stronghold he had over her throat.

The dark rim in her eyes closed in.

She gasped and coughed as the constraint suddenly relaxed around her throat.

Several more blows to her face followed before the attacker's bodyweight lifted from her. Just when she thought it was over, she moaned as the attacker stomped his feet on her chest. She heard the crack of her bones as the air was forced out of her chest, coughing out a mouthful of blood along with it.

After that, she could hear a clamor around her. But even when she pried her eyelids open, everything was in a blur. She tuned out the noises and tried moving her limbs; she barely had the strength to twitch her fingers.

Giving up, she closed her eyes and concentrated on not blacking out.

She wasn't sure how long she lay there. Perhaps it was just a minute; perhaps it was fifty.

Vaguely, she heard the door open and close. That was when she allowed the darkness to swallow her.

* * *

Evelyn, Dan, and Ryan sat around the kitchen table with the blueprint to the gym spread across it. Most of the renovation had already been completed, and they were simply running things through with Ryan.

Truth was, Evelyn didn't even have to be there. If Ryan wanted to make any changes, Kate had to be the one to do it. But Kate being Kate, she came up with all sorts of excuses to make Evelyn take her place, just so Evelyn could spend more time with Dan.

Evelyn wasn't completely useless either. She was able to help Ryan decide where the different equipment should be placed.

When the doorbell suddenly rang, the three of them glanced at each other, confused.

Marianne and Mr. Sawyer were in the other wing while Tyler worked in the study upstairs. The final two members of their group were at work, so there shouldn't be anyone ringing the bell.

The mansion was situated at the top of a hill, surrounded by acres of trees and nothing else. No salesman would bother to come all the way up to look for one potential customer.

"I'll get it," Dan said, pushing himself off the chair.

Evelyn swiveled around and watched Dan as he hastened toward the door. She couldn't see the main door from the kitchen, but still she stared at the walkway, expecting Dan to stroll back in with Joseph. Instead, she heard Dan talking to another man, followed by Marianne's voice.

The voices were hushed, and she couldn't hear what they were talking about. Curious, she stood from her chair. "Are you all right here?"

Ryan waved for her to go on while he scooped another mouthful of mango sorbet into his mouth.

She strode out of the kitchen and entered the living room just as Marianne disappeared up the stairs. She caught a glimpse of Marianne's frown and turned to Dan, only to find him as confused as she was.

Standing next to Dan was a man in his forties. The man's dark brown hair was combed back, and the edge of his hairline displayed signs of receding.

Evelyn gave him a look over, immediately concluding that he wasn't a salesman.

With his hands in his pockets, the man had pushed aside his charcoal-gray suit, revealing the vest within.

She didn't know much about suits, but she knew three-piece suits weren't common and didn't come cheaply.

Then there was the tip of a neatly folded white handkerchief peeking out from the suit's breast pocket, carefully folded and placed such that the monogram *D.M.* was displayed.

Without invitation, the man moved toward the couch and sat as if it were his own house. He crossed his legs and leaned back, taking a glance around the living room.

She moved to stand beside Dan. "Who's that?" She'd never seen the man before, but something about him seemed uncannily familiar. Despite his polite smile, Evelyn couldn't shake the urge to shiver.

"Some David Morgan."

The name sounded familiar to her, but she couldn't remember where she'd heard it. It couldn't be one of her clients; she would have at least remembered the face.

The answer hit her as she saw Tyler hurrying down the stairs.

It was the name she'd seen on Lydia's whiteboard.

Evelyn's eyes returned to David Morgan and she observed him, trying to figure out the sort of person he was.

Throughout the years spent in the foster system, Evelyn had learned that a person's behavior gave away many telltale signs of who one truly was. Words were easy. Words could form their own story, but behavior was always a whole other matter.

"What are you here for?"

"Tyler Hayes," David Morgan said, looking right at Tyler. Then his eyes moved toward Evelyn and Dan. "Dan Riley and Evelyn Jordan. Or should I address you as Mandy?" For a moment, his smile morphed into a smirk.

Although he was quick to remove it, his chin remained jutted in arrogance and his eyes scanned them with absolute contempt.

Dan immediately took a step forward, his hand stretched protectively across her waist.

"I hope you enjoyed my present for you. It's always nice to catch up with old friends, isn't it?"

Evelyn clenched her jaws.

Digging out her past wasn't an easy affair, and for this man to accomplish it spoke a lot about his connections.

The thought that a complete stranger held such knowledge of her past rattled her, but she was quick to take in a breath to soothe the anxiety from her face, leaving only the same polite smile that reflected David Morgan's.

It was then that she finally recognized the vibe he was giving.

There was something about him. Perhaps it was the emptiness in his eyes. Perhaps it was the way the smile hung on his face. She couldn't pinpoint exactly what set her off, but she finally recognized it—the aura of evil.

She couldn't believe it took her so long to place it. But now that she'd figured it out, she had no problem connecting him to another devil she'd once lived with.

Her smile faltered slightly at the reminder of Mrs. Moore, just slightly. She was no longer a kid, and this time she wasn't alone. Dan was right beside her, and she was certain Tyler wouldn't let her get hurt either.

Besides, who was more qualified to deal with psychos than she was?

"Look—" Dan began.

"Yes, I should thank you for that." Evelyn gently took Dan's hand away from her waist and stepped forward.

Dan took a step along with her, placing himself slightly before her.

She squeezed his hand, hoping he would get the hint that she wanted him to stay right where he was. "It wasn't nice seeing her, but it felt terrific to see her walk away, all flustered, after Dan nearly broke her arm. So, thanks," she said with a half shrug. "I guess it was kind of fun."

She sat next to David Morgan on the couch, propping her elbow casually against the top of the couch and leaning her head on her hand as if his presence was boring her.

From the corner of her eye, she could see Tyler moving behind David Morgan.

She didn't lift her eyes from the man in front of her. "I'm a straightforward person, so let's get to the point. If you're the one behind Amy, I suppose Lydia is getting close to something." She smiled and blinked, mimicking the facade of innocence that Kate had used on Amy. "You may have strutted in here with that smile and a five-thousand-dollar suit. But actually you're getting kind of worried, aren't you?"

It took much control not to smirk as Evelyn saw his arrogance faltering.

"You don't dare to take all of us on at one time, so you're starting with the weakest link?" She paused. "But they proved you wrong. So, back to Tyler's question. What are you here for?"

Evelyn stayed exactly where she was, her smile bright and brilliant, even when David Morgan's smirk morphed into a devious scowl.

"You think you're smarter than me?"

"No, I just don't think you are smart at all."

David Morgan shot to his feet and raised his hand. In the same instant, Dan moved forward, pulling Evelyn back, and Tyler moved in to grab David Morgan's hand.

Certain that Tyler had David Morgan under control, she patted lightly on Dan's hand. "How is it possible that someone like you can commit crimes and escape the law for so many years?" she said as Tyler shoved David Morgan out of the door that Marianne had opened.

"Not everyone is here today. Not everyone has someone to protect them right now." David Morgan straightened his suit, and the annoying sneer returned to his face.

Evelyn clasped her hands behind her, reining in her temptation to claw at the smirk.

Tyler didn't bother to ask. He slammed the door shut and started calling Kate right away. While he did that, Evelyn called Lydia. But neither Kate nor Lydia was picking up their phones.

"It's probably nothing. Kate's phone is always in her bag. She's always missing calls. Try the office," Evelyn said as she saw the disquiet on Tyler's face.

Evelyn redialed Lydia's number. When Lydia didn't pick up her call, Evelyn sent her a text, telling her to call once she saw the message.

"Just stay in the office. I'll pick you up. Everything's fine. No, just stay right where you are. Don't go anywhere until I get there." Tyler hung up the phone and grabbed the car key by the door. "You guys should stay here."

"Are they in danger? This can't be happening again," Marianne said.

"At least this time we know who we're dealing with. That was smart of you, Evelyn," Mr. Sawyer said.

Dan shook his head. "Smart? He could've hurt her."

"In that short conversation, Evelyn proved that Lydia had found something that was making him anxious, and she made him reveal who he was—someone insecure," Mr. Sawyer explained.

Dan sighed, and she could tell he didn't care what she'd proven, only that she could have gotten hurt.

She found herself wanting to laugh.

She'd heard Kate complain, time and again, about how irritating it was when Tyler could hear of nothing but the slim chance that she could have gotten hurt.

To Evelyn, it was important to size up the opponent, to know what kind of person she was dealing with. She'd come to the same conclusion that Mr. Sawyer had drawn, but she didn't think it was the time to bring that up.

She took Dan's hand and gave him a small smile. She'd watched how Kate dealt with Tyler whenever he got frustrated with her for, in his point of view, not putting her safety first. Evelyn thought it was a perfect time to put the gentle-tone-and-sweet-words tactic to use now. "I didn't step forward because I was stubborn. I stepped forward because I know that, between you and Tyler, there was no way he could've laid his hands on me."

She grinned as the frustration melted from Dan's face.

"We'll check that all the windows and side doors are locked," Marianne said, pulling Mr. Sawyer along with her.

"Let me call Kate; I think she must be going out of her mind."

For the first time, Kate picked up her call on the first ring. Evelyn put her on speaker while she told her what had happened. But before she could finish her first sentence, Kate cut her off.

"Eve? Is something wrong with your phone? You sound so far away."

"We're on speaker."

"Why would you do that?"

Why can't she do that? Evelyn thought. "Dan's here."

"Huh."

"What, huh?" Evelyn asked.

"Dan, she's never bothered to put me on speaker before. We always chat whenever we wanted for as long as we wanted."

Evelyn reached for the phone, intending to turn off the speaker when Dan snatched it from the table.

"She was talking to me," Dan said.

"Do you want to know what happened or not?" she shouted in the direction of the phone.

"Right, of course. What's going on?"

She took the phone back from Dan and gave Kate a summary of what happened. She offered to stay with Kate on the phone until Tyler got to the office.

But Kate refused, saying she was safe and there were still others in the office. "And I'm going to call Lydia until she picks up."

"Do you have her iTunes account?" Evelyn asked. Dan had already told her how Kate had tracked her to the meet up with Amy and how they found her after that.

"I'm sorry, Eve. We were worried and—"

"Save it. I would've done the same if it were the other way around."

"Right. Okay, but I don't have her password. So I'm just going to spam her phone now."

"Do. Not. Leave. The. Office. You understand me?"

"All right, I get it. I'll see you back at home."

Evelyn dropped her head back against the couch, frowning. "Don't worry, she'll be fine."

She nodded slowly. "Lydia said that David Morgan was suspected of quite a few cases of rape and murder. It isn't fair that scumbags like him get to walk around free while the women's lives got stolen."

Dan pulled her into his arms, his hand rubbing up and down her arm. "What about you? Knowing he was the one behind Amy's appearance," he asked after a minute.

Evelyn sighed softly and poked her tongue against her inner cheek. "I was a minor, so the records were sealed. If he can unseal it, I have no doubts that he's able to create more problems."

"Don't you mind that he knows?"

She thought about it for a moment. The only concern she had was the connections that allowed David Morgan to get the information. Besides that, she didn't seem to care.

Mandy Shannon would always be part of her, but she had left that chapter behind and was ready to move on.

Dan was right. She had a new name, a new life, but she had remained trapped by the life Mandy Shannon had.

She was done with that. "I guess it doesn't seem that important anymore."

Dan couldn't help but break into a wide grin. He lifted her chin, and she returned her gaze to him. "I'm glad to hear that."

He kissed her lightly on the lips.

"What's going on?"

They broke from their kiss to see Ryan hopping out of the kitchen. She'd totally forgotten about him, and he wouldn't be happy that he had missed the entire drama.

Chapter Eighteen

Evelyn, Dan, and Ryan all sat on the bed while Evelyn filled Ryan in on what had happened. He lapped up the details, but the curiosity in his eyes left and a seriousness, which Evelyn never thought Ryan had, took over.

He angled his face away from them, his eyes focused on the wall, seemingly considering what was going on. Then, in an instant, the solemnness in his eyes vanished and he smiled at her. "Don't worry. Like you said, Lydia probably has something on him already."

"How do you do that?" she asked.

Ryan glanced over at Dan. "Do what?"

"How do you brush your concerns aside and focus on the positive so easily?" Evelyn clarified.

"Which of you by worrying can add one cubit to his stature?" Ryan said.

"Did he just quote the bible?" Evelyn asked Dan. She hadn't read that verse before, but it sounded complicated and absolutely nothing like the words that usually came out from Ryan's mouth.

Ryan grinned. "I can't solve anything by worrying, so I prefer to focus my energy on something else and leave the solving part to God."

"I think Kate is playing too huge an influence in your life."

"Actually, he's always been like that," Dan corrected.

"Maybe that's why Kate and I are the happiest and most lovable people in this house."

Evelyn stuck out her tongue and pretended to gag.

"I know you can't admit it in front of Dan." He winked at her and laughed.

Evelyn grinned and shook her head, but she couldn't help thinking what Ryan had said was somewhat true.

"All right, you're clearly worried about something. What is it?" Ryan asked.

Her grin morphed into a wry smile. "Something isn't right; someone like him usually answers to someone else."

"What do you mean?" Dan asked.

She straightened and sighed as she thought about the whole encounter with David Morgan. "He isn't one who can keep his cool. He does stupid things like turning up here and letting us know Lydia was getting too close for his comfort. How is it possible for someone like him to commit crimes for so many years but never get caught?"

"Are you saying there's someone else? Like an accomplice?" Dan said.

"Like a mastermind, but I don't know. Something isn't right. If we were in a foster home, he would be picked on and bullied. He's like one of those idiots who think they're strong and almighty, but burst into tears at the slightest shove." She paused and shook her head. "Maybe I'm thinking too much," she said, returning to find support on Dan's arm.

Usually, she could easily forget a man like David Morgan. He was too rash and too idiotic to cause much harm, but the difference between him and other men like him was money.

Money could change a lot of things.

For one, she was sure David Morgan hadn't personally sent the threats that Kate had received and wasn't the one who set Kate's house on fire.

She didn't have any proof, but she'd caught a glimpse of the arsonist. He was calm and methodical, even a gunshot didn't frighten him off. That man set out to burn down the house with them in it, and he did it with the alarm ringing and the knowledge that one of them had a gun, nothing like how David Morgan had reacted.

"Something just doesn't sit right with my gut," she mumbled

under her breath.

Silence lingered as each of them seemed to think about what Evelyn had just said.

"Ryan? Dan? One of you should take this. It's Joe." Marianne stood at the door, her frown deepening the lines on her forehead. "I'll pack some clothes for Lydia."

"Pack some clothes for Lydia?" Evelyn said as Marianne handed the phone to Dan.

"Please don't tell me Lydia is at your hospital."

Dan's sigh was an answer that Evelyn didn't want to hear. She shook her head and gave a frustrated sigh. "Kate's going to freak."

"How bad is it?" Dan asked. His lips pressed into a thin line as he nodded away. "All right, we'll get there as soon as possible. No, it's fine. Eve will call Kate. All right."

"How bad is it?" Evelyn asked Dan once he put down the phone.

"He isn't sure; he hasn't seen her. She's being transferred there right now. But based on what he's been told, it's bad. Should we wait until Kate gets back before telling her?"

"You've got to be kidding. I'm not putting my neck out for that. We tell Kate, and we tell her right now," Ryan said.

Dan turned to Evelyn and waited for her to make the decision.

"He's right; we have to tell Kate. I don't look forward to her reaction, but we've got to tell her, now."

As Evelyn expected, Kate didn't want to wait for an update from Joseph. She insisted on heading down to the hospital immediately. Dan, Evelyn, and Marianne headed down while Mr. Sawyer and Ryan stayed behind at the mansion, in case any new surprises sprang up.

They waited for over half an hour before Joseph came out through the swinging doors.

He didn't smile even as he saw them. His face was clean of all expression, and the only sign of distress was the small sigh he gave before speaking. "She isn't in any danger, but she's hurt quite badly." His voice softened on the last two words, as if that would help to lessen any anxiety they had.

"What happened? Was it David Morgan?" Kate asked.

"She doesn't know. All she could remember was being shoved into her apartment while she was opening the door. The rest is a blur." He paused for a moment, allowing Kate to absorb the information.

Evelyn could tell he had more to say but was wondering if he should say it all at once. When Joseph's gaze flickered to her, she gave him a small nod. It was better to spill everything at one time. Kate hated having to sniff out information piece by piece.

"The paramedics said her house has been trashed, but her money and jewelry are still on her table. She didn't say anything except to send her here and gave them my name."

Kate took a ragged breath as her hand moved toward her necklace. She tugged on it, and the focus of her eyes drifted from him.

"Did she tell you anything else?" Tyler asked, his hand around Kate, holding her protectively.

"The assailant did give her a message—back off or pay."

Kate's face blanched. "Can we see her now?"

"Yes, but not all at once. Her throat hurts, so she can't really speak."

"Evelyn, would you go in with her? I need to talk to Dan," Tyler said.

Evelyn knew they were going to start planning their full security scheme that neither she nor Kate would have a say in. She went to her friend and looped her hand around Kate's arm, following Joseph toward the wards.

Even Evelyn couldn't help but gasp when she saw Lydia's swollen face. Her face was a mixture of purple and blue, and her skin had stretched to accommodate the swells. The whites of her eyes were barely visible, and when she forced her eyes open, all Evelyn could see was the crimson red in her eyes.

Kate couldn't even speak. She stared dumbfounded as tears fell.

"I'm okay." Lydia's voice was soft. As she spoke, her hand flew to her throat and she winced slightly. Phone, she mouthed.

Evelyn immediately stepped forward and handed Lydia the

phone. Lydia typed away on the phone before handing it back to Evelyn.

"I've synced all the info I had in all my devices and uploaded them to iCloud." Evelyn read out what Lydia had typed, then smiled before continuing. "Even if the person took everything, trashed everything, I can still get back every article, info, and interview I've conducted."

Despite the differences between Kate and Lydia, they had one thing in common—they always had a contingency plan. If anything went wrong, they'd be prepared.

"I guess that's a minor victory on our side," Evelyn said, controlling her urge to show any disapproval. She wasn't being unsupportive; she just didn't understand how Lydia could dismiss her attack and injuries so easily.

Kate pulled up a chair and reached over, cupping her hand over Lydia's. "We'll get the son-of-a-bitch."

Evelyn blinked, then laughed when she was sure she'd heard Kate swear. Lydia laughed, too, except hers became a soft cry of pain as her hand moved toward her chest.

"The police want to talk to her, but I told them they'd have to wait. And they refuse to place patrols for her until they're sure her life is still in danger."

"*This* isn't enough proof that someone is out to hurt her?" Kate said, waving her hands as though she was showcasing Lydia.

"That's just how they work. Can we take her home?" Evelyn asked. No point getting pissed off over the system. They had rules and procedures to follow. Though some of the rules and procedures were absolutely idiotic, the police would follow them anyway.

"I won't recommend it. I think she should stay and be kept under observation, at least for a few more days. Besides, she gets morphine here. She needs it."

Evelyn turned to look at Lydia then to Kate. "I think she should stay, too." She knew Kate would want Lydia to be well taken care of, but Kate couldn't leave Lydia here alone, not with everything that had happened.

"Dan and I will stay with her." Evelyn didn't want Kate staying over, not even if Tyler agreed. It was way too dangerous.

The last time Lydia meddled with the case, Kate's house got burned down. This time, Kate would probably be the next target as well.

"No, we'll—"

"No, I'll stay," Joseph interjected.

"But you've already been working all day," Kate pointed out.

He shook his head while he said, "You think I've never pulled a double shift before? Look," he said before either of them could continue, "go home, eat something, and get some rest. We'll talk tomorrow. She's not going to get better with either of you sitting here and worrying."

Evelyn nodded. "He's right, and I don't think it's safe for you to be here."

Kate rolled her eyes, and Evelyn quickly added. "They chose to come after you the last time. What makes you think this time it'll be any different?"

"You should go," Lydia said with her hand against her throat, and her brows puckered.

"All right, all right," Kate conceded. She gave Lydia a soft squeeze on her leg and stood.

Except for Joseph, everyone went back to the mansion. That night was the quietest dinner they'd ever had at the mansion. Though Evelyn wasn't physically harmed, she couldn't help but feel drained.

The ride back to her house was equally silent. Dan hadn't said much since dinner, and she knew he had something on his mind.

"Are you okay?" Dan asked as they entered her apartment. "You haven't said much since we left the hospital."

"Everyone was quiet. I'm tired, I guess. I don't know." She sighed and plopped onto her couch.

Dan walked over, pushed aside the pile of clothes on her couch, and sat next to her. "I'm not letting you stay here alone tonight; I'm not letting you stay here until this whole thing blows over. Why don't you pack some stuff and stay at my place for a while? I have a spare room anyway."

Her head snapped up, and she shook her head. "No, I'm not going to run. If he wants to send someone, let him come. I have a gun."

"You had a gun when Kate's house went up in flames."

She opened her mouth to retort, but was silenced by his kiss; a sudden, fierce kiss. A kiss of possession, fear, concern, and love.

"Don't fight me on this," he said. His voice was soft, but it was clear he meant it as a command rather than a plea. "You don't have to protect yourself. You have me now." His lips returned to cover hers.

Her heart thumped hard as her hands fisted in his shirt. She yielded to his kiss and felt herself being pulled closer to his chest, his arms enveloped her as his lips continued its unrelenting kiss.

"I cannot—no—I will not risk you getting hurt." He paused and gazed into her eyes. "I love you, Eve."

She hooked her arms over his neck and pulled his lips back to hers. She realized then that Dan was the first man who'd ever told her those three simple words. She grinned and held on to Dan, unwilling to let him go.

She almost agreed without a second thought.

But the accuser in her mind chided her. She should know better. With all her sleeping idiosyncrasies, she was only going to embarrass herself or scare the hell out of Dan.

Her arms dropped to her side and she leaned back.

"Dan, I get nightmares and—"

"I know and I don't mind. If you wake up from a nightmare, I can accompany you."

"When I sleep at a new place, I wake up at the slightest noise, sometimes at non-existent noise."

He shrugged. "Like I said, I don't mind."

"I may scream."

He grinned and moved in closer. "Just make sure that if the police show up, you don't let them arrest me."

She scowled at him. "I'm not joking."

"Neither am I." He removed his smile, and she closed her eyes as she felt his warm touch moving lightly down the side of her face. "Trust me."

* * *

The next morning, Evelyn walked into Kate's office, yawning.

"Didn't sleep well?"

"Didn't sleep enough."

"Marianne packed them for you." Kate pointed to the brown bag sitting on the coffee table, right next to a set of home decor magazines she'd fanned out, ready for clients to browse through.

There was a meeting room catered for clients, but sometimes the meetings clashed and Kate would require another place to speak to their clients.

It didn't happen often.

They met most of their clients in their own homes. It was more convenient for the clients, and Kate and Evelyn could see the house for themselves. But Kate still kept everything ready in case she had to meet a client in her office.

Everything in Kate's office had a place. Kate knew exactly where all the forms and contracts were. The portfolios of all their clients were labeled, arranged in alphabetical order, and placed neatly in the cabinets. When opening any of the folders, there wouldn't be any loose forms or papers chucked within. Everything would be filed neatly in the different sections she had labeled inside.

Evelyn had always found it scary whenever she called Kate to ask for a file, and Kate could tell her exactly which cabinet to open, which color the file was, and exactly which section she could get the document from.

Even the cabinets in Evelyn's office were packed and maintained by Kate.

They had a system between them.

Evelyn would stack everything in a corner of her desk until Kate got so irritated at the sight of the stack that she would file them for her.

Sometimes, Evelyn would return and think, for a moment, that she'd gone into the wrong office.

So when Evelyn strolled in, she immediately noticed the difference in Kate's office. A new laptop bag was leaning against the couch. Kate always placed her laptop bag under her desk so that it wouldn't look messy when clients or anyone else came in.

"Whose laptop is that?"

"Ty got it for Lydia."

"That's fast."

Kate nodded and got up from her chair. "He even downloaded all the stuff back into her laptop. Have you moved your stuff over to Dan's?"

"No, maybe tonight or something. I was too tired last night."

"Okay. Eat your breakfast, I'll make coffee."

Evelyn slumped onto the couch and opened the bag. It was a tough decision to skip breakfast. She really didn't want to miss Marianne's breakfast, and it looked like she didn't have to. She pulled out the three boxes and took in the aroma of the food as she opened them.

She held the fork in her hand and debated on which of the boxes she should attack, eventually popping a piece of peach with a piece of pancake into her mouth. She chewed on her food, enjoying the sweet spurt of juice from the peach, and was about to reach for the magazine when she noticed the laptop again.

Curious at what Lydia had been working on, Evelyn picked up the bag and took out the laptop.

She scanned through the different files and documents, not looking up even when Kate returned with a cup of coffee for her.

"I don't think you should look at that while you're eating," Kate said, placing the coffee in front of her.

Evelyn chewed on her lips and continued to browse through some of her documents. "She isn't just looking at your parents' case. She's looking into everything; she has all the information on the various victims and cases that your father believed David Morgan was involved in."

"She was trying to find evidence, so I guess she had to be thorough."

"No, it isn't just that. It seems like she's trying to solve all those cases as well."

There weren't just newspaper clippings. Lydia had done some serious research, trying to piece together the timing and whereabouts of David Morgan through various socialite parties printed in different newspapers. She even went to the detectives in charge of the different cases and interviewed them. She had collected detailed notes on every murder linked to David Morgan.

"Oh, no. Don't."

"Don't what?"

"Eve," Kate said, slamming the laptop close. "Don't get involved in the cases. I want to get whoever hurt her, but I don't want you to get involved in the cases. All this happened so many years ago. I don't want you to be chasing after ghosts as she is."

"I thought you wanted to catch the son-of-a-bitch?"

"I do."

"How are you going to get the guy if you don't help her?"

"There are cameras in her building. Someone must've seen something. There are other ways; we don't have to get involved. These cases are over a decade old."

"People like them don't stop, Kate. For all you know, he may still be killing, except he's gotten better and managed to keep it under wraps."

Kate pressed her lips into a thin hard line, the way she did whenever she disagreed with Evelyn.

"Maybe we're all wrong about Lydia. Maybe she isn't obsessed with your parents' case. Maybe she meant it when she went on and on about justice and all," Evelyn said.

"Maybe. But the women are dead. No matter what we do, we can't bring them back."

"So we should just turn a blind eye because we don't want to trouble ourselves?"

"Eve—"

"If my caseworker, teacher, or the school nurse had been half as passionate as Lydia is, maybe I would never have gone through what I did. Maybe that was why your father went ahead with the prosecution even though he knew the dangers he might face. People like your father and Lydia would've saved Amy, Leah, and me." She stared at Kate and continued when she saw her sigh. "We can't bring back the dead, but what about those he's still hurting? There's a chance he's still killing."

Kate scrutinized her face, then shook her head and sighed. "Ty's going to kill me. But if you want to do this, I'll do it with you."

Evelyn gave her a grateful smile. "You don't have to."

"And let you go crazy along with Lydia? Forget it; you're stuck with me to keep you two in line."

"Are you sure?" Evelyn asked.

When Kate's grandmother started to get confused due to her dementia, Kate began suspecting there was more to her parents' death than the car accident her grandparents' had told them.

Kate didn't know if she should find out the truth and fight for the justice her parents deserved. She had asked Evelyn, and Evelyn was the one who had told her not to chase after ghosts or burden herself with things of the past.

She knew Kate didn't want to dive into the case and be reminded of how her parents were ripped from her life. Kate was one who believed in holding on to the good memories; she would rather relive the wonderful times she had with them than focus on how she had lost them so suddenly.

With her own dark past, Evelyn was certain nothing good would come out from the past. There must have been a reason for Kate's grandparents to lie.

Now, after seeing Lydia's notes and perhaps with the change in perspective, Evelyn could see the reason behind Lydia's relentless pursuit and, in a way, even respect her for it.

But Evelyn didn't want to drag Kate through the past if she didn't want to.

"I wish my parents were still alive, but I don't blame them for dying. I didn't want to get involved because no matter what happens, I can't bring them back," Kate said. "But you're right. If he's still hurting someone now, we can't ignore it simply because it's the convenient thing to do."

Chapter Nineteen

That night, Dan and Evelyn ended up having dinner at a restaurant near her workplace. He'd sensed something was wrong the moment she got into his car.

She hadn't said much, only telling him about her day at work and the handcrafted chest she had completed.

But something was wrong; he could sense it. He kept glancing over in her direction even as he drove, trying to figure out what was wrong.

And Evelyn's continual avoidance of his eyes was louder than any of her words.

She was all smiles that morning. What could have happened to change her demeanor so quickly?

At the restaurant, she sat across the table from him, spinning the phone in her hand.

He sighed. Maybe she was having second thoughts about moving in with him. He didn't know what had happened during the day to change her mind, but he wasn't going to allow her to stay alone until the threat of David Morgan ceased to exist.

Going through the motions, he placed his order and waited impatiently for the waiter to repeat the order and leave.

He'd already come up with a list of logical reasons why she shouldn't be staying alone, and he was ready to start convincing her.

He took a deep breath and asked, "What's wrong?"

Evelyn stopped spinning her phone. "Nothing," she said and reached for the glass of ice water. She took a sip but continued to hold the glass to her lips after that.

He waited for her to begin the speech of how she was safe at her place and how she could take care of herself.

Instead, Evelyn placed the glass down and chewed on her lips, her hands returning to play with the phone.

Dan wondered if he had always been an impatient man. He never seemed to have a problem when negotiating with his clients, but waiting for Evelyn to speak her mind was exasperating. "Is this about moving over to my place?"

"No, of course not."

He was stumped by her answer. He had only considered that as the reason for her weird behavior, but perhaps it was more serious. Dan ran his hand through his hair and narrowed his eyes at her. "We had a deal; three months."

She broke into a smile and stopped twirling her phone. "Okay, I think I'm making it worse. I'm not freaking out about us." She reached over and gave his hand a squeeze. "It's about the David Morgan thing, and I'm worried that you won't like what you're about to hear."

"Anything is better than keeping me in suspense."

"I'll remind you of what you said." She grinned and continued. "I saw Lydia's notes today. She isn't just working on her parents' case; I think she's working to close the cases that her father was prosecuting as well."

"Okay. And?"

"And I want to help."

His brow arched, and he relaxed against the back of the chair, relieved that her behavior had nothing to do with them; not directly anyway. Then he smiled. "So you're worried that I would be unhappy? You're concerned about what I think."

She glowered at him. "Did you actually hear what I said?"

"Yeah, and it sounded as if you were worried that I'd be angry with you."

She sighed and rolled her eyes. "Yes, Dan. I was worried that you would disagree or get pissed that I'm sticking my nose into it."

"I was under the impression that you didn't agree with what

she's doing."

"I didn't. I thought she was using her so-called justice to defend her reasons for lying to Kate. Maybe it had started out that way. But based on her notes, she isn't just focusing on her parents. Maybe we're wrong."

"And you think she deserves a second chance?"

"Yeah. And I have this gut feeling that whatever David Morgan did, he's still doing it."

"And you want to help Lydia stop him?"

"Yes."

Dan considered Evelyn's words. He had to hold his tongue and stop himself from telling her that it was way too dangerous. "Did Kate ask you to help?"

"No, it was my decision."

"Why?"

"Because I don't want to turn away like how my teacher and caseworker did."

He nodded, not knowing what else to say.

She obviously felt strongly about helping Lydia, and it could help to heal her of her past. But a warning had clearly been issued through Lydia, and he didn't want to think about the consequences if they all dove in.

It was selfish, but her safety was his priority.

She must have sensed his concerns. She gave his hand another squeeze. "I'll be safe. I'll stay at your house, and you can be my chauffeur. And I promise I won't go anywhere alone. I'll keep you and Kate informed of my whereabouts."

"You came prepared."

"Kate and I went through it in the office."

"Huh," he said. "That's why we're having dinner outside. You don't want to be there when Kate gives Tyler her speech."

She bit down on her bottom lip as the corners of her lips grew into a smile. "She's already told him about it in the afternoon. *And*, I wanted to tell you this in private."

"That being the second reason."

"They were equally important."

"I'm sure." He scowled at her. "All right, so how close is Lydia to nailing that guy?"

"I haven't read through anything in detail."

"Take your time with dinner, then we'll go over to Ty's."

"Tonight?"

"I want to see what Lydia has and how we go about being amateur detectives."

For the first time in a rather long time, Dan had to ring the bell to the mansion. Marianne opened the door and cocked her head toward the stairs. "They're upstairs in the study. You kids want anything to eat?"

"Nope. We already had our dinner." Dan said. "How's Ty?"

"Was that why the two of you skipped dinner?"

Dan cocked his head over to Evelyn then exchanged a smile with Marianne before she returned to the other wing.

Taking Evelyn's hand, they headed up the stairs.

"What information do you want? Or am I supposed to pull everything I can find?"

Evelyn cast a quick glance over at Dan. "Who's that?"

He shrugged and led the way into the study.

"Whoa," Evelyn said, standing right by the door.

The study room had been completely transformed. The mahogany table had been shifted to the side. The things on the table cleared and replaced with three laptops. Boxes of iPads, with their plastic still wrapped around, were stacked against one of the walls while pieces of paper and photographs were sprawled across the floor.

A printer, perched on the edge of the table, continued to churn out paper as she and Dan stood dumbfounded.

Though this was the room least used by both Kate and Tyler, neither had been keen to redecorate the room into one they could use. Evelyn knew Kate simply didn't want to change the room that Tyler's grandfather used to be in all the time; Kate had spent a lot of time listening to the late Mr. Hayes's family stories right in this room.

Instead, they'd converted the attic into their study and workspace, leaving this room intact the way it was.

When Evelyn brought up the subject of changing the room,

Kate and Tyler would say they had no use of the room and would change it when there was a need to.

Now, the room was in a complete mess. Ryan's eyes were on an iPad, his finger swiping across the screen. Kate and Tyler were sitting on the only empty spots on the floor. A laptop was on his lap, his fingers busy typing away while Kate watched.

Behind the desk, sitting in front of one of the laptops, was a young man whom Evelyn had never met.

"What are you people doing?" Dan asked, his eyes giving the room another quick scan before stopping on the man seated before the desk.

All eyes turned to them, and Kate hopped to her feet. "Oh gosh, I'm so sorry! I know the room is in a mess."

"That's Ben, my Internet guy," Tyler said when he noticed their stares.

"Something wrong with the Internet? And what's with all this?" Evelyn said, pointing to the mess on the floor.

"Ty is downloading Lydia's research and interviews onto the new laptops, then he'll sync the info with all the iPads there," Kate said.

"We all get new iPads!" Ryan said, waving the one he was holding. "Early Christmas presents."

"Thought you didn't see the point of having one." Evelyn sat by the door. "And Ben is fixing the Internet?"

"He's good at finding info on the net," Kate explained.

Dan grinned at what Kate said. "You mean he's hacking."

"That would be illegal, so no, I'm not hacking. I'm just good at finding information people leave behind on the Internet. Things never disappear on the net; you think you've deleted it, but it's still right there. You just need to know how to find it," Ben said.

Evelyn shrugged and turned back to Kate. "How did you guys get this up in …" She glanced at her watch, then back up at Kate. "In two hours."

"Ty came back and set it up after lunch."

"From today onward, the two of you should avoid going anywhere alone or even together," Tyler said. "You'll be staying over at Dan's for now, right?"

She nodded.

"Good. Now for the homework," Tyler said as Kate crossed the cluttered floor and got two boxes of iPads for Tyler. "We're synchronizing everything. Read them once you get the time."

While Dan went over to help Tyler, Evelyn helped Kate transfer the photos on the floor to the wall. She pinned them up exactly where Kate instructed, with Kate adding additional Post-it notes to them, summarizing the different information and the title of the files where additional information could be found.

Soon, the plain white wall was transformed into a giant web of information.

Evelyn took a step back and looked at the well-organized info.

"I've already looked through the arson case. Everything had been destroyed. If there were any evidence, it would be long gone. So we'll focus on the rape cases and on David Morgan. Ben is working on getting more info on David Morgan, and Lydia already has plenty on the rape cases. She's interviewed several people. She even listed those who refused the interviews and her thoughts on them," Ryan said and stood, stretching his back.

Evelyn took the iPad that Dan handed her and scanned through the files randomly.

"You take care now," Ryan said to her as he half hopped across the room. Then he turned to Dan. "Call if you need anything. Unless it's urgent, then call anyone but the cripple."

That night, Evelyn stuffed some of her clothes and necessities into a bag while Dan watched her. He had offered to help, but she was certain her way was faster.

She was ready in less than fifteen minutes, and they headed off to Dan's house.

Once they entered the house, Evelyn headed straight for the couch. Having sort through all the information was exhausting.

"You can have the bed in my room; I'll sleep in the study."

She frowned and stared at him. "Why? Is your bed not big enough for both of us?"

"You're willing to share?"

"Is something wrong?"

He dropped the bag he was holding and went to sit by her side. "I just don't want you to … freak? I'm afraid that you'll think this is too similar to us moving in together."

She blinked and opened her mouth to speak, but stopped.

Chewing on her lower lip, she asked, "Are you afraid that I think we're moving in together?"

"No, I'm afraid you'll think I'm trying to push you into moving in. I'm afraid you'll think we're moving too fast."

"Hmm, you should stop worrying about that. I'm perfectly comfortable with messing up your house." She picked up one of the cushions on the couch and flung it across the room.

Dan laughed, but he lunged at her when she picked up another.

She shrieked and struggled under him, giggling.

He held his weight on his arms but kept himself close to her. "You know, the first thing I always see in your living room is your shoes." He kissed her down her neck, then slid off the couch to remove her shoes. Returning to her lips, he kissed her lightly and moved up her cheek. "Then, the rest of your floor is covered with your clothes," he whispered into her ear.

They didn't move to the bedroom until several hours later. By then, Evelyn was so tired that she almost had to crawl to take her bath and fell asleep once her head hit the pillow.

Sometime in the night, Evelyn jolted upright on the bed.

Dan's eyes immediately flew open. He sat up straight, staring at the door as Evelyn was. "Did you hear something?"

Her rigid frame relaxed the moment she heard his voice. She sighed, running her hand through her hair. "I don't know. I'm a little sensitive to noise when I sleep. It's probably nothing."

He pushed her hair back behind her ear and leaned over to kiss her on the cheek. "It's all right, I'll go check. Do you want to come with me?" he asked as he got off the bed.

Evelyn nodded and slipped off the bed, trailing after Dan.

Dan waited by the door and took her hand, leading the way. He switched on the lights before leading them down the stairs. Then he did a quick check of both the living room and kitchen to make sure that no one else was in the house and that all the doors and windows were locked.

"Feel better?" Dan pulled her into his arms and gave her a peck on her forehead.

She let out a nervous, embarrassed laugh. "I'm sorry, Dan. I just …"

"It's okay; I don't mind." Leaning against the counter, he held her close and waited for her nerves to ease. "Hungry?"

"No, I'm fine." Her words came out in a whisper as she laid her face against his chest, listening to the steady drum of his heart. "Thanks for doing this."

She never liked staying over at a new place. Her ears would sense every new creak in the house, drenching her with fear each time she woke.

"Wake me up anytime."

But she didn't have to.

When they got back in bed, she fell asleep in the security of his arms.

She still heard the noises. But each time she stirred, Dan would hold her close and tell her everything was all right. She wasn't even sure if he was awake or if he was simply responding instinctively. She only knew that with Dan's arms around her, no one would be able to hurt her.

Chapter Twenty

Evelyn and Kate strolled down the street where their client's house was located and waited by the curb on the main road. Neither of them had their cars, so their temporary staff became their temporary chauffeur as well.

"Yes, I'm with her; she's right beside me. She's on her way." Evelyn rolled her eyes while Kate sniggered next to her. "Yes, I'll text you once I'm in the car."

She hung up the phone and spun it around in her hand while she gave a frustrated sigh. "I think they're having a competition on who'll be the most annoying boyfriend of the year."

Kate laughed again. "For the year, huh? Looks like things are going well with you and Dan."

"You know, you guys can straight out ask me what I'm thinking instead of nit-picking at everything I say."

"Yeah, and you'll be all dodgy about it. Other stuff, you have no problem speaking your mind. Relationship wise …" Kate pinched her lips together and pushed the corners down, forming an inverted U.

Evelyn rolled her eyes at Kate.

"But since you said so, how does being in a relationship feel?"

She had to suppress the urge to shrug and give a nonchalant 'fine.' She hadn't put much thought into analyzing her relationship with Dan. It just felt natural, like it was supposed to be. "Strange."

Kate's brows furrowed, and she thought about her answer for a moment. "Good strange or bad strange?"

Evelyn twirled the phone in her hand and pursed her lips.

"Are you going to elaborate or do I have to dig it out of you?"

"It feels strange to have to be concerned about what someone else thinks. I can't just do what I want. The first thought that comes to my head is how he'll think or feel, not in a bad way, though. I don't mind having to do that …" She let her words trail when she realized she was rambling.

Biting her lips, she tried to organize her thoughts. But she found herself getting confused by her own contradicting thoughts.

She *should* mind the lack of freedom she used to have, but she didn't. She *should* mind having to explain her actions to someone, but she didn't.

Evelyn sighed, giving up on finding the right words.

"Are you happy?" Kate asked, seemingly noticing her lack of ability to form coherent sentences.

"Yes," she answered immediately. She *was* happy; that was something she didn't even have to consider.

"Then that's all that matters," Kate said as their temp staff pulled up in a black sedan. "Can we head to the hospital to visit Lydia instead of heading back to the mansion right away?"

Evelyn shrugged and said, "We should give Tiffany a raise."

"We should. I'm sure she didn't sign up for this."

When they got to the hospital, Evelyn pushed the door to Lydia's ward and found herself staring at the chest of a man clad in a dark blue T-shirt.

She glanced up at the man and noticed another pair of eyes studying her.

"Mrs. Hayes?"

"That'll be me," Kate said from behind Evelyn. "Ty got you here?"

The men nodded.

"So Joe went home?" Kate strode in while Evelyn continued to stare, more subtly, at the men.

Apparently, Kate had been with Tyler long enough to be so comfortable with such antics that she hadn't even blinked when she found out her husband had hired bodyguards to stake out the hospital.

"Yes, there are four of us. We'll take shifts so Miss Mitchell will have someone with her at all times."

Kate smiled at them before turning to Lydia. "Are you awake, Lydia?" Kate asked and softly laid her hand over Lydia's.

Lydia's eyes opened, but only slightly. The bruises seemed to have gotten worse. The purplish bruises had darkened into a deep eggplant-purple, and Evelyn couldn't help but draw a deep breath when she laid eyes on her. "Hi there. It's okay, just rest. Don't worry about us."

Her chin moved down slightly, and she sighed. Even sighing seemed to be causing her pain. "Did you get—"

"Yes, yes, we got all your info back. Don't worry," Kate said.

Evelyn moved to the bed and sat as lightly as she could without jarring the mattress. "We've looked through it. You've put a lot of effort in tracking down all those women. You do know that even if you solve the rape cases, you might not be able to prove anything for your parents' case."

Lydia blinked and nodded. "They deserve as much justice as my parents." Her voice was low and hoarse. Frowning, her hand moved to her throat.

"I get it," Evelyn quickly said, not wanting Lydia to exert any more strength in speaking.

Lydia swallowed, and her brows furrowed further, deepening the line between. "Talk to his wife, Melissa Rose."

"We'll do that. You have a lot more people helping you now. And with them." Evelyn cocked her head toward the men by the door. "You'll be safe here."

"We'll go now. Rest well," Kate said.

Evelyn stood as gingerly as she sat.

Lydia blinked, then suddenly stretched her hand out and grabbed Kate by her wrist. "I heard Mom. I heard her telling me to stay awake when I was attacked." She reached over to the necklace around her neck; the same necklace Kate used to wear. She opened the empty locket and touched the concave area where their family photo used to be. "Help me get the photo back, will you?"

"Of course." Kate gently tapped Lydia's hand. After saying their goodbyes, Kate and Evelyn left.

"Dan's coming to fetch us," Evelyn said as they strolled along the long walkway.

"Actually, Ty's coming. I've got a doctor's appointment."

Evelyn stopped walking and spun around so suddenly that Kate walked right into her. Evelyn held Kate by her shoulders and stabled her staggering friend. Then she narrowed her eyes and asked, "Why?"

"What why? It's a doctor's appointment."

"We have the same doctors; we always make the appointments together."

She knew her suspicions were valid when Kate's hand reached for her necklace.

"What is it? Oh my God! Are you pregnant?"

"Shh …" Kate said, glancing around at the stares they were getting. "I don't know."

"I want to be her godmother!"

"Eve, I may not even be pregnant and please stop shouting. You can't be her godmother; you're her aunt."

Evelyn froze for a moment before she understood what Kate was saying.

"Oh, you're the greatest! I'm going to be an aunt!"

"Shh! Why are you so excited? You used to hate commitments, relationships, and families."

"But she'll be *my* family! Why aren't *you* excited?"

Kate tried concealing her smile, but the corners of her lips inched up anyway. "Because I may not even be pregnant. Do. Not. Tell. Anyone."

"You have to call me once you get the news. Promise?"

"All right, all right. Promise you won't tell anyone."

"I promise."

"Okay. Oh, would you get the photo for Lydia?"

"Yeah, go for your checkup and call me once you get the news." Evelyn moved over to Dan's car as Tyler's car pulled up behind. "Remember to call me."

Once inside Dan's car, Evelyn closed the door and smiled. "Hi there."

"Why is Ty here? I thought we agreed I'd pick you ladies up."

She pursed her lips. She'd forgotten to ask if Dan was included in the 'anyone.'

"What?"

Oh, whatever. She tells Tyler everything anyway. "They're going to the doctor. Kate may be pregnant."

"Really?"

"Yeah, but she hasn't confirmed it yet. Oh, and we have to go over to Lydia's place first."

"Are you okay?" Dan asked as he pulled out from the hospital.

"Yeah, why?"

"Just asking."

Evelyn studied Dan's face for a moment. "Because I can't get pregnant and she is?"

Dan stole a glimpse of her before returning his gaze to the road.

She hadn't thought about that.

She smiled ruefully. "I am. Maybe a little jealous and a little sad, but I'm so happy for her." And she was. "I'm happy for myself, too." The baby was going to be her family.

She just didn't expect the jealousy.

When her doctor told her that she wouldn't be able to have children, she hadn't cared. She didn't even bother listening to what was wrong with her; she wasn't intending on having children anyway.

She had only asked if the condition would affect her health and had shrugged it off when the doctor assured her that it wouldn't.

But it wasn't until now that she realized how much she wished she could be a mother.

Then again, she didn't have to get pregnant to be a mother.

"Are you sure?"

"As you said, I can always adopt."

"I? Don't I get a say in it?"

Shaking her head, she said, "Most guys freak out when their girlfriends plan for the future."

"Then aren't you lucky to get such a uniquely wonderful boyfriend?" He grinned and winked at her.

She laughed and tucked her hair back behind her ear. "After stopping by Lydia's house, can we go shopping? I want to buy something for the baby."

"Eve, she may not be pregnant. Don't you think it's a little too early to be getting the possible baby a toy?"

She didn't bother to reply; she was already thinking about what toy to buy.

When they got to Lydia's house, they stood at the door and took in the sight of the wreckage.

"Was the person searching for something or was he simply trying to trash her house?"

Dan wrapped his arm over her shoulders. "Get the photo and we'll leave." He looked over his shoulder as she crossed over all the mess and headed straight to the whiteboard that was now lying on the floor.

Most of the information on the board had been torn off, but the picture was still taped to the middle of it.

She pulled it off the board and put it into her wallet as she returned to Dan. Taking a peek at her phone, she said, "Let's go shopping!"

Initially, Dan was worried about Evelyn's reaction to seeing all the baby's toys, but she was all smiles in the shops and was completely oblivious to how out of place the two of them were among the pregnant women and families.

He was thankful that they were out of the first store in less than five minutes. Apparently, the toys in the store weren't good enough because the materials weren't organic.

At the second store, after Evelyn had confirmed that all the toys were made from organic materials, she went around the shop, picked up every bunny she could find, and commented on how cute it was.

She didn't allow him to stay quiet either.

Every now and then, she would pick up two similar toys and ask him which was nicer.

He was sure the right answer wasn't the one he had in mind—they looked the same to him. He didn't think that a slight difference in the nose or eyes was a big deal. What would a baby know anyway?

Still, Dan bent forward and examined the two bunnies.

After years of experience with his mother and Joanne, he'd learned that by delaying time, he could wait for the woman to reveal the choice she was leaning toward. Then, an agreement was all that would be required of him.

He did that a couple of times and got away with it. So, when Evelyn picked up another two similar bunnies and asked him the same question, he did the same thing.

He leaned forward and narrowed his eyes. "Hmm …"

"I think this is cuter."

"Yeah, I think so, too." He flashed a grin when Evelyn frowned at him.

"Really? Why do you say that?" She blinked, feigning ignorance.

"Because I trust your judgment."

"You think a patronizing remark will get you out of it?"

His smile broadened as his arm looped around her shoulders, pulling her closer. "I'm sorry, but they all seem the same to me. Why do you keep picking bunnies anyway? I like that bear."

"But look at its ears. It's so soft and snuggly," she said while her fingers skimmed down the rabbit's ears.

"Are you buying it for yourself or for Kate's baby?"

Evelyn glowered at him and pulled the teddy bear from the shelf. "We'll get both."

"Can we go back for dinner now?"

"No, I can't go back. I'll end up blabbing to everyone. What if she isn't pregnant? I don't want to embarrass her."

"You told me."

"You don't count. She tells Tyler everything I tell her, too. We need to have dinner elsewhere."

He shook his head indulgently and wondered if Evelyn or Kate would be more disappointed if it was a false alarm.

During dinner, Evelyn's eyes flickered toward the phone every other second. She couldn't stop talking about how the study room would make a wonderful nursery and how she could make a special crib for the baby.

He reached over and took her hand, his thumb rubbing circles against her skin, while she continued describing the crib she'd make.

Seeing the smile and her glow of excitement, it was as if Evelyn were going to be the mother.

He couldn't help wondering what sort of mother Evelyn would be. Based on how she was behaving, she would probably spend way too much money on way too many toys.

"You'll have to set me up with your wood guy again."

"Organic wood?" He laughed when she saw her sudden pause and her eyes moving to the side as she thought about the question.

She didn't have to think long. Her phone rang and she snatched it off the table. "So?" She paused for a moment, then screamed, "Oh, congrats! I'm so excited. I bought her a toy already. Two, actually. Yup. Okay, I'll see you back at the mansion. All right, bye."

"It could be a him," Dan said as he gestured for one of the waiters. Getting a waiter's attention wasn't difficult. Evelyn hadn't been mindful of the decibel she was speaking in while on the phone with Kate, so everyone in the restaurant was already staring at them.

All the way back to the mansion, the smile was plastered on Evelyn's face. She wanted to let Kate break the news to everyone back home, but she knew she wouldn't be able to contain her thrill. So instead of heading inside, they sat in the car and waited for Tyler and Kate to get back.

Tyler had barely stopped the car when Evelyn went jumping out and running over to Kate.

"Congrats." He walked over just as the ladies finally broke their hug.

"Thanks," Kate said, her grin equally wide.

Evelyn took the bag he was holding. "Look at what we bought!"

Kate laughed, and the admiration of how adorable the soft toys were continued for a few minutes until Kate said, "Look what Ty bought."

She moved over to the trunk of the car and opened it. Within it, there were at least ten boxes of shoes.

"What's that for?"

"He's forbidding me from wearing heels, and since I don't have anything that's completely flat, ta-da!" Kate looked down at her feet and wriggled her toes. "I have this style in three different colors."

"And I was afraid that Eve was being a little too excited," Dan said when he saw the boxes of shoes.

Dan and Tyler took all the bags in while Evelyn told Kate about the crib she'd make for her baby. Leaving the boxes in the living room, they headed toward the kitchen.

"I'd appreciate it if you guys could inform me the next time you're going out on a double date. Look at all the food," Marianne grumbled.

"Ooh, Ty and I only ate a little. I'm starving." Kate sat on her usual seat, bringing a smile back to Marianne.

Tyler weaved his fingers into Kate's hair and ran them down her back.

"They have news!" Evelyn said as the rest of them settled into their seats.

Tyler grinned at Kate. "Kate is expecting."

Dan laughed when he saw the contrast in reaction. Evelyn was clearly waiting for everyone to erupt into some sort of cheer so that she could share her joy, but everyone else around the table appeared to be waiting for Tyler to continue speaking.

"That's the end of the sentence. She's expecting. The end," Evelyn added impatiently.

"Oh my God! Really? Oh, Kate." Marianne went over and hugged her.

"Marianne, you're choking her," Tyler said, prying Marianne from his wife.

"How far along are you?" Joseph asked.

Marianne ignored Tyler. She picked up Kate's plate and took

a little of everything on the table. "I know you can't eat when all the food gets piled up. You have your vitamins? Give them to me. I'll sort it out for you so you won't have to worry about that."

"Five weeks," Kate said as she took the plate from Marianne.

By the time Marianne was done fussing over her, Joseph had helped Ryan over and both gave her a hug. They had barely put their arms around Kate when Tyler pulled them apart, telling them not to suffocate her.

"Oh, we can go shopping for books that you can read up on. You love to be prepared," Evelyn said.

Kate chuckled, then leaned into Tyler's arm. "He's already ordered a Kindle for me, and we've bought over a dozen books."

"Why don't you just read it on the iPad?" Ryan asked.

Kate took a deep breath and said, "Someone says I shouldn't strain my eyes."

Ryan laughed and shook his head. "Good luck in surviving him for the next nine months."

Chapter Twenty One

Over the past week, the conversations around the dining table revolved mainly around two topics; the cases that Lydia was investigating and Kate's pregnancy.

When Evelyn found out that Kate was pregnant, she began having second thoughts about the investigation. It wasn't the right time to fight a battle, especially not when the other party had already attempted to kill them once.

Evelyn wanted to get David Morgan and make him pay for his crimes, but she wasn't willing to do it at the cost of Kate getting hurt. There was so much more at risk now.

Kate, however, was quick to shoot down her concerns. She insisted that they simply had to be more careful and said she didn't want to be looking over her shoulders for the rest of her life.

Marianne hadn't said much. As always, she supported them no matter what she thought. She had only one rule about the whole investigation; meals would only be served around the dining table. She was insistent that no matter what they were doing, no matter how close they thought they were to solving the case, they were to put the case aside and sit down for proper meals.

"Are you all right?" Ryan suddenly asked as they were going back into the study after dinner.

"Yeah," Evelyn said. "I just can't stand looking at those pictures." She tipped her chin forward, gesturing at the iPad. "You see all this at work all the time, but you are still so ... so cheerful."

"I'm not the one who set the fires. I do my best whenever I get to the scene, and I don't give up unless I have no choice. But beyond that, there's nothing I can do. I'm not God; I don't try to take up God's responsibility," Ryan said.

Smiling, Evelyn continued up the stairs, not saying anything else.

"I like to focus on the fact that I'm still alive and still in a position to help someone," Ryan added. "Like you are. I know what you've been through is horrible, but now you found the strength to help someone else."

Evelyn grunted softly.

"You know we're all in this because you wanted to get involved. And if we do help someone, either dead or alive, it's because of you."

Dan watched as Evelyn's smile grew into a grin.

Walking behind them, Dan smiled and shook his head. No wonder Ryan didn't have many friends outside their group.

Dan had always found it strange that for someone as gregarious as Ryan to have so few close friends. Now, he knew why.

Ryan was just too friendly with everyone.

If Dan hadn't known how loyal Ryan was as a friend, he would start getting worried.

Ryan returned his focus to his iPad as they entered the study.

Everyone had been pitching in wherever they could.

Ryan looked through the photos from the fire repeatedly, hoping he could find something that arson investigators had missed.

Kate put her organization skills to use, sorting out all the information, categorizing it, and placing it in the right files. Together with Tyler, being the fastest readers among them, they included a short summary of everything they had read and synchronized it with the rest of their iPads so that the rest of them could just refer to the summarized versions.

Tyler's computer guy was either some sort of miracle or an extremely creepy person that Dan didn't want to mess with. Ben had managed to dig up email correspondence, online purchases, and even tracked the websites that David Morgan had been accessing. He even set up some sort of script or program that would inform him whenever any news of the Morgans hit the internet.

Dan didn't quite believe that everything Ben was doing was legal, but Mr. Sawyer seemed to have questioned Ben in detail and hadn't brought up any objections.

The bulk of their investigation centered on the rape cases, and Lydia was adamant that David Morgan's wife might hold the key.

Dan didn't think that a wife would help outsiders take down their husbands. But Ben had discovered some scandals regarding a possible divorce, and the address that Lydia had written in her records showed that Melissa Rose was no longer staying in the same house as David Morgan.

If there were already discord between them, it would be much easier to convince her to take their side.

Everyone thought it was a good idea to pay Melissa Rose a visit. The only problem was the *who* factor.

Lydia had noted that Melissa Rose was unwilling to talk and seemed frightened. Knowing this, Kate wanted to speak to Melissa Rose alone or with Evelyn. But Tyler refused to let Kate and Evelyn go on their own. He wasn't even willing to wait outside in the car, insisting that he be right by her side.

When such situations occurred, Kate usually turned to Marianne for help. But this time no one was on her side, not even Evelyn. That resulted in an impasse. So until Kate could find another solution, Melissa Rose would be left alone.

The main conclusion they'd drawn, something that they'd already guessed, was that David Morgan had alibis for most of the cases; most of them being quite questionable.

"Look at this." Joseph suddenly stood with the iPad in his hand and moved over to Dan. "I knew there was something about the bruises; I just couldn't figure out what it was."

Dan peered over at the photograph on the screen, a closeup on one of the murdered victims.

"Do you see it?"

Dan continued staring at the photograph. All he saw was a huge patch of bruise.

"There's a strange bruise pattern along the neck of all the murdered victims," Joseph said, his finger pointing to different parts of the bruises. "Do you see it?"

No, he couldn't. Dan had no idea what Joseph was talking about.

Joseph probably saw the blank expression on his face because he jumped into a detailed explanation. Dan simply nodded away, still not quite getting what Joseph was saying.

Caught up in his excitement over the new find, Joseph turned to Evelyn. He flipped through the photos, pointing to the marks on the necks, again diving into all the details.

Even with his finger directing her eyes, there was no way she'd miss the horrors of the photo.

After all this time, Dan had learned Evelyn's sign of distress.

Most people had obvious reactions when they got uncomfortable or frightened. For Evelyn, her lack of expression was the sign. Sometimes, she'd hide behind a smile. But there would always be a moment where she would draw a slow, deep breath, and her face would go blank.

When he saw the same impassiveness on her face, Dan strode over, putting himself between Joseph and Evelyn. He mouthed 'enough' to Joseph before turning to Evelyn. "Do you want to go for a walk?"

Evelyn jumped at the chance to get some fresh air.

The only walk they took was from the study to the door. Once they were out of the mansion, Dan sat on the porch.

Evelyn still hadn't gotten used to the woods, and no matter the time of day, she wouldn't enjoy a stroll through it. Since the mansion was surrounded by nothing but trees, there wasn't anywhere they could go.

"Are you all right?" Dan asked the moment Evelyn settled beside him.

Her head dropped against his shoulder, and he shifted to put his arm around her, pulling her closer.

"Yeah, it's just the photos."

"I know. I'll talk to Joe about it later."

Evelyn chuckled softly, shaking her head. "There's no need for that. I'm sure he got the point."

He was still going to do it anyway.

Though Evelyn appreciated all their help with the Amy issue, she didn't like people helping her out with everything. He understood it was the need to hold on to her independence, to remind herself that she was no longer the young girl who couldn't protect or take care of herself.

Her willingness to move in with him was already a huge compromise, so he was careful not to overstep.

Still, it couldn't hurt if she didn't find out about it.

"So, have you told Kate about changing the study into a nursery?"

The change in topic immediately got her smiling. "Yeah, Tyler has no problem with it. It's actually Kate who's having a bit of a problem with letting go of some of the things in the room. She spent a lot of time in that room with Tyler's grandfather."

"You'd think he was her grandfather."

"In a way, he was. I'm thinking of taking the desk apart and using it to make the crib. That way, she's not giving up the furniture; it'll become a part of the new room."

"That's a great idea. I'm sure she'd love it."

"And Dan." She paused, spinning the phone in her hand. "There's something else I want to discuss with you."

"What is it?"

"I want to speak with Melissa Rose—alone. I'm sure Kate will be fine with it after some persuasion."

Dan frowned. The word 'no' was already at the tip of his tongue, but he managed to keep his lips sealed.

She was no longer the cryptic person who did things regardless of what others thought simply because she thought it was right. He was certain she'd thought things through and taken his feelings into consideration before speaking to him.

"You can drive me there, but I want to speak to her alone. I can call you on the phone and stay on the line while I go in. That way, you'll hear everything. If I get into trouble, you'll only be a few steps away."

The corner of his lips crept upward. "Thank you."

It was her turn to frown. "For what?"

"For compromising."

"It was really Kate's idea, just that you're not Tyler. I know you'll let me do it if you know that's what I want."

He considered the situation and the risk involved.

"Dan, I've been learning self-defense from Tyler and have been practicing with Joseph. I'm not saying that I'm an expert, but I'm pretty sure I can handle a woman for a few minutes."

"What if there are others in the house?"

"I thought Ben said she was living on her own?"

"He *believes* she's living on her own."

"Hmm …" She pursed her lips and thought about it for a moment. "I'll leave if I see anyone else inside. I'll ask her, too. That way, you can hear it on the line."

Dan nodded slowly. "All right, we'll do as you say. If Kate is agreeable, then I'm fine with it. *But* you have to be on the line at all times. If it gets cut, I'll go in after you."

Evelyn bit down on her lips, and Dan knew she was trying to stop herself from laughing.

"I'm serious."

"Okay. We'll talk to Kate about it."

Kate wasn't the only one who opposed to the idea of Evelyn meeting Melissa Rose on her own.

While Evelyn was worried about Kate, the rest of the guys had reminded Dan that things were different this time around and told him to be more alert.

Before, Kate was the main target; the threats and fire all aimed at her.

This time, the focus had shifted.

Evelyn had received the blackmail, and David Morgan had basically admitted being the one behind it all.

The guys turned to Dan, expecting him to put in some kind of protest, but he only shrugged.

"We're not letting you go alone," Ryan said.

"I'll be fine. Dan will be right outside."

"He goes in with you, or you don't go at all," Joseph replied.

Evelyn rolled her eyes at Joseph's condescending words. "Nothing will happen. Lydia went alone and she was fine."

"Fine? She's in the hospital now and doesn't look fine at all." Joseph turned to Dan. "You're okay with it?"

"No, I'm not. I don't want her to take the risk." He paused and raised his hand, palm out, when he saw Evelyn's surprise. "But, she's been practicing with you and Ty. Even if something does happen, I'm sure she can handle herself for a few minutes."

"Thank you."

Joseph opened his mouth to speak. Dan was sure Joseph would have a valid refute for every valid point they had, but he shook his head slightly and continued. "Let her go. She knows what she's doing."

"We've been through everything, and Melissa Rose is our only lead. Let's just get this over and done with," Evelyn said.

"If Dan's fine with it, then why not?" Ryan gave Joseph a mock punch.

"Then it's settled." Dan turned to Evelyn. "We'll go tomorrow."

That night, Dan and Evelyn lay in bed, neither saying anything.

He had supported Evelyn's plan because he knew Evelyn needed to do this. Logically, he knew the chances of the meeting becoming dangerous were slim. He knew Evelyn could handle herself in tough situations, and he knew they didn't have anything else to go on.

But … There was always a but.

"Can't sleep?" Evelyn asked as she moved closer, laying her head on his chest.

"You're still awake, too."

"I'll be fine. I'm just wondering if she would entertain my questions. And if she does, what will she say? What does she have over David Morgan?"

"She may have nothing. You do know it's just Lydia's hunch."

"I know."

He weaved his fingers into her hair. "Whatever it is, promise you'll be careful. Don't push her. And if you sense that something's wrong, you'll get up and leave immediately."

"I will." She lifted her head and kissed him lightly on his chest. "Goodnight."

The next morning, both Evelyn and Dan woke up without the help of the alarm. Sitting in the car, Evelyn read through the notes that Lydia had on Melissa Rose.

Lydia had every detail on Melissa Rose, from the date of birth to the current home address.

It summed up to a familiar entertainment-industry story; a former model who married a tycoon.

Ben had since added a few additional details he'd dug up. Small but highly revealing details.

Ben couldn't find much about Melissa Rose after her marriage. Besides the photos in highly publicized social events, there was barely any information on her. And for a while, Melissa Rose had dropped out of the social scene while rumors of a divorce speculated. Then she returned to the parties, smiling graciously beside David Morgan.

Evelyn stared at the photo of Melissa Rose and David Morgan on her iPad.

She recognized the smile on Melissa Rose.

A smile that didn't reach the eyes; a smile concealing a mixture of rage and despondency. The exact smile Evelyn used to wear whenever she was in school and around strangers, whenever she had to pretend that everything in her life was fine.

She glanced up from the picture when the car came to a stop.

"Are you sure about this?"

Nodding, she pulled out her phone from the bag. "Let's set up the call."

They adjusted their phones, testing to make sure Dan could hear everything while her phone was in her bag.

Dan wanted her to hold the phone in her hand, but she thought it was too obvious.

With the Bluetooth earpiece in her ear, she got out of the car and moved toward the house. Then she turned to wave at Dan before she rang the bell.

The door inched opened, just slightly, and a pair of skeptical eyes peered out from behind the door.

"Melissa Rose?"

"Yes?"

"I'm Evelyn Jordan, Lydia—"

The pair of eyes disappeared, and the door was about to slam close in her face.

"Listen." Evelyn pushed against the door, keeping the door from closing.

"Leave me alone," Melissa Rose hissed.

"Eve." She heard Dan's voice through her earpiece, and she knew he was a couple of seconds from jumping out of the car.

"I know what it's like to feel all alone, like there's no one to help and no way out."

The weight on the door lifted, but Melissa Rose remained hidden behind it.

"I can help. I have friends who can help you. You don't have to be alone."

Melissa Rose didn't reply.

There was no movement behind the door either.

Evelyn waited, giving Melissa Rose the time she needed.

Slowly, the door opened and Melissa Rose scanned the surroundings, her eyes stopping on Dan's car.

"That's my boyfriend. He's just waiting for me," Evelyn said when she noticed what Melissa Rose was staring at.

After a minute, with neither speaking, Evelyn continued. "Look, I know you want to leave, and I know you need help to do that. I'm offering you that help."

Again, silence fell between the two of them.

"Eve, forget it. She doesn't seem willing to talk."

Evelyn glanced over her shoulder at Dan, then back at Melissa Rose. "If someone had offered me a chance to get out of my situation, I would've grabbed it without a second thought. If you want to leave, I'm here to help." She looked Melissa Rose right in her eyes and waited.

Just when she wanted to turn around and leave, Melissa Rose

stepped aside for Evelyn to enter.

"Where's the Lydia girl?"

Pursing her lips, Evelyn tried to come up with something that wouldn't cause Melissa Rose to regret the decision of letting her in.

"Don't lie to me."

"I wasn't going to." She moved over and sat on the couch while Melissa Rose remained standing across from her. "She's in the hospital; she got hurt."

Evelyn saw Melissa Rose's eyes widening, so she quickly continued. "That was because we didn't know what she was investigating. She's safe now. She has two bodyguards with her at all times."

"I can't live with a bodyguard for the rest of my life."

"Then why don't you leave?" Evelyn noticed the wry smile on Melissa Rose's face.

Melissa Rose finally sat. She closed her eyes and shook her head slowly.

Evelyn scrutinized Melissa Rose. The dark rings under her eyes were obvious. She appeared so frail and brittle that it was as though one touch would cause her to shatter into a million pieces.

Melissa Rose continued shaking her head. The wry smile on her face disappeared, and she pursed her lips, her eyes revealing a pain of hopes being dashed.

Evelyn knew she was losing Melissa Rose. Anytime now, she'd be thrown out. She had to convince Melissa that she truly understood her fear and helplessness.

"This is a—"

"I do know what you're going through," Evelyn interjected. She told Melissa her story; she told Melissa how she was caged and tortured, how she thought every night was her last, and how she tried to get help only to find out that no one cared enough to fight for her and that she was all alone.

"So I wasn't lying when I told you that I understand how you feel. No one helped me when I needed it," she said. "Now, I'm offering to help you."

"What can you do? He won't let me leave. He wouldn't even let me get a divorce. I had to threaten him to let me stay here alone. Even here, he keeps track of my movements. He won't allow me to go to work. Like he said," Melissa turned and looked out of the window before continuing in a soft, pained voice, "I'm just a pet to him."

"If you put him away in jail, he'll lose his hold on you."

"He'll kill me before that happens. He told me so. And since we're still married, I can't testify against him."

"Then give me the clues and point me in the right direction. He doesn't have to know you're involved."

"I can't. He'll kill me if he finds out."

Evelyn nodded. She understood her fear; she had been through it herself. "I'm not pushing you to make a decision now. I have a friend who knows a detective well. We've got an experienced lawyer on our side. My friend can get you a place to stay and bodyguards until we put him away. When you are ready, you can leave this cage." Evelyn took out her name card and pushed it across the coffee table separating them. "Think about it."

"What happened to your foster parent?"

"I killed her, in self-defense." Evelyn stood while Melissa continued to stare at the card. "It's not too late. You can still leave if you want." She waited for a moment before moving toward the door. "Call me when you're ready."

Chapter Twenty Two

Evelyn looked through the drawings of the crib and dressing table for the baby. She calculated the amount of wood needed and crosschecked it with her measurements of the mahogany desk in Tyler's study.

It wasn't enough. She would have to take some material from the huge cabinets against the wall.

She did more calculations and figured that with the additional wood, she could fashion a small study desk for the baby to use in the future.

Looking up from her drawings, she glanced toward her cell phone.

The possibility of Melissa Rose calling was slim, but she couldn't help checking her phone to make sure she hadn't missed any calls.

She understood why Melissa Rose was so hostile to her.

Fear and loneliness were great wall builders. After years of being controlled by David Morgan, Melissa must have built up a strong barrier to protect herself.

"Miss Jordan, do you need anything? If not—"

"Go ahead, Tiffany. See you tomorrow."

The last of her staff left the office, and Evelyn returned her focus to her drawings. She was determined to get Melissa Rose out of her mind. She had done all she could; she had offered her help and could do nothing else unless Melissa was willing to help herself.

Her efforts to concentrate on her drawings weren't much of a success.

Since Dan should be arriving any time, she packed up her stuff, which mainly involved sweeping everything she wanted to bring home into her bag and pushing the rest of the paper and stationery aside.

She really should pack up her desk soon.

To convince herself that she wasn't a complete slob, she began arranging the few pencils she'd pushed to the edge of the desk, placing them in line with one another, from the shortest to the longest.

She fussed with them for the longest time, until her phone vibrated and saved her from the mundane task. She picked it up, seeing a text from Dan, telling her that he was there and would wait for her in the parking garage.

She frowned slightly at the text. Since Lydia's assault, Dan always came up to her office and walked her down.

Call him.

She laughed at how dependent she'd become. It wasn't a long walk to the parking garage, and she wasn't a baby.

Call him.

She shook the thoughts from her head, took her bag, and headed out of the office. She had just stepped out of the elevator and was scanning the parking garage for Dan's car when she felt a jab in her neck.

She flinched from the pain and turned, but everything swirled; and she found herself swaying dangerously to the side, unable to right herself. Almost immediately, a dark rim invaded her sight, quickly overtaking her vision.

Dan had just gotten out of his car when he felt a pair of bony hands clasp onto his arm. His head snapped toward the hands, and he glared up at their owner.

His glare must have been menacing, for she immediately let go and stumbled a few steps back.

"Melissa Rose?" He softened his looks and smiled politely at her, but the frantic look on her face didn't go away.

"Quick, you don't have much time. He took her."

"What? Who?"

"Miss Jordan! He took her!" She waved the crumpled name card in her hand. "I saw him; I saw him taking her. You have to find her. He'll kill her."

"Where did he take her?"

She blinked, seemingly caught off guard by his question, then shook her head. "I don't know …"

"Think!"

She shrank back from Dan, her chin tucked in. "I really don't know."

He wanted to step forward, to press her for more details, but she appeared so frightened that he didn't dare to risk it. With his eyes on her, Dan called Evelyn on her phone, but it was switched off. "He drove off in his own car?"

"No, he has another car for these things," she said.

"Do you know the number plate of that car?"

She chewed on her lips and took another step away from him. "No."

Dan needed information, but he was afraid that Melissa might take off running if he pushed her any further. He'd take her to Kate and search for Evelyn while Kate grilled her. "Please come with me, Miss Rose."

Her head swiveled to the side as her eyes appeared to be searching for a way away from him.

"Eve would help you. If things were the other way around, Evelyn would do everything in her power to help you."

Melissa Rose hesitated for a moment before nodding. She hurried over to the passenger side and got into the car, clutching her handbag against her chest.

"We'll head over to where our friends are," he said while pulling out of the garage and calling Kate.

"Hey, Dan," Kate's chirpy voice filled the car once the line went through.

"Trace Evelyn's phone. Do what you did the other time."

"Why?"

The words were already ringing in his head, but he couldn't get them out of his mouth.

"Dan? Are you still there?"

He forced himself to swallow hard before saying, "He got her."

No further explanation was needed. The sudden silence on the other end of the phone was deafening.

"Kate."

"I'll do it now," Kate said.

"I have Melissa Rose with me. We're heading over."

"All right, drive safe. I'll update you if I get a location."

Hanging up the call, he slammed on the gas pedal.

Kate must have been keeping watch from the mansion's window. The moment his car went around the bend, Kate stepped out of the house with Tyler and waited for his car to pull up front.

When Melissa Rose saw Kate, her shoulders relaxed. The resemblance between Lydia and Kate was obvious to all.

Kate rushed up to Dan as he stepped out of his car.

He held his breath, hoping Kate wouldn't turn hysterical. He needed all the help he could get, and the last thing he wanted was to waste time calming Kate down.

He sighed, relieved, when Kate simply ran her hand down his arm with a tense smile and nod before turning to Melissa.

"Miss Rose, you have to help us find her."

"I don't know what I can do."

Kate placed her hand lightly on Melissa's arm, leading her toward the house. "Tell us everything you know." Returning her eyes to Dan, she continued. "Her phone is switched off, but I've set the email notification."

Kate ushered Melissa into the house and sat her down in the living room.

"Miss Rose—"

"Melissa."

"Melissa." Kate took her hand and squeezed it gently. "Point us in the right direction. We're digging up everything, but that'll take too much time."

"I'm sorry, all I know is that I lied to provide him with an alibi whenever he needed one."

"But you know something; a wife always knows something."

Melissa reached into her handbag and took out a DVD that had a line of numbers written across it. 15042009. "This is my trump card. This was how I got him to let me move out."

Dan grabbed the DVD.

His haste startled Melissa, and her eyes widened, staring at the DVD.

"We'll give that back to you." Kate patted Melissa's hand softly. "I promise."

Though Melissa was clearly much older than Kate, Kate spoke to her like a mother coaxing a child. "This is Marianne. I need to help them out. Will you be all right here?"

Dan didn't wait for Kate. He headed up the stairs and toward the study, grabbed one of the laptops, and played the video that the DVD contained.

All the guys dropped what they were doing and crowded around the laptop. Kate joined them just as the video began playing.

The screen was black for the first few seconds before a new scene suddenly cut in.

Dan's heart dropped.

He had seen the photos, seen the cuts and bruises, but he wasn't prepared for the scene in the video.

A woman in her twenties was strapped to a chair. No matter how she shoved, turned, and twisted, the chair didn't budge.

Tears were streaming down her cheeks, smudging the mascara and messing up her face. Though the same gray tape that strapped her to the chair was across her mouth, it was clear she was screaming or perhaps begging.

Dan was glad he was seated as he felt the blood drain from his face.

He knew things weren't good when he found out Evelyn had been taken. But somewhere inside, he'd hoped it was simply another threat. He'd hoped she would turn up by the side of the road. Even turning up at the hospital in the same state as Lydia was a better alternative than this.

But if Melissa held such evidence, if Kate's house was a warning, and if Lydia's attack was a taste of the worst to come, he couldn't help thinking this was a showdown.

Evelyn wouldn't be turning up by the road or hospital. She might not be turning up at all.

"It looks like a container," Tyler said.

Tyler's words took his eyes off the woman and onto the background.

The walls appeared to have white wallpaper over them. Unlike those found in homes, they weren't matte. There was a light sheen as though it was waterproof. The most telling of it all was the floor; the undeniable metal wavelike structure.

"He owns a logistics firm. It's probably one of his trucks," Joseph added. "We'll watch this. Ben managed to find some information about the firm. There are tons of logs and other things to look through. Why don't you help with that?"

He knew Joseph was trying to get him away from the video. He wasn't interested in watching the video, but it didn't seem right dumping such a task on Ryan and Joseph.

"We've seen all sorts of injuries at work. Leave this to us," Ryan assured, taking the laptop from Dan. "We won't miss anything."

Tyler and Ben went back to their computers while Kate looked at a stack of logs, taking a quick glance at each page before flipping to the next.

"What's that?"

"Ben managed to get us the logs of the trucks' records."

"Are you looking for something?"

"There's something about the schedules. Look at the dates. Logistics firms operate 24/7, right?"

Dan nodded.

"I can't find a single day where the trucks return to the office on a Wednesday. The schedule seems to be arranged such that the trucks are out every Wednesday," she said while she continued flipping through the pages.

"They have two cleaning companies, both outsourced. Perhaps it's for the cleaning of the trucks," Mr. Sawyer spoke up, and for the first time, Dan noticed he was in the room.

Dan thought about it for a moment. It wasn't right. He

provided tools and trucks for his workers, too, but he wouldn't bother with finding someone to clean them for his guys.

Keeping the trucks clean would be the driver's responsibilities.

"It can't be. Ben, can you find more information on the two companies?"

Mr. Sawyer scribbled down the names on a piece of paper without even looking through the documents and handed it over to Ben.

Ben took it, and Dan crouched over him to stare at the computer.

He didn't understand a single thing Ben was doing. Ben's fingers were typing away on the keyboard, but everything on the screen meant nothing to Dan.

Despite that, his fingers drummed against the desk while he continued staring at the screen, waiting for something to happen.

He couldn't stand around and do nothing. The image of the woman was quickly morphing into images replaced by Evelyn in that chair. He had to keep himself busy.

From the corner of his eye, Dan noticed Tyler scribbling down something on a piece of paper.

"What's that?"

"All the container trucks have built in GPS tracking except for these two. Kate, check if you can find either of these trucks entering the warehouse."

Thank God for technology, data, logs, and all that paperwork he hated, that Kate and Tyler seemed exceptionally good at.

Dan grabbed the note and gave it to Kate, staring at her while her fingers skimmed down the page. Once her index finger reached the bottom line, she continued on to the next page. "Are you sure? I think I saw—"

"Dan, I read a lot. I'm good at speed reading. I know you're anxious, but you need to trust me."

He knew that, but he needed something to do.

Kate studied him for a moment, then took out a small stack from the one she was holding and handed it to him. "Search through these."

His fingers went through the logs, going down line by line.

He was too slow.

He could hear Kate flipping through the pages, and he tried doing what she did, only to find himself moving back up the column to look through it again.

"Can't we just use the find function on the computers?"

"It's not in excel form. Everything is taken from their company's program or something. I don't even know how Ben printed it out."

Dan sighed as Kate reached over to take the stack he was holding.

He itched to leave the room, to do something, to be out there searching for her instead of looking through papers in the room.

It was pointless to drive around when he had no idea where she could be, but he was getting more restless with each passing second.

"Nothing," Kate said. "Nothing on those trucks."

Just as Dan's hopes rose, Ryan sent his hope crashing. "He knows his wife has this," Ryan said. "Won't he move? This video is from a couple of years back. If I know my wife has this DVD over me, I'll change the way I operate."

"I'll talk to her." Kate got up and shook her head at Dan before he could push himself off the floor. "She looks frightened around you. I don't think she'll talk with you around."

He exhaled heavily and nodded.

Looking around the room, his eyes fell on Ryan. *God, if you are really as great as what Ryan and Kate make you out to be, then don't let him hurt her.*

Chapter Twenty Three

Kate hurried down the stairs and found Melissa staring at the cup of tea in front of her. "Melissa."

Her eyes shot up. "Was that helpful?"

"Yes, but I need to ask you something. That video, it was from a few years back. Do you think things have changed? Could he have found another place or—"

"He knows all I have is this DVD. I don't know much, so I don't think he'd change anything."

Evelyn's words ran through Kate's mind. *He's the arrogant sort; the kind who thinks he'll never get caught.* "He's arrogant."

Melissa nodded. "I'm sorry I can't be more helpful."

"Forgive me for asking this, but why didn't he kill you? After what he'd done to all those women."

"I'm a public face. I still show up with him at social events. If I die or go missing, there'll be news." She chewed on her lower lip and took a deep breath before saying softly, "My death would be an inconvenience to him."

Kate didn't know how to react. She wanted to give Melissa a hug and tell her that everything would be all right, but that wouldn't help her in any way.

Inconvenience.

Then Kate thought about Evelyn, and she wanted to cry for her best friend as she thought about the demeaning life Evelyn was forced to go through.

No wonder Evelyn wanted so badly to help Melissa.

Jesus, please don't let him hurt her. Kate stood and was heading up the stairs when she turned back to Melissa. "How long does she have?"

"Sorry?"

Kate didn't want to ask that question; she didn't want to be prepared for the worst. She wanted her best friend back, but she had to know. They needed to know how long they had to figure things out. "How long does she have?"

"I don't know."

That can't be true, Kate thought. "I suppose you began suspecting when he asked you to be his alibi? You must have gone digging for this DVD; you must have seen the news about the murdered women."

Melissa nodded slowly.

"Then you know the timeline. The alibi you provided was probably when a woman went missing. From the date that you had provided the alibi until a body showed up."

Melissa pursed her lips as her gaze fell to the floor. "A day or two."

Fighting back her tears, Kate nodded.

"You still have time."

Kate swallowed her tears, gave Melissa a wry smile, and ran up the stairs.

"So?" Dan asked the moment Kate reentered the room.

"She doesn't think so. We should call Detective Allen."

Dan was on his feet and ready to leave the room. "I'm going there now."

"Where?" Kate stepped in front of him.

"The company. Their trucks are huge. You can't just park them anywhere; people will notice," Joseph said.

"And one of the cleaning companies is a shell company, the other one cleans the main office. So there's no reason for them to arrange the schedule that way," Ben added.

"Yeah," Ryan said. "He's probably using that as an excuse so he can wash out his truck, and no one will suspect if the floor is wet or if there's a weird detergent smell."

Kate shook her head. "How are you going to get in? There's security. No one's going to let you in. If you make a big deal and she's inside, don't you think it'll only make things worse for her? Look at what he did to that woman. He'd kill her in a second if he knew we were coming."

"I can get you in." A small voice came from outside the room.

Everyone turned to see Melissa Rose standing by the door.

"I've been with him to quite a few company parties. The security and staff should recognize me. I don't think there'll be a problem."

"Won't it be weird for you to bring a man into your husband's company?" Joseph asked.

"I know how to pretend. After all these years, I think I've become a pretty good actress. I'll have no problem taking him in."

"Let's go, then."

Kate opened her mouth to protest but decided against it. Dan should know how dangerous it was. She didn't have to remind him. If things were the other way around, he wouldn't stop Tyler; he'd go along with him.

And there wasn't time for her to sit and think through every aspect. She didn't want Evelyn to go through any of what she'd seen in the video.

She reached out and held Dan's arm. "Bring everyone back safe and in one piece," she said, again swallowing her tears. "And Melissa, thank you."

Dan was already halfway down the stairs when Melissa nodded and trailed after him.

Kate watched their figures disappear from her sight before turning back into the room. Tyler was already on the phone with Detective Allen.

For now, there was nothing else she could do.

Taking a deep breath, she closed her eyes and clenched her jaws.

Time wasn't on their side, and breaking down wasn't going to help bring Evelyn home.

"I should go with him. It isn't safe for him to go alone," Joseph said. "Ty and Ryan will stay here with you."

"Where are you going? You won't be able to get in."

"Then I'll wait outside. At least if something happens, I can be there."

Kate nodded. She wanted to go along with them, but she was certain none of them would allow it.

"Don't even think about it. Even if Ty allows it, I'm not. You're pregnant; you're in your first trimester. It isn't safe. Evelyn will kill herself if anything happens to the baby," Joseph said.

"He's right. You're going to sit this one out," Ryan said and gave Joseph a nod. "We'll call you once there's news."

Her fingers played with the pendant on her necklace. *Please bring them back safely, Lord.*

Evelyn opened her eyes and stretched out her legs, immediately hitting the edge of something. She retracted her legs as grogginess swarm in her head. She blinked and struggled to keep her eyes open with the bright light blaring right at her.

When her full vision returned, she was stunned for a moment.

The metal grills. The tight, confined space.

She turned, and the same grills met her.

The haze that shrouded her mind dissipated. She pushed herself off the ground and onto her knees. She jammed her fingers through the squares and gripped onto the cold, hard metal grill.

Then, she found her voice. She screamed and shook the cage. She should know her actions were useless. She'd tried it before, and it had never accomplished anything except to drain her strength.

But she couldn't stop herself. She couldn't control her actions.

She didn't know how long her delirium lasted when she finally heard the still small voice she'd heard at the office.

Calm down, Evelyn. Don't be afraid. Save your strength.

Curling her legs up against herself, she leaned against the cage and took a deep breath.

Calm down, everything will be fine.

She drew slow, long breaths through her nose and forced herself to focus.

The cage was larger than the one she had been in, but it

yielded the same results. She couldn't stand without bending over, and she couldn't stretch her legs.

She looked around, squinting when she turned toward the source of light; a spotlight shone directly at her. She used her hand to shield herself from the direct glare, trying to look at what was beyond the light. Regardless of how she tilted her head from the light, she couldn't see anything.

She glanced in the opposite direction to escape the light and allow her mind to process the situation.

The walls of the room were close, too close, and it seemed elongated.

She'd seen enough rooms in her work to know something wasn't right. It wasn't a room; she was in some sort of container.

A little farther down the container, a single stool stood between the walls.

Confusion and fear compounded and exploded into a migraine that made thinking impossible.

She shook her head and, again, forced herself to breathe. She tried to concentrate and think about what got her here.

The last thing she remembered seeing was a text from Dan. Then, the rest of her memories poured in. The voice she'd heard; the voice she should have trusted. Exiting the elevator …

Her hand moved up her neck, and she winced as she felt the swollen bump.

None of her memories brought any comfort. It didn't take long for her to figure out who put her in the cage.

She knew at once that she was in danger.

There would be no message for her to send. She would be made to disappear or turn up in a morgue. That realization sent her heart racing, but she was quick to quell her fear and anxieties before they spiraled out of control.

Now wasn't the time to break down.

David Morgan put her in a cage for one obvious reason—to break her.

The stubborn streak in her wouldn't allow that to happen. If she could survive the torture for three years, she could survive this.

And above all else, she was no longer alone. Dan would come for her. Kate would find a way. Tyler, Joseph, and Ryan wouldn't give up on her. All she needed to do was to hang on.

She was sure they were already working on getting her home. Dan would be here anytime.

Then, despite being caged up like an animal, she found the strength to smile.

The sudden gush of air caught her attention, and her head snapped toward the direction of the light. She hadn't realized how stuffy the air was until the sudden injection of warm air.

She still couldn't see anything, but she heard the heavy feet landing on the metal base. She felt the slight vibration and the almost negligible dip of the floor. "Back of a truck."

"Very smart."

The voice confirmed her suspicion. "Hello again, David Morgan."

His heavy footsteps continued, sending the clang of metal echoing in the tight space each time his feet landed.

She didn't bother to watch him. She already knew she couldn't see anything beyond the blinding spotlight.

When the focus of the spotlight shifted, she turned and watched as his silhouette slowly appeared while her eyes adjusted.

She kept her eyes on him until she noticed a tiny red glow beside the spotlight.

He wasn't working alone. Someone else was watching.

"I hope my reaction didn't disappoint."

"I love breaking people down. I haven't had a feisty one for quite a while now."

Taunt him.

Evelyn snorted and smiled. "Is this the only way you can feel good about yourself? Did your mommy bully you? Is that why— Oh no, you didn't have a mom. So … daddy disapproves?"

"Shut up!"

She was glad her captive was an absolute moron. She was merely guessing, but his reaction gave her the answer she needed.

"What did he say about you? Hmm, let me guess. Did he say you're stupid?"

Her cage suddenly came alive as David Morgan rammed his feet against it. The cage throbbed and a buzz filled her ears.

She'd expected his violent reaction and shifted away from the edge of the cage before his leg hit it. "So is absolute control the only way you can deal with women? Is this the only way women pay attention to you? Tying them up to chairs or locking them up in cages. Sad, really."

His silence confirmed her suspicions about the chair.

The inevitable would come.

If the chair was the usual set up, then this cage was meant for her. She had no doubt he knew every single detail regarding her past. Amy would have given it up for a few quick bucks.

The torture would soon follow.

Just keep him talking.

If she could keep this idiot talking, she could delay it.

"I can have anyone I want," David Morgan suddenly said.

"Not everyone. I can easily name three you'll never have and one who can't wait to get away from you. She has something important, doesn't she? That's why I'm here. Lydia found her and she got beaten up. I went to look for her and now we're here. She's going to help me. Even if you keep me here, my friends will find her, and she'll help me."

David Morgan burst out laughing. "If you're relying on her, then you're done for. She knows what's happening. She doesn't know the details, but she knows what's going on. Yet all she asked of me when she got her hands on the evidence was to let her leave. She didn't even get her wish; she's still my pet. That's the kind of person she is—weak and pathetic."

"Like you? Daddy's pet, weak and pathetic?"

"I'm her owner! I own her!"

"No, you don't. She was alone; she didn't think anyone could help her. She believed me when I told her that we could and we would. I could see it in her eyes. She needed hope and I gave it to her."

"And when she realizes what happened to you, which she will, she'll watch out for herself and forget all about you."

If this had happened a year ago, Evelyn would believe that.

She would believe Melissa wouldn't think twice about self-preservation. She would believe she was all alone and her time was up.

But everything had changed.

Tyler, Joseph, and Ryan weren't just Kate's friends. She'd thought them to be just that. Now she understood that they didn't protect her because *she* hadn't allowed it. The walls she'd built had served her so well for so many years that she didn't give anyone else a chance.

But even when her walls were still up, they had gone ahead and helped her without being asked.

"That's the problem when you've only got one person whom you can't trust to rely on. Even if Melissa doesn't come for me, Dan and Kate will. Everyone back at the house will do everything to bring me home. While you, you'll only have someone watching remotely and never approving."

Just then, his phone rang and he hurried to answer it. The call lasted for a few seconds, and he didn't say a word throughout it.

"Daddy called? Disapproved of something again?"

"Shut up."

David Morgan moved to the corner of the truck and bent over a duffle bag.

She hadn't noticed the bag until now. She'd dragged it out as long as she could.

It was time.

A tingling sensation ran down her spine, and she couldn't help but shiver.

Don't be afraid.

She scoffed at the voice. *Don't be afraid?* she thought to herself.

She'd lived through the nightmare once. She'd felt the sting of electricity racing through her body. She'd felt the cuts and still remembered the sensation of warm blood trickling from her wounds.

She was older now. Her capacity to handle pain would probably be better, but it was still impossible to shake the fear.

Dan's coming for you. Keep talking.

The whole situation was so absurd that she hadn't realized she was speaking to herself, or maybe it was her gut. Whatever it was, the voice was right at the office. She'd ignored it then and ended up here.

She wanted to heed the advice, but she didn't know what to say.

The fear was raging wild under her placid exterior, and she couldn't think. *God, if you're out there, please help me,* she thought. *Tell me what to say.*

Taking a deep breath, she ignored the chill in her skin. She opened her mouth, not having a word or sentence prepared. "Your father's smart, coming up with this truck idea after you screwed up."

That immediately caught his attention.

"I came up with this idea! I was careful! I didn't screw up!"

She gave him a condescending laugh. "Oh, please. You did." She didn't allow herself to look at him. The presence of the bag of torture tools brought back too many nightmares.

She had made sure she removed all fear from her face, but she didn't trust her eyes. She couldn't risk letting David Morgan detect any ounce of fear, so she kept her face away.

Thankfully, the idiot was easily manipulated.

He stood, empty-handed, and returned to the side of the cage. "I did not screw up," he said, enunciating each and every word.

"So you're saying your father did?"

"I didn't say that!"

"Aw, you really are his pet, aren't you? Don't dare to say anything bad about him because he's watching?"

With him right beside her cage, she could see his face turning red. He started kicking the cage, hollering like a deranged man. "I didn't screw up! I'm not his pet! He should be proud of me! I did this for him! I got him the girls! I made everything possible!"

She wanted to laugh as his outburst continued.

The cage that was meant to imprison her had become her protection against his insanity.

His phone rang again, and this time Evelyn was quick to interrupt. "Oops. There he is again, calling to tell you what an idiot you are. You'd better pick it up before your master gets angry."

Instead of picking up the call, he sent the phone smashing against her cage, stopping the ringtone.

"Shut up! Shut up! Shut up!"

"Are you talking to me or your father? You be careful now; he won't be happy if you're rude."

"I'm the one in control! I created all this!" His hand waved about as if he were showcasing a piece of art. "I made it possible for him to enjoy everything without lifting his finger, without dirtying his hands!"

The phone rang again, and Evelyn had to thank God for the timeliness. "I don't think he agrees."

He stepped toward the phone and stomped on it, smashing the phone and shutting it up permanently.

"You talk a lot about making all this possible for your father. But look at the facts: He didn't get caught; he wasn't even a suspect, but you were. *You* messed up; *you* got the police's attention; *you* were charged."

"He messed it up! He insisted on taking that girl. I told him it would bring attention; I told him we should find someone else. He screwed up, but I took the fall for it!" He paced up and down the length of her cage. "Then, I solved it," he muttered under his breath.

"By killing the lawyer."

"And he said I was stupid. It stopped the entire case, didn't it?" he said, almost in a whisper.

Evelyn turned away and swallowed hard. She wasn't afraid of him when he was yelling, but his hushed utters were giving her shivers.

There was such frenzy in his eyes that it worried Evelyn. She was afraid he was coming unhinged.

She wasn't sure if she should push him any further; he could snap, and he would become unpredictable then.

Keep doing what you're doing.

She sighed softly, then licked her lips and continued. "I think you meant delayed. Lydia picked it up. She's on the case again. And trust me, nothing's going to make her give up. So I hate to admit it, but I think your father was right."

"Last time, the warning wasn't clear enough. This time, when they see your body and your wounds, they'll stop."

"Wrong. If you turn up dead, your father probably won't give a damn. But do you know why we stuck our noses into the investigation even when we had once told Lydia to back off?" She paused and smirked. "Because you were stupid enough to send someone to hurt her. And because of that, we're fighting back. That's what families do—something you'll never understand."

He opened his mouth to retaliate, but a shrill scream cut him off. His head turned toward the entrance of the truck, then he returned his focus to her. Suddenly, all his rage was directed back at her.

He's here. Keep talking. Blame his father.

"Looks like your father found someone else to play with."

The frown he was wearing deepened. With a growl, he turned away from her and pushed the heavy metal doors wide open.

Evelyn sighed heavily. She closed her eyes, and the fear she had been suppressing surged to the surface. *Please let it be Dan.*

She pressed her face into her hands for a moment before pushing her hair and emotions from her face. David Morgan could come back at any moment.

She got onto her knees again and crawled over to the mouth of the cage.

What was the use of all those self-defense lessons? She should've learned to open a lock with a pin or something.

She lay on her back and pulled her knees toward her chest. Taking a deep breath, she kicked as hard as she could. The lock shook; the entire cage shook, but that stubborn silver lock remained exactly where it was.

Cursing under her breath, she tried it again before making herself stop. She should conserve her energy.

It's okay. You're safe now.

Thus far, the voice had kept her from harm. She had no reason to doubt it. So, she sat up and closed her eyes, listening for anything that would give her a clue to what was happening outside.

Chapter Twenty Four

Dan drove the car right up to the gantry as Melissa had instructed. He held his breath as the security peered out from the booth and stared right into his car.

Beside him, Melissa poked her head over the driver side and smiled sweetly at the security guard.

"Mrs. Morgan? Is everything all right? It's so late—"

"Yes, I'm just picking something up for David."

The security guard hesitated for a moment, and his eyes darted toward Dan for a second.

"This is Dan, my cousin."

"Okay," the security guard said hesitantly.

"If you need to, you can call David to check. Just do it fast, he's waiting for us back home."

Dan struggled to appear indifferent. He really should have more confidence in Melissa.

Throughout the whole drive, Melissa had kept to herself. Not once did she even glance over at him.

Then right before speaking to the security guard, her whole demeanor changed. She smiled and spoke confidently; a complete opposite of the frightened Melissa he'd seen over the past few hours.

"No, no. I don't have to do that." The security guard went back into the booth and lifted the bar.

"Thanks," Melissa said and waved as Dan drove by.

"You're good," Dan said as they got into the lift.

"If I couldn't pretend well, I would've been dead a long time ago."

Dan cracked a small, apologetic smile.

Following Melissa's instructions, Dan parked the car and got into the lift that would lead them down to the parking garage where the trucks would be.

"Thank you, Melissa," Dan said as they exited the lift. "Stay here. I'll find Evelyn." He immediately noticed the fear in her eyes. "I'll come back for you. It's safer to be by the lift."

Her head inclined slightly.

"Scream if you need anything," he said as his eyes scanned the parking garage from the elevated platform where they were standing on.

The parking garage was relatively empty, with only a handful of trucks in the garage.

Shouldn't be too difficult to find her, he thought.

He hopped down from the platform and treaded as lightly as he could. He went up to one of the trucks and pulled on the handles, but the door refused to budge. He moved on, feeling that his hands were too empty.

He should've brought a gun or something.

Then, he heard a muffled voice and a thumping coming from one of the trucks.

He paused and listened.

In the large parking garage, the sound traveled and spread out across the place. He couldn't make out which of the trucks the sound originated from, but it confirmed his suspicions—Evelyn was somewhere inside the garage.

He started jogging from truck to truck, moving close and listening for any noise. But the only sound he could hear was the thumping of his own heart and the silence of the largely empty lot.

"Come on, come on," he muttered to himself.

Shhh … pay attention.

The soft echo of the thumping came back, and he continued his jog among the trucks.

He held his breath as he neared one of the trucks and sighed as he pressed his back up against it, feeling the pulsation of the truck against his skin.

Dan moved over and was about to open the door when a scream froze his hand. He spun around and hesitated for a moment. Evelyn was so close; he could get her first.

Go. Evelyn is safe for now.

He ran his hand through his hair. "Hang on, Eve." He sprinted back in the direction he came from. From where he was, he could see a gray-haired man standing over Melissa. She lay curled up on the floor, her hands raised over her head, bracing for some form of attack.

That was when Dan saw the gun.

"Hey!" he shouted, bringing attention to himself.

The old man turned around and, without even aiming, fired a shot in his direction. He dropped to the ground and heard the bullet chip off a piece of concrete floor somewhere near him.

He had to get behind one of the trucks.

He got to his feet the same moment the old man was ready to pull the trigger. It might be too late, but he started running. He heard another shot and felt the burning sensation of hot metal skimming across his arm.

Before he could catch his breath, the corner of his eye caught a movement. Instinctively, he tried to dodge the blow. Tucking his chin in, he raised his arms and prepared for the oncoming impact.

But he wasn't fast enough.

He felt the blow on his cheek and the sudden jolt of tingle that shot right up to his brain, disorienting him. He shook his head and kept his hand raised over his face to prevent further blows while he tried to get his focus back.

He wasn't sure what happened, but he felt a shove and felt himself falling.

Muscle memory drilled in by years of training kicked in. He shifted his weight to the side, landing on his arm.

Other than the rough landing, no damage was done.

There was another scream from Melissa.

Dan opened his eyes to see David Morgan flinging himself over him. Dan couldn't help but grin at the fool. Being trained in

Judo, fighting on the ground was his forte. And for a moment, he almost felt sorry for the guy.

Dan didn't even have to think. Before David Morgan could raise his hand, Dan flipped him over, his arms easily finding their positions.

He pinned David Morgan's neck against his arm and locked his free hand against his wrist.

Dan pulled back on the guillotine chokehold he had on David Morgan.

David Morgan wasn't puny by any count, but Dan's arm fitted snugly against his throat, cutting off all oxygen supply. Unless David Morgan knew the right method to escape the chokehold, there wouldn't be much he could do.

He felt David Morgan's fingers digging into his arm, trying to pry it away.

Seconds later, David Morgan's body went limp in Dan's arms and another gunshot went off.

Dan released the unconscious David Morgan and stood just as Melissa sank her teeth into the old man's arm.

The gun dropped to the floor, sending another shot into the air.

He wasn't sure which direction the bullet was flying toward, but he ducked anyway.

Before he could get up and help Melissa, Joseph emerged from behind a truck, slammed the old man onto the ground, and picked up the gun.

Joseph stood in front of Melissa, his gun pointed at the old man. Glancing over to Dan, he shouted, "Go. We're fine."

Dan sprinted over to the truck and swung himself into the container. "Eve!"

"Dan!"

He went up to the cage and tugged on the lock. "Are you hurt? Where's the key?"

"I'm fine, but I don't know where the key is."

"It must be with one of them. I'll be right back."

He got out of the truck and returned to search the unconscious David Morgan. Once he found the key, he hurried back to get Evelyn out of the cage.

Taking Evelyn's hand, he helped her out of the truck before pulling her into his arms. "Are you all right? Are you hurt?"

"I'm fine. I knew you'd come, and that idiot kept on talking." She paused, taking a step back, and gave him a look over. "Your arm."

Dan had completely forgotten about it. "It's nothing."

Evelyn leaned in to check his wound, but he wrapped his arm around her and held her tight against his chest.

"Kate? Is she all right?"

"She's fine. She's still at home, I believe."

"Good."

"Melissa, I'm sure you can find some duct tape in the truck. Can you get that for me?" Joseph's voice caught their attention.

"I'll get it. I think I saw it in the bag," Evelyn said.

Dan allowed Evelyn to step out of his arms, but he kept her half a step behind him as he got back into the truck to retrieve the duct tape and return to tie the Morgans up.

"How did you get in?" Dan asked while looping the duct tape over David Morgan's legs.

"Ben found the blueprint, and Tyler found the loophole. There's a small, out of sight entrance. Probably for them to get in and out without having to pass the security guards. It was easy to climb over. Are you hurt?" Joseph lowered the gun when both the Morgans were taped up and moved toward Evelyn.

Evelyn shook her head and stretched her legs. "I was sure you guys were on the way. Melissa, thank you."

"You would've done the same for me. Besides, I didn't do much."

Evelyn laid her head on Dan's shoulder as the paramedics walked away. She looked at the Morgans in the police car, the older man staring straight ahead while David Morgan continued hurling who-knows-what.

When the police arrived, there was a slight confusion. It was the Morgans' office building, but their mouths, hands, and legs were taped while Joseph held the gun.

The confusion was quickly cleared when another policeman found the setup in the truck.

With the DVD Melissa had and the things David Morgan had said while they were in the back of the truck, there should be more than enough evidence to put the Morgans away for a long time.

"Are you sure you're all right? I know the cage and everything …"

"I was scared. But something in me, a voice actually, kept telling me that you were coming, that I just had to keep him talking."

He grinned and draped his arm over her shoulders. "I'm just glad you weren't hurt." Dan leaned in and kissed her lightly on her lips.

"Dan?" Evelyn said between kisses.

"Yes?"

"Will you marry me?"

Dan straightened and looked right at her. "Did you just propose or was that a question like would I someday marry you?"

That wasn't the reaction she was hoping for. "Depends on your answer."

"No."

"No? You don't want to marry me?"

"No. No, because that's my question to ask, not yours."

She scowled at him.

"You haven't even met my parents."

"Oh, I have. Your mom tried to slap me, remember?"

Dan laughed, but his laughter only irritated her further. She looked away and saw the silver beamer pulling up.

"Kate's here, and I'm done talking to you." She pushed herself off the ambulance and hugged her best friend. "Look who finally showed up."

Kate stepped out of their hug and twirled her around. "Not a scratch," she said with tears brimming in her eyes.

"Not a scratch."

"I'm sorry you had to go through that. It must be horrible."

Evelyn shrugged it off. At the moment, she was consumed with indignation at Dan.

"Are you all right?" Kate asked.

"Yeah." Evelyn smiled. "Don't cry, I'm fine."

Wiping off the tears hanging by the corners of her eyes, Kate sniffed and said, "I expected you to be happier than this, or maybe a little upset. But why do you look angry?" Kate narrowed her eyes and stared at her. "What's wrong?"

"Later."

"Okay, then. Let me fill you in." Kate hooked her arm around hers and walked toward the silver beamer. "We were with Detective Allen. We showed him the video, and he got a warrant to search the house. They found proof, more than enough to keep David Morgan away for a long, long time."

"Perfect. What about the older Morgan?"

"What older Morgan?" Kate asked.

It was Evelyn's turn to fill her in.

"There was nothing on the videos to indicate that anyone else was involved," Kate said.

"So he'll be freed?"

"I'm sure Detective Allen will do everything he can."

For now, that was good enough. Though David Morgan committed the horrible acts, she was sure Richard Morgan was behind it all. He was the ultimate mastermind; it wasn't fair that he was going to get away with it.

Then again, that was life.

Evelyn turned to look at David Morgan and found space in her heart to pity him.

She used to think that Amy got off easy. After what Amy had done to her, Amy's only punishment was counseling. Now, she realized it wasn't Amy's fault. Perhaps it wasn't just self-preservation. Perhaps Amy was simply yearning for the acceptance that none of them ever had as a child.

She sighed and pushed the thoughts from her mind.

For now, the chapter with the Morgans was over.

Her mind went on to brood over how blatantly Dan had rejected her. Wasn't he the one who wanted a proper relationship and a family? She was giving him what he wanted, wasn't she?

Then the self-conscious voice that she hadn't heard in a while dropped an idea in her mind.

Maybe she wasn't the one he was looking to have all that with. "You know what? I'm so tired. I'm going home."

"Eve, are you all right?" Kate asked again.

Evelyn smiled and gave Kate another hug. "I'm fine. I'm just … tired." She saw Kate reaching for her necklace. "Kate, I'm fine. I swear."

"All right, but call me if you need anything."

"Right now, I need you to go home and get some rest."

Chapter Twenty Five

Dan pushed the heavy glass door open and entered the store with the rest of the guys. Instead of having bright spotlights, the store was set in a low yellow glow. Spotlights were only found in the display cases, casting off brilliant sparkles.

The contrast between the dim lightings of the store and the display only emphasized the dazzle of the diamonds.

"Good evening, sir. Can I help you?" The sales assistant clad in his well-pressed suit and white gloves smiled politely at him.

"I'm looking for an engagement ring."

"Ahh …" The sales assistant's brows rose. "Right this way, sir. Do you have any design in mind?"

"No, he doesn't have a clue," Ryan answered for him.

Dan shot Ryan a glare. Though it was absolutely true, there wasn't a need for Ryan to announce it to the world.

He hadn't dared to entertain the thought of proposing to Evelyn. Even when she'd proposed after the incident with David Morgan, Dan had thought she was merely reacting to the scare she went through.

Besides, Evelyn never brought that subject up again. He assumed she had recovered from the episode and was glad that he hadn't taken it seriously.

He had even half expected Evelyn to move back home the moment David Morgan was arrested. When she didn't, he'd concluded that Richard Morgan was the reason why she was still there.

Then, he received that crazy phone call from Kate. She had

gone on ranting without even explaining to him what was going on. He'd simply allowed her to continue, thinking it was her hormones going crazy. It was a good ten minutes into the call before he realized it was over Evelyn's proposal and his flat-out rejection.

Once he got over the initial surprise and disbelief, he started planning. The proposal was the easy part; the specifics of the ring were what he had no idea of.

Dan turned back to smile at the assistant. "I want something special, not like the normal bands you see."

Stopping by a section, the sales assistant nodded. "Let me see." The sales assistant studied the rows of rings and pulled out several display trays, laying them on top of the clear glass.

All the guys bent over the trays and stared at all the bling. They continued staring for a minute without anyone offering any suggestions.

He should have brought Kate instead, but he didn't really have a choice. He needed Kate to distract Evelyn with some shopping so that he could plan his surprise.

Standing there with the guys who had gone mute, he realized he should have at least brought Marianne.

He turned to them with a raised brow and noticed that Tyler wasn't with them. Looking over his shoulder, he noticed Tyler over at the earrings section. With all the time Tyler had on his hands, he had to choose this moment to buy something for Kate.

Dan turned back to the rings, still completely clueless.

The sales assistant must have noticed. He smiled and asked, "Does your girlfriend prefer simple or slightly flashier designs?"

"Simple."

Reaching below the shelf, the sales assistant pulled out an empty tray and set it before Dan. He picked a few of the rings and slotted them into the ridges on the empty tray. "Then I would suggest solitaire or trinity rings without any side diamonds on the band. And if you're looking for something special, this one has a unique band."

Dan grinned the moment he saw the last ring being placed onto the tray. He took it in his hand and turned the ring around,

Closing Books

scrutinizing it.

The square-cut diamond was set in a band that curved away from each other, twisting the diamond diagonally.

"This is nice," Joseph said.

"Yeah, I think so, too," Ryan added.

Dan was certain they would agree with whichever ring he picked up. "When it's your turn, I suggest you guys bring Marianne or Kate."

"Right, we know you're actually grateful for our wise insight," Ryan joked.

Dan couldn't stop himself from shaking his head. He was tempted to take a photo of the ring and send it to Kate, but it was too risky. Kate was such a bad liar. Besides, she rarely checked her phone.

Placing the ring back onto the tray, Dan gave the other rings another look. He liked the first one he'd picked, but he wasn't sure.

"This one looks good," Tyler said, pointing to the ring Dan had just placed back.

"You're done choosing Kate's present?" Dan couldn't hide the frustration in his voice.

"They're wrapping it. This is good." Tyler picked up the ring. "It's different."

Just like her, Dan thought. "But I thought bands were supposed to be one complete round, like … I don't know … together forever kind of thing?"

Ryan and Joseph became mute again.

"Kate would say that it's like two different people on different paths coming together to become a family," Tyler said after a while.

Dan looked over at Tyler. He wanted to tell Tyler that Kate was the best thing that happened to him. But instead, a corner of his lips sneaked up. "I love Kate." He knew that would irritate the hell out of Tyler.

"Everyone needs to stop loving Kate."

That brought about a round of laughter from the rest of the guys while Tyler went off to pay for the pair of earrings he'd picked out.

"I'll take this," Dan said, his heart already pounding with excitement. The moment he made the choice, he could see Evelyn wearing the ring.

She would love it—that was if she still wanted to marry him.

Evelyn's phone vibrated as she dropped her shopping bags onto the chair. The cafe was abuzz with customers, and she was glad there were still seats available. Her feet were aching from all the shopping, and she desperately needed to rest them before they fell off her.

She took a glimpse of her phone and handed it to Kate who was just settling into her seat.

Evelyn was sure her number was second on Tyler's speed dial. Whenever he couldn't get Kate, which was quite often, he'd call her.

Kate took the phone from her. "Sorry," she said when she saw Tyler's name on the screen and answered the call.

"Chamomile tea?" Evelyn mouthed.

Kate nodded. "Thanks."

Evelyn moved toward the counter, checking out the menu hung on the wall. She didn't want to be drinking coffee so late at night, but the aroma of it was so strong and tempting that she gave in to it.

When making her way back after the purchase, Kate was off the phone and was staring at her engagement and wedding rings.

Evelyn sighed quietly as Dan's rejection came back to mind.

After Dan had rejected her proposal, she had convinced herself that it was for the best. She wasn't in her right mind when she had asked him; it was probably the result of impulse.

Dan seemed adamant about putting her question behind him as well. He hadn't brought up her proposal since that day.

His silence on the topic brought about waves of insecurities, and the thought in her head soon dropped into her heart. She wasn't the one Dan wanted all the relationship stuff with. He'd tried it out with her and realized it wasn't what he wanted.

Or maybe she was too late. Maybe she'd pushed Dan away so

many times that he didn't think they could ever move beyond their current status.

"Do you think I should move back home?" Evelyn asked as she set the tray down on the table.

"No."

"I moved in because of the whole David Morgan issue. Now David Morgan is locked up and—"

"And Richard Morgan?"

Evelyn placed Kate's tea and her coffee onto the table and handed the tray back to a staff passing by. "Thanks."

The evidence they had on David Morgan was enough for the judge to deny him bail, but they didn't have much on Richard Morgan, and the district attorney was reluctant to charge him.

Turning back to Kate, she smiled. "I was just asking; just a random thought."

"And does that random thought has something to do with your question to Dan?"

Evelyn took a sip of her coffee and shrugged.

"He isn't having second thoughts, Eve."

"And how would you know that?"

Kate reached for her necklace and Evelyn continued. "See, you don't know that. You're merely trying to make me feel better."

Dropping her hand, Kate scowled at her. "I didn't reach for my necklace because I was guilty. It's just a habit."

"Right."

"When David Morgan got you, I saw how worried Dan was. He went after you. He didn't let you down."

Evelyn leaned her head lazily against her hand but said nothing.

"You knew he would come for you, and that kept you sane. It gave you enough strength to keep yourself from falling apart."

She did know Dan would come for her, and that did give her strength to hang on, to keep herself calm and hold her wits together.

She wasn't in complete control, though. She had a little help. "There was a voice that I kept hearing. I …"

"I know, Dan told me."

"I didn't think that God existed until the fire at your house, until I saw your necklace. Even after that …"

"I know. You just didn't believe that He cares about you," Kate said. 'But He does," she added with absolute confidence.

"Thanks for your present. I'm sure you put a lot of time and effort into it, and I'm sorry I took so long to open it."

Kate's brows furrowed for a second before her eyes widened. "You mean the Bible I gave you?" She laughed, shaking her head. "I thought you'd thrown it out."

Evelyn rolled her eyes. "I won't do that. I just chucked it away in my drawer." She grinned and twirled her phone around on the table.

"When did you open it?"

"Not too long ago."

Kate smiled and nodded. "Humans are funny creatures, aren't we?" she stated. "We don't look to God until we're at our wits end. I'm sorry you went through all that heartache with Dan, but I'm somewhat glad that it led you to open the Bible."

"Don't you think He's rather cruel to let me go through all that just to reach out to me?"

"Eve." Kate pushed her cup of tea aside and leaned forward on her elbows. "He has been trying to reach out to you. Through me, He has shown you that He exists and He protects His children. But you refuse to believe it for yourself. Maybe, just maybe, this was the only way you would turn to him."

Evelyn licked her lower lip and reached for her coffee.

"He didn't put Mrs. Moore in your life, He didn't send Amy to you, and He definitely didn't set David Morgan up to kidnap you. But He delivered you from all of it. And through all these, He showed you that you're not alone, that He has placed you with the best people on earth." Kate laughed softly. "It may not be in the way you had expected things to turn out. But I think He has shown you that even in your deepest valley, He is there with you. Even when you think He didn't care, He was always there watching over you, waiting for you to accept His protection."

Evelyn held the cup to her lips.

"And because of you, because of what the devil had made you go through, you stopped a monster. Who knows how many more people David Morgan would've gone on to kill?"

Scoffing, Evelyn shook her head. "I didn't do anything except get myself locked up in a cage."

"Seriously? Is that what you think?" Kate leaned back, and her fingers returned to play with her necklace. "If it weren't for you, none of us would have jumped in on the case. Everything that followed only happened because you made it your business to get involved."

Evelyn wasn't sure of everything Kate had said, but she was certain of one point; God had placed her with the best people on earth. Kate had always been her support. And through Kate, she now had a family.

"It doesn't matter what you believe; all I care is that you're safe. *And* you're going to keep staying at Dan's, or I'm not going to accept the baby crib you're making."

"That's not fair."

Kate smiled sweetly and fluttered her eyelids. "I know," she said. "As for the situation with Dan, maybe it's time to pray instead of listening to whatever crazy thoughts that are going through your mind."

Evelyn didn't say anything. *All I have to do is ask for help?* she thought. *Well then, God, I want to get married.*

Chapter Twenty Six

Evelyn was exhausted after a full day of work and a whole night of shopping. When Tyler had picked them up, she'd expected him to send her back to Dan's place. Instead, he dropped them off at the mansion and said he had to make a trip to the office to solve some problems.

Evelyn couldn't help feeling that she was being kidnapped as Kate pulled her into the house and made her look through all the drawings for the new room.

She tried paying attention, but she wasn't in the mood to discuss the room. All she wanted was to go home and sleep.

The thing about being such great friends was that Evelyn had no problem telling Kate how tired she was, but neither did Kate have any problem insisting that she stayed.

Kate never asked anything that would inconvenience anyone unless it was important.

For a moment, she thought herself to be an awful friend. Of course Kate was excited about the room; it was their first child. Evelyn was thrilled for them as well, and she shouldn't allow her doubts about her own relationship to dampen Kate's mood.

So she stayed, smiled, and gave as many suggestions as she could.

As time dragged on, Evelyn became suspicious that Kate was keeping her around on purpose.

"Is something wrong?" she asked, cutting Kate's speech about the clouds she wanted to paint on the ceiling wall.

Kate paused and opened her mouth.

Evelyn waited, but no words came out.

Then Tyler suddenly came in, telling Kate that it was late and he should take Evelyn home. He didn't wait for either of their replies. He stretched his hand to help Kate to her feet. "Let's go."

Evelyn thought Kate must have gotten into a squabble with Tyler, but the smile that Kate was giving him said otherwise.

Something was wrong.

She wanted to stop Kate and ask her what was going on, but she was dead tired.

Tomorrow, she thought. Tomorrow she'd ask Kate about it.

"Evelyn."

She felt a light tap on her shoulder and sprang upright.

"It's just me," Tyler said. "You're home."

"I fell asleep."

He nodded.

She stretched and leaned forward.

Tyler immediately put his finger to his lips and said, "She fell asleep, too."

"Thanks for sending me home," Evelyn whispered and pushed the car door open, then closed it softly behind her. Heading up the stairs, she dug into her bag for the key that Dan had given her.

There wasn't any hint of light behind the windows, so she assumed Dan had gone to bed. She opened the door as quietly as she could, but gasped the moment she stepped in.

From the edge of the door, two fake walls covered the entire living room except for the narrow path leading to the kitchen and the staircase leading upstairs.

The fake walls were overlaid with wallpaper. On the wallpaper was a blossom tree; its branches stretched across the length of the walls. Stenciled words of various colors and size were written across every plain surface.

Petals of red roses were scattered across the narrow path, and small tea candles placed in transparent glass tubes lined the edge of the floor.

She ran her fingers under the first message. *You make me the happiest man on earth.* She smiled and moved along, reading every message on the wall.

When you're in my arms, every worry melts away.
Waking up next to you is the best thing in life.
Your smiles light up my day.
You're always on my mind.

No one had ever done anything like this for her. Her tears fell as she read the messages, and all the doubts she had about Dan and her completely faded. She picked up her pace and moved toward the kitchen. She couldn't wait to see him and go into his arms.

Pushing aside the translucent white drapes painted with small golden flowers, she entered the kitchen and skidded to a halt.

A crystal chandelier hung from the ceiling, holding five tea candles, illuminating the entire kitchen in a dim glow. Every inch of the countertop's surface was covered with tiny red flowers. In the middle of the kitchen, where the dining table used to be, stood a tree with the same flowers that were on the countertop.

Christmas lights were draped across each branch, adding to the orange glow in the room. She stepped toward the tree and ran her hand down the trunk. She already knew it wasn't a real tree, but she couldn't figure out how Dan got it in and managed to get it standing upright in the kitchen.

"I know you don't believe in fairy tales," Dan said, turning her head.

The transformation of the room had captured so much of her attention that she hadn't realized he was standing by what used to be the fridge.

"So I created one for you." He took a step forward and gave her a bouquet of peach and white roses.

"If you allow it, I'll make sure that from this day forth, every day of your life will be lived happily ever after." Getting down on one knee, he opened the black box he had been holding. "Eve, will you marry me?"

She couldn't stop the tears from slipping down her cheeks. Neither could she stop herself from smiling.

Right now, with him, she did feel like a princess in one of those fairy tales. "Yes, of course I'll marry you."

Dan's smile was as wide as hers. He slipped the ring onto her finger and stood. Gently, he wiped the tears from her face. "I love you."

"I love you, too." She threw her arms around his neck and kissed him; her own prince charming, the beginning of her own fairy tale.

The sun had risen for hours before Evelyn and Dan got to the mansion. Evelyn ran in ahead of Dan, but she was surprised to see Kate missing from the entourage in the kitchen.

"Congrats!" Ryan and Joseph exclaimed.

"Thanks." She grinned, then glanced over at Tyler.

"She just woke up. She's in our room," Tyler said without her asking.

Turning around, she rushed out of the kitchen and up the stairs. She burst into Kate's room without even knocking.

Kate smiled and sat up on the bed. "Let me see your ring!"

Evelyn hopped onto the bed, settling beside Kate. "Why are you still in bed? Not feeling well?"

"Just feeling lazy. Ty told me to rest for a while longer. It looks great on your hand! Do you like it? Ty helped."

"Yeah, I heard. And I love it. You should see what Dan did to the house!" She pulled her cell phone from the back pocket and showed her all the photos.

"Wow, he did that in one night? Ty's description didn't do it justice." Kate took the phone from her hand and examined the photos. "He put in *a lot* of work on this. Do you know how heavy the tree was? It took all of them to move it."

"I never thought I'll get married. I never thought I'll be so happy. Oh, Kate, you made a great decision to move in here."

"Aww … I've never thought about things that way. But yeah, and who was telling me that it was a horrible idea?"

"I was wrong, so wrong. Thank God, you never listen to me."

"Hey!" Kate elbowed Evelyn softly before tossing back her phone.

"I was thinking—"

A few soft raps on the door cut Evelyn's sentence, and they

both turned toward the door as it opened.

Tyler stepped in, and after a quick glance at Kate, his eyes moved onto her. "Detective Allen is here. He's hoping he can speak to you for a few minutes."

"Ty—"

"It's okay." Evelyn gave Kate a pat on her leg. "Don't worry, I'm fine. I know all of you think I shouldn't be, and I know I shouldn't be, but I really am."

She meant every word she said.

The whole episode should have scared her beyond all imagination. Though she'd somehow found the courage to keep her wits together while she was in the cage, she should have broken down after that. Her nightmare should be plaguing her every night. She should be waking up in the middle of the night, quivering with fresh fear sparked off by the whole event.

Instead, she found it easy to forget about David Morgan.

The only memories she held from the kidnap was the reinforcement that she wasn't alone anymore. She not only had Kate, she had friends who knew about her past and still defended her. And she knew no matter what happened, Dan would be there for her.

Above all else, she realized that Kate might have been right about God all along.

She gave Kate a quick hug and left her with Tyler while she went out of the room.

Evelyn grinned as she saw Dan leaning against the wall. "Why didn't you come in?"

Dan laughed softly and led her down the stairs. "While he's willing to extend the courtesy toward you because of Kate, he won't be that kind toward the rest of us."

She looked up at him, wondering what Dan was talking about.

"He's an extremely private person. No one goes into his room. If we wanted something in his room, he'd get it. He's weird like that." Halfway down the stairs, Dan paused and took her hands. "Are you sure you're all right with this? We can just tell him that you don't want to talk about it anymore."

"Don't worry. I want to help put them away. If it's going to take a thousand interviews, then that's what I'll do."

Dan squeezed her hand and lifted it up to his lips. "Sometimes I forget how amazing you are. But promise me, anytime during any of these interviews, if you get upset or if you just need some fresh air, let me know."

"I promise."

They headed down the stairs and saw Detective Allen speaking to Mr. Sawyer.

Ben and Tyler had handed over all of their own and Lydia's findings to the police. Mr. Sawyer had convinced Detective Allen that everything was legal and that they wouldn't have a problem using the findings as evidence. He even found some precedents on evidence provided by civilians being admitted for court trials.

When she had decided to help Lydia on the case, Mr. Sawyer began keeping tabs on everything they were doing to make sure they wouldn't end up getting into trouble with the law.

She remembered Mr. Sawyer talking to Ben at length, asking in detail how he obtained the information and so forth. She'd thought Mr. Sawyer was merely being curious. But in fact, while they dove head first into the case, Mr. Sawyer had made sure that their backs were covered.

"Hi, Detective."

"Sorry to disturb you. I was actually here to update Mr. Hayes about the case, but since you're here, I thought …"

"Don't worry about it. What can I do for you?"

They moved over and settled on the couch.

"Let me give you the good news first. The D.A. is sure we have everything we need to put David Morgan away."

"But?" Evelyn asked. Whenever someone wanted to give the 'good news' first, there was bound to be a 'but' behind.

Detective Allen took a sip of his coffee and sighed. "We can't find anything to link any of the cases to Richard Morgan. We went through the house and office, but we couldn't find anything on him."

"David Morgan admitted it when we were in the truck."

"We only have his word. Besides, he's keeping his mouth shut now."

Her hand twirled the phone she was holding as she thought back on everything David Morgan had said. She was sure Richard Morgan was behind it all. There must be a way to prove it. "The footage from the camera in the truck was being transmitted somewhere. He was watching. Whenever David Morgan got too chatty, Richard Morgan would call."

"It was streamed to a computer in David Morgan's office. The security camera was switched off. We can't prove Richard Morgan was in the office."

"Then how did he see us? He kept calling just moments before I heard Melissa screaming. He must have seen Dan and Melissa going into the building."

"Circumstantial at best," Mr. Sawyer said.

"Look at the old cases. David Morgan said something about his father screwing things up. That was why Kate's father could take them to court. He didn't say exactly what Richard Morgan screwed up on. But whatever it was, it must be something damning."

"That case revolved around one witness, Suzanne Harrison. She was the one woman who got away. When Mr. Mitchell died, Suzanne Harrison backed out and the case went cold. I tried looking her up, but she simply insisted that she didn't want anything to do with it and slammed the door in my face."

"Then why was only David Morgan charged?"

"The evidence wasn't strong enough. I think Kate's father was trying to deal with David Morgan first, then see if he could turn David against his father," Mr. Sawyer said.

Detective Allen nodded. "It seems that way. According to the statement, David Morgan tortured her. She was kept in a room without windows, so she didn't know how long she was held captive. It was only after she escaped that she realized it'd only been a couple of days."

"How did she get out?" Dan asked. "They were all strapped to the chair."

"She couldn't remember. She was pretty doped up. All she remembered was Richard Morgan strangling her. He must have thought she was dead, but she woke up a while later and caught him off guard. Then she ran out and managed to get help before he could react."

"That sounds pretty damning to me!"

"Problem was, she was heavy on drugs. She couldn't get the details of her escape right. It would be easy to refute her claims."

There must be a way. After all that the Morgans had done, both of them should be behind bars. "What if David Morgan confessed?"

"If I'm on the defense, I'll say Richard Morgan knew nothing about what was going on and David Morgan is just pushing the blame so that he can escape the death sentence. All you need is for the old man to shed a few tears or choke up when he's speaking. No jury will send a frail old man away or issue a death sentence unless they see something concrete."

Evelyn saw Detective Allen's head bobbing up and down. That must have been the same dilemma Kate's father had faced before the trial.

"The frail old man took a couple of shots at me," Dan said.

"He claimed that he saw you through the security system and thought you were breaking in."

"And Melissa? He had the gun pointed at her."

"He said he was about to put the gun down when he saw that it was his daughter-in-law, but then he saw you."

"Seriously? And you let him go because of that?" Evelyn shook her head, irate at the justice system.

"We let him go because there isn't enough evidence to hold him. And now, he's hiding behind a legion of lawyers."

"I may be able to help."

Everyone looked up as Joseph hurried over with his iPad and that day's newspaper.

"Remember the unusual bruises I mentioned? Those on the victims' necks? Look at what Richard Morgan is wearing." Joseph pointed to the picture that took up nearly half a page.

It was a close-up of Richard Morgan using his hand to shield his face from the camera. His palm was facing out, and the ring that he wore on his index finger was smacked in the middle of the picture.

"It matches! The moment I saw the picture, I knew this must be it. See the unusual wave of the ring? The thickness, the pattern; it all matches!" He placed his iPad, which displayed a zoomed-in version of the bruise, alongside the newspaper.

Everyone's head hovered over the pictures, but Evelyn couldn't give any comments. The bruises just seemed like every other bruise, and Joseph must have seen the confusion on everyone's face.

"Look," he said, pointing to a particular point in the bruise, showing the darker lines amid the light purple bruises. He traced the darker lines then moved to the ring, tracing the same pattern on the ring. "Do you see it?"

"I think so …" Evelyn said.

Detective Allen got to his feet. "Does the M.E. have these photos?"

"It's all in the files that Lydia found."

"Good." He took the newspaper from Joseph. "Do you mind if I take this?"

"Go ahead."

"Will that be enough?" Evelyn asked Mr. Sawyer as Detective Allen went hurrying out.

He considered for a moment before answering. "They'll have to prove that he was wearing it during all those years. He's been to many social events, so finding pictures of him wearing the ring shouldn't be too difficult. They'll also have to prove that it's a one of a kind ring; that only he has it. Otherwise, it's enough for reasonable doubt."

Evelyn smiled. She had a good feeling about this.

It was clear that David Morgan's suit was tailor-made. Even the walking stick that Richard Morgan was holding appeared to be custom-made. The handle had a clear monogram with the letters R. M.

They tailored their suits and have monograms on the things they owned. Surely Richard Morgan wouldn't settle for a ring that anyone else could buy in a store.

Chapter Twenty Seven

The front page news had been dominated by news about the Morgans. With the logs that Tyler and Ben found, Detective Allen managed to dig in further to find a link to human trafficking; the supply for the Morgans' sadistic fetish.

Though both the Morgans were hiding behind their lawyers, the evidence that the police had was quickly mounting against them.

Using the new lead given by Joseph, the medical examiner got inspired and started looking through old crime photos. Besides proving that the ring was custom-made, the walking stick, which had been a constant companion of Richard Morgan, made an undeniable imprint across the right temple of Suzanne Harrison's face.

That evidence backed up Suzanne's theory. With the Morgans safely behind bars, and with some persuasion from Lydia, Suzanne Harrison agreed to take the stand again.

Everything was leading to a happy ending in this case. Even Melissa got a million-dollar book deal to write about her life with David Morgan, exposing everything about the father and son.

Evelyn had also been offered quite a large sum of money for interviews and book deals, but she wasn't interested. She wasn't keen on dwelling on what had happened anymore. All she wanted was to focus on her wedding; a small wedding ceremony held by the beach.

Before they dove right into their plans, Dan and Evelyn took a trip to visit his parents.

She found herself feeling more anxious about seeing them than being caged up by David Morgan. Even before this meeting, she'd already chalked up quite a number of demerit points.

It started when she took Kate's side while Joanne created waves of trouble with Kate. Though Joanne had made up with them, she couldn't say the same for Dan's mother.

She was certain that to Dan's mother, she was the one who bullied her precious daughter, then fed her daughter all sort of nonsense to send her halfway across the world.

Dan couldn't stop thanking Evelyn for getting through Joanne's head. He had thought Joanne would waste her life away in front of the mirror and couldn't be happier that she had found something else to pursue.

Though it was probably wrong to think so, Evelyn was glad that Dan's parents had decided to neglect him. The lack of smothering from his mother had turned him into the responsible, self-sustained man that he was.

"Are you sure you want to do this? I can return another time and let them know about the wedding. And depending on their reactions, we'll decide our next move."

"We're not playing chess, Dan. I'm fine. I know your mom won't be pleased to see me, but I can handle it."

She didn't know how wrong she was.

Ten seconds of being in his parents' house had her wondering what she'd gotten herself into.

The already small, thin-lipped smile that Dan's mother had the courtesy of displaying vanished in an instant and the shouting began.

"What the hell were you thinking? She's the woman who took my baby away from me! She sent her all the way to Paris so the Kate girl could get together with your friend! You should be helping your sister, not hooking up with the slut!"

Evelyn rubbed her fingers against the tip of her nose, hoping her hand would conceal the smile on her face.

For heaven's sake, Kate and Tyler were already married, and they were starting their own family. There was nothing her *baby* could have done to change any of that.

"Don't talk about her that way. I brought her here as a matter of courtesy," Dan said, pulling Evelyn behind him.

"Courtesy? You never think about my feelings! How do you expect me to react when you bring home the woman who put crazy thoughts into my baby?"

Evelyn suppressed the urge to roll her eyes each time Dan's mother referred to Joanne as her baby. Joanne was merely a few years younger than she was, which makes Joanne way too old to be called a baby.

When Dan had told her that his mom was dramatic, she'd believed him. But his mom had managed to exceed beyond all expectations. She bit on her lips to stop the bubble of laughter from escaping her mouth. Perhaps Dan's mother had watched too many soap operas for her own good.

Then, in the midst of the crazy yelling, she heard Dan's low, steady voice. He wasn't shouting, but the calmness in his voice was so much louder than the hysteria his mother was throwing in their way.

"I said to stop speaking about her that way."

Evelyn smiled as she watched Dan speak to his mother. He stood up to his mother, not allowing his mother to put her down, but his words contained no anger. He spoke in his calm voice, speaking his mind without getting drawn into his mother's drama.

His unflustered, unruffled manner captured all of her attention.

Dan's mother went on and on as though she didn't hear a single word that Dan had said.

"We're not staying. I'm not letting her listen to your rant." Turning away from his mother, Dan placed his arm over Evelyn's shoulders and pressed her close against him.

Dan said to his father, who had been standing quietly behind his mother, "I love her. I love her more than anything in the world. And if you can think reasonably, you'll know what she did for Anne was better than what you guys could've ever done for her. We're getting married. You're both invited, but I won't lose any sleep over either of your missing attendance."

He didn't linger for another second. Once he'd said what he wanted, they were out of the door and back in the car.

"Eve?" His finger skimmed down her jaws.

She closed her eyes and enjoyed the warmth from his finger.

"Are you all right? I'm so sorry about my parents."

"You need to stop asking me that." She opened her eyes to see Dan gazing back at her, frowning slightly.

"I don't understand."

"Since the whole thing with David Morgan, all of you keep asking me if I'm all right. I am." She grinned mischievously at him. "You were really hot in there. The way you spoke to your mom." She sighed softly and leaned toward him. "You were so strong, so calm, so—"

Dan laughed before she could finish her sentence. "You never react like normal people do." He cupped his hand over her neck and closed the distance between them. "I love you."

With a quick peck on her lips, Dan's hand moved to turn the key in the ignition.

Evelyn reached over and placed her hand on Dan's arm. "Dan, are you sure you want to leave here like this? I can apologize to your mom. Maybe she'd—"

"No, you have nothing to apologize for. I don't care what they think. They don't know you like I do, and there's no way I'll let you go in there to apologize."

"They are your family. I don't want to be the reason for you to lose them."

"They lost me years ago. You see Kate as your sister because she has been there for you and will continue to be. By that definition, my family is probably all back at Ty's house, waiting for Marianne's next meal."

Epilogue

Twisting the flowers in her hands, Evelyn exhaled slowly through her nose. She smiled as she looked into the mirror, seeing herself in the long, white gown.

She had never thought she'd someday become a wife and have someone who still loved her in spite of her past.

Closing her eyes, she thought about everything she'd been through and about all the events that led her here. She found herself smiling at all those faces that should have scared her; Mrs. Moore, Amy, and David Morgan. They all played a part in getting her here, in helping her learn that the eventual victory belonged to the good.

That morning, she received the best wedding gift.

The front page of the newspaper was plastered with the trial of David and Richard Morgan. Neither had been convicted as yet, but she was sure that the mountain of evidence was enough to ensure they would never be able to harm another person.

The article about the Morgans was short.

Instead of going on about the downfall of the rich and famous, the reporter wrote a special piece about the victims. The reporter reminded everyone of the lives lost and the justice that was long due.

Lydia cried when she saw the piece. The justice that she had so adamantly believed in had finally been served.

Just as the ceremony was about to begin, Kate delivered another piece of wonderful news. Joanne had managed to get back in time to attend their wedding, and she'd turned up with

Dan's father.

Dan's father then came by and gave her a quick hug, thanking her for helping Joanne. He even told her that Dan couldn't have chosen a better bride.

"Ready?" Kate asked as she lifted the train of her dress.

"Yes." She took a deep breath and stepped out, beginning the new life she never imagined she could have.

Note To Readers

Hi there!

Thanks for giving my book a chance, and I hope you enjoyed reading it.

I know the descriptions in the book inclined toward a darker side. But the aim of my story is to show that no matter what one has gone through in life, it is never to late to begin anew.

Sometimes, life doesn't go the way we want or expect it to. Sometimes, there is so much baggage from the past that we think we can no longer fulfill the purpose that God has for us.

But that's not true.

God knows the destination He has set for us, and nothing on earth can stop you from reaching the good life that Jesus had died to give us.

You may have gone on a detour. But when you're ready, God is ready to set you on the right path. No matter how far you've strayed, God can and will bring you back. All you have to do is ask and He will be there.

Feel free to drop me an e-mail and let me know what you think of the book!

With love,
Trisha Grace

Trisha@trishagracenovels.com
http://www.trishagracenovels.com

P.S. Honest reviews on Goodreads and Amazon.com are always appreciated.
P.P.S. The third book is out as well! You can read the except of it at the back of this book!

Growing Up
© 2014 Trisha Grace

Ryan Faris is a self-proclaimed bachelor, enjoying his life. Over the past few years, he has seen his closest friends fall in love and get married. But that isn't a life he wants.

Marriages never work. Maybe they will work for his friends, but not for him.

Besides, he doesn't need love or marriage to have a good life. He is surrounded by great friends and has started a business that is growing every day.

Things couldn't be better in his life.

Then Ashley Frost walks back into his life, with a child in tow —his child.

Enjoy the following excerpt from Growing Up:

Chapter 1

Marianne opened the door just as Ryan was stepping out of the car.

"Thanks." Ryan entered the house and closed the door behind him.

Marianne started to reach for the remote control with the hand in a cast, but changed to the other hand after a split second.

"Still not used to it, huh?" Even Ryan wasn't used to seeing Marianne's hand in a cast.

Last week, while she was looking for clean towels in the laundry room, a cabinet collapsed on her. Thank God he was around and heard the crash, and he was able to send the unconscious Marianne to the hospital. And since she got back from the hospital, no one had allowed her to do anything but rest.

"How's your hand?" he asked as he settled on the seat, putting down the file he'd been holding.

She switched off the TV and turned to him. "It's fine. You don't have to ask about my hand each time you see me. That's at least twice a day, and it's beyond irritating."

Ryan grinned.

Marianne was always harping on every tiny aspect of their lives, but it seemed only she was allowed to do that.

"All right," he said and pushed the file across the coffee table to Marianne. "These are the final three poster designs. We can either pick one and print all the flyers in that design, or we can split our order between these three designs."

"Won't that be more expensive?"

He leaned back with a bright smile. "Kimberly says she'll do that for us for no additional charge."

Marianne narrowed her eyes. "Don't lead people on just to get some benefits."

"I never led her on. I didn't ask her out, and I didn't ask for a discount either. She offered it to me."

"But she likes you." Marianne looked through the designs. "What do you think? Should we print one or three?"

Ryan shrugged. "I'm fine with anything."

Marianne pinched her lips together. "What does Joseph say?"

"He thinks we should print one. But we'll print some posters with the three different designs and put them up in the gym."

"That sounds good." Marianne looked up at him. "Which design does he prefer?"

"He says you can choose the design."

"Hmm …" Marianne flipped through the designs again. "I like this one."

"Great." Ryan took the file and folded down a corner of the design Marianne had chosen. "By the way, Kate reminded us to proofread the poster before confirming the final print. Joe had already read through it, but you can check them again since you're so free and all."

Marianne stared pointedly at him. "Leave it. I'll do it later."

Ryan clapped his hands together. "All right, so we're all set for our new venture."

"Venture," Marianne said and laughed. "Sounds so adult, especially when it's coming from you."

Ryan grinned. He'd never thought he would end up as a business owner, and he hadn't expected the success of the gym. When he and Joseph decided to open a gym, they were prepared to go without pay for a year or so.

They weren't too worried; they could simply sponge off their richest friend, Tyler, as they always did. Since high school, he, Joseph, and Dan had always gathered at Tyler's place.

Tyler wasn't living in this huge mansion then, but his housekeeper, Marianne, was already their favorite chef. And Marianne had always taken care of them as if they were her children.

Now that Tyler had inherited the mansion, the guys had all become semi-permanent residents. All thanks to Tyler's wife, Kate, of course.

Tyler was someone who needed his private space, but Kate loved having people—specifically them—over. And so they were always in the house. They all knew the password to the security system, and they were free to use the house as if it were their own.

"Is Kate bringing back dinner tonight?" Ryan grabbed the remote and switched on the TV.

The first few days after Marianne got injured, they had ordered takeout. Then Kate suddenly announced that she had found someone to cook for them. So for the past couple of days, Kate had been bringing food back to the mansion from the mysterious Ashley-the-chef.

"Whoever this Ashley is, she's a great chef. Not as good as you, of course." He winked at Marianne.

A corner of Marianne's lips curled. "I just hope she doesn't mess up my kitchen."

"Ashley-the-chef is coming over today?"

Marianne nodded. "They should be here soon. I have to show her where everything is."

Ryan frowned at her. "Sit, watch TV, and relax. I'm sure Kate can handle it."

"I've already been sitting around all day."

"You're always complaining that you work too much. Now you're complaining that you rest too much? Nothing can please you, Marianne." He grinned and jumped from his seat before she could knock his head. "Do you want anything from the kitchen?"

Marianne shook her head.

He laughed quietly as he went into the kitchen. He was pouring himself a glass of orange juice when he heard Kate's voice.

"Hi, Marianne. Ashley is right behind me. She brought her son along."

Ryan returned to the living room when he heard Kate's voice. He leaned lazily against the wall as Kate turned and waved at who he assumed was Ashley-the-chef.

He had always liked the name Ashley. He smiled as he thought of the Ashley he once knew.

"Here." Kate stepped out of the house and came back in with a handful of bags.

He took a mouthful of orange juice and was about to step forward to help Kate with the bags when Tyler came down the stairs with his newborn, Nathaniel, cradled in his arm.

Ryan hadn't even known Tyler was at home. But since his help wasn't needed, he returned to his lazy position against the wall and waited for the mysterious Ashley-the-chef to make her appearance.

Tyler leaned over and gave Kate a peck on the lips while taking the bags in her hand. As Kate went over to give Nathaniel a kiss, Tyler glanced out of the door and froze.

That immediately piqued Ryan's curiosity. He'd never seen Tyler this surprised.

"Ryan." Tyler strode over.

"Everyone, this is Ashley," Kate announced.

Ryan raised his brows at Tyler when he remained quiet. Instead of saying anything, Tyler merely stepped away from his line of view.

Ryan's eyes widened when he saw Ashley.

"And this is Blake."

Ryan's eyes moved to the young boy with light brown hair and teal-green eyes.

Those eyes …

Before opening the gym, Ryan was a firefighter. He had been in countless burning buildings and life-threatening situations, but he'd never felt the blood drain from him as it did right now.

Kate immediately noticed the icy atmosphere the moment Ashley stepped in.

No one moved or said anything.

Kate glanced at everyone in the room, stopping at Tyler. "What's wrong?"

"Come on, Blake. Let's go."

She looked back at Ashley. "Wha—" Kate moved aside as Marianne brushed past her.

"How old is he?" Ryan asked, still staring at the doorway that was now empty.

Kate frowned. "Six. Why? What's going on?"

Tyler wrapped his hand around Kate's shoulder and leaned close to her ear. "They used to date, around six years ago."

"Oh." Kate glanced at Blake's back, then turned back to Ryan. "*Oh.*"

"Did you know?" Kate asked.

Ryan's jaw dropped slightly as he tried to form a sentence, but all that came out of him was a huff of air.

She nodded and headed out the door.

By the time Kate got to Ashley's car, Ashley had Blake seated in the back seat and had loaded the groceries back into the trunk.

Marianne was right next to Ashley, asking her to calm down.

"Ashley," Kate said.

Ashley moved past her and Marianne without looking at either of them. "We're leaving."

"Ashley, please. I'm sorry about how things turned out, but you're scaring Blake," Kate said softly. "Let's just all take a deep breath. Maybe we can go back inside. I'll get Blake a bowl of ice cream, and you can maybe have a talk with Ryan."

"I don't need to talk to him. I need to get Blake home." Ashley reached for the door handle.

"Ashley." Marianne moved to stand between Ashley and the door. "Is he Ryan's? They have the same eyes and hair."

Ashley swallowed hard and cleared her throat. "Please let me leave."

Marianne hesitated, but stepped away after a moment.

With her hand on the handle, Ashley turned to Kate. "I told you this would end disastrously." Then she got into the car and closed the door.

Kate and Marianne stood and watched the car pull away from the house and disappear around the bend.

Once the car was out of sight, Marianne turned and marched toward the house.

"Marianne." Kate wasn't sure what Marianne was about to do, but she'd never seen her this angry.

Marianne entered the house, glaring at Ryan. "You'd better not have known she was pregnant," she said in a low but deadly voice.

"I didn't," Ryan said, his face blank. "Is he mine?"

Marianne licked her lips and turned to Kate. "Do you know where she lives?"

"No." She stepped closer to Tyler. "I only know where she works and where Blake goes to school."

Marianne nodded as she drew a deep breath. "You'd better put this right." She jabbed her finger right in the middle of Ryan's chest.

"What do you want me to do?"

Kate cringed at Ryan's question. That wasn't a question he should have asked in front of Marianne.

Ryan's gaze met hers, and she shook her head. She pinched her thumb and index finger together and slid them across her lips.

"You step up and be the father Blake needs," Marianne said.

Kate took Nathaniel from Tyler's arms and walked over to Marianne, shaking her head when she saw Ryan open his mouth.

Ryan sighed as she handed Nathaniel to Marianne.

Kate planted a light kiss on Nathaniel when he burst out crying, then cocked her head to the side and dragged Ryan toward the stairs. "Honey," she said to Tyler. "Can you order pizza?"

Tyler nodded and moved to stand right in front of the stairs, preventing Marianne from going after them.

Once upstairs, Kate pointed to the couch, and Ryan took a seat without any argument.

He ran his hand through his hair and stared blankly into space.

Kate cast a glance down the steps to make sure Marianne didn't follow them up, then she joined Ryan on the couch. "First things first. You didn't know she was pregnant, right?"

"I swear I didn't."

"What are you going to do? You'd better have a good answer before Marianne kills you."

"Why didn't she tell me?" Ryan said to no one in particular, his eyes staring into space.

"Maybe she hinted. Maybe you broke up with her before she could tell you."

Ryan's head shook slowly side to side. "She broke up with me. Her parents were staunch Christians. They were always telling her that if she didn't see her relationship heading toward marriage, then she should end it. So I thought she was simply listening to them."

"She's all alone. At least that was what we heard," Kate said. "You're going to do the right thing, right?"

"What if she doesn't want me to get involved with Blake? Maybe that was why she kept me in the dark."

Kate licked her lips. "That sounds an awful lot like an excuse. Blake deserves to have a father."

"I grew up without my father. I think I turned out pretty well."

Kate shook her head. "If you'd said that with Marianne around, I think your head would be rolling on the floor now. And what do you mean you grew up without your father? I know your parents were and are barely around, but you have some sort of a father."

She had been rather upset for Ryan when his parents failed to show up for the gym's opening. They kept going on and on about how exciting it was, how they couldn't wait to see the place, and how they wouldn't miss it for the world. But they didn't turn up. They didn't even bother to send Ryan a text or give him a call.

Regardless, he still had a father.

He frowned at her. "They are free-spi—"

"Yeah, yeah. Free-spirited people and all. Point is, you have a father. Blake—"

"The father you see in the photos isn't my biological father. He's my stepfather. My father walked out on me when I was eight."

"Oh, I'm sorry. I didn't know that."

"They seemed to be doing fine without me."

Kate grabbed one of the pillows on the couch and slapped it into Ryan's chest. "Stop. Stop talking like the selfish brute Eve was complaining about."

Ryan's brows drew closer. "What are y—"

"They aren't doing well. Blake was almost thrown out of school because Ashley couldn't pay the school fees."

"What? Schools do that?"

Kate nodded. "We'd just come out from the bathroom when we heard Ashley pleading with someone. Eve thought she was in trouble and went out the back door to help. She hadn't worked for a couple of months because of the accident, so—"

"Accident?"

She sighed and waved it off. "You need to step up."

"What if she doesn't want me to get involved? She's been keeping it from me for so many years. She must have her reasons."

"I don't care what her reasons were, and I don't care if she has a valid reason now," Marianne said as she walked over with Tyler right behind her. "All I know is that I don't want to hear any excuses from you." Marianne's loud statement startled

Nathaniel, and he began crying in Tyler's arm.

"Shh …" Tyler's hand cupped over Nathaniel's head, and he gave him a kiss.

"You do what is right," Marianne continued, softer this time.

"And what's that? Marry her? My mom was so unhappy in her marriage. She fought with him all the time. They were always screaming at each other, and she was always crying. Maybe Ashley didn't want that for her life; maybe that was why she kept me in the dark."

Marianne's chest rose sharply, and she turned away, seemingly to stop herself from strangling Ryan. After a moment, she clenched and released the fist that wasn't bound by the cast before turning back to Ryan. "You may think that the system your mom and her boyfriend has is perfect, but it isn't."

"She is happy. I don't ever see them get into a fight."

Marianne threw her hands in the air. "Because when either of them gets remotely angry with each other, they split." She had kept her voice low, but it was still harsh.

"They have been together for nearly two decades."

Marianne scoffed. "Is that what you think? Your mom and her boyfriend have broken up more times than I can remember. Remember all those times when she dropped you off at Ty's old place? That was when she'd tell me how upset she was and how she needed time alone. I know you think your mom and your so-called stepfather are the most fabulous people in the world, but I'm telling you right now that they are the most irresponsible people in the world."

"They just want to be happy. What's wrong with being happy?"

Kate shook her head. She had never seen the stubborn side of Ryan.

Ryan was always open to input on whatever decision he had to make. He didn't concern himself with trivial things, and he always seemed to know what to say in every situation.

But in defense of his parents, Ryan seemed to have turned into a whole other person.

"They weren't pursuing happiness, Ryan. They were

pursuing thrill and novelty, and they pursued it at your expense. I know you have been a happy-go-lucky person your whole life, and you're really sweet to want happiness for your mother. But think about it.

"How many times did she pull you out of school because she didn't feel like staying in the same place anymore? You changed schools more than seven times in two years. Your mom wanted to take you away from here as well. I was the one who persuaded her to let you stay. I promised I'd take care of you. Your mom barely knew me then, but she agreed without much thought. I'm not bragging, but you grew up all right because you had the boys and me.

"I wouldn't have cared if you chose to remain a bachelor. I'd love for you to have your own family, but if remaining a bachelor was what you wanted, I would've been fine with it. But now, it isn't just about you; it's about Ashley, and it's about Blake. And I'm not letting you be the irresponsible parent like your mom was. You do the right thing, or I don't want to see you around here anymore."

Kate drew a deep breath through her nose as Marianne went down the stairs.

Her hand moved to her pendant, and she leaned against Tyler's arm, not knowing what to say.

"I should go," Ryan said.

"Ryan," Kate said. "She didn't mean it."

"She meant it, all right." Ryan got up and went down the stairs, and Kate realized he was angry as well.

"This is the first time I've seen him angry. It's kind of scary." Kate turned to Tyler. "Don't you want to stop him or something?"

Tyler took a deep breath.

"What is it?"

"I need to talk to him."

"Then go." She reached out for Nathaniel, but Tyler shook his head.

"Later. I'll go to his apartment."

She frowned. "Why?"

He pulled her close and kissed her. "I'll tell you when I'm back. I need to talk to him first." Then he stood and headed to Nathaniel's nursery.

Chapter 2

"You're the last person I expected to see," Ryan said to Tyler, then moved aside for him to enter the apartment. "Did Kate send you?"

Tyler didn't say anything. He settled on the couch and waited for Ryan to do the same.

"Marianne sent you?"

"Nobody sent me. I'm here to return a favor."

"Return a favor?"

"I wanted to leave you alone, but I was afraid it'd take you a little too long to figure it out."

Ryan smirked as Tyler said those familiar words. He'd once said that to him when Tyler had gotten into a fight with Kate. "So what am I not figuring out?"

"You have no right to be angry with Marianne, and it's time to grow up."

Ryan sighed. "I wasn't trying to fight Marianne. My mom took me with her when my dad walked out on us. She could've left me with him and pursued whatever dream she wanted."

Tyler took a deep breath as he stared at Ryan.

"What?"

Tyler leaned forward, resting his arms on his legs. "I only knew this because I overheard Marianne on the phone. I didn't quite understand what she was saying until I was much older." He paused and hesitated.

This was the first time Ryan had seen Tyler hesitate when saying something.

"Your father didn't walk out on you. Your mom took you and left. She took you because she wanted to punish your dad."

"What?" Ryan laughed and reached for the remote on the coffee table. "You're crazy."

Tyler snatched the remote from him. "Your dad was a

policeman, right?"

Ryan had never told any of them that. He didn't like talking about his biological father. He figured that if his father didn't care enough about him to stay, then he shouldn't care enough about his father to keep him in his mind.

"Your mom was bugging your father to quit his job and go to Paris so that she could paint and learn music. Your father refused because he had enough common sense to know it wasn't a viable dream. He knew they didn't have the money for that, but your mom kept going on and on about it. Then, she had an affair—with your now stepfather."

Ryan shook his head.

"I heard both sides of the story."

"You met my father?"

"I didn't actually see him. I was outside my room and overheard them. Marianne didn't want you to be pulled from place to place, so she found your father and asked if he would take you from your mom. That was when your father came over and said he'd been searching for you since your mom took you."

Ryan stared at Tyler. He wouldn't have believed it if anyone else had told him, but he had known Tyler for a long time. He clenched his jaw. "And you never thought to tell me about it?"

Tyler straightened. "Marianne confronted your mom and made a deal with her; a deal your father agreed to. Your mom would stop pulling you from place to place. If and when she wanted to leave, she had to leave you with us. And your mom agreed to this on one condition; that your father never see you again."

"And Marianne agreed to that?" His question came out louder than necessary.

"She told your father, and he agreed it was better for you. He hadn't seen you in years, and Marianne had told him the story your mom fed you. He didn't mind being the bad person."

"Then Marianne should've told me when I got older."

Tyler inhaled deeply through his mouth. "Your dad got shot in the line of duty. Your mom had taken you on a holiday then. When you came back, you were so happy and the funeral was over …"

"And you decided to keep your mouth shut as well."

"Your father instructed Marianne not to say anything. He wanted you to be happy. If you were happy with the story your mom fed you, then he was fine with it." Tyler paused and looked down for a second. "And Marianne made me swear that I'd never tell you this."

Ryan shook his head. "Get out."

"I never spoke to your father, and you haven't seen him since your mom took you away. But even then, he put you first. You're a father now. It's time you put Blake first."

"Get out."

Tyler nodded, then got up and left without another word.

Ryan sat where he was and watched Tyler close the door behind him.

There was no reason for Tyler to lie. But if that was the case, then his mom had been lying to him throughout his life. And Marianne knew, and she'd kept it to herself.

He exhaled heavily, the anger rolling in heated waves over his tongue.

How could Tyler keep his mouth shut until now? Were they going to hide the truth from him forever?

He had no right to be angry with Marianne?

He had every right.

How could she make that decision for him? He went into his room, grabbed his gym gear, and headed out.

Ryan switched on the lights in the gym and headed in. He started out on the treadmill, then went on to the bench press. He was all alone in the gym, but he still added more weights than he was used to.

He knew he shouldn't, but he wasn't in the mood to think logically. He continued lifting the bar until his hands shook so badly that he almost dropped it.

When he finally placed it back onto the rack, he sat up and jumped. "Kate, gosh. I thought I saw a ghost."

Kate looked up from her Kindle and smiled. "I'm alive and

am definitely a human."

"How long have you been sitting there?"

"A while. Ty allowed me to drive here on my own."

He shook his head at the mention of Tyler. "How did you know I'd be here?"

"I clean when I need to vent. You're the most muscular among the guys. It isn't difficult to imagine what you do when you need to vent."

"Are you here to hand out advice as well?"

"You haven't seen Ashley for a while. How do you think she looks? Any different from when you were dating her?"

He realized he hadn't thought about that.

He was still simmering in shock when he'd been besieged by Marianne on what he should do.

He never considered himself a rebel. He had always been a rather easygoing kid. But when Marianne demanded that he'd better do the right thing, he couldn't help but feel frustrated. He hadn't known about Blake, so why was it suddenly his fault?

And of course, that wasn't enough.

He had to find out that everything he'd known in his life wasn't true.

With all that had happened, he hadn't given much thought to anyone but himself. And with that one question, Kate made him realized how selfish he'd been.

"She looks good," he said. "She used to only wear dresses, which was what her parents told her girls should wear."

Kate nodded.

"She still looks amazing, though." And she did. Even with her hair tied up in a low bun, even in just a plain T-shirt and a dark pair of jeans, she looked great. "How's she doing? Besides money, that is. And you mentioned something about an accident."

"She was minding her own business when a truck crashed onto the walkway, almost ramming her right into the wall. Thank God it only clipped her arm, causing a fracture. But the injury did keep her from working for a couple of months, which was why she couldn't afford Blake's fees."

"Blake," he said. That was the first time he'd called him by name.

"Blake's a very understanding boy. After school, he sits in the diner and waits for Ashley to be done with work. Ashley doesn't even need to remind him to do his homework and all, and I've never seen him throw a tantrum."

Kate sighed softly. "Tyler told me everything. He only told me after he'd spoken to you, of course. I can tell he's feeling awful."

"That's the real reason why you're here."

"I came to check up on you."

"You think I should forgive him because he feels awful? He lied to me. He and Marianne somehow thought it was right to decide my life for me."

"Really?" Kate said. "You're still protecting your mom now?"

"What?"

"They didn't lie to you. Your mom did. Your dad and Marianne did what they thought was best in the situation."

"And after I grew up? They didn't think I had the right to know?"

"Marianne was doing what your father wanted—for you to be happy. Do you think it's been easy for Marianne to carry this secret all these years? She had to pretend to be cordial to your mom. She had to see and keep her mouth shut about your misplaced admiration of your mom and hatred of your father."

"She should've told me."

"Maybe. But she didn't tell you because she wanted to protect you. That's better than any reason your mom has."

"Kate—"

"Ryan, you're not stupid. I know you joke around a lot, but I know you can sit and think. I need you to stop pumping your muscles and just think. You have more information now. You can look back and think about what your mom said and did or what Marianne said and did. Don't act on your first instinct and get busy trying to blame Marianne and Tyler."

He took a deep breath.

Kate got up and walked over to him. "I'm not going to give you a hug because you're disgusting right now," she said with a smile. "I'll go now. I'll keep my phone close to me. If you need anything …"

"Thanks."

Her hand moved to give him a pat on the arm, but she stopped before she actually touched him and pulled her hand back. "Goodnight."

He grinned. "Goodnight."

Kate walked over to the glass doors and turned back to him. "If I were Marianne, I would've done the same. I would've carried the secret to my grave if it meant you'd always be happy with thinking your mom was the greatest person on earth." Then she allowed the door to swing closed behind her.

Ryan picked up his bottle and took a gulp of water.

Kate knew what it was like to keep a secret. Until last year, she had kept a secret for her best friend and business partner, Evelyn, for years. And he'd seen the pressure on her and the tension caused within the group, especially between her and Dan. But still, she'd kept her mouth shut for Evelyn.

He sighed. Maybe Kate was right. Maybe Tyler was right.

Then, for the first time in years, he allowed himself to think about his father, about what he could remember of him.

He couldn't remember much, but he did remember he was always playing with him; baseball, basketball. His father also taught him how to ride a bike.

He hadn't ridden a bike since his father—no, since his mom took him away.

He and his mom had constantly moved around since then, and it wasn't viable to carry his bike wherever they went.

He wiped his sweat off on the face towel he'd brought.

He knew his mom was the free-spirited sort. He'd always been grateful that she brought him along and tried to take care of him, and he'd always made sure he didn't give her too much trouble because he knew he was already a burden to her.

His mom had always told him how his father left because he didn't want either of them anymore, and he didn't care enough about them to stay. And she had always gone on about the sacrifices she'd made to keep him.

Suddenly, all the reasons he'd given to explain his mother's behavior and actions, even his explanation of her being free-spirited, sounded like nothing but excuses.

Marianne was right.

It was the right thing to do, and he wasn't going to allow himself to become an irresponsible person. Marianne had brought him up to be a better man than that.

Chapter 3

"Bye mommy." Blake kissed Ashley on the cheek and got out of the car.

She put on her brightest smile and waved. "See you later."

She watched for a moment, then pulled out before someone had to blare the horn at her. She called her mother on her cell phone and counted the number of rings.

She never waited until she got transferred to the voicemail. She counted to five, and if her mother didn't pick up the call, she'd hang up.

Three.

"Ash," her mother's whisper came through on the line.

"Is it all right for you to talk?"

"Not for long."

Ashley looked at the clock on her dashboard and frowned. Her father should be out of the house by now, but she didn't want to waste precious time asking pointless questions. She knew the risk her mother was taking by answering her call while her father was still at home. "Are you free to meet?"

"Maybe in an hour. I have to go." The call ended abruptly.

She sighed and drove toward the place she used to call home while she called Jim and told him that she'd be an hour late. She needed to talk to her mother, even if it was for five minutes.

She stopped outside a diner and turned off the ignition.

The diner was a ten-minute drive from her parents' house, so it would be easy enough for her mom to rush back home if there was a need to.

Ashley slumped back against the seat, propped her hand against the window, and bit down on her index finger. Despite a whole night of tossing and turning, she still hadn't been able to decide what she should do.

In the end, all she could do was to shut her eyes and wish for that whole day to be nothing but a nightmare.

She exhaled heavily.

It was strange to see all the guys and Marianne again. She never imagined she would see them again, and she never thought Ryan would remain here. She had assumed he would travel the world like his parents did. After all, he was always telling her about their adventures and how much fun they always had.

She wasn't sure what she was supposed to do now.

She had promised Kate that she'd help with the cooking until Marianne got better, and as she'd seen for herself, Marianne was still wearing that bulky cast on her arm.

She sighed softly as she tilted her head back and considered how she should deal with Ryan.

Maybe, she thought, maybe she wouldn't have to. Maybe Ryan would simply go on living his life as if he hadn't seen her and Blake.

It wasn't that far-fetched. He had always enjoyed his freedom; he had always considered the traditional family unit as something that would never work.

And last night, even after seeing Blake, he hadn't bothered to come after her.

Maybe she could continue to cook for Kate and all of them and treat it just as she would with anybody else—as another job and nothing more.

She smiled, pleased with the decision she'd made.

Just then, her phone rang, and she picked it up almost immediately. "Are you on your way?"

"Ashley, Ryan's here," her mother's hushed and trembling voice came through the line.

"At home?"

"Yes! Hurry." The call ended.

Ashley threw the phone onto the passenger seat and pulled out of the lot. She hadn't ever driven this fast before. And for the first time in over seven years, she turned a bend without slowing down.

Once the car came to a stop, she jumped out and hurried over, just as her father was shoving Ryan back. "Ryan, what are you doing?"

"I knew you must be nearby. I've told you once, and I'll tell you again; you're no longer welcome in my house, and you won't get a single cent from me. How dare you still show up here after disgracing God and me?"

"What?" Ryan turned to Ashley, then back to her father. "I didn't come here for your money."

"Enough, Ryan," she said.

Her father took a step toward her, and Ryan moved between her and her father. This time when her father shoved at Ryan, he remained right where he was.

"Ryan, get back into the car. We should go."

Ryan's face turned to her, but his body remained facing her father, blocking her from her father's direct yelling.

"Yes, get back into your cars and get out of here. Don't you people ever show your faces here again."

"She's your daughter. There isn't any need to talk to her this way."

"She's no daughter of mine. She's going to hell. All of you are going to hell, including that offspring of yours."

"That's enough." Ryan took a step forward. "I've allowed you to yell at me because you're Ash's father, but there are lines I won't allow you to cross."

A strong sensation of someone staring at her pulled Ashley's attention toward the second-floor window.

Behind the curtains, her mother stood, looking down at her with a hand clutched on the cross pendant around her neck and another hand across the front of her waist.

Making her father angry would only cause problems for her mother.

"Ryan." Ashley grabbed his arm. "Let's go." She didn't wait

for his response. She headed back to her car while her father continued yelling at them.

She let go of Ryan's arm as they neared her car; then she got into her own car and drove off with Ryan's car tailing hers.

She returned to the diner where she had parked her car while waiting for her mother, and stepped out.

She couldn't believe Ryan would go over to her parents' house, and she expressed it in the most controlled tone she could manage when Ryan got out of his car.

"I didn't know where to find you. I thought you'd be—"

"You could've asked Kate or Evelyn."

"Right, I should have," he said. "Your dad threw you out? Where have you been living?"

"Look, Ryan—"

"Why didn't you tell me?"

She sighed. "And what would you have done? You were always telling me that marriages never work, that your parents are happy because they aren't married. There was no way I could've stayed on with you and still have Blake. Having Blake was sin enough already."

He clenched his jaw. "I don't know what I would've done, but I definitely wouldn't have let you deal with this whole thing on your own," he said and ran his hand through his hair. "I can't believe your father threw you out."

"He's always been religious." She paused and took a step away from him. "He gave me a choice; get rid of Blake and promise never to see you again, or get out of the house and never see them again."

Ryan rolled his eyes. "Isn't abortion a sin as well?"

It was, but it was a sin that wouldn't publicly humiliate her father. "I don't want to discuss that anymore." Either way, she was going to hell. What was the point of discussing the details?

Ryan reached out and took her hand. "Ash."

His warm touch surprised her, and she almost tightened her hand around his and stepped into his arms, just as she used to do.

But that was years ago. She pulled her hand from his and took another step back. "I can't do this today," she said, even as her fingers curled around the warmth that still lingered on her hand.

"Wait. Please, Ash."

She opened the door of her car and stepped in. "Let's just continue with our lives as if yesterday and today never happened."

"That's not going to happen. He's my son, Ash."

She turned to him. "He's *my* son." She didn't understand why she was suddenly so defensive.

Ryan nodded. "Yes, he is. But he's my son, too. Let me do my part; let me help."

"Are you seeing anyone now?"

"No," he answered.

She smiled. "Have you had any relationship, besides with the group of guys, that lasts longer than six months?"

"That doesn't mean I'll only stick around for six months."

"You hate responsibility, Ryan. You adore the lifestyle your mother has. How does having Blake as your son fit into that lifestyle?"

"It doesn't matter. I don't get to choose."

"See!" Ashley threw her hands in the air. "You don't want to have Blake around. You just think this is what you have to do."

"No, that's not what I meant."

She turned her back to him. "Just pretend you haven't seen us." Then she got into her car and drove off.

"You have to work on your drawings, Mark. Look at this." Kate pointed to the drawing in front of her. "This shouldn't be visible from the front view. Miss Jordan is really unhappy with your work. She says she doesn't understand what you're drawing."

That was among the many other things Evelyn had said.

Mark studied the drawing in front of him. "I'm so sorry."

The door to her office opened, and Ryan strolled right in. He settled on the couch with a nonchalant "Hey."

Kate stared at him for a moment, but he had leaned back on the couch and shut his eyes. "You'd better clean this drawing up before giving it to her again, or you might find yourself out of a job," she said to Mark.

Mark pulled his eyes from Ryan and turned back to her. "Yes, Mrs. Hayes." He stood and left the room after casting another look at Ryan.

"Hey," she said to Ryan after Mark closed the door. "Making yourself comfortable?"

He shook his head and stared at her. "I'm a dad."

"According to Eve, all you are right now is a sperm donor." She smiled when he sighed.

"So I suppose everyone's been updated."

"I didn't say anything about your parents."

Ryan continued lying on the couch.

"So, what are you going to do?"

Ryan sat upright, reached into his pocket, and pulled out a small black box. He placed the box on the table and slid it toward her.

"Is that what I think it is?" Kate stood and went over to the couch. She sat and picked up the box, inhaling deeply when she opened it. "I hope you bought this as a gesture rather than an expectation of an actual engagement."

"I'm ready for responsibility. I'll marry her and take care of her and Blake."

"And you think she'll say yes? Ryan, I don't know Ashley well, but I seriously doubt it." She set the box down on the table. "But," she quickly added when Ryan looked as if he would protest. "But it's a good gesture to prove you're trying. It's a good start."

"It was my fault that she didn't tell me she was pregnant. It was because I kept telling her that marriages don't work. And because of that, she thought for sure I wouldn't want to have anything to do with Blake."

"How do you know that?"

"I saw her this morning."

"This morning?" Kate's head tilted to the side. "How did you find out where she lives? Please don't tell me you made Ty run a check on her."

Tyler owned a large security firm that had everything needed to run a background check on someone. And one of Tyler's staff, Ben, was so good with computers that the FBI had tried to hire him several times.

Ryan's brows rose, and Kate surmised he'd just realized he could.

"I went to her parents' house," he said.

"She's no longer living with her parents, right? I heard they threw her out or something like that."

Ryan nodded. "But I didn't know. Her father said a whole load of crap to my face, then she showed up a few minutes later, and we both got chased away."

"Gosh … What was her reaction?"

"Angry that I showed up at her parents' place. Then she told me to pretend that yesterday didn't happen and to go on with my life."

"So she doesn't want you around Blake."

"She thinks my interest in stepping up won't last."

"And will it?" Kate asked.

"He's my son, Kate. I'm not going to let him grow up without a father. Unlike my mom and stepfather, I'm going to be there for him."

Kate arched her brow. "That's a pretty drastic change in opinion from last night."

"I had a pretty drastic change in perspective."

She nodded. "But she doesn't want you around."

"Because she doesn't think I want the responsibility."

"And that's why you bought the ring," Kate said. "Please don't think the ring will change anything. You need to come up with an actual plan; you need to think of something that will prove you're serious and in for the long haul."

"You're a mother now. Tell me what I should do."

She narrowed her eyes and stood, then slapped him lightly on the head. "I'm not a problem solver. This is your problem; *you* need to come up with the solution."

"That's not helpful at all."

"I'm helping you right now. Ashley thinks you're not ready to grow up, so imagine her reaction when she finds out that whatever you're going to do is because I told you to do it."

Ryan lay back down on the couch, his feet threatening to kick Kate over if she didn't move.

She smacked his leg, but stood and went back to the seat in front of her desk. Ryan already treated all of their homes as his own; apparently her office was his office now. "Told you to allocate some space for your own office and you refused."

"I don't need an office."

She glared at him, but Ryan was oblivious. He hooked his arm behind his neck and closed his eyes as if he were taking a nap. "Is there a guidebook I can buy? Like a how-to-be-a-father-for-dummies book."

It was kind of uncanny to see Ryan so comfortable in her office. Even Tyler didn't lie down on her couch this way—even *she* didn't take a nap in the office.

She glanced out of her office and noticed a few of her staff staring. She wasn't sure if she should fog up the glass.

It looked weird having Ryan on her couch, but fogging up the office seemed worse.

"Kate." Evelyn opened the door, another person who didn't bother knocking when entering her room. "I'm heading to the stu—what is he doing here?"

"He screwed up a meeting with Ashley this morning," Kate answered.

"What's this?" Evelyn strode over and picked up the small black box.

"According to Kate, a stupid idea," Ryan said.

"I didn't say that."

"I summarized it."

Evelyn grabbed Ryan's legs and pushed them off the couch to make space for herself. "It is stupid," she said. "So, have you decided on what you're going to do? Besides this stupid ring idea."

Kate brought Evelyn up-to-date.

"That's good." Evelyn nudged Ryan with her shoulder. "I knew you'd do the right thing."

"Really?" Ryan's brows drew closer, and he stared at her.

"All right." Evelyn shrugged. "Kate knew you'd do the right thing."

Kate rolled her eyes. "You need to think about how you can be a father to Blake and at the same time help Ashley. Maybe you can start by babysitting. He's always sitting in the diner all day doing nothing."

"True." Evelyn nodded. "I'm sure she needs help with money, too. But right now, I doubt she'll trust you enough to let you help."

"Neither of you are being very helpful."

"You just need to start doing something. Show her you're serious about stepping up," Evelyn said.

"Autumn break is coming up," Kate said. "You should start there."

"I don't know if I'm the best person for him to hang around with. What if I screw up? What if I drop him?"

"Then don't carry him in the first place. Problem solved." Evelyn's brows flickered up.

Ryan's head tilted, and his non-interested eyes shot a pointed glare at Evelyn.

"Oh, sorry. I'm not used to you being so serious."

Kate shook her head. "Ryan, just be yourself. You're fun; you love having fun. And kids are all about having fun. Being yourself will be enough for him. Blake will love you."

The boyish grin that Kate was so used to finally returned. He got up and gave her a hug. "See, I knew there must be a reason why I came here."

Kate laughed, and he broke from the hug.

Evelyn shook her head. "If Tyler didn't trust you enough, I bet he'd think the two of you are having an affair."

"I'm sorry, Kate. I can't, everything is just too complicated now."

Kate slapped him on the arm. "Get out of here."

Ryan shrugged and went over to the door. Then he turned back and flashed a mischievous grin. "I'll call you later," he said loudly.

Kate frowned, wondering what he was up to.

"I love you," he announced, and his grin grew wider.

Kate rolled her eyes and looked over at Evelyn.

"Someday, Tyler's going to kill him," Evelyn said. "All right, I got to go, too. I'll give him another slap if I bump into him in the parking lot."

To continue reading Growing Up, you can get it at Amazon http:// amzn.to/2tQa2XR

More Books

Other titles by Trisha Grace

Now available:
Ghost of the Past (Book 1) - Moving On
Ghost of the Past (Book 2) - Closing Books
Ghost of the Past (Book 3) - Growing Up
Ghost of the Past (Book 4) - Believing Again
Done Being Friends
A Fresh Start
Sing For Me
Shine Series Book 1 - Mr. Bad Influence
Shine Series Book 2 - Mr. Playboy

You can find Trisha's books on Amazon here: http://amzn.to/ 2tQa2XR

Coming soon:
Shine Series Book 3 - Mr. Golden Boy
Shine Series Book 4 - Mr. Party
Ghost of the Past (Book 5 & 6) - Lydia and Joanne

About Author

Trisha Grace graduated from Bradford University with an Accounting and Finance degree. She has always been an avid reader and has a passion for writing. After being a tutor for over six years, she finally sat down and penned her own novels.

53181737R00181

Made in the USA
Columbia, SC
11 March 2019